Lynne Graham was born
has been a keen romance
is very happily married to
who has learned to cook since she started to write!
Her five children keep her on her toes. She has a
very large dog who knocks everything over, a very
small terrier who barks a lot, and two cats. When
time allows, Lynne is a keen gardener.

Lorraine Hall is a part-time hermit and full-time
writer. She was born with an old soul and her
head in the clouds—which, it turns out, is the
perfect combination for spending her days creating
thunderous alpha heroes and the fierce, determined
heroines who win their hearts. She lives in a
potentially haunted house with her soulmate and
a rumbustious band of hermits in training. When
she's not writing romance, she's reading it.

ALTAR OF SCANDAL

LYNNE GRAHAM

LORRAINE HALL

MILLS & BOON

First published in Great Britain 2026
by Mills & Boon, an imprint of HarperCollins*Publishers* Ltd,
1 London Bridge Street, London, SE1 9GF

www.harpercollins.co.uk

HarperCollins*Publishers*, Macken House, 39/40 Mayor Street Upper, Dublin 1, D01 C9W8, Ireland

Altar of Scandal © 2026 Harlequin Enterprises ULC

Unveiling the Wrong Bride © 2026 Lynne Graham

Secretly Pregnant Princess © 2026 Lorraine Hall

ISBN: 978-0-263-41764-7

01/26

MIX
Paper | Supporting
responsible forestry
FSC™ C007454

This book contains FSC™ certified paper
and other controlled sources to ensure responsible forest management.

For more information visit www.harpercollins.co.uk/green.

Printed and Bound in the UK using 100% Renewable Electricity
at CPI Group (UK) Ltd, Croydon, CR0 4YY

UNVEILING THE WRONG BRIDE

LYNNE GRAHAM

MILLS & BOON

CHAPTER ONE

'IT'S WHAT YOU'VE been waiting for!' Aldo Renzetti proclaimed to his grandson. 'Tomaso is finally willing to sell up.'

'Only because he's on the edge of bankruptcy,' Tore Renzetti responded drily, a lean, powerful silhouette as he lounged like a fluid, graceful panther in the doorway of his office that connected with his grandfather's, who was head of the board and president of their vast company. 'But why now? He's had a standing offer from us from the day he opened for business. What's changed?'

Aldo winced. 'He's gotten older. Maybe he's ready to retire,' he suggested of his former childhood playmate and business partner. 'Regardless, it means you can get his voting shares back and take our company to public when you take over. There is, however, one major drawback. Tomaso had made the offer conditional on you marrying one of his two granddaughters.'

Tore straightened to his full six foot five inches and stared back at the older man in absolute amazement. 'You're kidding me…right?'

Aldo grimaced. 'I wish I was. But I assume that Tomaso is trying to conserve his legacy through his family and pass it down.'

'What legacy? His failing company?' Tore parried with disdain. 'But for those voting rights, he has nothing else to tempt us with.'

'But he was *here* right at the very beginning of Renzetti Pharmaceutical,' Aldo reminded him with his ever-present regret for that lost partnership and old history.

'And you bought him out when he chose to walk away,' his grandson reminded him flatly, the dying sunlight of the day gleaming over his cropped silver-blond hair, accentuating his bronzed, hard-boned features. 'You owe him nothing else.'

'It wasn't that simple,' the older man sighed unhappily.

Tore didn't want to encourage his grandfather to get down and dirty all over again in the long-distant past. Aldo was a sentimental man, prone to guilt and regret. Tore knew it all by heart in any case. That friendship and business connection had broken down when both men fell for the same woman, and that woman had become Tore's grandmother, Matilde. Tomaso Barone had moved to England and set up his own company while retaining his voting rights in Renzetti Pharma, indeed insisting on retaining that link against his former partner's wishes.

'A marriage of convenience!' Tore commented instead with sardonic bite. 'We're not living in the Dark Ages anymore when women were bartered like sheep. I'm twenty-eight. I'm not prepared to marry some stranger, and I can hardly credit that that stranger would be willing to marry me!'

Aldo averted his gaze in silent disagreement. In his opinion, Tore was a huge trophy on the marriage market, being the CEO of a thriving global company worth billions, who enjoyed an enviable lifestyle. He knew that, Tore had to know that and presumably his former partner knew it, too, *knew* what a big ask he was making while no doubt hoping that it would hurt. That unexpected demand had warned Aldo that Tomaso was still as bitter as gall over the way their respective marriages and business investments had turned out.

'Apparently, *both* granddaughters are willing to make the sacrifice,' Aldo informed his grandson wryly. 'But Tomaso suggested choosing the eldest, who is apparently a less complex young woman. I don't know what that means and I have no idea what either woman's motivation might be.'

'*Money,*' Tore framed with raw distaste. 'What else?'

'Well, that's for you to discover if you have the interest. If not, we'll leave this discussion there. I'm not planning to put any pressure on you to meet Tomaso's arbitrary demand. If you do consider it, though, note that he's only specifying that the marital connection should last a minimum of five years,' Aldo imparted uncomfortably. 'In other words, it wouldn't be a life sentence.'

Like that changed anything! Tore reflected in disbelief as the older man departed, seemingly impervious to the size of the bombshell he had dropped on his grandson. No pressure? Was Aldo serious in that claim? Tore's green eyes flashed like emerald lightning in his lean, darkly handsome face.

How could there be anything other than pressure? Everything he was today was due to Aldo and Matilde's care and concern for him. Aldo had liberated Tore from sordid circumstances as a young child, saving him from those who only sought to use him for his inheritance. Aldo had done what it took to stage that intervention even if it had entailed breaking the law. And that kind of action from a man, who toed the very letter of the law in every other field of his life, proved how desperate his grandfather had been to give his only grandchild a fighting chance to move beyond his unstable beginnings and flourish into something more. Thanks to Aldo, Tore had learned what it was to have security, love and education. Indeed, every good feature in Tore's life had stemmed from his grandparents' generous, tolerant and forgiving hearts. Their son, Marco, might have proved a grave disappointment but they had still given *his* son, Tore, the opportunity to prove that he could do better.

Aldo and his wife could have reacted very differently to Marco's illegitimate child, born from a brief fling with a Norwegian fashion model. Marco had settled sufficient money on Tore's mother to keep his child's existence out of the newspapers. But then, unhappily, Tore's mother had died when he was a toddler and he had become her sister's responsibility instead: a sister who dabbled in drugs, bad men and crime; a sister who liked to live on the edge while using Tore's ever-growing inheritance to keep her comfortable. Having exhausted all legal processes, Aldo had paid off Tore's aunt to get her to sign over custody to his grandparents.

And magically, literally overnight, Tore's troubled, frightening childhood world had been transformed.

He owed more than family loyalty to his grandparents. He owed more than he could ever repay, so naturally, he would agree to this foolish marriage because for Aldo Renzetti, such an agreement would finally bring closure to that nasty partnership breakdown light years in the past. Tomaso would be paid handsomely for those precious voting shares, and his granddaughter would get to make a tiny marital footnote in the Renzetti family bible and leave the Barone family again royally enriched by her temporary rise in status.

Yes, he would agree to the marriage for Aldo's sake but he would only do it on his own terms, and those would be business terms. *Strictly* business. He would pick the less complex candidate as advised by her own grandfather. She would get nothing but his name and lifestyle out of the deal. He would stick her in the south wing of his London mansion where she could moulder undisturbed until her time was up. There would be no mingling of any kind, not in their daily lives. However, possibly there would be the occasional social appearance as a couple to support the concept of normality, he conceded. After all, he couldn't simply ignore the woman completely, could he? He hoped he had better manners.

Even so, he saw no reason why he should even meet his future bride before the wedding. It didn't matter what she looked like, how she dressed or spoke, because he was stuck with her regardless, he reflected, subduing his rage at that lowering truth while he tried not to wonder if she would be an embarrassment. But he would, however, negotiate on that lengthy marital term. Five years was too long a period to be tolerated in such an empty marriage. Three years would be ample, even generous on his part. She could live high on the hog on his money. Sadly for her, however, the prenup would be a labyrinth of legalese complexity, guaranteed to hog-tie even the most rapacious of women into good behaviour for the duration of their union.

So, potential problem solved, he reflected on the back of gritted teeth and a searing current of his innate efficiency at plotting his next moves. His eager bride would shrink so far back into the wallpaper, she would be barely visible in his life. He would manage her in very much hands-off mode and she would not cause him the smallest inconvenience.

Violet clattered up the stairs to her flat, her back aching after her eight-hour shift, which had started at four in the morning. Being a baker was no job for a slacker who liked to lie in bed, but Violet was now so accustomed to the labour of early starts and busy hours in the bakery that she thought nothing of it, choosing instead to be simply grateful that there was money in the bank and no debts.

And very sadly, she owed all of that security to her best friend, Isabel. Unhappily, Isabel and her partner had not lived long enough to enjoy the success of the business they had built. The couple had died in a car accident the year before, only days after the birth of their daughter, Belle. Having long worked by her friend's side, Violet had been nominated as guardian to Belle and had inherited the bakery in the little girl's stead, which had made it financially possible for her to take on the responsibility of raising a young child alone.

It was a surprise for Violet to walk into Isabel and Stefan's former apartment above the bakery and find her sister waiting for her rather than her tenant and childminder, Joy.

'Relax, nothing's happened. I told Joy she could leave early. She'd already given Belle her lunch and put her down for a nap,' Tabitha explained, easily interpreting her sister's expression of dismay at her unexpected appearance. 'I have something to tell you.'

'Oh…' Violet's tension drained away and she dropped down into an armchair with a sigh. 'What's up?'

Tabitha winced and then darted off to the bathroom in haste where her sister heard her be sick. Frowning, Violet followed her and stilled in the doorway. 'What's wrong? Have you caught a bug?'

'Get me a glass of water while I freshen up,' her twin urged.

Violet poured a glass of water and handed it over when her wan sister appeared back in the snug little sitting room. The apartment was a rabbit warren of small rooms because Isabel and her partner had put their money into improving the bakery rather than their living accommodation.

'It's not a bug,' Tabitha shared tautly, her lovely face troubled and embarrassed. 'I wouldn't be visiting if I had anything contagious. No, the truth is that I'm pregnant.'

'Pregnant?' Violet gasped in disbelief. 'But *how*? I mean—'

'Not a virgin anymore,' Tabitha cut in somewhat bitterly. 'You have to remember me saying that there was no way I was going into this marriage a virgin and staying that way for another three years!'

Violet frowned. 'Yes. Of course I remember that but I didn't see why it should be a problem when this marriage is a business deal rather than a normal one. Nobody's expecting you to sleep with the wretched man!'

'So you assumed but who knows?' Tabitha asked. 'And even if he doesn't push the sex idea, it means that I can hardly be an unfaithful wife while I'm with him, and I couldn't stand the idea that I would be trapped in celibacy as well for the next three years. So, I decided I would get rid of the problem.'

Violet groaned out loud. 'It's not a problem, not something you should think of in terms of getting rid of.'

'I'm only doing what *you* did,' Tabitha condemned with flushed cheeks. 'Didn't you sleep with your high school boyfriend because you thought it was time?'

Violet turned scarlet with embarrassment but the less said about that unwise decision of hers the better, when she had never come clean with her sister about what a disaster that had proved. 'So, if you're pregnant, who's the father?' she asked instead.

Tabitha grimaced. 'Someone I met at work who was just passing through. I thought he would be perfect as I'd never see him again but my birth control let me down.'

Her twin studied her with sympathy. 'What are you going to do?'

'It's more a question of what *you* are going to do,' Tabitha stated, turning the question back on her. 'After all, I can't marry Tore Renzetti now that I'm pregnant. It would be a breach of the contract I signed and I can't hide it, so I'll have to fess up and then the marriage won't go ahead and that means we don't get the money up front.'

Violet slumped in horror. 'Oh, good heavens...' she whispered, aghast at that prospect for they were depending on that money for their mother's benefit.

In recent years, Lucia Blessington, Tomaso Barone's only child, had had every cancer treatment available in the UK and her health was still failing. But there was a clinical trial of a new experimental drug taking place in America that could save their mother's life. Unfortunately, it took serious money to win a place on such a trial, and the Blessingtons were poor as church mice.

Through their grandfather's lawyer, Tabitha had agreed to reduce the length of the agreed marriage to a three-year maximum and in return had demanded a very large up-front payment of cash. With that safe in the bank there would be sufficient money to fund her mother's place on the trial, and there would also be enough for her mother and her lifelong best friend to live on while she received treatment. That was the only reason both sisters had been willing to marry Tore Renzetti, because their grandfather had agreed to help his daughter and had then backed out on the agreement. Either twin would have done virtually anything to give their mother even that slender chance of survival. Their childhood might have been pretty miserable, but throughout it all their mother had been a beacon of love and support.

'Now it's your turn to step up,' Tabitha remarked with a guilty grimace. 'And we dare not tell Tore Renzetti in advance in case he refuses to do a swap.'

'But why should he? He couldn't be bothered meeting either of us!' Violet reminded the blonde tartly. 'He doesn't care who we are or what we look like or if we come with dependents. His lawyers never asked, did they?'

'No, they didn't, but it's going to be a headache getting the relevant paperwork changed in time from Tabitha to Violet. I've already committed you,' her twin announced, throwing her a remorseful glance. 'I had to sign the prenup this morning to ensure that that cash payment was transferred in time, and I panicked and forged your signature.'

Violet paled. 'But that's against the law.'

Her more impulsive and less careful sister shot her a silencing glance. '*So?* We can't take the risk at this stage that Renzetti will back out.'

'But *would* he? He must want those shares pretty badly to agree to this in the first place. And how am I supposed to pretend to be you when I'm six inches shorter and as dark-haired as you're fair? His legal team *has* seen you,' Violet reminded her in dismay.

'For the wedding, we'll stick you in high heels and a blond wig with a veil on top. We can swing it if we try hard enough,' Tabitha declared with characteristic fortitude.

Violet surveyed her twin with a sinking heart but not a word of argument could she come up with. How *could* she argue? Tabitha had been willing to sacrifice three years of her life, and it went without saying that Violet should be equally willing. Just because she was the less daring twin, didn't mean she had to be useless, did it?

It could work. It would *have* to work, wouldn't it? She would bring Belle into this stupid fake marriage and since Tore was based in London, she would keep on running the bakery as usual. As Tabitha was already telling her, no problem was insurmountable.

Violet felt sick on the way to the wedding. Actually being alone with her bad-tempered, sour grandfather was a source of stress. He was virtually a stranger. Indeed, they had only met once before and she was now pretending to be her sister, hence the wig and the veil that screened her face.

'I realise you've got a cold but can't you talk at all?' her grandfather queried peevishly, his low tolerance threshold challenged by her ongoing silence. 'You'll have to speak to give your responses at the altar.'

'Yes,' she said gruffly. 'I'll manage.'

She sat shivering in the fancy wedding dress, which had been bought to fit Tabitha. On Violet, it was too tight over the bust and too long. Those differences had forced her to wear six-inch heels, which she could barely walk in and a blond wig because she was a brunette. All she had to do, she reminded herself, was get through the ceremony without anyone realising that she was the original imposter bride.

And then Tore Renzetti would make that all-important up-front payment, and they would be home and dry. It didn't matter how he behaved or what he said afterwards once he realised he hadn't gotten the sister he had expected: She could take it. Of course, she could take anything the horrible man handed out in punishment! Her heart hammered inside her too-tight bodice, and her narrow shoulders braced.

The entire deception would have been much easier had her grandfather not insisted on a church wedding with the accompanying guests. There were too many people who would recognise that the bride was not the woman she was supposed to be. Shy, socially awkward Violet was cringing in horror at the threat of a public scene and of being exposed in public by an irate man. He might not have bothered to meet either twin but ultimately, he was sure to spot the difference between a five-foot-five-inch blonde and the less than five-foot-nothing brunette who had literally stepped into her sister's shoes. She could only be grateful that her grandfather, Tomaso Barone, barely knew her or her sister, having disowned their mother long before they were even born.

And anyway, what did any of it ultimately matter? Tore Renzetti and her grandfather *wanted* this marriage, and it was immaterial to both of them which sister he wed. Tabitha would've been a stranger, too.

'The full veil is a little theatrical,' her grandfather complained.

'I don't want anyone to notice if I cry,' Violet declared defensively.

'Why would you cry? You're marrying a hugely wealthy man with high-society status and the blessing of your family. You'll never want for anything again. It'll be a big change for you. No outstanding debts and the very best of everything. You've got it made. You should be *thanking* me for setting this up for you!'

Violet winced. Tomaso Barone was proud as punch of selling her off like a product because he was delighted that she was marrying into wealth and class. This wedding meant something to him while it meant nothing to Violet or her sister. Although that *was* an actual lie, she adjusted with a pang of discomfiture as she thought of her mother's frail health and wondered if they were chasing windmills while inwardly praying for a good outcome for the older woman. Even if the treatment were only to grant Lucia a couple of extra years rather than cure her, she reasoned heavily, it would be worth it.

She stumbled walking into the church. The heavy lace veil covered her face but made it hard to see steps. Her ankle twingeing as she shakily moved on, she accepted her grandfather planting her hand on his forearm and breathed in with a shudder at the foot of the aisle. Her future husband awaited her. Tabitha had looked him up online and announced that he was gorgeous, but doubtless that had been her lively sister endeavouring to make her sacrifice seem less of a sacrifice. Violet was ashamed to admit that she still hadn't looked because she was already too intimidated by the whole process. And then she looked ahead to the man at the altar...

Shock gripped her for a split second. The man awaiting her bore more than a passing resemblance to one of the elegant elves in her favourite *Lord of the Rings* movies. Very tall, very fair, very, very beautiful. No, she hadn't been expecting that; she hadn't been expecting that at all. She stared, helplessly entranced, marvelling that there wasn't some kind of crown on his silver-gilt hair and actual magical sparkles surrounding him. Just a stupid flight of fancy, she told herself off, but in truth she had been so terrified entering the church that anything that warded off the ice-cold taste of fear was welcome.

She didn't like angry men, having grown up with one in the person of her father, and her bridegroom promised to be very angry indeed at the deception practised on him. A man like him, rich, arrogant and hugely sought after by ambitious women, wasn't accustomed to receiving less than he saw as his due. And Violet had known since childhood that she wasn't the beautiful twin, blessed with that angelic fairness that distinguished Tabitha. No, she was short and dark and infuriatingly curvy.

Tore surveyed his bride approaching in literal astonishment. Her gait was awkward and stiff and the obscuring ornate veil she wore put him in mind of the Bride of Frankenstein. How many women covered their face that much in this day and age? Right, he reflected impatiently, *obviously* she was plain and had no looks to speak of. Maybe she was stupid as well, not to have

registered that her appearance was absolutely mean-
ingless to him. Even if she looked a bit ridiculous? He
gritted his teeth; possibly he would never take her out
in public. She was visibly shaking like a leaf. Tore gritted his teeth again, thinking of that up-front demand of
cash, reminding himself that this woman was an unashamed, tawdry gold digger. He reached down and
grasped her hand.

He had never seen such a small hand except on a
child and it was ice-cold, lost within his, fingers con-
vulsing like he was threatening her in some way. He
breathed in deep, ignored it and the ceremony began.
She spoke her responses in a strange little gruff voice.
It made him want to rip the veil off and offer her a
glass of water. It hugely irritated him. Perhaps there
was something wrong with her, physically, mentally…
How the hell was he to know?

And then it was done and he was threading the ring
on a tiny finger. He hadn't bothered with a ring for himself, had no intention of acting like a married man in
any way. He refused to change his own life. His bride
could have the trappings but nothing else. She got the
name, the ring, the money, the houses to share and that
was that. Tore Renzetti did not do parasites, unwilling
to work for a living.

Work was the spice of life to Tore. Aldo was forever
urging him to take it easy, to relax, to make something
of his free time, but Tore had never wanted free time.
For him, there was always another mountain waiting to
be conquered just ahead. He was purely goal oriented,
always had been, always would be, and no woman had

ever challenged that and probably never would. Tore had long since worked out that he was cold as ice in the heart department. Even in adolescence he had been blessedly free of crushes and infatuations because he was intensely critical and more prone to spotting flaws than perfections. And he liked himself that way; his cool, shrewd intelligence protecting him from the mistakes that others less blessed screwed up their lives with.

But by the time he stepped with his bride into a rear room to sign the register, the final legal step of their cursed alliance, he was out of patience. He watched her sign her name, except he was too clever not to notice that it was the wrong name and immediately he picked her up on it.

'It's not Violet,' he told her with amusement because what else could it be but a silly mistake. 'Your name is Tabitha—'

'Er…no, it's not, it's Violet,' she said in a very small, squeaky voice as he signed in his place.

'And lift that stupid veil!' he told her abruptly, marriage apparently conferring on him the right to speak to her as if she were a very young child. 'It looks like something you'd wear in an amateur stage production of *The Corpse Bride*.'

Violet trembled and began to fuss with the edges of the heavy veil.

Her bridegroom hissed something in a foreign language and impatiently tossed up the veil for her. It was too sudden a movement for the weight of the veil and the heavy long blond wig beneath it, and the whole lot went flying off the back of her head, leaving her fully exposed in the skull cap restraining her black hair.

'What the hell...' Tore exclaimed in disbelief.

'Violet?' Her grandfather demanded from the other side of the table.

'Where's Tabitha?'

The other older man, Tore's grandfather, was simply wide-eyed at the other side of the table where the signing had taken place. 'Is there something wrong?' he asked hesitantly.

'It's some kind of a scam,' Tore declared with distaste, whipping off the skull cap so that a torrent of blue-black wavy hair fell round his bride's pixie face and tumbled to her waist. And there she was, like something he dimly thought might pop out from behind a tree on a moonlight walk with her enormous blue eyes.

He had never liked blue eyes, he reminded himself. His vicious aunt had had blue eyes. He remembered the look in those eyes when she slapped him for getting in her way or seeing something he shouldn't have seen. He had seen stuff at four years old that no child should be allowed to see, and he had never forgotten those seedy glimpses of adult life. Forgiving, tolerant of those who broke the rules of decency, he was not, and would *never* be that way inclined. You got one chance with Tore Renzetti. Blow that chance and you never got another.

'I'm s-so s-sorry,' Violet stammered unevenly.

'You're not,' Tore informed her in a wrathful undertone. 'But you will be...'

And with that disturbing assurance, Tore lifted her

right off her feet so that her borrowed, rather too large, shoes fell off and he stormed for the exit door.

'But what about the reception I've organised?' Tomaso Barone demanded in a panic from behind them.

And Tore said something unrepeatable about what he could do with his wedding reception.

CHAPTER TWO

VIOLET WAS AGHAST as Tore strode back down the aisle of the crowded church, impervious to the startled gasps and the astonished speculation of their guests. Her cheeks burned hotter than fire with mortification. *Kill me now*, she thought. *I've married a drama queen.* No quiet chat and explanation for Tore Renzetti possible or allowed, no matter the public nature of the exhibition that he was making of them both. And what a temper! Goodness, those startlingly green eyes of his had sizzled into her like accusing arrows tipped with poison.

You're not sorry. But you will be...

Her empty, unsettled tummy lurched. She wasn't a heroine. If he had set her down on her own feet, she would've run like the wind, even though she was barefoot. A gleaming silver limousine drew up at the kerb. A man came out of nowhere to yank open the passenger door, at which point Violet was stuffed onto the seat with all the finesse a bag of groceries might have required. The door slammed and she grabbed the handle, suddenly convinced that it would be madness to stay with this lunatic, but the handle wouldn't move.

Tore swung in beside her from the other side and treated her to a razor-edged half smile. 'You're not going anywhere until I have this sorted out,' he assured her, unfurling a cell phone and within seconds commencing a dialogue in what she suspected might be Italian, of which she spoke not a word. Her anxious gaze welded to his classic profile, she recognised that his rage was only growing. A faint flush edged his high cheekbones now, a leaping tension surrounding the corners of his shapely mouth, not to mention the fact that he was clutching his phone like he might crush it. In haste, she looked away.

Tore set his phone into her nerveless hand. 'Type out your full name and birthdate.'

'But you already know it,' she pointed out weakly.

'Do as I ask,' he instructed. 'Naturally, I wish to establish whether or not that marriage ceremony was legal.'

Violet winced, belatedly recalling him christening the change of brides as a *scam*. She typed out her name and birthdate, passed it back in silence.

'So,' he recapped in the most sarcastic of tones, 'instead of Tabitha I've got Violet Grace Blessington.'

'That would be correct,' Violet stated. 'But you know there was absolutely no need for that melodramatic exit from the church. Tabitha and I made sure the paperwork was in order.'

'Is that a fact?'

'Yes…er, we didn't want any mistakes made. One of us *had* to marry you, so I'd be surprised if the marriage turned out to be illegal in some way,' she dared.

'In other words, you wanted that cash payment badly,' Tore interpreted unpleasantly.

'Yes.' Violet saw no point in lying about that necessity because she had an awful suspicion that Tore would drag every last detail out of her, even if she kicked and screamed during the process. He would make her pay the piper, regardless of how she felt about it.

Her conscience stirred. Wasn't he entitled to feel angry? Tabitha *could* have told his lawyers the truth and taken the risk that he would agree to the last-minute swap... But leaving their mother's health to rely on that necessary agreement when there was so little time to spare had proved too much of a challenge for both sisters.

A few minutes later, Tore was back chatting on the phone, presumably to a lawyer if he was still checking out the legality of their marriage. Violet swallowed hard, wishing she had a phone on her because Tabitha might well hear about the contretemps at the church. Her sister hadn't attended because she could scarcely put in an appearance as a guest when she was supposed to be the bride. However, their grandfather was unlikely to go in search of her sister, she reflected. He might be miffed at not getting to show off Tore Renzetti at the wedding reception, but he would be content enough once he was reassured that the marriage to Violet would stand. Tomaso hadn't cared which one of his daughter's twins chose to marry Tore.

'Why am I married to you instead of your sister?' Tore demanded abruptly, tossing his phone aside.

Violet shrugged a slight shoulder. 'Tabby agreed in good faith to marry you and then found that she couldn't go through with it a couple of weeks ago.'

'Why?' Tore shot back at her baldly.

Violet compressed her lips. 'Unexpectedly, she fell pregnant.'

'I suppose I should be grateful to have escaped that car crash,' Tore retorted unfeelingly.

'Yes, and if she was sitting here now, she would be equally glad to have escaped you,' Violet sniped, unable to bite back the response and stay polite.

'If your sister was sitting here now, this situation wouldn't have arisen. She didn't keep her word and the two of you chose to deceive me instead of being honest. That tells me all I need to know about your characters,' Tore derided. 'You chose to disguise yourself in the most ridiculous manner for the wedding. You completed the changes to the paperwork behind my back. You deceived me and your grandfather. At no stage did either of you consider the option of telling the truth.'

'While you're reading the riot act,' Violet said with new daring because her temper was bubbling like lava below her nervous exterior, 'could you tell me where you're taking me?'

'Home to where you will be living for the next three years.'

'Gosh, I can almost hear the rattle of the jailer's keys in that tone,' Violet slotted in helplessly.

'I will need your address so that your belongings can be conveyed to my home,' he told her coldly.

'Were you planning to pack my daughter in a cardboard box for conveyance as well?' Violet enquired dulcetly, beginning to get the measure of his polite passive-aggressive attitude to his clearly unwelcome bride.

Tore swung round to face her. 'You have a *child*?' he raked at her in unhidden horror.

'You see that there is the big problem of choosing not to meet either woman you might have married beforehand. You miss out on the little details,' Violet pointed out with satisfaction.

Tore sat in brooding silence and fumed. A kid? She had a kid! A child could not be as easily located in a distant wing of his house and forgotten about. Children were lively, noisy and demanding. Tore knew nothing about kids but he had occasionally been forced to socialise with friends who had reproduced, and what he had witnessed had not warmed him to the idea of sharing his life with little people. He liked his life just as it was: smooth, efficient, static. He liked his routines. He did not like surprises or disruption of any kind. His household ran with clockwork efficiency, he reminded himself soothingly. His staff would deal with the hassle created by a child.

'When can I expect to be in a position to be reunited with my daughter?' Violet pressed curtly.

'You should've thought of that before you married me.'

Violet reared round to look at him like a tigress protecting her cubs, blue eyes lightened by sudden fury, her face flushed, her tiny hands in fists. 'You will *not* keep me from my child!' she hissed back at him.

Taken aback by that startling burst of aggression, Tore studied her with academic interest. Not quite the nervous co-conspirator he had assumed; not quite the fearful victim she had been playing. 'Obviously, I am unlikely to do something which I have no power to do,' he breathed thinly.

Thoroughly rattled at the way *she* had allowed him to frighten *her*, Violet whipped her head away again, accepting that truth. But the smouldering blaze of his emerald-green eyes stayed with her. Nobody had ever looked at her before with such hostility and distrust. Belatedly, it occurred to her that having married Tore Renzetti in a deceptive manner could well make life very uncomfortable for her and Belle. The prospect of three years living in such an atmosphere left her bereft of breath and her usual optimistic spirit. It was time, she thought unhappily, to regroup. But she was stuck continuing in their marriage because she had signed a legal contract and accepted payment for doing so.

'I'm sorry that you feel…er…threatened by what my sister and I chose to do. No offence was intended.'

His perfectly sculpted lips compressed. 'I am not feeling *threatened*. I abhor lies and avarice. You deceived me for money. I cannot and will not respect that.'

Violet pictured herself telling him the truth behind their *avarice* and cringed at the concept of plucking a thousand violin strings with their story. Tore wouldn't respect that, either. She suspected that he was a man who only saw in shades of black and white and nothing in between. He criticised, he judged, he wouldn't try to *understand*. In his opinion, she had wronged him, even though she could not think of any lasting harm coming from that sisterly swap in brides.

'You're a very stubborn man,' she muttered unevenly. 'But you must see that if we're stuck with each other for the next three years, we have to—'

'I don't intend to be stuck with you in any guise for that length of time,' Tore framed with dulcet precision. 'We will live in separate wings of my home here.'

Violet's delicate profile tensed and she turned round to look at him and almost smiled. 'Oh, that's a very good idea,' she told him cheerfully as if he had handed her a beautiful bouquet of flowers.

Tore was taken aback, not having discarded the notion that his bride might strive to make their marriage into a real marriage by being sexy. After all, the more he looked at her, the more on some subconscious level he was aware that she was *not* unattractive. That mane of wavy, tousled blue-black hair was glorious, the blue eyes enormous in that pointed little face, her mouth ripe and pink. She had curves, a faint hint of cleavage peeking from the straining bodice of her gown, but she was small, slight in stature, the very last kind of woman Tore went for with such height and width of his own. She looked downright *breakable* and that was not a trait that fired his libido. He preferred tall, graceful women and she was neither. She would never appeal to him, he assured himself calmly. If she had any seduction plans, she would soon find herself barking up the wrong tree.

The tip of Violet's tongue slid out to moisten her taut lower lip beneath Tore's burning scrutiny. She didn't know why those sharp green eyes were staring, but she didn't like the sensations he aroused within her. A sort of warmth was snaking up through her, making her tummy tumble, her dress feel constricting, her very hands restive. It was truly uncomfortable and in haste, she looked away. *No, I do not fancy him; no, I do not*, she told herself firmly. And she knew it was a lie even while she was telling herself that; one of the biggest lies she had ever told herself because he was absolutely drop-dead beautiful from the dark brows and lush black lashes that framed those stunning eyes below that unexpectedly pale hair to the high cheek-bones that led to such facial definition that it was a challenge not to stare back.

In an uneasy silence, the limousine drew up in a driveway and stopped dead at a front door. A massive double front door beneath an imposing portico. The door beside Violet cracked open and she stepped out, not remotely inhibited by her bare feet, her gown trailing round her ankles.

Trailing like a shroud, Tore reflected as he automatically swept her up into his arms again, striving to do the newly married thing even though there was nothing remotely romantic about either of them. He wondered why in that initial glimpse she seemed to have shrunk when she had not been very tall even to begin with. He was startled when a small fist struck his shoulder hard.

'Put me down!' Violet demanded.

'Act like a bride,' Tore told her drily. 'This is what you're getting paid for.'

Furious pink lit Violet's cheeks and she set her teeth together. 'I didn't know that acting was included.'

'Then you didn't read the paperwork. Behaving like a normal wife is part of it.'

'While we inhabit separate wings of your gigantic house? Is *that* normal?' Violet asked snidely as he strode indoors because the more she glanced around herself the more she realised that she had never seen such a large house beyond her tour of a handful of rooms at Buckingham Palace.

Tore ignored the comment and lowered her to the ground, belatedly noticing that she wore no shoes, wondering what had happened to them but not really caring because his bride was not at all what he had expected. There was a sort of angry insouciance about her piquant little face as she gazed up at him with a fixed, utterly unconvincing smile. She didn't like him either and the knowledge startled him. He had been prepared for all sorts of behaviour from the unknown woman he had to marry but not the same rancour that he was also experiencing. He had expected sweet as sugar submission or provocative sex appeal, all the wily lures of the determined women who usually chased him…but he wasn't getting *any* of that.

'What happened to your height?' he framed abstractedly, noticing that she had shrunk to alarmingly tiny proportions.

'My sister's a few inches taller,' Violet revealed between gritted teeth.

'What height are you?'

'None of your business,' she whispered in embarrassment. For someone who had told her to act he wasn't doing a very good job in front of his hovering staff: an older man garbed like a butler and a middle-aged woman with a polite smile of welcome.

'You're not even five foot, are you?' Tore gritted like height was next to godliness.

'I'll leave you to guess but I suppose you could say that we're not a match made in heaven. You're much too tall,' Violet pointed out with pleasure. 'Now, do you think you could have me shown to my room and given some food because I'm starving.'

'Please show Mrs Renzetti to her quarters,' Tore instructed curtly. 'And feed her!'

As he stood in the grand hall, a peal of chiming laughter sent his head back around. His bride was clinging to the balustrade and giggling like a drain. *'Quarters?'* she queried with amusement. 'Am I in the army now?'

'I'm Dora, Mrs Renzetti, your husband's housekeeper. The other member of staff is Mr Jenkins, who is in charge of the household,' Dora told her chattily, guiding her across a massive landing and down a corridor that led through another door. 'I do hope you like the rooms prepared for you.'

'I need a bedroom for my daughter,' Violet announced. 'She's eleven months old.'

'A baby!' Dora carolled in apparent delight at the news. 'We'll all very much enjoy having a child in the house. When will she be arriving, Mrs Renzetti?'

'This evening,' Violet decided, for while Tabby was available to look after Belle, Violet wanted her adored little girl back under the same roof as fast as possible. 'I'll need transport for my possessions and to collect her.'

'I'll inform Mr Jenkins immediately,' Dora told her,

pushing back a door and allowing Violet to precede her into the most lovely room set up with the kind of colour scheme and furnishings that took Violet's breath away.

'This is…*gorgeous*,' Violet pronounced truthfully because around her she was seeing the grace and beauty of a decor enabled by unlimited wealth. Silk-draped curtains, fresh flowers, antique furniture and paintings. It was all so far beyond her personal experience that she was tempted to pinch herself at the idea of actually *living* in such a room.

'Let me show you the rest of it,' Dora urged.

And there was a lot of *the rest of it*, Violet registered as she was shown a second bedroom that would have to house Belle, and a large sitting room, dining room, study and a very nice, spacious kitchen, which made her eyes flash with appreciation. She could bake here in her new home if she put in an industrial oven and then go to work as usual. It also dawned on her that with such rooms put at her disposal, her bridegroom clearly didn't wish to see her at all and her chin lifted at that obvious point. Being married to Tore promised to suit Violet perfectly.

'Mr Renzetti's grandmother does have a good eye for decoration,' the housekeeper confided. 'A lovely lady as well, very down-to-earth.'

Well, that news was something. Violet hoped that she wasn't already so prejudiced against Tore that she assumed his family was all cut from the same cloth.

'Now, what would you like to eat?' Dora asked in completion.

'If there's food in the kitchen I can look after myself.'

'But why would you when we're here to do it for you?' the older woman quipped and asked her again what she would like to eat.

Violet conceded the point, not wanting to behave like a lodger in the household when she was supposed to be its new mistress, even if the staff had to suspect she wasn't going to be a normal wife when she had her own wing to occupy. Thirty minutes later, Dora had helpfully unhooked her wedding dress, and Violet had changed into serviceable jeans and a long-sleeved top. She ate her perfectly cooked omelette with satisfaction and sped downstairs at the news her transport was waiting for her. Three years of someone cooking for her? Oh, she could definitely get with such a programme, she decided with determined cheer. She spent enough time in the kitchen at work and had little enthusiasm for doing it outside work as well. There would be no cleaning, either, she reflected. She would get her evenings back again...

Tabby rushed to the door to greet her when she arrived at her former flat. Her twin had decided to move in the week before the wedding when Violet had begun to panic because Joy, Violet's childminder, tenant and a part-time student had decided to move home and live with her parents to save on expenses.

'I've been climbing the walls since Grandfather phoned me and asked me what was going on!' Tabitha exclaimed. 'And then I didn't hear a word from you. What's he like?'

Violet correctly interpreted that question as relating to Tore rather than their grandfather. 'Obnoxious, arrogant—'

'Pretty good-looking, though, isn't he?'

'Don't see what that has to do with anything,' Violet parried, stooping to grab Belle, who had crawled into the hall to greet her with enthusiasm. She gazed down into that lovely little smiling face and hugged her daughter, suddenly happy for the first time that day. 'Tore is none too chuffed that I've got a kid, but it doesn't matter because he's put me on what seems to be the opposite side of his extremely large house with my own accommodation.'

'Oh, that's brilliant!' Tabby gasped, hugging both her and Belle. 'I was feeling so guilty and worried about you. You know, that he might push the sex angle,' she extended with a wince.

'Oh, no worries there! He's far too superior to want anything of that nature from me,' Violet laughed. 'He couldn't get away from me fast enough after the ceremony at the church!'

Across London at the same moment, Tore was struggling to handle a situation he had never expected to arise. 'But it's a marriage of convenience,' he reminded his grandfather on the phone. 'We won't be *having* a honeymoon.'

'Why not?' Aldo Renzetti enquired mildly. 'At least getting to know each other as friends will make the next three years more bearable for both of you. And there's a little kid involved now, a baby, I understand. You can't ignore the needs of a child for three years. You're a stepfather now, Tore. Surely, I don't have to tell you that you have a duty to be present for that little one?'

Tore wanted to tear his hair out, scream, shout, violently disagree but of course, as usual, he forced himself to live up to Aldo's old-fashioned ideas of family, duty and honour. 'No, you don't,' he murmured as gently as he could when he was furious and fighting to hide the fact. 'Very well. Violet and I and her *little one*,' he voiced with a grimace, 'will be delighted to accept your generous gift.'

'You've always loved the *castello*, Tore. We spent many happy summers there with you. Make the most of the opportunity not to turn your wife into an enemy for the future,' Aldo advised sunnily.

Tore breathed in deep and raw as he tossed his cell phone down. He wanted to kill someone. He was taking the wife he despised and her child on a honeymoon he didn't want. Why? He was too much of a coward to tell his grandfather that he didn't intend to take his gold-digging wife to the foot of the street if he could help it. Aldo would consider such feelings cruel and insensitive even though Tore had told the older man about that up-front demand for cash. But then Aldo was the same man who had stepped up without hesitation to accept the responsibility of raising his late son's child. Naturally, Aldo now saw Tore as an acting stepfather. He was that kind of man, decent, kind and honourable, the same man whom Tore loved like the father he had never known, and the only reason Tore had accepted this marriage of convenience.

Aldo regarded all women as innately fragile and in

need of loving, caring support and loyalty. The fact that Tore had planned to spend his wedding night with a leggy blonde in unashamed adultery would horrify Aldo. Well, now he wasn't going to be horrified because Tore would not be spending a single night with a leggy blonde in London. Evidently, that ring on his finger was cutting him off from sex as well, which for Tore was a truly appalling development.

Of course, he hadn't ever planned to be faithful! Any more than he had planned to bed his wife! He might be married to an undersized, mouthy single parent but he did *not* see himself as a married man or a potential stepfather to a young child. Not in this particular marriage, anyway.

Clearly, Aldo and Matilde, his grandparents, had yet to absorb that hard fact. Yet, as grandparents they were relatively young being only in their fifties, but they were probably hoping for some miracle to occur and provide them with great-grandchildren. Why else had his grandmother also chimed in during that unwelcome phone call to confess that she couldn't wait to meet Violet's baby? The baby he didn't even know the name of, which Agnese Renzetti had censured as a glaring omission.

'You mean you didn't even *ask*, Tore?' she had gasped in dismay. 'What were you thinking?'

That had long been Tore's burden in life, he acknowledged. He was in possession of wonderful, unbelievably nice and loving grandparents but they would never ever know—if he had anything to do with it—that their beloved grandson wasn't remotely nice or loving. Except towards them…

* * *

'You're the most beautiful little girl *ever*!' Violet ex-claimed as she planted a noisy raspberry kiss on Belle's plump little tummy and the baby chortled full of glee, rolling over to move off under her own power. Fed, bathed and into her giraffe jammies, Belle would soon be ready for bed.

Violet massaged her aching back. With her sister's help she had packed all their belongings and the baby equipment and it had taken the afternoon to bring it all back to Tore's house. She had unpacked the necessities with Dora's assistance, and Belle's cot was set up in readiness. Luckily for Violet, Belle was a sociable, easy baby and change didn't freak her out.

A knock sounded on the door and on her knees, still tidying up all the paraphernalia that went with babies, she swivelled. 'Come in,' she called.

Astonishment gripped her when Tore strode into her new sitting room. Her first thought was, shame-fully, that he was off-the-charts *hot*, particularly when he was more casually clad in light chino pants and a long-sleeved top, his luxuriant white-gold hair a little messy and damp, she surmised, from a shower. The embarrassment of that thought suffused her cheeks with colour.

'We're flying to Italy later this evening,' he an-nounced.

'I beg your pardon?' In disbelief at that declaration of intent, Violet scrambled upright, barefoot in her jeans and no makeup, once again feeling outclassed and caught unprepared.

Tore dealt her a sizzling appraisal. 'You heard me fine.'

'Yes, I did but I couldn't believe you were serious. Why would I travel to Italy with you?'

'You're supposed to be my wife.' His big frame tensed as a baby crawled from behind a chair and moved towards him. He endeavoured to ignore it. It was tiny, *another* member of the tiny family with a tousled cloud of brown curls and a huge smile as it crawled over the top of his shoes and hovered looking up at him with big, expectant blue eyes. It was not a fan of being ignored because it let out a little shout as if it was trying to grab his attention. A little girl, he reckoned.

'Agreed, but we both know I'm not a real wife.'

'It felt shockingly real in that church,' Tore contradicted. 'In any case, I don't care how you feel about a trip to Italy because you're going whether you like it or not.'

Violet's blue eyes sparkled at his arrogance as he spoke to her as though she were an employee without choices about where and when she went. 'For how long?'

A broad shoulder shifted in a shrug. 'A month at most.'

Belle let out another shout that had the edge of a shriek and Tore flinched. He surprised himself then, dropping down into a crouch and saying, 'And what's your name?'

'Belle,' Violet supplied, watching her daughter stretch up a tiny hand to Tore's knee.

Tore scanned the huge smile and invitation of the raised arms and leant in to lift the baby up. Belle squealed in delight and kicked her legs. 'She weighs nothing,' he commented with a frown. 'Is she healthy?'

'Totally, but she's very like her mother in build— naturally slender and light in weight. Look, Tore, I want to be reasonable but I can't *possibly*—'

His ebony brows had pleated. 'You're *not* her mother?'

'I am but I'm not her birth mother. I started adopting her after my best friend, her mother, died,' Violet extended. 'Isabel and her partner nominated me as her guardian in their will.'

Realising that the baby was still dangling, Tore shifted her experimentally closer and like a puppy she pawed her way up his chest and into the crook of his neck, burying her head there and slowly slumping against him.

'She's tired. If you give me five minutes, I'll put her to bed and then we can talk about Italy. It would be *impossible*,' she could not help telling him in advance. 'My business couldn't run without me. I work with an assistant but he couldn't bake or decorate cakes as well as me. He's not experienced enough yet.'

'You own a business?' Tore was disconcerted enough by that news to follow her into the bedroom next door.

'Yes, but strictly speaking it's not mine. The bakery belonged to Isabel and her partner. They left it to me, which has allowed me to be able to raise Belle, but once she grows up it should go to her because it's her inheritance from her parents,' she explained as she tucked Belle into her cot, switched on the glowing sheep toy that played soft music and backed away to close the drapes. 'Night, night, baby.'

Belle snuggled in, clutching a shabby dinosaur, and simply closed her eyes. Having been told that he was a challenge to get to sleep as a little boy, Tore was impressed. And Violet was not at all the feckless, idle, spoiled young woman he had rather unpleasantly assumed she would be as Tomaso Barone's grandchild. She ran a bakery and obviously baked as well. Not for the first time, he cursed the arrogance and the anger that had prevented him from having both sisters fully investigated in advance of the wedding. He should've *known* something of that nature when he was marrying the woman. Instead, he had chosen to work off biased assumptions rather than fact, and that oversight infuriated him.

'I can make arrangements to make the Italian trip possible,' he asserted, accompanying her back into the sitting room.

Violet dealt him a pained look. 'It's not possible. I've got cake orders coming in, decorating to do, deliveries to do, payroll, bank visits.'

'If I'm willing to pay enough I can get it all taken care of for you,' Tore imparted with unblemished confidence. 'Experts are always available for hire for the right price…'

'But why would we even want to go to Italy?' she prompted. 'I know it's your home and I wasn't being rude *but*—'

'My grandfather has signed over to me the property in Calabria where I spent every summer growing up,' Tore countered. 'It's a wedding gift, a big gesture when you consider that this is not the usual marriage and he knows that.'

'So, if he knows that why is he making the big gesture?'

'He witnessed our exit from the church,' he reminded her, with that beautiful mouth of his compressing, emerald eyes narrowing, only making her more aware of the lush curling black lashes he rejoiced in. 'I would imagine he doesn't want us to be at each other's throats for the next three years and he's done it for *our* benefit. He's a kind, thoughtful man.'

'Something my grandfather doesn't suffer from,' Violet remarked helplessly, her eyes clouding with bad memories. 'He cut off my mother when she was only a teenager and never forgave her for marrying someone he didn't approve of. Although history proved that he was totally right to make that judgement, my mother suffered a lot without family support when we were little.'

'Some of us find it equally hard to forgive mistakes,' Tore commented drily, his tone shaking her back out of the past to the present. 'We'll be leaving for Italy tonight as soon as my pilot can find us a slot at the airport.'

'I don't want to go to Italy,' Violet reiterated, tilting her chin, standing her ground. 'Right at this minute it's out of the question. I have responsibilities.'

'And what about your responsibilities in this marriage?' Tore cut in with lethal bite. 'You're my wife. We only got married today. I believe I'm owed more than the hour the church ceremony took of your time.'

Violet paled. That word *owed* reminding her of the enormous sum of money that her sister had demanded from him before she signed on the dotted line of matrimony. She was equally aware that the agreement they had signed had taken for granted that *she* would fit in with *his* life and not the other way around. That would've suited her twin but unfortunately, Violet had less freedom. 'Yes, you do have some grounds for believing that *but*—'

Tore slanted her a hard, glittering green glance. 'No objections. Even if you're not the original intended bride, you *will* meet the obligations you agreed to. It can hardly escape your attention that your business difficulties are nothing to do with me, and my offer to take care of those problems was exceedingly generous of me in the circumstances.'

Violet sucked in a deep breath. 'Yes, but this is my livelihood and Belle's,' she pointed out uneasily.

'My staff will nail down a replacement for you and you will fly to Italy.'

Involuntarily, Violet spoke again. 'But not in the middle of the night, not with a baby in tow. It'll upset her. Couldn't we leave in the morning?'

Tore clenched his teeth together on the desire to maintain his schedule as he had already decided. As a rule, he was not flexible. But while it may not have been his choice, yes, he now had the needs of a baby to consider. He wasn't so stubborn that he would punish a baby, too... *Was he?* He knew very well what it was for a child to suffer a guardian's mistaken choices. That was the life he had lived unhappily with his mother's kid sister. He might not want to be a stepfather but he would not make an innocent child pay for Violet's sins. He was neither that selfish nor cruel.

'We'll make it an early departure first thing in the morning,' Tore decreed, still irritated that he was even making that concession. Violet had chosen to replace her sister and had inherited her commitments and that was definitely *not* his problem.

CHAPTER THREE

VIOLET LOOKED AROUND with interest as the SUV that had collected them from their flight delivered them into a green, elegant space sheltered by towering stone walls and filled with a beautiful traditional Italian garden complete with low box hedging, fountain, shaped beds and gravel walks.

'Is this a hotel?' she asked automatically.

'No, this is the property.'

'But it's a castle,' she pointed out gently as though he might not have noticed.

'*So?*' Tore shot back at her, far from reasonable after a four in the morning departure from his London home.

Slap it into you, Violet reflected with satisfaction. He deserved to be irritable after losing a night's sleep, particularly when there had been no logical reason for such a very early departure. There was no emergency, after all. She had simply married a very strong-willed, stubborn guy. Compromise, *sensible* compromise, was still a skill he had to learn in personal relationships but so far, it seemed that Tore was the type who only forged a straight line between objectives and was aghast at the prospect of accepting the smallest change to his routine. And she just bet that routine was set in stone.

Belle had adjusted by going straight back to sleep within minutes of being roused. Violet, accustomed to predawn starts but used to working them, had finally dozed off during the flight. Tore, however, nowhere near as sensible, had worked throughout.

'You could've mentioned that your grandfather's property was a castle.'

'Would it have made any difference to your attitude towards coming here?'

'Probably not,' Violet conceded equably, for work also always came first in her world. That said, however, Violet was thrilled to find herself on the grounds of an inhabited castle by the sea and on the edge of a small town in Calabria.

'*Castello di Renzetti* was my grandfather's ancestral home and birthplace,' Tore imparted grudgingly.

'Lucky man,' she remarked, gazing out at the pristine gardens and the spick-and-span outer walls, eager to see the interior and what she imagined would be spectacular views.

'He wasn't. The family were penniless back then and the castle was pretty much a ruin,' Tore admitted curtly. 'Once he began to make money, he poured back as much as he could into this place. It's very important to him. That's why we had to immediately visit and demonstrate our appreciation.'

That was interesting news. Cold, judgemental Tore turned human and sympathetic and mindful of other people's feelings once his grandfather entered the picture, Violet noted, suppressing a grin with difficulty. So there were limits to that almost robotic outlook on life in general. *Some of us find it hard to forgive mistakes*. Yes, and one of them was sitting right beside her. Unluckily for him, Violet had grown up facing male disapproval and criticism and she was proofed against it. First had come her grandfather's longstanding rejection of his daughter, Lucia. How much better all their lives might've been had their grandfather responded more kindly to his daughter's pleas for help!

Although, would they have been? Violet asked herself wryly. Possibly, their grandfather had known his own daughter better than most. In fact, their mum had still stood by her loser of a husband and their father long after most women would have thrown him out. Lies, cheating, thefts, not to mention alcohol and physical abuse had destroyed what should've been their safe home. But Lucia Blessington was the kind of woman who had stuck by her man through thick and thin for far more years than she should've done. Intensely loyal and loving towards her children but also, unfortunately, towards her undeserving husband.

Indeed, Violet wasn't sure that if her father hadn't himself walked out for another more promising prospect of a woman her mother wouldn't *still* be by Sam Blessington's side, wearing her wedding ring. Her father had pushed for the divorce although his affair had died soon after it was granted. High on his latest acclaimed exhibition as a leading artist, their father had put both ex-wife and daughters behind him for good. That had proved a relief to his daughters, if not their mother. Violet didn't dislike anyone as much as she disliked her own father. She was always aware that he had made both her and her twin unjustly wary of and distrustful with men.

Holding a drowsy Belle in her arms, Violet clambered out of the car.

'Do you need any help?' Tore asked without noticeable enthusiasm.

'Yes, thank you.' Violet handed over her daughter with a bright smile. Tore was exhausted and cross and he was still doing the courteous bit, and in Violet's opinion that deserved a reward and there was no greater reward than Belle. Belle patted his cheek and tugged at his bright silvery hair, equally impressed. Until now there had been no men in Belle's world, and she had taken a liking to Tore at first sight.

They mounted the steps below the clear blue sky with the heat of the sun beating down on them. They were greeted in the ancient stone-tiled hall by a clutch of staff, all of whom crowded round Tore to volubly admire Belle even before greeting Violet.

'Please may I hold her?' a young woman urged, holding out her arms to Belle.

Belle turned her head away because she obviously preferred Tore. Violet smiled and laughed.

Introductions began. 'Violet, this is Stella, who swears she's a baby whisperer after all the babysitting she's done over the years.'

Violet lifted Belle out of Tore's arms, ignored her daughter's little sound of protest and handed her to the young woman. 'I'll show you the nursery,' Stella offered.

They climbed a twisting stone staircase, ornamented

with narrow window casements and oil paintings and there on the first floor was a full-blown nursery, which took Violet by surprise.

'Little children in the family visit often,' Stella told her cheerfully.

And Violet, misery that she was, wondered if that meant, as Tore now owned the castle, that it would be *their* role to entertain those children and their parents. She wouldn't have thought like that if she and Tore were a normal married couple, but keeping up the act that they *were* in front of potential family members would be more challenging.

And there was everything in that room from a beautiful cot and junior beds to a wide selection of toys and necessities. A sound alerted her to Tore's arrival. He stood beside her, his shapely mouth compressed into a tough line while Stella finished settling Belle in her giant cot. The young woman departed then, seemingly as aware as Violet of the new castle owner's ominous mood.

'What's up?'

'Our housekeeper has informed me that we're still in store for all the usual family visits this month, which means that we will be meeting every near *and* distant member of my family and entertaining them. I *never* visit during July!' Tore gritted out between hard-clenched teeth.

'Not the sociable type?' Violet guessed with rueful amusement. 'So, Mr Grumpy Pants, how do we handle the situation since you evidently have inherited the responsibility?'

'I can hardly cancel them at the last minute!' Tore bit out with barely leashed rancour. 'That would distress my grandparents.'

'You have been *had*,' Violet murmured with wry sympathy. 'Your grandparents are being more appropriate than you assumed. This arrangement will hardly qualify as a honeymoon and it's a neat way of getting you to conform to expectations that you have, clearly, previously ignored. *Family time…*'

Tore swore vehemently under his breath in Italian and swung round to her, one hand momentarily brushing her shoulder to ensure that she turned to face him. 'Did you think I hadn't already worked that one out?' he raked furiously down at her, green eyes flashing sparks in that lean, darkly handsome face.

'Don't put angry hands on me or raise your voice,' Violet told him in sharp, icy warning. 'I won't stand for being treated like that!'

Tore gazed down at her in total shock at the sudden alert and he stepped back a pace. 'I barely touched you,' he objected straight off. 'And I was only expressing my annoyance. It was *not* directed at you personally.'

'I'm sorry…you unnerved me there for a moment. I don't like tall, angry men getting too close,' she admitted uncomfortably.

'Who taught you that lesson?' he prompted with a frown of censure.

'My father. Let's just say that he was a terrible husband and parent,' she replied flatly.

'I would never *ever* lose control of my temper with a woman or become physical,' Tore assured her squarely.

'I'm not built that way. I may storm up and down a little and curse but that's the height of my flaws in that field.'

'Good to know,' she muttered, pink-cheeked with embarrassment that she had been forced, in fairness to him, to admit her father's appalling parental failures. She had heard enough of Tore's comments concerning his grandparents to know that an unhappy home life with them was far removed from his experience and that felt humiliating to her just at that moment.

'There is another problem,' Tore murmured very quietly as he preceded her out of the nursery. 'We can't occupy separate bedrooms with family members under the same roof. I also doubt if there would be enough rooms free to accommodate the guests. Although my grandfather added an extension when I was a child, it's still not a large property.'

Violet breathed in slow and deep but inside herself she was secretly filled with amusement. Tore was no longer on the front foot. His grandparents had stymied him by landing him with a month of happy family to-getherness, which he craved about as much as he craved a broken leg. She hoped she was a more generous person than he was in adversity.

'If you can respect my privacy, I can respect yours,' Violet responded quietly.

'*Seriously?*' Tore countered in apparent wonderment. 'You're not about to pitch a five-act tragedy over this?'

'I don't think you could do anything that would make me pitch one of those,' she answered truthfully. 'I'm quite a quiet person and usually non-confrontational.'

So take that and stop jumping down my throat look-

ing to fight, she wanted to say but she was not that blunt.

Tore breathed in deep and slow. 'I apologise for making that scene at the church but the awareness that I had seemingly married the wrong woman, and a woman wearing a disguise, overcame my good manners.'

'That's okay. Nobody died, nobody was hurt,' Violet responded more sunnily. 'I did understand how you felt.'

'But you still haven't explained why,' he reminded her.

'Maybe someday,' she said dismissively, recalling how sarcastic he could be and shrinking at the prospect of describing her mother's frail health in what would probably strike him as the ultimate sob story. And then she would be so angry she would lose her temper and she did not like to lose her temper, it being the only thing she seemed to have inherited from her horrible father.

Tore cast open a door, wondering what other murky secrets she was still hiding from him. Although there was nothing murky about a bakery, he conceded as she walked into the spacious bedroom they would be forced to share. Surely, Aldo Renzetti, quite a prudish older man, could not have thought *that* through!

'The bed is big enough for three or four of us. We'll manage,' Violet framed with determined calm even though she had never ever shared a bed or a bedroom with an adult male. Wild horses could not have dragged that lowering truth from her. But honestly, for the past few years with her mother's illness, her friends' deaths, the bakery and her daughter, Violet hadn't had the space for a personal life. That was something other young single people got to have while she had little but heavy responsibilities on her plate.

'I appreciate you not freaking out about this whole situation,' Tore conceded, suppressing the suspicion that she might want something from him in return, striving to be a little more gracious to match her.

Violet gave him a huge smile and her slight shoulders lifted.

Green eyes narrowed and Tore's big powerful frame tensed. The smile lit up her little face like sudden sunlight. *Little*, he reminded himself fiercely, in danger of being squashed if he got too close. Why was she looking sexy all of a sudden? Was it the hair, that generous fall of waving ebony silk? The big blue eyes he had told himself he didn't like? The sheer delicacy of her in miniature? Or the surprisingly full thrust of her breasts and the curve of her hips? He had no idea; he only knew that he was without the smallest warning, hard as a rock. Well, there wasn't going to be *any* fraternising of any kind. She would have to drug him to get him in that mood...only apparently, not this time.

Tore had gone silent and it unnerved Violet. 'I'll just unpack, get comfortable.'

'There'll be an early lunch served in an hour.' There was a kind of intensity in those startlingly green eyes that held her fast where she stood. He had very thick, dark lashes, which accentuated them up close. Her tummy flipped, her nipples tightened; the kind of heat she didn't want to notice caused an ache between her thighs. Her face went scarlet and she turned away to the luggage, determined to stop looking at him. So he was beautiful like a fantasy, and fantasies were harmless. They weren't real. She recalled her late friend talking about being sex-starved when her partner was abroad visiting family, and she smiled down at her case contents. *Obviously*, she was sex-starved and that was all that was wrong with her. And it didn't matter anyway because Tore was not available. He was as safe a target as a hot pin-up poster on the wall, she reasoned.

She had gone very pink, Tore was thinking as he took his leave. Because he had been staring at her, his brain pointed out. He absolutely should not be doing that but for the first time he was thinking that the lack of sex in his life might not be as sensible as he had assumed. For years he had been of the opinion that sex was genuinely not a necessity, and bedding women who universally viewed him as a trophy because of his wealth and status, had not changed his mind. He had had all kinds of sex and almost all of it had been vaguely disappointing, not at all what he had hoped lay ahead of him as an adolescent. If lusting after the wrong woman was the punishment, he needed to think again. When was a wife not a wife? *His* wife. Their marriage contract excluded sex.

Stella acted as translator for her mother, the housekeeper Sofia, and the two women began to lead Violet on a tour of the castle before lunch. As far as Violet was concerned, she thought, unlike Tore, that it was a very large property but grasping that Tore's relatives visited in family groups helped her understand his point. They were in a long stone corridor when Tore strode out to join them and spoke to the two women.

'I'll show you the castle,' he spoke in English to bring her up-to-date.

And he did, pausing to show certain paintings that displayed the main characters in an ancestral saga that spanned several hundred years, explaining how his grandfather had tracked them down once the family impoverishment was at an end. He showed rooms like the one set aside as a game room for the teenagers, the snooker table, the library stuffed with recent literature, and she realised that it was very much a *family* holiday home. It might be in apple-pie order and lavishly furnished but the accent was on character and comfort, rather than grandeur or a desire to impress.

'It's a really lovely house,' Violet acknowledged as he reached over her head to open the narrow door set between massive walls that they had paused in front of. An odd little chime sounded and just as she was wondering what it was and hastening to precede Tore through the door, he was suddenly, unexpectedly wedged in the same too-small space of the doorway with her.

Jarred by the startling heat and strength of his very tall and powerful physique locked against hers, Violet blinked up at him, disconcerted that he could've pushed his way in front of her to get through the door first.

'The bolted door and the alarm are a warning that it's dangerous. That's why I tried to go ahead of you,' Tore explained in a somewhat raw undertone. 'There's a flight of stone stairs to your immediate right and only one child had to fall down them for Aldo to appreciate that he needed to block off this entrance to the extension. Only adults and staff use it. Access isn't a problem on the ground floor.'

'Oh…' Violet barely stirred, paralysed where she stood with Tore's body heat leaking into her every skin cell and setting off what felt like a chain reaction inside her: the warm flush of her skin, the goose bumps on her bare arms, the dangerous flutter in her belly. And still locked against her, *him*, all that was lean and hard and masculine, tearing apart her equanimity.

'Am I allowed to…to kiss you?' Tore breathed in a fractured undertone, glorious green eyes blazing down at her with desire.

Violet may not have been around the block very much but she had long waited the advent of a man who would study her as if she were his very last meal, as if she *meant* something more than a fleeting notion. 'Why not?'

'It's against the rules—' Tore glowered down at her as if she should know what he was talking about.

'Oh, for goodness' sake!' Violet hissed, rising impatiently on tiptoes, but even that wasn't sufficient to overcome the difference in their heights, and his hands dropped to her waist and he lifted her up in an effortless movement that in some mysterious way was incredibly sexy.

And then he kissed her, bracing her spine back against the thick stone wall that bounded the doors. He went for gold like an Olympic swimmer, pressing even closer, welding every inch of her into his powerful body until his mouth connected with hers. Firm and soft, assured but gentle, and she leant into that kiss like a trouper. A split second later, fireworks went off in the pit of her stomach, exploding through her limb by limb until there wasn't a single part of her, it seemed, that wasn't on fire for its continuance.

His tongue skated across the roof of her mouth and then plunged and then she was spun into a fierce maelstrom of hunger that left her quivering and breathless. She wanted more; she wanted *so* much more. One hand lifted and speared into his springy silken hair and the other braced on his shoulder, closed in place, gripping the tensile steel of muscle there. Nothing had ever felt like being in his arms; nothing had ever been so exciting, so fiercely compelling, that she simply couldn't resist it. But *he* was. And that truth was a revelation that stunned her out of what little remained of her wits.

A sound interrupted them and Tore lowered her carefully back onto her own feet again, turning to address the housekeeper, who had a crisp stack of fresh bedding in her arms.

Sofia beamed at Violet and for just a moment, Violet was in such a daze at the disruption that she couldn't work out why. Of course, the newly marrieds finally acting like honeymooners! What people expected even if nothing about that experience had proved to be what *she* expected.

'Let's get lunch,' Tore said, smooth as glass and stretching down to reach for her nerveless fingers. 'I don't know about you but I'm hungry…'

CHAPTER FOUR

VIOLET DIDN'T KNOW which one of them felt the most awkward during the hour of dining that followed. She had stolen Belle from Stella, who had been about to feed her daughter in the kitchen and had insisted on feeding her in the dining room instead. With Belle in her high chair, wanting to feed herself but not yet capable of getting a spoon to her mouth, there was no room for conversation. There was a lot of pretend airplane flying with the spoon, even more silly noises and several angry tussles with Belle. In between times, Violet swallowed the occasional sip of wine and a mouthful of the delicious savoury tart provided for her own meal.

'If you don't want to talk about something, just tell me,' Tore informed her as he set down his coffee cup to leave the table and rose to his full intimidating height. 'You don't need to hide behind a baby.'

Face aflame, Violet watched Belle trying to crawl across the polished floorboards in fast mode to follow Tore from the room. He didn't miss much, did he? He had seen right through her foolish pretence. And what had he taken from that avoidance tactic of hers? That she didn't want another kiss?

Pale now, Violet scooped up her disappointed daughter, who had not been able to catch up to Tore. *It's against the rules*, he had told her. His rules? Her rules? Whose rules? What on earth had he been saying? My goodness, for all she knew he already had a girlfriend somewhere. Their marriage was fake, she reminded herself with a faint pang of rejection, which was even more stupid. Feelings weren't involved in their relationship. And if Tore was involved, the *rules* were probably forged in steel. So no more feelings, no more kisses. He was a breathtakingly beautiful guy and totally her fantasy male, but that didn't mean she had to make a fool of herself and expose her reckless fascination. A guy with looks of that ilk had to receive many promising offers from women, and he didn't need to settle for a small, curvy baker with little experience with men.

She was in bed before she saw Tore again. She had had a busy afternoon. Stella had accompanied her down to the beach and through the little town. On the street she was disconcerted by how many people acknowledged her and paused to be introduced to her by Stella. Locally, the name of Renzetti was much respected, and Stella told her how much the interest of Tore's grandparents in the town had accomplished there. She did wonder if Tore, a workaholic running a multibillion-dollar earning industry, would ever emulate the older generation.

That evening, she climbed into the big bed, clad in unremarkable pyjamas, and put out the light. When Tore arrived, he crept about in darkness until she gritted her teeth and sat up to put on a lamp. 'It's all right. I'm not asleep yet.'

'I thought you could be faking it to avoid me again. Although I do owe you an apology for kissing you.'

'Oh, don't be ridiculous,' Violet muttered before she could think better of it. 'It was a kiss. We're both adults.'

'Well, *be* an adult and tell me how you felt about it.'

'I thought that was obvious… I liked it,' Violet replied uncomfortably.

And Tore was stunned by that very honest response. *I liked it.* She had said so in spite of the marriage contract and hadn't denied enjoying it to make a point. He didn't think he had ever been with a woman who was that open and straightforward. It was an amazingly attractive quality. There was no faking a front, no flirtation in such an answer. She was putting herself out there…*the way you wouldn't*, he acknowledged, a touch uncomfortable with that truth.

'But it goes against what you—or should I say your sister—agreed to in the marriage contract, which we both signed.'

'I'm only marginally aware that there was an actual contract signed,' Violet admitted, slumping down on the pillows, wishing Tabitha had shared more with her. But then Tabitha always focused on the big picture, not the little details. She suspected that Tore might well have ended up strangling Tabitha had he married her. He might prefer rules, but rules and unnecessary detail inflamed her twin. Tabitha had been a total rebel at school and anywhere else where people tried to tell her what she could and couldn't do.

'There was a clause within the contract specifying that there would be no physical intimacy.'

'Tabitha couldn't have read it properly,' Violet told him with confidence, recalling how her sister had been concerned that her bridegroom might be expecting sex from her.

'She didn't read it but she signed the document?' Tore queried in apparent disbelief.

It was incomprehensible to Tore that anyone could sign a legal agreement that they hadn't fully *read*, Violet recognised. However, he had not had the specific stress of knowing, as Tabitha had, that she *had* to sign regardless of what was in that document. It was for their mother's sake and the sole hope of obtaining the money they needed for her treatment. Tabitha had known that she had no choice.

'My sister gets irritated with stuff like that. She's very impatient.'

'You're not,' he remarked.

'No. We're non-identical twins. We don't look like each other and we're also quite different people but we love each other to bits anyway,' she completed, her breath feathering in her throat as he dragged off his shirt.

An acre of naked male flesh swam into view, spanning toned biceps, prominent pecs and the sort of taut abdominal muscles, flat stomach and lean waist that belonged on a giant movie screen. Violet endeavoured not to stare. She wasn't a teenager, for goodness' sake! Her response to the thrilling expanse of Tore's bronzed magnificence embarrassed her. Out of the corner of her eye she caught the removal of the sleek suit pants below and she shut her eyes fast, listening to him trek into the en-suite bathroom.

'Will it keep you awake if I go for a shower?'

My goodness, he was so polite. 'Not at all. Go ahead.'

Now she had to think of him stark naked in the shower! Did he have no sensitivity? Or was she the only one of them starved of such thoughts and promptings for far longer than she cared to admit? She rolled back and forth in the bed, striving to get comfortable with the situation while adhering strictly to her side of the mattress.

'So, I've been thinking...' Tore mused as he sank down into the bed mere inches away.

Violet was busy wondering what he was wearing and telling herself that it was none of her business. 'What about?'

'I don't know why I was thinking about that marriage contract—'

Well, if he didn't, Violet did and she said, 'You were thinking about it because you like rules, legal rules, whatever...so, what about that contract?'

'It doesn't apply to us because you didn't actually sign it. I'm married to you, not your sister. We won't make new rules. We'll let everything progress naturally. I will try to loosen up a little on the rule front,' Tore conceded because he was still hearing *I liked it* somewhere in the back of his brain and just then it sounded like a remarkably soothing refrain.

It was strange how he no longer felt quite so trapped in the marriage, he acknowledged in surprise. The anger had gone. Violet was so grounded that she calmed him. She wasn't creating a fuss about anything... Why should he? After all, if she could make him feel what she had made him feel when she was in his arms, she was more of an ally than an enemy. As for that demand for up-front cash that had once enraged him? Possibly, he was more than a little spoiled by the fact that large sums of money had always been available to him. He had never known poverty. And the way his bride dressed herself and the baby, she was pretty poor. He had already made arrangements to deal with that problem.

Progress naturally? What did he mean by that? No more rules?

'I don't really understand what you mean by—' she admitted ruefully '—progress naturally?'

'If we want to kiss, we kiss. If we don't, we don't,' Tore framed crisply, his dark, deep drawl curling up her spine like a caress.

Violet curled up sleepily. 'So, no rules, then,' she mumbled in relief.

And she fell asleep right there and then. Tore was rather disconcerted by that discovery. He remembered suspecting that his ambitious-to-keep-him bride might try to use sex to manipulate him and a quiet laugh escaped him. No, he didn't think Violet in her alphabet pyjamas was likely to be involved in that power play. But over the years he had had more than one sexual partner who sought to manipulate him.

A week later, Violet traced her fingertips across the neat piles of silk, lace and the finest cashmere in her walk-in dressing room. An array of summer garments hung in the closets for her: pretty dresses, formal evening wear, beachwear and more luxury lingerie than she had ever seen outside a shop. There were even rows of footwear of all descriptions and handbags galore. It was time to have a word with Tore in private.

She descended the curving stone stairs, crossed the hall and traversed the lower floor corridor into the extension where Tore kept an office suite. Phones were ringing, quickly answered by formally dressed staff. Computers were humming. It was all business. There was a beautiful beach outside and the sun was shining, but inside the office space they could have been in any city location. Tore was dealing with a herd of guests under his roof by continuing work as usual. He wasn't entertaining or rediscovering old childhood haunts with the guests, either; goodness no.

'I'd like to see Tore…my husband,' Violet added as a harassed assistant set down the phone and regarded her and the baby in her arms in open dismay.

The woman dealt a tentative knock to the closed door behind her and Violet slid in front of her and simply opened it, espying Tore lodged by the window while he dictated something into a phone. Sheathed in a dark grey suit, a midnight-blue shirt and silvery tie embellishing the slice of broad chest visible, he turned, enquiring emerald green eyes to her. Such beautiful eyes, jewels of light in that lean bronzed face, black lashes dipping as he studied her.

And that was a cue for butterflies in her tummy and a touch of overheating to kick in, a bit of a flush. With those physical reactions came uncertainty and a discomfiture, which she valiantly fought off. 'Tore…'

Belle let out a squeal and opened her arms wide.

Almost unbalanced by the little girl's welcoming gesture, Violet set her daughter down on the wooden floor
beneath her feet. Belle scrambled in Tore's direction.

'How can I help you?' he asked pleasantly, tensing
a little as Belle got closer.

Violet could have given him a list of how he was
not helping her with *his* guests, *his* relatives, whom
he was ignoring, but the new wardrobe of clothes was
currently top of that complaint list. 'It's the clothes,
the new clothes you appear to have bought for me...'

Tore lifted a sardonic brow in apparent surprise.
'And?'

'Obviously, I don't need all that stuff,' she objected.

Tore surveyed his bride, clad in faded jean shorts
and a rather washed-out tee and flip-flops. 'You need
new clothes and it's my role to provide them.'

'Since when?'

'Since I decided I didn't want to see my wife and
her daughter less well dressed than our guests. It's a
superficial thing and I don't usually worry about those
but I need to see you turned out correctly as my hostess...and squash any unpleasant rumours that I could
be a tight wad,' he quipped with amusement as Belle
crawled across his feet and then when he didn't appear
to notice her arrival, turned and did it again.

Violet lifted her pointed chin, blue eyes flaring. 'I
wasn't expecting you to buy me clothes, Tore!'

'Seems remiss of you not to have guessed that I
would take care of a problem like that,' Tore countered, admiring the pink in her cheeks, the brightness
of her eyes. Her black hair was piled in a messy bun

on top of her head, odd little tendrils curling round her small ears, dark against her pale Celtic complexion. He throbbed against his zipper, reminding himself that she was in his bed at night but always fast asleep by the time he got there and still asleep when he rose at dawn. He was going to have to rearrange his routine, cut the very late nights and possibly the early starts as well. Evidently, she needed a lot more sleep than he did while he had decided that he needed rather more of her.

'It wasn't a problem,' Violet contended curtly. 'I'm quite happy wearing my own clothes.'

'But I'm *not* happy with you or Belle looking shabby.' Tore finally bit the bullet and just came clean as Belle loosed a squeal of frustration. He dropped down and grabbed Belle where she was now clinging to his trouser legs, precariously standing and proud of the fact. 'What are you complaining about?' he asked the little girl as he swung her up into the air and she giggled, her rounded baby face a picture of delight. 'Who lifted you out of your cot this morning when you were desperate to escape?'

Cheeks still burning from that label, *shabby*, Violet frowned. 'You...*did*?'

'*Si*. I felt sorry for her and Stella wasn't up yet. Belle and I had breakfast together,' he shared with amusement. 'I gave her a banana and water to keep her happy until Stella appeared.'

'That was very kind of you. I should've been up... but the clothes? You really think they're necessary?' Violet prompted uneasily.

Brilliant green eyes rested on her. 'I do and because

I have no idea of your style, there's a selection and you can return anything that you dislike. In the short-term, though, it means you have something to wear for every occasion.'

Violet lifted her arms to reclaim her daughter. That word, *shabby*, had hit her pride squarely where it hurt and she knew it was true. She didn't spend money on clothes for her or her daughter. She was used to making do with what she had and that was a habit engrained from childhood when money had always been in short supply. Even though the bakery was doing well financially, she still didn't spend on anything other than necessities. Now she reckoned she should have splashed out on some smarter clothing for her and Belle before the wedding. Tore had won the battle, she reflected tartly. No, it wouldn't be fair to expect him to be embarrassed by his wife's *shabby* appearance.

'You should come down to the beach with us this afternoon,' she suggested because she had already developed the habit of letting Belle play in the sand and dip her toes in the surf for an hour every afternoon.

Tore stiffened. 'Maybe another day.'

'I thought so,' Violet sighed. 'Don't be offended but you should be giving your relatives more than your company over dinner.'

His ebony brows, such a stark contrast to his light hair, pleated. 'If they've got you, it lets me off the hook.'

Violet hadn't been prepared for him to be that frank. 'Yes, but they're family, Tore. Family won't always be there, so you should appreciate them while they are.'

Tore went rigid. 'I couldn't care less.'

'You will when your grandparents arrive because I gather they *do*. It's one month in the year,' she reasoned. 'Surely, you don't have to work this hard every day of the week?'

If she'd been his real wife, he assumed he would feel differently. He knew he was neglecting her and their guests. But he reminded himself that Violet and Belle would be gone in three years. That reality cost him the oddest sharp pang. Certainly, life was less boringly predictable with them around. They lightened the atmosphere, smoothed some of his rough edges into something more socially acceptable than his usual hermit habits and touched his conscience.

'I'll begin taking more time off,' he told her, exhaling in a rush. 'I promise.'

Satisfied, Violet departed but Belle wailed. Tore groaned, running long brown fingers through his pale, already tousled hair. And later, he watched his unwanted wife walk out onto the beach, Stella in tow with the baby and someone else dragging a load of bags of essentials. He watched a tall man in bathing trunks leap up to stride forward and greet her and he frowned. Sandro, his cousin Sandro Rossi, newly popular television star and famed pastry chef. He had an ego that could probably be seen from the moon.

Of course he and Violet would have stuff in common, not least the fact that Violet was baking the household's bread and Sofia had been furious when Sandro tried to take over the job, pointing out to Tore that Violet was a much better baker. The intense loyalty the staff had already developed towards his unexpected

bride had made Tore smile in appreciation. He watched
Violet throw back her head and laugh and it annoyed
him.

'His favourite is red velvet,' Violet informed Sandro,
who irritated the hell out of her with his superiority. It
was Tore's birthday in two days and she was baking
his preferred cake. According to Sofia, he wouldn't
want purple grape or orange or almond ricotta cake.
He would want the favourite he had enjoyed since he
was a little boy.

'But that's not Italian and it's not very sophisticated,'
Sandro pointed out while his adoring mother backed
him up in that conviction.

'Doesn't matter,' Violet said mildly. 'He's getting
what he likes. If you want, you can decorate it.'

Sandro threw his handsome dark head back in dismay. 'My assistants do the finishing stuff like that. I
don't.'

'I'm quite happy to do the whole thing,' she replied
in a tone of finality. 'But thank you for offering your
expertise and advice.'

Sandro sighed and returned to flirting with her.
Eventually, irritated by his persistence, Violet got up
and walked down to the shore to enable Belle to dip
her bare toes in the rushing surf. Her chortles of glee
released Violet's tension and she smiled. She fooled
around with her daughter for twenty minutes, enjoying her baby innocence, thinking with pained regret of
how much Isabel and Stefan would have enjoyed such
an outing with their child. She was blessed, though, to
have the time to play with Belle, she reflected, appre-

ciating that her enforced break in Italy had provided unexpected benefits.

A swanky baker from Italy was currently providing the bakery's sale produce while Tabitha took care of the business side and the staff. Her twin was a hard worker and that awareness was allowing Violet to relax. Her mother had begun her treatment at the cancer centre in Massachusetts and it was too early for any prognosis as yet, but at least a start had been made. Certainly, Lucia's spirits had lifted, Violet had deduced from their various phone chats. This time, her mother was daring to hope.

Violet decided to bake Tore's cake before dinner. It would have to be a large cake because they had a castle full of guests. For forty-eight hours, there had been a constant procession of arrivals and Belle was no longer alone in her nursery. The aunts and the uncles, the adult cousins and partners and their children had contrived to fill every spare room in the castle.

'We've never had so many guests,' the housekeeper had proclaimed with pride and satisfaction at the large turnout. 'It's because *Signor* Tore has married you. Everyone is curious.'

For curious, read downright nosy, Violet thought for she had had to fend off far too many intrusive questions. How many weeks/months had it taken for Tore and her to realise their futures were aligned? Did she want children? How was Tore adapting to being a stepfather? Considering that she had only met Tore on their wedding day, it was challenging to handle the assumption that she knew everything there was to know about her husband. Everyone believed they had been together for months yet had married in indecent haste. Cue many curious glances in the direction of her not quite flat stomach.

After the beach, Belle went down for a nap and Violet hit the kitchen to begin baking. Unfortunately, Sandro soon found his way there, too, and joined her, sitting at the table with his coffee to watch her work while sharing both criticisms of her method and what he viewed as motivational tips. Violet gritted her teeth and just got on with her task, ignoring him to the best of her ability while tossing him the occasional polite smile.

Tore paused in the doorway when she was laughing at some story Sandro was recounting, a dusting of flour on the tip of her nose. Sandro, in the meantime, was busy admiring Violet's bare shapely legs and curvy bottom as she ambled between sink and table. Something about that scene infuriated Tore and filled him with distaste.

'May I have a word with you, Violet?' he asked.

Her smooth brow furrowed as she looked up from her labour and focused on him. So tall, and dark and effortlessly suave. 'Er...okay.'

'In private,' he specified, urging her a few feet down the corridor.

'I'm kind of busy,' she admitted, wiping her hands uneasily down the sides of her shorts, wondering what was amiss.

Tore wasted no time in telling her. 'It is not appropriate for you to be working in the kitchen. We have a full staff here,' he reminded her, gazing down at her with fierce green eyes, his exasperation unhidden.

'I like to bake. I'm afraid you're stuck living with that,' Violet replied curtly.

'I'm hoping you'll be reasonable about this,' Tore informed her.

Faint pink entered her cheeks. 'Not feeling reasonable. When are you reasonable? When you're working eighteen-hour days even though we have a houseful of guests? Is that your version of reasonable? People in glass houses shouldn't throw stones.'

'Violet—'

'No, don't say my name like that as if you're scolding a little girl.' Violet lifted her chin and stared up at him, her blue eyes wide with annoyance. 'Don't make me lose my temper with you. I have a terrible temper.'

'You are my wife—'

'Don't remind me of what you won't allow me to forget!' Violet exclaimed, her trembling hands settling on her slim hips, her voice steadily rising in volume.

'We'll discuss this upstairs,' Tore breathed with resolve.

'I won't be any more reasonable upstairs. Even gagging me won't shut me up. If I want to work in the kitchen, I will work in the kitchen and there's nothing you can say or do to stop me!' Violet lashed back at him furiously, his unyielding stance and tough gaze merely making her feel more angry. 'You are a bully, Tore.'

'I am not a bully,' Tore fielded speedily and then he bent down and simply swept her off her feet to stride down to depress the button on the lift that went up to the next floor.

As he draped her over one broad shoulder, Violet just lost it. Her temper surged to the top of the scale and screamed inside her in desperate need of escape. She thumped his back with balled fists and shrieked, *'Put me down!'*

Tore strode into the lift and lowered her back to the floor. 'You do not need to be working in the kitchen,' he informed her stubbornly. 'You're my wife, a very wealthy wife. We employ people to take care of all the domestic tasks. Your personal involvement is in no way necessary.'

'Tell all that to someone who wants to listen!' Violet hissed, spinning where she stood to brace white-knuckled hands against the steel wall in frustration. Anger was writhing inside her like a wildfire, seething and burning out of control.

'You weren't joking about the temper,' Tore remarked, disconcerted by the level of her ire and her obvious struggle to put a lid on her emotions. Violet, so quiet, so calm. Had he done this to her? Driven her into a rage?

Violet had told him the truth when she told him that she didn't like to lose her temper. Very rarely did she make that mistake. She didn't want to get angry and lash out at people because invariably that led to regret and apologies. But when she did get angry it reminded her of her childhood when her drunken father's rages and assaults had terrified them all. Thankfully, that rage was the only thing she had inherited from him and in the aftermath, she always felt wrung out like an old dishcloth.

She stomped down the passage and preceded Tore into their bedroom. 'Why did we have to come up here?' she demanded, refusing to look directly at him.

'The staff were peering out of doorways. If we fight, it should be in private,' Tore decreed.

Her gaze moved up to his lean, dark face, his eyes bright as gemstones. He stood back from her, his suit jacket flipping back to show a slice of shirt-clad chest and a silky lining as he pushed long fingers into the pocket of neat-fitting pants, drawing the fabric taut across his groin.

Pink and uneasy, Violet shrugged and glanced away from him. 'I have nothing to say other than that I plan to continue treating this place as I would treat my own home. It's wrong to expect me to behave differently here. And if you could prevent your smarmy slimebag cousin Sandro from stalking me, flirting like mad and telling me risqué jokes and stories, I would be very grateful,' she added in a rush. 'Although I suppose it's possible that he's feeling sorry for the new wife, whose husband rarely puts in an appearance. Maybe he thinks he's doing me a favour by showing me so much attention.'

Tore's shapely mouth went taut at the reference to his cousin and faint colour edged his high cheekbones. He would certainly ensure that Sandro did not make any more of a nuisance of himself. He suspected that Violet's refusal to be impressed by the younger man had pushed Sandro to ever greater efforts. Sandro did not like to be ignored.

'I believed I was doing you a favour because you don't need kitchen duties on top of everything else you're handling here.'

Violet winced. 'But I *enjoy* baking. Did you think you were rescuing some poor downtrodden Cinderella from kitchen labour that you consider too humble for your wife to be seen doing?' She breathed in deep, feeling the last of that insane anger draining away and sighed. 'What I really need to tell you is that that contract Tabitha signed does not mean that you *own* me body and soul.'

Tore went rigid. 'I know that.'

'I'm not sure that you do,' Violet confided. 'I may only be your wife for the present. But I'm *not* an employee who has to do everything you say and follow your every guideline. Is it really this much of a challenge for you to show me some respect? I treat you with respect. I also try to see your viewpoint. You should at least have *asked* if I considered baking a pleasure or a punishment.'

Tore raised both hands in sudden apology. He felt slightly battered. Only his grandfather had ever dared to rake him down in such a way. He saw that he had erred in his view of his bride right from the first mention of marriage. He had considered only his own comfort, his own needs, his own wishes. He had not made allowances for hers and yet how could she remain part of his life for three years without negotiation and compromises on both sides? He knew that he could be selfish. It had been a means of survival while he was a child, but being raised by adoring grandparents had possibly allowed that fault to linger longer than it should have done.

'I should've asked,' he conceded. 'But I will repeat… I am *not* a bully.'

'Perhaps not. It may just be the sheer physical size of you that intimidates me,' Violet countered ruefully. 'And that's not your fault, any more than it's my fault that I'm shorter than most people. Well, at least you didn't lose your temper, too. Look, I have to get back down to the kitchen to finish what I started.'

The cake complete, Violet went upstairs to dress for dinner where she was intercepted by one of Tore's cousins, who told her apologetically that later they would all be heading to a family party at her boyfriend's parents' home. Sheathed in a black, quite sparkly cocktail frock that bared her back and her legs, Violet sat down to dinner with the heady knowledge that once the meal was over she was free from the responsibility of acting as a hostess. A night off her duties and she would make the most of it with a long, luxurious bath and a good book.

'You're free to go back to work,' she told Tore cheerfully as he rose from his seat, having assumed that he had been bored stiff with the inconsequential chatter that had distinguished the gathering.

'And what are your plans?'

'A lazy bath and a book I've been saving,' she confided lightly.

'That dress is lovely on you,' he murmured, sharply disconcerting her with that personal remark. 'And I spoke to Sandro. I doubt if he'll make you uncomfortable again.'

The compliment embarrassed Violet. She wasn't used to compliments. There had been no loving father or admiring boyfriend to build up her ego. She told herself that the beautiful new wardrobe was worth its weight in gold. She was also relieved that he had taken the step of warning Sandro, having been unsure of how best to handle an actual pass if Sandro dared to push that far with her.

Thirty minutes later, she slid with a sigh of bliss into a richly scented bath. The water brushed against her skin like silk and she had even laid out a fancy nightdress and wrap to don afterwards. Luxury, sheer luxury, she savoured. That bath had been calling to her since the day they had arrived because as far back as she could remember she had only lived in accommodation with showers. She had sampled one of the decorative bottled bath oils to try. An hour later, she clambered out, moisturised all over, dried her hair and put on her new slithery lingerie, an artful confection of lace, silk and ribbons in a soft blue shade, the likes of which had never come her way before.

There was a glorious seating area by a fireplace in the bedroom and she sank into an opulent sofa, clutching her romance novel, and put up her feet with a groan of pleasure. Perfect peace she was savouring just as the door opened and Tore strode in.

CHAPTER FIVE

'AM I INTERRUPTING YOU?' Tore enquired.

Violet sat up, her cheeks flaming, suddenly very aware of how little she was wearing and the sheer nature of the garments. She hadn't thought that through very well when they were forced to share the same room and bed. She didn't want him to think that she was being deliberately provocative.

Tore absorbed the pert jiggle of her surprisingly full breasts and went taut, infuriated by the fact that he only had to get within five feet of Violet to start thinking about sex. In fact, he only had to *look* at her and his logical brain went illogically blank and then haywire. His bride might be little in stature but she took up way too much space in his head. He thought about how she had looked even from a distance in a bikini on the beach, recalled Sandro's indefensible excuse that his wife was *gorgeous* and his shapely lips compressed. He also remembered her saying, *I liked it* and all of a sudden all he wanted to do was give her more to like.

'What are you reading?' he asked, using the query to break out of his paralysis and bend to scoop up the book she had thrown aside.

The cover depicted a half-naked, very muscular

male, and his mouth quirked with appreciation. He skimmed the page she had been perusing and his ebony brows lifted in surprised satisfaction.

'It's a romance,' she said lightly.

'Raunchy stuff,' he remarked, resting the paperback down again where she had left it.

She went pink, obvious discomfiture gripping her. 'I-I—'

'I was teasing,' Tore qualified. 'Nothing wrong with a raunchy read.'

'I know.'

'I came up for a shower...' Tore hesitated, glancing back at her when he entrapped the deep blue eyes resting on him. 'And here you are, sitting in a little pool of light looking absolutely edible in little wisps of fabric.'

'They're not little wisps,' she argued tightly. 'It's all full length but maybe I would've covered up more if I'd been expecting you to walk in.'

'Doesn't matter how covered up you are. I have a great imagination and you shouldn't have to think like that anyway. This is *your* room in which you should be able to relax. Forget about me.'

'That's kind of a challenge,' Violet acknowledged uneasily, her breathing coming a little quicker through her lungs as she collided head-on with shimmering emerald green eyes accentuated by lush black lashes.

Tore swung back round. 'I'm sorry. That's my fault. No matter how hard I try to ignore it, I'm extremely attracted to you. I'm not telling you that to make you uneasy. I can and will control that side of myself but there's no escaping the truth when it's just the two of us.'

'It's only curiosity,' she assured him, confident of the fact. 'Living like this in such close proximity and pretending to be a normal couple is a strain for both of us. Maybe we should just simply get rid of the curiosity and do what everybody assumes we're doing anyway.'

Tore struggled to untangle that statement and came up not quite believing that she could've meant what she had actually said. 'Not sure I grasped that.'

Violet laced her trembling fingers together tightly. 'We're not kids, Tore. It's only sex making stuff feel awkward between us, nothing more important. I bet if we get that childish curiosity out of the way, we'll find out that we can manage fine.'

'There's nothing childish about the way I feel about you,' Tore countered, sliding out of his suit jacket and hooking it on one finger.

She studied his lean, powerful physique and the sheer energy he emanated with fresh understanding and a small pulse of superiority. She knew she was right and that he was wrong. Adults living so close to each other questioned and resented boundaries imposed. It was common sense to her way of thinking. Once they had established that sex between them was nothing exciting, they would both be cured of the craving that itched in her every skin cell. Was he the same? she wondered helplessly. Or was it only because he was a guy that he couldn't handle the proximity?

'It's only curiosity,' she assured him again as she stood up. She found him equally attractive and she wasn't prepared to lie about that when he had been honest. And really, what was the big deal? She had

had sex before and it had been a huge disappointment. It might be marginally better with Tore because she was much more drawn to him than she had ever been to Damien but even so, it wasn't as if she was expecting meteor showers raining down from the heavens. She wasn't that naive anymore. Nor was she a nervous teenager who had little idea what she could be inviting. And once they had experienced that intimacy together, perhaps they would both feel more relaxed with each other.

Tore dropped his jacket and stalked forward to reach for her and that fast she was in his arms, shaken and stirred by a sudden burst of anticipation. He lifted her up into his arms and crushed her parted lips under his, his tongue dipping and delving and setting off a riotous reaction through her quivering body.

'I like the way you kiss,' she muttered unevenly as he lifted his head.

Tore slanted her a frankly irrepressible grin that made his lean, dark, serious features shed years. 'I know,' he said with pleasure.

'I don't like big egos,' she warned him, forefinger poking his shirtfront in warning.

And he brought her down on the bed with a simmering smile that fired up every nerve cell she possessed. 'Not one of those…although, I can't say that Sandro emerged from our chat feeling as good about himself. Since he got that TV show, he's had an army of fans and their adoration has made him believe that his charm is universally appealing.'

'He was getting on my nerves,' she confided. 'I

mean, he's family but no offence intended, he's definitely a bit of a perv.'

'My grandfather, Aldo, would revel in that description,' Tore laughed and he went back to kissing her while she worked, somewhat absentmindedly on his shirt buttons, loosening them, sliding them free, spreading her fingers across warm male flesh. He dug something out of his jacket and tossed it down beside the bed and she squinted, recognising that it was contraceptives and relieved that he was prepared.

Tore dragged the sleeves of her wrap down her arms with an imprecation. 'You might as well be wearing a shroud,' he complained, impervious to the fluttering attractions of the garment.

'You're impatient,' she complained.

'I feel like I've been wanting you for a lifetime,' he breathed rawly, an uncertain note in that admission as he made it without consciously thinking it out. And then he immediately thought that he shouldn't have said that because it made it sound like what they had was special and obviously being the kind of cold-hearted bastard he was, there was no such thing as any woman who was more special than the previous. Yet, the bite of craving her naked in his arms had persisted day and night. Acknowledging that made him feel antsy.

'Sounds good. Nobody has ever wanted me that much,' Violet confided, thinking wryly of her first and only lover, Damien.

Damien had needed a lot of encouragement to get that intimate with her and only the idea of going off to college still being a virgin had motivated him. Of course he hadn't wanted her *enough*, she reasoned, and she hadn't wanted him that way, either. They'd been best friends but a bad mix as sexual partners, she conceded because the sex that had followed had been a major disappointment to them both. And only months later, in his first weeks away from home, Damien had informed her that he was gay, which had explained a lot from her point of view. In truth, Violet had never before been able to luxuriate in the conviction that a man truly *wanted* her.

Tore ripped off his shirt and cast it aside, dealing with her robe in a similar fashion. He covered her breasts through the lace of her nightgown with big, gentle hands. 'Just a glimpse of these drives me crazy,' he growled. 'If I was to see them in a bikini on the beach, I could be uncontrollable.'

'How?' Violet asked in honest wonderment. 'It's only flesh—'

'*Heavenly* flesh,' Tore contradicted, tugging down the slip straps to bare his bounty and nuzzle against the firm mounds with his unshaven chin. His mouth landed on a pouting pink nipple and conversation ceased as that tugging turned into an incendiary burn between her thighs and gave Violet something else entirely to think about.

'I love your breasts,' he groaned.

'Yes, got that message,' she whispered in disconcertion, not at all certain what to do with such admiration when it had never come her way before. 'And your bottom,' he confessed, moulding the rounded generous globes with appreciative hands while he tugged her down the bed.

At that point, he shocked her, roaming to a place that wasn't on her mental map of sex. She shifted, awkward, embarrassed, trying to close her thighs again.

Tore lifted his tousled silvery head and murmured. 'I want this… I need to taste you… You won't regret it.'

And in receipt of that sincerity, Violet's objections were quelled because what did she really know after one less than successful experience? Insecurity made her loosen her hold on her trembling body.

He went there to that most private place and ravaged her flesh as though she were a feast he was celebrating. Shock held her fast and then the quivers of response and reaction began to hit her in waves. Every wave built up to the next and long before she knew what was happening to her, she was flying up into the sun and an explosion of unbelievable pleasure was blasting through her every limb and rendering her helpless. She flopped back into the pillows like a boneless rag doll.

Tore shifted over her and bent his tousled head to extract another deep, driving kiss filled with hunger. And panic claimed her then because she knew that she hadn't been a partner in any sense of the word. She hadn't touched him; she hadn't touched any part of him. While he had given her pleasure, she hadn't reciprocated and that awareness shamed her.

'Tore…' she began as he twisted away to don protection.

'You're amazing,' he turned back to tell her in a ringing surge of unconcealed approval.

Long fingers fluttered at the sensitive heart of her, toying with the newly tender flesh, stoking her earlier arousal afresh and adding a new urgency to that need that she had never felt before. An ache began to build low in her belly. He slid over her and a fleeting memory of the pain once before made her tense in dismay.

'You're very tight,' he breathed in a roughened undertone. 'Are you a virgin?'

'Of course not,' she declared with confidence in that fact at least.

He eased into her degree by degree and she tried not to tense at the sting of his entrance. Even so, her body felt like one giant howl of craving that could only be sated by him sliding inside her. But it felt like there was far too much of him and that added a faint edge of panic to her anticipation. Keen to get over what she expected to be an anti-climax, she parted her thighs more and tilted up her hips to encourage him. Finally, he buried himself deep. An unexpected burning sensation made her flinch and then there was a sharp little pain that made her whimper in dismay.

Tore froze and gazed down at her, intense green eyes holding her fast. 'Are you sure I'm not your first? I hurt you.'

'Only a little. It's been years,' Violet admitted grudgingly. 'Ignore it, don't stop.'

His ebony brows pleated into a frown.

Violet was fearful of being categorized as a freak then and she shifted her hips up again in welcome, keen to push the encounter to its usual denouement. He shifted his hips, rolled them and the strangest sensation of pleasure feathered through her lower body. She closed her eyes, giving herself up to that sensation, wanting so badly to feel what she knew some other women felt.

'I can still stop,' Tore breathed in a raw undertone.

'No!' she answered fiercely, convinced that she was doing absolutely the right thing and ridding them both of that dangerous curiosity that was making life difficult.

He tugged her thighs up even higher and surged deeper still. The unfamiliar sensations came in a ripple that washed through her and then centred low in her belly like a little spark that was catching eager to burst into a flame. And she discovered that once the discomfort and the stress had gone, she liked what she was feeling. The weight of him over her, the provocative slide of his male body over hers, the piercing pleasure starting to pool like warm honey low in her body.

A frisson of excitement rippled through her. 'Don't stop,' she warned him.

He startled her by sliding off her and flipping her over, pulling her up on her knees and sinking back into her in an urgent, commanding thrust. As long fingers brushed the bud of her clit, she gasped and the backwash of delight almost swallowed her alive. His ferocious control was elemental and raw and savagely masculine, filling her with sensual energy and enjoyment. His every movement controlled the enervating flow of that sweet pleasure and she ran with that earthy pull of sensation, losing herself in it, yielding control, wanting more and more until she reached the peak her body was unconsciously striving to attain.

A climax engulfed her in a surging rush of feeling and she cried out, her voice breaking in shock as he surged inside her one more time and groaned, attaining his own orgasm. Soon afterwards, she slumped, utterly empty of response but luxuriating in the blissful aftermath of satisfaction. *Well, wasn't exactly prepared for that*, was her first coherent thought.

Tore strode into the bathroom but quickly rejoined her. He pulled her close and rolled her over, throwing back the sheet, his keen gaze homing in on the blood stains. 'You were a virgin. You should've warned me. I would've gone slower and been more gentle—'

Violet's eyes flew wide and she sat up. 'I wasn't... I couldn't have been. I had sex when I was seventeen!' she protested.

Tore tugged her back down to him. 'Well, it didn't take,' he reasoned, closing both arms round her. 'Let's not argue about something immaterial to the present.'

Violet wanted to argue but she was remembering back to that night when Damien had lost interest, as it were, and they had drawn back from each other in mutual discomfiture that they had so misjudged their friendship that they had conducted such an experiment. But it had hurt, she recalled, which had convinced her that the deed had been done and she was no longer physically innocent. Now she didn't know what to think because at the time there had been no embarrassing evidence on the bedding.

'I hurt you... I wish I hadn't,' Tore continued.

'I'll recover,' she muttered drowsily. 'Well, have you conquered your curiosity?'

Tore laughed softly above her head. 'It's a little too early to say but I should admit that I'm already thinking of how much fun it would be to do it again…of course, awaiting your…er recovery.'

Violet tensed. 'That's not what I was hoping would happen.'

'Does it matter right now?'

And just at that moment, warm and secure in his arms, nothing seemed to matter. She postponed any regrets to be dealt with the next day and drifted off to sleep. She only hoped that their new intimacy wouldn't make it harder for them to endure three long years together. If she was right in her earlier conviction, it would make them more relaxed and comfortable with each other. But was it to only happen once? Hadn't that been her first assumption? Or would they continue to have sex? She supposed it was more what they both decided on and that she was probably worrying about nothing.

The next morning, while she was in the shower, aware with every tiny movement that she still ached between her thighs, she told herself squarely that she wasn't going to do any morning-after regrets over what had happened between her and Tore. It would be pointless to regret what couldn't be changed. Hopefully, now that curiosity had been sated, she and Tore would be less awkward with each other.

Tore, of course, had already vanished from their room to make his usual early start. It wasn't a promising new beginning but it was a gorgeous day and she chose a spicy red sundress to wear with sliders on her bare feet. Belle was already gone from the nursery and everyone else seemed to be still asleep, so she went downstairs for breakfast as quietly as she could.

Stella was just settling Belle into her high chair when she arrived. Tore was seated with his coffee.

'You should've woken me,' Violet told him just as Belle squealed at the sight of her and tried to get out of the chair again.

In the ensuing fuss, Violet lifted her daughter to share their usual morning cuddle while Stella fetched the little girl's breakfast. Tore poured her coffee and she studied him. Heat mushroomed between her slender thighs as brilliant green eyes assailed hers. For a split second, she couldn't quite credit that the intimacy of the night hours had actually happened. Without warning their whole relationship had gone from distant to much, much closer and she wasn't quite sure how to handle that.

'Where do we go from here?' she heard herself ask uncertainly as Tore surveyed her with his characteristic cool, assessing gaze, and she lowered her head and began to feed Belle to occupy herself.

His lean, hard-boned features tightened. 'No place different from where we were last night,' Tore imparted with succinct bite.

Violet felt a little like she had been slapped down because on her terms, *everything* was different. But Tore was evidently telling her that *he* didn't want it any different outside the bedroom door. Obviously, he wasn't feeling the sense of closer connection that she was experiencing. That physical togetherness had meant nothing to him.

'I can tell you, though, that today we're cutting out on our guests and having a day for ourselves,' Tore continued smoothly, seemingly unaware that he had said anything likely to annoy or distress her.

'Oh…?' she said, off balanced by that statement.

'We deserve an escape and some sightseeing. This is your first trip to Italy yet you have been nowhere and seen nothing. That's pretty bad for a honeymoon that's already more than a week old,' he completed.

So once again, Tore was thinking of appearances, about adding a firmer foundation to the reality that they were newly marrieds and ensuring that they looked and behaved more like the average new couple. It was his birthday tomorrow. She would decorate the cake that evening, she decided numbly.

'You didn't want to get married, did you?' she heard herself comment.

'No, but neither did you and now we're simply making the best of difficult circumstances,' Tore pointed out without expression.

'That makes me feel like the last resort in the bedroom,' Violet whispered truthfully.

Shimmering green eyes caught and held hers in reproof. 'It shouldn't. We're stuck in this situation and we're dealing with it in the most practical way,' he argued.

Violet totally blamed herself for the hurt he had inflicted as she went upstairs to dress her daughter in something pretty. She had made the decision, the *choice*, to be with him the night before but still she contrived to be *hurt*. She had travelled at speed from her raunchy novel to the exciting reality of Tore and had got her fingers burnt. She hadn't thought far enough ahead. Had it even crossed her mind that once she cancelled those boundaries, putting them back up again would be an impossible challenge?

And why would Tore say no to commitment-free sex when he had no other female outlet? He was a normal guy with a libido and she had handed herself to him on a silver platter, thinking that she was being daring, practical and sensible. But maybe all that she had really been thinking about was that she was hugely attracted to Tore. She had been all too willing to find a good excuse to allow herself to explore that attraction.

Honestly, what had she expected to happen the morning after? They were locked together in a *temporary* marriage and Tore was telling her right now up front that he didn't want that to change. He wouldn't suddenly fall in love with her and decide that he wanted to keep her. No, Tore was still looking forward to the freedom he would reclaim in three years' time. She was the fool who had briefly toyed with the dangerous suspicion that he might want something more from her than her body. Unfortunately, she hadn't even admitted that truth to herself.

As Violet finally grasped what had upset her most about his chilly, adamant declarations, she paled and guilty unease gripped her. She couldn't afford to catch feelings for Tore. Succumbing to that stunning beauty and shocking sex appeal of his was one thing; feelings of attachment entirely another. She gave herself a good, hard talking-to.

In recent years, she had often been lonely. The weight of her obligations had made it impossible for her to enjoy a normal social life. What free time she had, had been spent with her mother, her sister and Belle. Therefore, it made sense that she would be more likely than most women to fall for the first handsome man who paid her attention. It was just unfortunate that that man should also be the guy she had married as part of a business deal. Tore was extremely unemotional about their connection, and she would have to learn to think and behave like that as well. Not only for the sake of conserving her pride but also out of a very real need to look after herself. Three years down the road, Violet had no plans to reel away from their divorce with a broken heart.

Belle in her arms, Violet clattered back downstairs to be slotted into a very large and comfortable SUV. When they stepped out at their first stop, she was surprised when Stella emerged from one of the cars behind them, immediately moving forward to ask if there was anything she could do to help.

'Thanks, but if we're only here for a walk, we're fine,' Violet said lightly, choosing not to comment on the new designer stroller that had appeared for her daughter's use and settling her into its pristine interior.

She had not realised that sightseeing with Tore would require an entire cavalcade of cars, staff and security. He grasped her hand and planted it on his arm and they strolled along the promenade. She still had to almost trot to match his pace and it was too much for her in the heat. At one point she paused to catch her breath and stood by the railings on the esplanade. The views of Sicily were utterly spectacular. It was a clear day and Tore pointed out Mount Etna, and she smiled as the sunlight glanced off the pale turquoise water of the sea and almost blinded her.

When a paparazzo darted up waving a camera, one of their bodyguards prevented him from taking a photo. He was soon followed by another paparazzo and then another. A literal mob of the cameramen gathered to hover on the pavement outside the promenade café where they'd stopped for cold drinks.

'Now I understand why we haven't been going out,' Violet admitted, striving to act as if the amount of attention their party was receiving wasn't spooking her. But it absolutely was.

'I have a much quieter location picked for the afternoon,' Tore imparted, stroking a forefinger across the tense clenched back of one of her hands where it rested on the table. 'Relax. I rarely appear with a woman in public. Now that news of our marriage is out, you are a major source of interest. Belle is an added draw because they haven't worked out yet where she fits into the picture.'

'I had no idea it would be like this for us,' Violet muttered, goose bumps breaking out on her arm beneath his careless touch and an awareness of him blossoming that she was trying fiercely to ignore. 'I'm not used to being stared at.'

'This is your world for the next three years,' Tore pointed out wryly, his attention locked to her soft pink mouth like a laser beam and making her feel intensely self-conscious. 'We can only enjoy privacy within our homes but don't let it get to you. Privilege has to have a downside.'

CHAPTER SIX

'SO WHERE ARE WE?' Violet asked as the car drove up a long, twisting, steep lane to pull up outside a weathered sprawling farmhouse. The creamy stone walls were draped in climbing plants, and flowers were everywhere she looked. It was very picturesque and redolent of southern Italy.

'While the Renzettis lived at the castle, this farm supplied the family food. After the castle became ruinous my grandfather persuaded his mother and siblings to move back here and live in greater comfort. They lived here for a decade,' Tore explained. 'Of course, they all felt that it was a terrible humiliation. They had been born into a certain stratum of society and then lost status through lack of money.'

'Your grandfather was wise. A castle is not impressive as a home if it's falling apart,' Violet agreed.

'And the original Renzetti *was* born here, a farm boy who became a soldier and climbed the ranks. Only when Aldo went into business and succeeded beyond his wildest dreams were the Renzettis able to reclaim the castle.'

Climbing out of the car behind them, Stella hurried

towards them. 'Can I take Belle into the house to meet my family?' she asked hopefully.

'Your family lives here?'

'Stella's family runs the farm,' Tore explained.

'Of course you can take her,' Violet said warmly.

'And I'll give you the official tour,' Tore told Violet, closing one hand over hers to move her on to a worn path that wound farther uphill. 'Nothing very exciting, I'm afraid. Some Roman ruins, the fruit orchards,' he extended, turning to indicate the points of interest. 'We grow clementines, mandarins, oranges and lemons here. Aldo extended the farmland over the years.'

'By the sounds of it, you are a regular visitor.'

Tore dealt her a wry smile. 'Aldo first brought me here when I was four years old to show me where the family started out and impress on me the conviction that any kind of honest labour was worthwhile. I was far too young to take on board those ideas. Back then I hadn't been living with my grandparents for very long and it was a very awkward conversation. My Italian was still very poor and his Norwegian was even worse.'

'I didn't realise that you'd lived with your grandparents,' Violet admitted.

'They brought me up from the age of four.'

'And you spent your early years in Norway? Tell me about your parents,' she urged.

Tore winced as they reached the viewpoint at the top of the hill. 'They were never together in the usual sense of the word. My father, Marco, was only eighteen, my mother, Ingrid, only a few years older. She was a model. They had a fling one weekend in Rome and I was the result. I imagine that I wasn't the most welcome surprise to my father because he never made the effort to see me or have anything further to do with me...'

'Gosh...' Violet muttered, unsure what to say to such a wounding admission.

'But I can't really complain about Marco because he did provide handsomely for my upbringing. He *did* accept responsibility for me. Unfortunately, however, he didn't tell my grandparents that I existed. I was his grubby little secret to be hidden away in another country forever.'

Violet winced. 'Oh dear...'

'Within a year of my birth he died on the track racing cars. That was his dream but he wasn't very good at it. He was still very young but quite a challenge for my grandparents. He refused to consider further education and had no interest in business.'

'He could've grown out of all that and matured,' she said in all fairness as he led her down through an alley of ancient oak trees, the blessed shade welcome. 'So, what happened to you and your mother?'

'I remember her as warm and loving. She passed away from a nasty bout of flu when I was two years old,' Tore related more slowly. 'Her kid sister took me in...because of the money that came with me. It enabled her chosen lifestyle and those were the bad years.'

As he led her out onto another slope where a rug was spread and a picnic basket and cooler awaited them, she was too involved in the story to concentrate and she asked, 'How did your grandparents find out about you?'

'Essentially, they followed the money. Questions were asked when my father's estate was being wound up because a lot of cash was missing. The trail eventually led to me,' Tore explained. 'And they were astonished…and *hurt* that their son hadn't told them that they had a grandchild. They tried to get legal custody of me and failed. They couldn't get enough evidence to prove that I was in an abusive home. In the end, they circumvented the law to get me away from my aunt and I'll always owe them for being willing to go that extra mile for my sake.'

Abusive…the bad years he had said and she could only wonder what that had encompassed when he had been so very young, indeed still only a baby in many ways. Regardless, he had endured and won through to gain a happier life with his grandparents. What had those unpleasant experiences taught him? They had both survived unhappy, difficult childhoods. She had learned to be afraid of angry men and wary of strangers because her father hadn't always brought the most decent people into their home. She had learned to save rather than spend. She had learned that she, like her mother before her, had to work hard to keep herself. And finally, she had learned to forgive her mother for loving their father so much that she'd stayed with him to the detriment of both her and her daughters.

'Do you want to explore the amphitheatre now or after lunch?' Tore enquired.

'Let's do it now. I'm not sure I'll have the energy after I've eaten,' Violet warned him as she looked downhill to the large angular structure poking up out of the rough grass. 'Although that means climbing back up the hill again...and I'm not sure I could.'

Tore laughed. 'I'll carry you if necessary.'

'Take off your jacket and tie at least,' she urged him. 'You should've worn casual clothes.'

'I was brought up to always be prepared for a board meeting,' he teased, shooting an amused green-eyed glance at her. 'You look amazing in red. It accentuates your light eyes and black hair. Which parent do you take after?'

'My father. Mum's blonde and Tabitha looks exactly like her. All I inherited was my mother's lack of height.'

'You never mention your father.'

'If you've nothing good to say, say nothing,' she quipped. 'He is a drunk, a liar and a womaniser and when he was in the wrong mood, which was all too often, he hit my mother. My sister and I have had no contact with him for years and that's how we prefer it.'

Tore grabbed her arm to steady her before she could head down the steep slope, and he guided her over to the worn steps that led into the structure. 'It doesn't sound like he was much of a loss.'

'He is a remarkably talented artist when he chooses to work. But he'll always be the man who told me and my sister that he never wanted children and that we were my mother's responsibility.' Pale at the memory, Violet held her head high and forced a smile. 'My goodness, how did we get so serious today?'

Tore watched her lean back against the worn, weathered stone of the inner wall. In that colourful dress, she looked like a living flame against the grey backdrop.

She kicked off her shoes and flexed her bare toes in the soft grass, innocently sensual in her enjoyment. The longer he was with her, the more boxes she ticked on his list of what made a desirable woman. She was a great mother to her adopted daughter, a hard worker and universally polite and pleasant to all. His attention rested on her vivid face, her skin flushed from the sun and exercise. There might not be much of her but she was a beauty and she had tremendous spirit. He had never liked yes-women or the bootlickers of the world. And the more he liked her, the more he reacted to the sexiness of that pouting pink mouth, those slender, shapely legs and the sparkle in those big blue eyes... And the more he knew that he needed to push her away.

Why? She would never settle for the little he had to give in the emotional field. And he didn't want to be married, at least not until he was in his forties, when he would be mature enough to choose wisely. He had long accepted that eventually he would marry and provide his grandparents with at least one great-grandchild. And when he was older, unlike his youthful father, he would make a better parent. But he wasn't ready for all that yet. He wasn't ready to be a committed husband or father, nor was he ready to turn his back on his freedom and belong to one woman alone. Violet had just come along at the wrong time, he reasoned tautly.

Although she was even younger than he was and she hadn't done much with her freedom, had she? Not only had she come to his bed untouched and ignorant enough not to even know it, but she had also taken on the burden of a child when many women would have been aghast at the responsibility. No, he needed to keep his distance or he would risk getting in so deep with Violet that he would have to stay with her. So he was making his choice, staying in control, being decisive. He would be single for at least the next decade.

As they walked back, Tore told her about the archaeological excavation that had been completed on the farm twenty years earlier. The remains of an early fortress and a settlement had been discovered, and several finds were currently on view in the town museum.

'When did you arrange the picnic?' she asked him as she threw herself breathlessly down on the rug.

'When I got up this morning. I thought we would be glad of a little laziness after we'd done the scenic tour.'

'It's hot,' she complained as she pulled a bottle of cold water out of the cooler and pressed it against her brow before gulping back some water to quench her thirst. Mercifully, they were seated in the shade of a thin belt of trees.

Tore rolled up his shirtsleeves and undid another button on his shirt.

'Take it off, for goodness' sake,' she told him. 'I don't care.'

Tore stared at her and then his expressive mouth quirked and he peeled off the shirt to pitch it aside.

'It's not as though there's anyone to see!' she mocked.

An irresistible grin slanted his lean, darkly attractive face. 'You're very welcome to take off that dress...'

Violet, flushed from more than the heat, busied herself opening the picnic basket. She set out the tempting contents with little ooh's and aah's of appreciation while ignoring his challenge to strip to her underwear. 'I'm starving,' she confided.

'A glass of wine?'

Violet nodded as he drew a bottle from the cooler and she set out the glasses. 'Heavens, this is very civilised.'

Violet unfastened the straps on her sundress, seeing no reason to invite tan lines. Tore set out the plates as she sipped her wine and tried not to pay too much heed to his marvellously muscular torso. There was no word for a temporary husband, she acknowledged, but she supposed it meant that he was more like a casual boyfriend than an actual husband. She wondered if that meant that she should make hay while the sun shone or whether she should back off now and figure out what she was doing in the near future. The intensity of his gaze on her made her want to preen and at the same time, laugh at herself for being so susceptible.

Yes, it was nice to be admired, but essentially it meant very little. He might want her right now but he didn't want her to start thinking that he was eager to keep her. He saw no future for them as a couple. Tore Renzetti had no small opinion of his own worth. Didn't it occur to him that *she* might not want to hang on to him, either? In fact, why would she choose to stay married to him? Yes, he was gorgeous and sexy but he was also a workaholic and not particularly social. He was good with Belle, though. At least he didn't ignore Belle like her father had ignored his twin daughters, only acknowledging them with an angry reprimand if they got in his way or made too much noise.

Both men in her family tree, her father and her grandfather, had let Violet down by neither loving her nor even taking an interest in her. That had wounded her deeply and she didn't want to put herself in the same position with Tore. She didn't want to fall for him and develop expectations and then get disillusioned all over again by a man.

Pleasantly mellow from the wine, the delicious snacks and the heat, Violet rested back on her elbows on the rug. 'I suppose we should return to the farmhouse and collect Belle, though I bet that by now, Stella's fed her and put her down for a nap.'

'She'll phone if there's a problem,' Tore asserted, rolling over to gaze down at her, brushing a strand of hair slowly behind her ear, his shimmering green eyes intent on her flushed face. 'I want you, *lucciola.*'

Playing for time, Violet lifted a questioning brow.

'Firefly,' he translated. 'Tiny and hot. It suits you. In more ways than one.'

Something had clenched taut between her legs and she pressed her knees together, fighting the pulse of arousal and awareness he had awakened. After all, she was still tender from that unexpected initiation the night before. Regrettably, she had not appreciated that the pressure of the desire he aroused in her would still make her crave more of him than was healthy. And now that craving was there inside her like a turncoat, a pool of liquid honey heat collecting at the very heart of her, wanting, *needing*, what she knew could well be bad for her.

Tore leant down and tasted her parted lips with re-strained hunger, the fierce desire he was controlling held back. But even so, he was fighting a hunger more ferocious than anything he had ever felt for a woman and it unnerved him a little. Her hands drifted up and her fingers speared into his tousled silvery gilt hair, rejoicing in that silky luxuriance even as her curvy body lifted up beneath his. His mouth travelled down her extended throat and his teeth grazed the tender muscle underneath the skin, making her gasp and in-stinctively lift her hips.

And at that point there was no further restraint from either of them. Tore groaned against her parted lips as he dragged down the bodice of her dress, baring her plump pouting breasts. He worried at a straining pink nipple with his mouth while his fingers pinched at its tender twin. Just as suddenly, they were rolling over and he was reaching below her skirt to remove her panties, wrenching them out of his path, momen-tarily shifting away from her to unzip and reach for protection.

Her blood felt as though it was pounding through her veins, and her heart was racing. She found his sensual mouth again for herself while he was establishing just how ready she was to take him again.

Groaning with pleasure, Tore went in for another driving kiss as he arranged her under him. 'I've never wanted anyone as much as I want you, *lucciola*.'

Her head tipped back as he lifted her hips and drove into her without hesitation. Blissful sensation engulfed her in a surge of intense pleasure, her body jolting, receiving and finally embracing. Nothing had ever felt quite that good and she was on fire with the sheer thrill of it. Mindless moments followed while her body raced to the heights and over the peak in an explosive climax that left her shuddering and convulsed in the wild tide of pleasure. Tore sank into her one last time with a growl before he attained his own release.

For a moment, Violet was in a daze of shock and pleasure and disbelief. They were outdoors where they might have been seen or heard, and she was aghast at how reckless they had both been. Tore shifted off her to dispose of the condom and slowly, clumsily, she sat up, glancing down at her bare bosom in horror before hastily yanking her dress back into place, lingering to refasten the straps. And all the time she was still thinking… *I didn't do that, I didn't allow that* but intelligence was telling her that she was guilty as charged. Guilty of getting so out of control that she had lost her dignity, she reflected with self-loathing as she wriggled into her discarded underwear.

'That was *amazing*,' Tore told her in a raw undertone of appreciation, making it crystal clear that his thoughts were completely out of step with hers. 'Sex has never been that exciting for me before.'

In a series of sharp little movements, her cheeks burning over that uninvited accolade, Violet slid her feet into her shoes and stood up. She had lost control and that shook, mortified and agitated her all at once. Here she was in a relationship that had no boundaries unless she set them. After all, why would *he* set boundaries when he was enjoying uncommitted, casual sex?

'We were irresponsible,' she pointed out tautly.

'No, we weren't,' he contradicted with amusement. 'I used protection.'

Her heart skipped a beat. 'But it's not always sufficient and I'm not using anything. We don't want consequences,' she muttered, thinking in horror of what a disaster it would be if she inconveniently conceived. Tore might have warmed up to Belle but not to the extent that he wanted a Belle of his own to cherish.

Out of the blue, they were both caught up in an almost uncontrollable passion for each other, Violet acknowledged as she watched him lift and put on his shirt, lean, strong muscles rippling below smooth olive-tinted skin. Even taking her eyes off his beautiful physique was an unforgettable challenge.

'There will be no consequences,' Tore asserted. 'I don't take risks in that department.'

'I would feel better if we contained this attraction and put an end date on it,' Violet told him truthfully.

'An *end* date?' Tore shot her a questioning glance from sizzling green eyes. 'Just because we both got a little carried away?'

'A...*little*?' Violet piled the picnic plates and glasses into the basket, her body aching and tightening at the recollection of how abandoned she had been in the fierce hold of that explosive passion.

'Leave this stuff here. It'll be picked up,' Tore informed her in an exasperated undertone as he grasped her hand and walked her back up the hill through the alley of trees. 'Nobody fights about sex that spectacular!'

'I'm not fighting with you. I just don't want us forgetting that what we have is only a temporary arrangement.'

Tore expelled his breath in a slow hiss, wondering why she was raking up unnecessary stuff all of a sudden and sizing up their situation from an irrelevant angle. 'I'm not about to forget that.'

Violet was still thinking frantically hard. 'I think a good end date for this sort of togetherness would be when we leave Italy to return to London.'

Tore stopped dead. 'Violet, you can't put a lid on an attraction like this.'

'I thought you preferred clear rules,' she argued unevenly.

'Not if it's likely to keep me out of your bed,' he admitted tautly. 'Possibly, I tend to be more realistic than you are—'

Violet stiffened and ignored that insinuation. 'So while we remain in Italy this can be the equivalent of a holiday fling,' she replied stubbornly. 'But once we return to London at the end of the month, we go back to our own lives and forget about this.'

'If that's what you want—'

'That's what I want,' Violet responded without hesitation, determined to ensure that she didn't develop any kind of emotional attachment to him or dependency on him. A holiday fling was fine; anything lengthier sheer insanity. Once they were back in London, occupying separate bedrooms at opposite ends of his massive house, there would be no temptation and she would recover.

Yes, already she could feel herself getting danger-

ously soft and warm and forgiving towards Tore and
she really, really didn't *want* to fall for him. If she was
truly that susceptible to his appeal, she needed to protect herself from getting more emotionally involved
with him. Furthermore, there was absolutely nothing
more sobering than Tore's utter indifference to such
finer feelings.

Tore wasn't risking anything in continuing to have
sex with her. He had one of those divided brains with
business on one side and leisure time on the other.
And she was the fool who had placed herself in an ir-
retrievable position, assuming that she could have sex
with him without feelings getting involved. Only now
was she appreciating that she wasn't able to stay that
detached from him.

'It's entirely your decision,' Tore murmured tautly,
wondering why he wanted to argue with her so badly,
why he was already thinking ahead to that rejection
awaiting him at the end of the month.

Obviously, it was a form of rejection and he wasn't
accustomed to that experience but over the next couple
of weeks, he would *become* accustomed to the concept,
he assured himself fiercely. Or possibly Violet would
discover that once you let a lion out of a cage, it was
a challenge to get it to step quietly back into captiv-
ity again.

The passion she inspired in him was a revelation.
Amazing sex was a hell of a draw, he acknowledged.
Setting up an artificial barrier between them at a date
only a couple of weeks ahead of them struck him as
weird, *unless*…

'Are you falling for me or something?' Tore shot at her with startling abruptness as they reached the front of the house. 'Is that what's spooked you?'

Violet settled her face into an expression of polite disbelief and turned to look at him, her blue eyes wide with surprise. 'Falling for you? Falling for the guy who likened me to the corpse bride on our wedding day?' she asked with a forced laugh. 'You have just got to be kidding me!'

And although Tore was relieved by that response there was an edge of annoyance in his reaction as well. Granted, he hadn't been the smoothest and most charming bridegroom at the outset, but hadn't he since made up for that poor start? And considering that she had told him that sex was a good idea, why was she suddenly backtracking on that decision? The lowering suspicion that the sex had not been as good for her as it had been for him could only linger…and sting.

CHAPTER SEVEN

THE FOLLOWING EVENING, Violet was, for once, proud of her appearance. Clad in a short silver iridescent dress from her new wardrobe, she felt young again for the first time in more years than she cared to count. She might only be twenty-two but too many of her teenage years had been weighed down with adult burdens. It was Tore's birthday dinner, and the night before she had decorated the cake she had made. After the meal they were heading out to a club with their younger guests to a surprise party.

'What do you mean by saying that I shouldn't dress up for dinner?' Tore prompted with a frown.

'It's your birthday and we're going out after we've eaten,' Violet informed him. 'You don't need to wear a business suit to a club.'

'A *club*?' Tore stressed incredulously as if she had suggested some extremely decadent location that shouldn't be mentioned in polite company. 'I don't dance or do clubs.'

Violet retained her bright smile with difficulty. 'Luckily for you, I do, although it's been far too long since I was actually free to go to one. It's a surprise party, Tore. I wish I could've told you in advance so that you could invite any friends you wanted to join you, but your relatives really wanted to surprise you,' she explained.

'As I said, I don't do clubs or dancing. I'm not very fond of surprises, either.'

Tore stood there in front of her like a very tall monolith of ice that cast a lowering dark shadow, green eyes glittering censure in his lean bronzed face.

'Well, tonight you're going to break those rules for the sake of our guests, who are accompanying us,' Violet continued, staying steady in the face of adversity, refusing to be cast down by his lack of enthusiasm.

'*All* of them?' he demanded in frank dread of such an event. 'Isn't it enough that I put up with them at dinner every evening?'

'Only the younger set are coming.'

'Bloody Sandro!' he exclaimed, actually flinching at that prospect. 'What a way to celebrate my birthday! And my grandparents will be arriving in the midst of it.'

Violet frowned. 'Your grandparents? You didn't mention that they were coming here tonight.'

'They never miss my birthday even if it entails flying to London to corner me,' Tore volunteered.

'Well, I didn't *know* that!' Violet gasped. 'Why didn't you warn me?'

'I assumed they'd give it a miss this year because we're supposed to be on our honeymoon,' Tore countered as if that were excuse enough for his silence on the topic.

'I wouldn't have let anyone arrange a night out for

us if I'd known your grandparents were coming!' Violet huffed in defence.

'Oh, don't worry about them,' Tore urged with a sardonic curl of his lips. 'They'll be quite content to relax and walk along the beach. They will thoroughly enjoy the concept of me celebrating my birthday in a nightclub. They adore surprises. In fact, I wouldn't be shocked if they put someone here up to the idea of this outing tonight.'

'I have to do my makeup.' Violet walked into the bathroom with a downcurved mouth. He didn't like dancing, clubs or surprises. Well, he could just put up with his disappointment, she thought in exasperation. He was only twenty-nine years old, not ninety-five. When did Tore celebrate still being young?

Thirty minutes later, Tore appeared in the doorway as she was slipping on her very high pearlized leather sandals. He was still wearing a suit, she noted but it was a very fashionable, fitted suit that simply accentuated his big, powerful physique and made him look utterly gorgeous and cool. She smiled at him.

Tore gritted his teeth after only one good look at her. Although she was eager to tell him what not to wear, he had been denied the chance to express his opinion about what she wore. There wasn't enough of the dress as far as he was concerned. It showed off her fabulous legs, outlined her curves and bared a certain amount of cleavage. Sandro would be all over her like a rash. Although not while Tore was around, he reminded himself.

'I have a gift for you,' Tore recalled, stepping back into the bedroom.

'You can't give me a gift on *your* birthday!' Violet objected in astonishment as she followed him. 'Particularly when all I've done for you is bake you a cake!'

'Don't be a party pooper, *mia lucciola*,' Tore urged, extending a jewellery box stamped with the logo of a famous designer.

Violet backed towards the bed and sat down to open the gift. A cobweb-fine diamond collar and matching earrings lay on a bed of satin. She blinked in amazement. 'I can't accept something this valuable from you.'

'Of course you can…you're my wife and you have no jewellery aside of your wedding ring. That looks strange.'

Violet reddened at that bold, unapologetic statement. 'Does it?'

Tore strode forward and lifted the collar to thread it deftly round her slender neck and fasten it. 'It's pretty,' he pronounced. 'It suits you…'

Violet darted over to the mirror and studied the rainbow effect of the sparkling ribbon of diamonds catching the lights at her throat. 'It's beautiful,' she muttered tautly as she extracted the earrings and carefully attached them. 'I suppose I can't say no if you think I look odd without any jewellery, but I can always leave them behind when we split up.'

Tore tensed. 'I can't understand why you would want to do that. It's not as though I'm likely to give them to anyone else when I specifically chose them for you.'

Violet tensed at that assurance, discomfiture feathering through her slight frame. 'You've been very generous,' she said uncomfortably, knowing that much like the clothes he had purchased for her and Belle, there was no way she could ever repay him for such gifts. 'Thank you.'

When we split up, Violet had said casually as if both phrase and action referred to the utmost trivia, Tore mused. Was their relationship that unimportant to her? And why was he worrying about that? Shouldn't he be relieved to see her display that attitude? Did they even have a relationship? He supposed there was no escaping the fact that they definitely did. Tore frowned, still unsure as to why he was annoyed that she should take their eventual divorce for granted. Shouldn't that be what he wanted? Why was he feeling as though she had stolen his momentum? He was very logical. Why did it offend his pride and even annoy him on some level that she was already calmly referring to their future parting?

They headed down to dinner with Violet pausing on the way to check on Belle, who was fast asleep, snug in her cot. They were about to enter the dining room when Sofia hurried past them, addressing Tore in a surge of Italian.

'My grandparents have arrived,' he translated.

'Oh my goodness, where are they going to sleep?' Violet hissed at him.

'Is that really your first thought?' Tore asked in wonderment.

'Of course. Every bedroom is occupied until tomorrow morning before the next batch arrives in the evening.'

'Evidently, Sofia has you brainwashed into the perfect hostess. I should imagine they will be staying at the farm in the guest suite there tonight, at least,' he suggested as Sofia opened the front doors and two smiling people bustled into the hall.

Violet only vaguely recalled Aldo Renzetti from that scene at their wedding when Tore had questioned the name she signed. She hadn't registered quite how much smaller he was than Tore at that first glimpse. But the two men could not have been more different. Aldo was a stockily built man in his fifties with greying hair and lively brown eyes. His wife, of a similar age, was elegantly dressed in a designer frock and some very sparkly jewellery. She was a slim brunette, a little taller than her husband, and she had warm eyes.

'I'm Matilde. I'm sorry we've been so last minute about this,' she began to say in easy English as the dining room door opened and the relatives flooded out to greet the older couple. Much hugging and back patting took place.

Two more places were set at the dining table and there was no getting a word in edgeways as catching-up chatter in Italian crossed back and forth between the different parties. Coffee was finally served and Violet's cake was brought in complete with burning candles. The cake resembled a man's business jacket with a collar and tie and there was much laughter at that apt, if irreverent choice. As Tore ate a slice and pronounced it the best he had ever tasted, Violet leant closer to say, 'If I had stayed out of the kitchen as you wanted, you wouldn't be enjoying that.'

Small gifts were produced and then Aldo slipped out and reappeared carting what was obviously a wrapped painting to present to Tore. 'For your collection,' he said, beaming a bright smile at Violet. 'One of your father's creations. A true, traditional Sam Blessington from the days before he decided to become more cutting edge.'

Violet froze and lost colour as the picture was revealed. 'That's my grandfather's home,' she proffered shakily and in an effort to be polite and suitably grateful, added, 'What a wonderful find!'

It was a relief when some minutes later, their younger guests began to make their apologies and bid the senior Renzettis good-night as they rose from the table.

'Taking Tore to a nightclub?' Matilde commented to Violet in a tone of delighted approval. 'You're going to be so good for him!'

'They think I work too hard,' Tore remarked apologetically on the way out the door as she donned a short jacket that matched her dress.

'You do,' Violet confirmed.

In her high heels, she clambered with difficulty into the low-slung Bugatti La Voiture Noire sports car that awaited them outside.

'Sorry about that painting. Aldo must've looked into your parentage. By buying it, he meant to compliment you and make you feel like part of the family,' Tore explained. 'I'll have it hung in a dark corner somewhere you don't have to see it.'

'No, I'm not that sensitive,' Violet hastened to tell him. 'I know that your grandfather didn't mean to hurt

me. He was so obviously pleased as punch when I recognised the house and yet even though my mother grew
up there, I've never been in it.'

'*Ever?*' Tore queried in surprise.

'He never forgave Mum for marrying my father. He's
not a forgiving sort of person.'

'I know that. He was Aldo's childhood playmate and
he turned his back on their friendship when my grandmother chose to marry Aldo rather than him.'

Violet winced in dismay. 'So, two friends fell for
the same woman?'

'That's what caused the final breach between our
grandfathers. Aldo bought yours out of our business
and Tomas moved to the UK to make a fresh start
alone.'

'It didn't do him much good,' Violet sighed. 'He
ended up marrying a much younger woman who
worked for him and she ran off with another man and
left their daughter—my mother—behind for him to
raise when she was still a kid. Mum was never close
to him but she said that he was always an unhappy,
harsh man.'

Her grandfather, she reflected, was also a liar. He
had told his granddaughters that if one of them married
Tore, he would give them the money to cover the cost of
the clinical trial in the USA for their mother. Only once
Tabitha had agreed, he had said that they would have
to wait for a few months until he could afford to hand
over such a large amount of cash. As if they had been in
any position to wait when their mother was dying and
time had been of the essence! That was why Tabitha

had demanded the up-front payment from Tore before she signed the marriage contract with Tore's lawyers.

'Your mother wasn't at the wedding, was she?' Tore commented.

'No, she wasn't.' Violet was picking her words carefully. 'Right now, she's on a clinical trial in Massachusetts. She has cancer.'

Tore glanced at her in surprise. 'How is the trial going for her?'

'It's too early to say but at least her body isn't rejecting the treatment,' she shared.

'Aldo informed me that he and my grandmother will be staying at the farm for the whole of their visit although they plan to join us for dinner most evenings.'

Violet smiled. 'They seem warm and friendly and they keep the conversation going. Do you know how lucky you are to have a family that close and caring?'

'I *do*,' Tore stressed as he shot the gleaming car to a halt in front of a brightly lit building. As she climbed out onto the pavement, bodyguards shielded her from the surge of paparazzi trying to take photos of their arrival. Tore tossed the car keys to a hovering valet and curved an arm round her to lead her indoors.

Bright lights and noise assailed them in the foyer. A cord was detached for them to be ushered away from the queue of partygoers awaiting entry. They climbed stairs to an opulent seating and viewing area on a balcony above the dance floor. As a bottle of champagne arrived at their table, Violet took off her jacket.

'I want to dance.'

'No,' Tore told her simply.

Violet dealt him a cheeky grin and her sheer appeal in that moment left him breathless. The sparkling eyes, the pink pout of her lips, the way she wrinkled her little nose in defiance. 'I don't need permission,' she said, standing up.

Tore captured her hands and tugged her gently down on top of him. In those heels, it took very little to unbalance her and she collapsed on his lap with a startled squeak of surprise. Lean, strong hands framed her flushed, stubborn face. 'Happy birthday, Tore,' he teased. 'This is how I like to celebrate. No clubs, no loud music or prying spectators. I only need you and I will quite happily carry you out of here and take you home. I want you, *just* you all to myself, *mia lucciola.*'

Violet connected with those mesmerising emerald green eyes set between ebony lashes, and her heart skipped a beat, anticipation running like a flame up through her body. Without hesitation, she stretched up to find his mouth for herself and that connection sent an instant electrifying jolt of excitement travelling through her. Her hands rose to lace into his hair and hold him as his tongue delved in an exploration of her mouth that drove her wild. She wanted to rip him out of his suit and do all sorts of things she had never gotten to do before. With Tore there was an enormous sense of freedom to be herself, to simply relax and go with the moment.

In a sudden movement, he ripped his lips off hers again and as she lifted her lowered lashes, she blinked at the flash of light that almost blinded her.

'I think we have now provided the ultimate lusty

honeymoon photo,' Tore commented very drily as he carefully lifted her off him to set her down by his side.

'Is that why you kissed me?' Violet demanded, her voice brittle with sudden hurt.

'You kissed *me,'* he reminded her.

Violet reddened, looked away and lifted her champagne glass, bubbles bursting against her lips while a server hovered to top it up if necessary. All of a sudden and a little too late she was accepting that they were on show in a public place. But he was perfectly correct: She had been the instigator.

'Not that I was objecting,' Tore quipped. 'A little enthusiasm goes a long way with me. We could leave early…'

'We've only just got here,' she protested in shock at that suggestion and colliding with those glittering jewelled eyes of his, she knew he wasn't joking. 'Our party hasn't even arrived yet.'

'But I want you…' An arm closed round her narrow spine, a big hand covering her thigh. 'I'm as hard as a rock and I keep on thinking that this is my birthday and I should be allowed to do whatever I want. And right now, at this moment, I just want to be inside you again.'

Violet's mouth fell open and then she was saved by the arrival of Tore's relatives. They had added to the party with various boy-and girlfriends, and a slinky blonde in a rather revealing red dress took advantage of the fact that Violet had stood up to greet everybody and slid in beside Tore with a flashing smile to introduce herself.

'Your girlfriend?' Violet asked Sandro, who settled down beside her.

'Wish she was. Angelina's an actress. She jumped at the chance to meet Tore,' Sandro informed her with a grimace. 'He's always a target when he goes out in public. He might as well be wearing a flashing billionaire sign above his head.'

'He's also very good-looking,' Violet interposed, disliking the suggestion that Tore would only be desired for his wealth.

'Well, look after him. She's like a guided missile locked on a target when she wants to impress.'

'Why don't you make a move on her?'

'I love to be seen out with her, but she's not interested,' Sandro admitted ruefully. 'She sexes up my image but it's only a show for the headlines. I owed her a favour and when she asked if she could come with me to meet Tore, I couldn't say no.'

Angelina was chattering to Tore while he was hailing the waitress to order drinks for their table. The owner of the club came up to speak to him personally, positively fawning over the blonde's graciously offered hand. Violet chatted as best she could to Tore's family members in the midst of the noisy party atmosphere. Angelina's girlish giggles sounded in her ear several times and when two of the other women got up to dance, Violet accompanied them down to the dance floor. She was irritated when she noticed that one of their bodyguards had stationed himself by the wall nearby. It made her feel a little like a prisoner out on parole but still under supervision.

She stayed on the floor a long time because she was enjoying herself and had no idea when she would get another chance to dance since it was obvious that Tore was not a fan of such venues. The bodyguard signalled her.

Out of breath from her gyrations, she approached him. 'Mr Renzetti would like you to rejoin the party upstairs,' he shouted in her ear.

'Sorry, no...' Violet framed without hesitation.

She wasn't a little girl to be called to order, summoned like a servant to do as she was told. Oh, hell no! If she wanted to dance, she was entitled to dance and as she was with two of Tore's family members, she already had a pair of literal chaperones.

Exasperated by the actress's persistent attentions, Tore vaulted upright and strode to the balcony to see why Violet had yet to return to his side. He saw her at the edge of the floor, lights flashing across the neckline of her dress and highlighting the firm little mounds of the breasts shifting beneath the fine fabric as she moved. And then he watched her spin and twerk. *Dio mio*, his wife was twerking like a teenager in public! He blinked and looked again but it was happening, the hem of the dress riding up to show rather more of her slender thighs than he liked on view. Tore breathed in deep and slow. Was he being too conservative? Too controlling? But Violet down on that floor alone felt absolutely wrong to him. So obviously, he was an old-fashioned guy...was he? Since when?

Evidently, since he had married Violet, who unfortunately loathed anyone trying to tell her what to do.

She had said that that rebelliousness was a trait of her twin's, even though it was painfully obvious to Tore that she was exactly the same. And he had a bad habit of shooting out orders and expecting them to be immediately obeyed. He knew that that tendency was something he needed to work on when it concerned a wife. As she had already told him, she was not an employee of his.

But still, he went rigid as a young man began to dance up against her. Dark primal fury surged up in a tidal wave inside Tore. That someone should actually touch her was beyond his tolerance level and he strode down the stairs to retrieve her. Was he a possessive man?

He had never thought he was before he met Violet. He couldn't have cared less about the various women who had amused him during his rare leisure moments. He had never had to pursue one of them. He had never had one who answered back and defied his wishes, either. Violet was in a class of her own. It was a marvel to him that such a small body could house such a huge personality. Only that feisty persona didn't show on the surface. He had initially thought that she was rather timid and quiet, but dare to cross Violet and you soon found out that she had inner fire and a passion for defending her rights as an individual.

Violet saw Tore watching her from the edge of the floor, ebony brows pleated, disapproval emanating from every inch of his big, powerful body. She moved away from the guy who had been trying to get her to dance with him and sped towards Tore, holding out her hand, wanting him to take it so that he could join her on the floor. Tore reached out and grasped her fingers but used them merely to tug her even closer.

'Tore!' she exclaimed as he simply bent down and swept her off her feet to carry her in his arms.

'Don't be stupid…put me down!' she instructed.

'Not until we reach the car,' he asserted. 'If I put you down, you'll run away again.'

'Tore…think about this,' she urged. 'What does this look like?'

'Like a guy retrieving his wife. Perfectly normal,' Tore declared confidently.

'Someone might take photos of us!' she warned him.

'Couldn't care less,' Tore countered truthfully, striding towards the exit after giving a nod to the club owner, his security team falling in around them to break through the crush.

'We're supposed to be hosting a party!' she slammed up at him in disbelief.

'Nobody's going to miss us.'

'Angelina will miss you,' Violet told him snidely.

'Yes, where were you when I needed you?' Tore enquired, green eyes gleaming bright with condemnation in his hard-hewn handsome face. 'You could've chased her off and instead you abandoned me.'

'I know you,' Violet argued vehemently. 'You were perfectly capable of chasing her off without anyone's help!'

'I expect my wife to stay by my side.'

'That sounds very Victorian and unreasonable.'

'I don't like you dancing with other men.'

'I was trying to discourage that guy without being rude or making a scene,' Violet informed him in a superior tone.

'He's lucky I didn't plant a fist in his smirking face!'

'I was tempted to slap you but I was too conscious that we were in a public place,' Violet responded, sounding even more superior. 'I wanted you to dance with me.'

'Don't play games with me, *lucciola mia*. I have a temper, too,' Tore warned her. 'One of our guards will retrieve your belongings from our table.'

'I wasn't ready to go home,' Violet complained.

'Then why are you stifling a yawn?'

'It's the one night out on the town that we've had.'

'There will be others.'

'I don't believe you,' she declared as the Bugatti filtered up to the pavement outside, eliciting a fair amount of excited comments from onlookers.

'I don't want to see you dancing with another man again,' Tore stated, slowly, carefully setting her down in front of him before reaching for her jacket as it arrived and deftly winding her into it.

'That's excessive,' she protested. 'Particularly when you don't dance.'

'It is what it is. I'm a possessive husband and you're stuck with me for at least three years,' he reminded her almost cheerfully as he walked her out to the Bugatti.

'That is not something to celebrate,' Violet replied crushingly.

'No? I think your attitude to me has changed since our wedding day. I know that I've changed,' Tore admitted.

The street lights illuminated the car interior and she

looked up at him unwillingly. 'I really was ready to slap you.'

'I know but you didn't because you have to be aware that I wouldn't like another man putting his hands on you.'

'Why would you care?' she dared to riposte.

'I don't know but I definitely do…while I dream of having a wife who obeys my every command like I'm a god in the flesh.'

'Dream on…'

Long brown fingers tipped up her chin so that their eyes collided and those crazy butterflies went insane in her tummy and her heartbeat pounded. He brought his lips down on hers and ravished them apart with a hungry groan of need. Any desire to slap him or indeed obey his every command evaporated. But the need to hold on to him when he felt like the only stable element in her new world simply increased a hundredfold. Her body pulsed with a life of its own, pushing forward demands and a need to fulfil them that was insanely new to her experience.

'So, even in this car, it will take almost forty minutes to get home,' Tore pointed out, settling her back into her seat and reaching across her to fasten the seat belt as he dragged in a ragged breath.

'Forty minutes,' Violet repeated slowly.

'And if waiting forty minutes to sate our urgent desires seems right now like waiting to go over the edge of a cliff, only imagine how we'll feel at the end of the month when such desires become forbidden,' Tore urged in a roughened undertone.

Violet breathed in deep and slow. 'Doesn't matter how we feel. It's the right thing to do before what we're feeling now gets out of control.'

Tore almost groaned. 'It's *already* out of control, *mia lucciola*.'

Violet rested her head back and struggled to relax, which was a massive challenge when every skin cell in her body seemed to be pitched on high alert. He ran a fingertip slowly along the line of her thigh, setting up a melting pot of sensation low in her pelvis, and then he pulled out onto the road to join the flow of traffic. He was arguing with her in silence by showing her how weak she could be made by a single fleeting caress.

'Agreed,' Violet conceded softly. 'Which is exactly why we need boundaries. If we're lucky this attraction will just burn out by the end of the month.'

Tore said nothing. He was wondering why he would want the best sexual connection he had ever had to burn out anytime soon. He was wondering why she was weaponizing sex. He had already made several obvious deductions from the likely consequences of the boundaries she was determined to set. Perhaps they would occur to her before the end of the month... He could only *hope*. If something was good, why on earth would you bring it to a premature end? It would be senseless self-denial and how would it improve anything between them?

CHAPTER EIGHT

IN THE EARLY hours of the next day, Tore wakened to the sound of a baby crying and he slid out of bed at speed and switched off the monitor. Violet lay fast asleep, bluish shadows like bruises below her eyes revealing just how tired she still was.

Belle was teething and not having an easy time of it. Tore was convinced that he could handle the situation on his own but he intended to talk Violet into hiring a proper nanny when they returned to London. An extra pair of hands would be welcome, if Violet would just accept that help. Violet only allowed Stella to assist her during the day because Violet believed that she should be her daughter's main support at night. But on this particular night, Violet was exhausted. The champagne and dancing had taken it out of her, not to mention the activities that had followed.

Tore, a quick learner under Stella's teaching at breakfast time, changed Belle's nappy and lifted her. With a muffled little sob, she buried her face under his chin and he sat down to use the teething gel on her sore gums. Afterwards, she slumped against him, still emitting the occasional stray whimper. He smoothed her back, marvelling at how little and delicate she was, and she sighed heavily. After a while all the tension drained out of her small body and she slept, splayed like a star-fish over his chest. He intended to get up and put her back in her cot but he decided to give her a few more minutes to settle safely into slumber.

Violet woke with a start, checked the time and pan-icked. Belle should've woken up and she reached for the monitor, taken aback to discover that it had been switched off, something she never did. Grabbing a wrap, she pelted down the corridor to the nursery and stared in shock at the sight of Tore lying fast asleep on the recliner with her daughter draped over him.

Yes, she had to admit it, he was a much better fa-ther figure than she would ever have dreamt and yet, she would never have asked him to step up to that role. After all, she couldn't forget that their marriage was only a short-term arrangement. In three years, Tore would be gone, gone, gone and poor little Belle would have to learn to get by without him. And of course, Tore was a source of fascination for the little girl be-cause prior to Violet's marriage, Belle had lived in an all-female world.

For a stolen moment, she surveyed the two of them. Tore was bare chested and clad only in a pair of plaid pyjama pants, his tousled silvery hair glinting in the early light filtering in round the edges of the curtains, black lashes lying like fans above his high cheekbones. The epitome of masculine beauty and animal sensu-ality, he looked delectable, sin personified in human flesh and he tempted her like no other man.

She would never forget the wild passion that had

sealed them together like magnets the night before. They had raced up to their bedroom, ripped each other out of their clothes and come together like starving animals let loose on a long-awaited feast. And the pleasure had been indescribable and so intense that even now in recollection her body quickened and her breathing roughened. She snatched in a breath, struggling to stave off the sheer physicality of the memory. She had never dreamt of experiencing that kind of enjoyment with a man. Her expectations of intimacy had been much more prosaic. Her expectations had not extended to a force of nature like Tore, who had absolutely no inhibitions.

Hearing steps in the corridor beyond, Violet reached down to grasp Belle, who let go of Tore with a sleepy little sound of complaint. His lashes lifted, revealing his pure green gaze, and he blinked in bemusement.

'You fell asleep with Belle,' Violet clarified as he sat up, all rippling lean muscle and still-drowsy male.

'I need a shower to wake up,' he muttered, vaulting upright just as Stella came into the nursery and hovered uncertainly by the door when she saw both of them there.

'Belle woke up during the night and Tore took care of her without waking me.'

'You need more sleep,' Tore interposed drily. 'You could go back to bed now.'

Stella held her arms out for Belle. 'I'll get Belle dressed. Signora Renzetti said she might drop in for breakfast.'

'She probably will. Belle is the closest she has ever

come to having a great-grandchild and she adores babies,' Tore told Violet. 'I suspect you won't get near
your daughter for the rest of the day.'

'I'd be delighted if your grandmother took an interest
in her,' Violet admitted, walking back to their room,
thinking that her mother had been unable to spend
much time with her adopted granddaughter. While the
older woman remained vulnerable to infection, Violet
had had to keep her parent and her child apart.

'You slept in the diamonds,' Tore noted, stepping
behind her to unclasp the jewellery still at her throat.

'*And* in my makeup,' Violet groaned in a scandalised
undertone of guilt as she took a reluctant glance at her
reflection in a mirror, wincing over her messy mop of
hair and her raccoon eyes smeared with shadow. 'I fell
asleep. You should've woken me up.'

'It was my fault you were so tired,' Tore pointed out,
stepping out of the pyjama pants to stalk naked and
bronzed into the bathroom.

'You should never switch the baby monitor off,' she
reproved from the doorway.

'She would've woken you up and all she needed was
a little attention. I wanted you to have an unbroken
night of rest. You deserve it.'

When she considered how many orgasms he'd given
her, she reckoned that she had deserved it no more than
he but then, Tore seemed to thrive beautifully on fewer
hours of sleep than she did.

Forewarned of Matilde's likely visit, Violet picked
what she deemed to be suitable clothing before she went
for a shower. Tore's grandparents might as well have

been his parents. As they seemed kind and friendly in spite of the peculiar circumstances of Tore's marriage to a stranger, she was keen to act her part. A tailored pair of shorts teamed with a silk T-shirt struck her as smart but appropriate for most activities.

By the time she got down to the dining room, Belle was settled on Matilde's lap getting cuddled while Aldo was juggling condiments in an effort to lure her on to his lap. Their obvious interest in Belle and acceptance of her warmed Violet's heart. She munched on a delicious cinnamon roll and enjoyed a rare breakfast freed of her daughter's demands.

After the meal, their departing house guests said their goodbyes and Tore went off to the office suite with his grandfather.

Matilde wasted no time in suggesting a walk along the beach. Tucking Belle into her all-terrain stroller, Violet was happy to join her.

'First, tell me how Belle ended up with you,' the elegant older woman asked curiously.

'I met her mother, Isabel, at school. We went on a pastry chef course together and we were very close. She grew up in foster care. She had one living relative, an elderly uncle who didn't feel able to give a little girl a suitable home. He visited her, though, and he owned a bakery. After completing her training, she went to work for him. I found work at a hotel. Her uncle died only weeks later from a heart attack and Isabel inherited his bakery and the apartment above it. I gave up my hotel job and went to work with her instead,' Violet related, enjoying the warm sea breeze on her skin because she could feel the heat of the day slowly building on her back.

'That must've been fun.'

'Yes, it was an exhilarating time. The bakery was very old-fashioned and Isabel was keen to renovate it. She fell in love with the builder who came to do the work,' Violet explained. 'They were married within the year and soon afterwards, Isabel conceived. Belle wasn't a planned baby. They had intended to wait for a few years but once she was on the way, they came round to the idea and got very excited…'

'And then something went wrong,' Matilde guessed as Violet's voice trailed off into silence.

'Two days after Belle was born, Isabel and Stefan's car was hit by a drunk driver. They had gone out to pick up her pram and had left Belle with me,' Violet explained tightly, her eyes stinging at the memory of receiving that tragic news. 'Afterwards, I was most shocked that she had had the foresight to write a will and leave the business and her daughter to my care if anything happened to them.'

'A huge responsibility for a young woman of your age to take on.'

'It was. Initially, I was doing it for Isabel's sake but looking after Belle, I began to love her as if she was my own child. I have no regrets.'

'You're quite mature for your age,' Matilde remarked.

'Tore's been very good with her,' Violet shared. 'He wasn't expecting me to arrive with a child as I'm sure you know, but he came round to the idea surprisingly quickly.'

'My grandson is not as hard as he likes people to believe. He did have a tough upbringing and it taught him to distrust people, which is unfortunate. He spends too much time working, not enough time relaxing. I think you and Belle could be exactly what he needs,' Matilde informed her.

'Hopefully, we will be for the next three years,' Violet replied, dropping in the timely reminder that she was well aware that there was an end date to their fake marriage.

'That was the most amazing birthday cake last night,' Tore's grandmother responded, stepping neatly away from the previous controversial topic of conversation. 'And your cinnamon rolls are to die for!'

'Tore tried to stop me baking,' Violet confided with a twinkle in her eyes. 'It didn't work. He thought it was beneath his wife to be working in the kitchen even though it was my choice to be there.'

Matilde laughed. 'Obviously, you disabused him of that conviction.'

'I did…we had a huge row.'

'It will do Tore no harm to have someone willing to stand up to him now and again.' The two women began to walk back along the shore. Belle was getting restless and Violet unclipped her harness, took off her socks and let her dip her toes in the water. Delighted baby chuckles rewarded them.

Over a light lunch, Aldo announced that he and Matilde planned to immediately move back into the castle to host the family guests, who would be arriving for the rest of the month.

Tore glanced at the older man in astonishment.

'You've done very well or should I say… Violet has done very well?' Aldo quipped with a rueful glance at his grandson. 'But you deserve a break from these responsibilities. You're newly married. You have our blessing to go somewhere else to enjoy your freedom without the burden of entertaining visitors.'

Tore gave the older man a sudden slashing grin. 'Admit it, you missed playing family host.'

'No. I'm simply letting you off the hook.'

'If you're sure that this is what you want to do,' Violet murmured uncertainly.

'We are,' Matilde assured her. 'And I would offer to look after Belle but I shan't because she'd miss you too much. Perhaps we could do that for you when she knows us better.'

'If the opportunity arises, that would be wonderful,' Violet replied, grateful for the offer but not knowing if she would ever take it up. After all, just as she was a fake wife, Tore's grandparents were only temporary grandparents-in-law because they knew that she would only feature in their lives for a short space of time.

'I'll organise our departure,' Tore announced over coffee.

'I'll pack. Any hints about where we're going?' Violet asked.

'We're heading to my house in Tuscany. What Nonna calls my restoration project. But I assure you that very few areas in the house still require work. We will be perfectly comfortable there.'

'Tuscany,' she repeated. 'That would be quite a long drive.'

'It would be but we're not driving there. We're travelling by helicopter. More suitable for Belle. I'll ask Stella if she would like to accompany us,' he added.

'Oh, I could manage—' Violet began.

'Do you like Stella?' Tore asked and waited until she had nodded. 'And do you approve of the way she looks after Belle?'

'Yes, she's marvellous with her *but*—'

'I want you to have a proper break before you return to running the bakery. It would also be good to go out occasionally and not have to worry about childcare.'

Disconcerted by that statement from a man who acted like it would take a hurricane to separate him from his desk and his phone, Violet simply nodded again and sped upstairs. She rang her sister first to tell her about the approaching move and heard about how flirty the Italian baker Tore had hired was being with her. After that she called her mother, who was at the clinic and had left her phone behind. Instead, she spoke to her mother's friend, who told her that her parent's blood count was showing promising signs of a positive response to the new medication. After saying she'd call back later to speak to her mother, Violet began to pack.

They left the *castello* mid-afternoon when the helicopter arrived to collect them. Stella was brimming with excitement at getting to leave home for a couple of weeks. The helicopter landed in a grassy clearing surrounded by trees. An SUV awaited them and their luggage and once the transfer was made, they drove through the woods and up a driveway lined with cypress trees towards a sturdy classical house of substantial size.

'This is much bigger than I was expecting,' Violet admitted.

'The Villa Renzetti is used for other purposes as well. The Summer Ball will be held here next month and the proceeds will go to the prison rehabilitation charity that was selected this year. We'll be attending and you'll meet my friends and executive colleagues at it. Our company headquarters is based in Siena, which isn't far from here,' Tore explained. 'I live at the villa six months of the year now that it's habitable again.'

Violet said nothing because there was too much to unpack in those statements. She knew that she had assumed without evidence that Tore spent most of his time in London and that she would easily be able to continue running the bakery. Now she was finding out different and wishing that he had been more up front about how and where he lived. Only perhaps she or Tabitha should have asked more questions beforehand and clarified the situation. Both of them had been ridiculously naive about what the marriage would entail. Why the heck had Tore been so stubborn that he had refused to even meet his future wife ahead of the wedding?

But would prior warning have changed anything? She hadn't had a choice, she reminded herself ruefully, not if she wanted her mother to have one last chance at a cure for her disease. Or at the very least, a period of remission. How wonderful it would be if her mother, after her miserable marriage, were to have the opportunity to rediscover her joy in life. That possibility inspired both Violet and her twin and had made every sacrifice of their interests acceptable.

Tore lifted Belle out of her car seat as Violet leant in to release her seat belt. Belle planted both hands against his cheeks and smiled up at him in reward.

'I bet she's walking by the time we return to London,' Tore forecast. 'She tries to pull herself up against everything.'

'When did you buy this place?' Violet asked as they mounted shallow stone steps to reach the arched loggia, which fronted the house.

'A few years ago. I was out driving around and I saw it. The for-sale sign had rotted in the ground and I climbed over the wall and wandered round it.'

'You trespassed. More daring than I would've been,' she remarked.

'If the temptation is strong enough, I can break the rules,' he quipped. 'I climbed in through a back window and when I walked through the place, I fell in love with it. It was so sad to see the wonderful workmanship that was being left to rot. Aldo came to view it and said it would be a lifelong project. He may be right but I've enjoyed the challenges.'

'Saving a building from destruction would be fascinating. I didn't realise you liked old buildings. Of course I should've done with the *castello* in the family.'

'This place isn't as old but I'm sure Aldo's constant work on the *castello* influenced me. I like the location, too,' he extended. 'You can walk down into the village from here and I set up several workshops in traditional crafts and skills while restoring the villa.'

Stella was awaiting them at the top of the steps and Violet hurried to join her, pausing in front of the array of staff awaiting them in the loggia, her eyes flying to the colourful frescoes on the wall and the alcoves displaying classic sculptures. It was imposing and elegant. Tore introduced her to everyone but the only name she matched to a face was Alfredo, who managed the household. They moved into an interior courtyard full of tropical plants thriving in the sunlight filtering down through the glass roof above that was clearly a more recent addition.

'I'm afraid the furniture brought in for Belle may be below your standards,' Tore murmured, leading her up a stone-and-wood staircase. 'I've lived here alone and I've never had overnight guests or children staying.'

'Oh...' She wasn't surprised but felt that she had to say something.

On the landing, Tore paused to study her. His wife. He was discovering that more and more he was thinking of Violet as his wife. Not as his fake wife, his contract wife or even his gold-digging wife. No, Tore thought of her simply as *his* wife and even more to his disconcertion he liked having her and Belle around. Yet, he had never thought he could be a family man or that he could like any woman enough to have her around all the time. With Belle and Violet, life had become less predictable, less routine. And the more he saw of her, the more he looked at Violet, the more he wanted her. All cute and fragile in her fancy shorts and light top that showed off her slim curves and gorgeous legs. Her glorious hair cascaded round her piquant features; those big blue eyes hauntingly expressive. She inspired a hunger in him that was wildly out of proportion within a temporary alliance.

With difficulty, Tore mastered his wandering thoughts. 'We may have to go shopping tomorrow to buy baby equipment.'

'Is there a cot?'

'Yes, but it's on loan,' Tore shared in some embarrassment.

'From whom?'

'One of our staff, who has grandchildren.'

'Well, be sure to thank them. We'll manage,' Violet said calmly as he walked her into a big empty room. A fabulous mural of a forest glade adorned with cute fluffy animals covered the entirety of one wall. 'Oh, that painting is amazing!'

'This room was designated to be a nursery and when the frescoes were being restored, there were several different artists working here. I asked one of them to come up with a suitable children's painting. At least Belle will have something interesting to look at.'

Stella was already there and Belle was down on the floor with some toys.

'She'll be fine. We're not fussy,' Violet said as he led her on across the corridor into a giant, magnificently furnished bedroom. 'This house is a revelation, Tore. I'm learning that in private, you like to live as grandly as an eighteenth-century king.'

Her appreciative gaze scanned the scarlet drapes and

the huge, carved four-poster bed with its gilded accents and superb golden pleated canopy. 'That is the most amazing bed *ever*,' she commented.

'I converted the room next door into a bathroom and dressing room.' As he threw open the doors on further opulent appointments, Violet was enthralled and soon making plans for the stunning sunken bath in front of her. No, he had not lied; they would certainly not be roughing it once they obtained some necessities for Belle's room.

'I'll take you downstairs to see the rest of the house.'

'I'd like to see the ballroom,' she admitted. 'I've never been in a ballroom before.'

'It took three years to restore it but it looks incredible and it opens out on to the terrace, which has wonderful views of the forest and the village.'

In the ballroom, she leant back her head to appreciate the incredible painted ceiling and the carved stone pillars that ran round the perimeter. She was picturing ladies in beautiful gowns whirling round the room, sitting down to catch their breath on the velvet couches or to enjoy a drink in the conversational areas. She suppressed a sigh, thinking for the first time of how very privileged she was to be enjoying such experiences as part of Tore's life, and how hard it would be to adapt to a more normal lifestyle again.

'The main salon, the dining room and the library are all fully furnished and decorated,' Tore assured her. 'I've only furnished the rooms I had a reason to use.'

'Are you telling me that there's no office sitting here in readiness for you to use?' Violet teased.

'No, there isn't. When I need to work I go to the main office outside Siena.'

'If Stella's all right keeping Belle for another hour, I'm going for a bath,' Violet decided on the spur of the moment.

A maid was already unpacking luggage in the dressing room. She gathered what she needed from a case and ran the bath. In the midst of her preparations, Tore knocked on the door and asked if he could use the shower. 'Of course,' she said and she waited until he had stepped behind the marble shower wall before doffing her wrap and stepping down into the warm water that was foaming with bubbles.

'There's a swimming pool behind the villa. It's welcome on hot days,' Tore told her some minutes later as he reached for a fleecy towel.

'Unfortunately, I can't swim.' Violet rested back in her bath like a queen and stretched out her toes, blissfully relaxed. She collided unexpectedly with scorching green eyes, enhanced by the darkness of his lashes and she tensed, a little curl of heat coiling and tightening low in her tummy. Desire was always there on some level with Tore, she conceded ruefully. Every time their eyes met, their bodies brushed, every time he laid a hand on any part of her... And when it hit, it threatened to consume her.

'That's not a problem. I'll teach you.' Looping a towel round his waist, Tore gazed down at her. 'Promise me that you won't go near the pool without another adult present.'

'I tend to steer clear of large expanses of water, so don't

worry about that,' Violet countered, her cheeks burning at the admission she had felt forced to make. 'When my class was getting swimming lessons, I was off school with glandular fever, so Tabitha can swim and I can't.'

'It would be safer for you to learn.'

'Agreed, particularly with Belle on the brink of walking…in case there was an accident and she was to fall in or something,' she muttered with an unconcealed shudder.

'The pool's walled off for safety and bristling with alarms.'

A knock sounded loudly on the bedroom door and Tore went to answer it. When he returned, he told her that dinner was being served early because it was the chef's night off.

'You have an actual chef here?' Violet gasped in interruption as she sat up.

'I can't cook.' Tore handed her a towel.

Having given up on her peaceful bath when she realised that their evening meal would soon be ready, Violet slowly raised herself out of the water and wrapped herself in the towel. She was awesomely aware of Tore's gaze gliding over her wet, gleaming curves. He rested lean hands on her damp shoulders and stared down into her misty blue eyes. A jolt slivered through her, provoking an ache between her thighs and a surge of dampness. Painfully slowly, he bent and dropped his hands to her waist to lift her up against him.

And he ravaged her parted lips slow and invasive in the very best way, and something inside her just melted into a puddle of liquid heat. 'Tore…' she began.

'I've got it,' he asserted, backing into the bedroom, resting her back against the wall and dropping to his knees in front of her.

As he tugged loose her towel, something akin to panic momentarily gripped her. She felt out of control and excited and she didn't like it how often that happened with him. But when his mouth found the wildly responsive heart of her and then his fingers slid into her slick centre and she was struggling to stay upright and simply breathe, conscious thought abandoned her. All of a sudden, she was simply living for the next moment and the *next*. Sensation controlled her, driving her needy body up to a tormenting high, and then she was falling over that orgasmic edge, crying out, gasping, leaning back against the wall simply to stay upright on shaky legs.

Tore was moving up and away and she couldn't bear that and she caught him by the waist and forced him still before dropping to her own knees. She found him with her lips and her hands and for once a nervous fear of her own ignorance wasn't muting her every action. Just for once, she wanted to return the favour and to offer reciprocal pleasure. Tore had a bad habit of giving her everything in bed and not giving her the opportunity to match him. And this time she was determined to match him.

He growled deep and rough as her tongue twirled round the crown of his cock. The muscles on his torso rippled as he leant back and arched his hips. Wicked satisfaction warmed her core, turning her molten as she teased him. And then just as suddenly, he was breaking away from her again and across the room, rustling through a drawer to return to her, biting off the edge of the packet, sheathing himself and then reaching for her.

'Dinner!' she gasped the reminder, a rather belated recollection.

He said something unrepeatable about that reference and while he was doing so, he was lifting her clean off her feet, bracing her spine against the wall and bringing her down on him. Her arms fell round his neck as he penetrated her deep and fast, and her whole body rejoiced in that urgency of his and that sudden satisfying sensation of being stretched and full. From that point their movements merely grew more frantic as if they were battling for supremacy. She was in awe of his strength as he supported her before she was utterly engulfed by the pounding excitement of his urgent possession. In the safety of his strong arms, she came apart in a thousand pieces, surging up to the highest point and then tumbling down again into deep, abiding satisfaction as he, too, achieved release.

'*Madre di Dio, sei cosi sexy,*' Tore ground out, kissing her and lowering her slowly back to the floor. 'Nobody has ever got to me the way you do!'

Violet clenched her teeth. 'That sounds painful.'

'All we have to focus on now is getting downstairs for dinner,' Tore informed her, only slightly out of breath, reaching out and tugging her close. 'I can't keep my hands off you. This is new to me, *mia lucciola.*'

'And me,' she breathed, stepping away as he vanished into the bathroom and she tried to think about getting dressed. But it didn't seem important, what she wore, how she behaved. Tore was in the hold of a sexual infatuation, the same as her. That was all it could be, all she would let it be. Her sanity depended on her being sensible. Only she knew that she was neither maintaining control nor being sensible. In short, she was surrendering to responses that seemed as natural to her as they seemed deadly.

'But I'm enjoying this connection,' Tore admitted as he pulled out clothes in the dressing room. 'What do we have to lose? Friends with benefits is better by far than enemies.'

Violet nodded even though her stomach was turning over. She had never, ever aspired to being a friend with benefits with any man. That concept went against everything she believed. She was not lost to her body, nor did she put those physical needs above other more important, *lasting* elements in a relationship.

But all over again she was understanding why she had chosen the end of the month as the finish date for their intimacy. She was too close to getting hurt, too close to wanting more than she could have, and Tore was essentially still cool as ice on the emotional front. He wasn't agonising over what he deemed to be a temporary sexual obsession and when it suited him, why would he be?

CHAPTER NINE

BELLE COMPLAINED VOCIFEROUSLY about being harnessed in the stroller when she could now walk.

Tore laughed as he bent down to lift the toy that Belle had tossed out in a temper. 'You'll get over it,' he told the little girl cheerfully.

Two weeks had passed since their arrival at the villa. On the second day, Belle had walked her first lurching steps into Violet's arms. Belle might be able to walk but she wasn't up to the challenge of walking amongst other people and if she met a dog, and she had never met a dog she didn't like, she was likely to sit down in front of it and try to cuddle it.

Violet glanced at Tore, still barely recognisable to her in close-fitting jeans and an open shirt, his formality abandoned. He didn't wear suits at the villa. It was, she appreciated, the place where he truly felt at home. And why wouldn't he? Everyone knew him in the area. Renzetti Pharma was a major local employer, and then there were all the villagers who either worked at the villa or in one of the traditional workshops Tore had set up. Her fingers briefly strayed to the gold ruby pendant she wore, a present from Tore from a jewellery

designer he had backed. It was a stunning gift and it
looked terrific with the red sundress she wore.

The two weeks had flown by so fast that she couldn't
believe it. They were leaving tomorrow. They had furnished the nursery for Belle. That had been their first
outing and a practical one. But the outings hadn't ended
with the practical options. She had had a grand tour
of Renzetti Pharma and had enjoyed a glass of wine
with the delightfully welcoming Aldo, who had flown
up specially to see them. They had gone out on scenic
drives and lunched in village restaurants in the hills.
They had visited several Tuscan vineyards and dined
out at little candlelit restaurants in Siena.

But most of all Violet had enjoyed their time alone
together at the villa. She had had swimming lessons
in the pool and if she was now not quite a fish in the
water, she was certainly a lot more comfortable and
Belle, free of fear as only a baby was, adored the pool.
And there had been walks through the trails in the
forest where there was a seashell-studded grotto in a
cave and various weatherworn mossy statues placed
in glades to honour ancient gods. They had dined most
evenings on the loggia beneath the vines that blocked
the sun, intimate chats over wine. Tore had made a real
effort to get to know her and in the process, under fire
from all that innate charisma of his and dizzy from all
the unexpected attention she was receiving from him,
Violet had fallen head over heels in love with her husband—the husband who wasn't a husband in reality.

Tore expertly took hold of the stroller and steered
it through the little café out to the rear courtyard gar-

den where they could free Belle from her restraints. The baby gave a delighted shout of recognition of her surroundings and no sooner had Tore snapped free the harness than she was climbing out to stumble across the grass to greet the labradoodle that lived there.

'She needs a dog,' Tore said for the tenth time.

'I couldn't cope with a dog and her at work.'

'The staff will take care of the dog when you're out,' Tore scoffed. 'And I suspect that Stella is very much hoping that we will invite her to travel with us back to London, so you wouldn't need to take Belle with you to work.'

Violet compressed her lips and said nothing, which was her usual reaction to suggestions that might seem great in the present but wouldn't stand the test of time once they parted. The dog was sadly a no-no. Stella, however, was a different question. 'If she's interested, I'd like Stella to come back with us.'

Tore unfurled his phone there and then and embarked on a conversation in fast Italian, of which she only recognised a few words. She had learned a basic vocabulary through communicating with the employees and meeting people, but she knew she would need to take lessons to gain a proper grasp of the language. Their super-fancy coffees arrived, delivered by the proprietor of the café, which was always buzzing with trade. Violet sat back in her comfortable padded wicker chair and relaxed.

'I have a question to ask you, a big question,' Tore imparted softly.

'Oh…' Violet squirmed in her seat and frowned behind her sunglasses because the last time Tore had framed a question that way, it had embarrassed the hell out of her.

He had asked about her first lover, Damien, and she had to tell the sad little tale of two underage drinking best friends and teenagers deciding that it would be a good idea to say goodbye to their innocence before moving on into their adult lives. That impulsive decision was quickly regretted once she found that introduction painful, and Damien lost interest in trying to take the experiment any further. Learning that there had been little foreplay involved and that Damien had later decided that he wasn't into women, Tore had had the bad taste to laugh and make Violet feel ridiculously foolish for her ignorance.

'It's a serious question,' Tore murmured with gravity. 'I've been waiting for you to tell me about it yourself but on this score, you seem shy. But why *did* you want all that cash paid in advance of our marriage? And what are you planning to do with it? Was it intended as a future security blanket or are you or your sister in actual debt?'

Violet had frozen in dismay where she sat and recognised that it was time she came clean. 'I know it must've looked bad but we needed the money to pay for Mum's inclusion on the clinical trial and to cover her stay in the USA.'

His level ebony brows drew together in bewilderment. *'But—'*

'When our grandfather approached us, the only reason my twin and I were willing to agree to the marriage in the first place was for Mum's health. Tomaso said he would cover the cost of the clinical trial but when it actually came to crunch time, he said we'd have to wait a few months for the money he'd promised…but Mum was dying. She mightn't have had a few months left.'

Something flashed in Tore's simmering emerald gaze. 'Why would he have had to ask you to *wait* for the money? We paid millions for his company and his voting rights—'

Violet winced. 'I don't know anything about his financial situation but I do know that he refused to help Mum with money on a couple of other occasions when she approached him for help. We grew up in debt, Tore. My mother worked in low-paid jobs while my father drank and played and never once worried about how the rent would be paid or how we would eat. My grandfather is very much a man who believes that when you make your bed you have to lie on it. He's not sentimental. He blamed Mum for making a bad marriage and for not taking his advice.'

Tore was stunned by what he was learning about her upbringing. 'He *refused* to help his own daughter?'

'No, he said he would and then retracted his promise and demanded we wait, which is why Tabitha asked your lawyers for the money instead.'

'You do realise that when I heard that demand, I assumed that you were a shameless gold digger through and through,' Tore countered censoriously. 'What else was I going to think about such a request before we had even reached the church?'

Violet flushed a deep, hot pink and got up to retrieve Belle from the dog before the animal got irritated by her approaches. A *gold digger*? That angle hadn't occurred to her although it should've done, she conceded ruefully. After all, marriage to Tore had already endowed her with a string of credit cards and a huge monthly allowance currently piling up in her bank account because she wasn't comfortable with such generosity. A request for cash beyond those lavish offerings had understandably given Tore the wrong impression of her and her sister.

'I'm sorry. I should've told you sooner but I come out in a rash when I have to tell Mum's sad story. People get tired of hearing about it and it depresses them. Tabitha and I have learned not to talk too much about her treatments and prognosis. Mum's been ill for years now. My grandfather made us feel about an inch high when we asked him for help. It was humiliating…and, of course, at the end of the day it may prove to be wasted money because there *is* no guarantee of a positive result,' she advanced awkwardly.

'I understand but that money being demanded in advance of the wedding gave me a poor opinion of you and coloured my whole attitude towards you,' Tore framed with barely restrained anger, his lean, strong face taut. 'My mother's sister only took me on because I was the egg laid by the golden goose. Without my money, she would never have fought to keep me. But at the same time, she resented the burden of a young child in her life. Naturally, I have a low opinion of those who will do anything for cash.'

'Naturally,' she echoed weakly, striving not to cringe at that admission as she sipped her coffee. Belle fixed little fingers to Tore's knees and settled big brown eyes on him, begging him to lift her.

'She's a very pretty baby,' Tore commented, grabbing her up. 'And she already knows how to use those eyes of hers.'

'She already knows they work on you. No, don't give her your phone,' Violet urged. 'Because she'll create merry hell when you want it back. Let her wander and explore.'

'The only thing she wants to explore is that poor dog.'

Even so, he let her daughter down again and watched her stumble like a determined little drunk across a flower bed. There was a chorus of complaint from her when they put her back in the stroller. Tore bought her a wooden train in one of the workshops and she made a fair approximation of the *choo-choo* sounds he taught her before she dropped into a nap. Tore exchanged greetings with various acquaintances, stopping occasionally to introduce Violet and chat for a few moments.

In the faded denim jeans that fit his lean, powerful frame like a glove and a casual blue linen shirt, his silver hair glittering in the sunshine, which accentuated his classic features, Tore looked heartbreakingly beautiful. Just glancing at him quickened Violet's heartbeat and sent the blood racing through her veins as a wicked pulse of arousal assailed her.

They strolled back to the villa in the sunshine, although Tore was the one strolling with Violet walking at a faster pace than normal to keep up with his impossibly long legs. 'Slow down...it's too warm for this much exertion.'

Tore sent her a smouldering look from hooded eyes. 'I'm sad to hear that. Possibly, I was looking forward to a little afternoon delight,' he teased.

A flush warmed her already warm body. They had been intimate every day and in every place possible. Nobody could say she had been half-hearted or less than adventurous. Tore seemed to want her round the clock and she found him equally irresistible. More and more she appreciated that the moment she recognised the beginning of her emotional attachment should have been the same moment that she told him that sex should be taken out of their marriage. For her sake, not for *his*. But she couldn't have admitted that, could she have? Even she had her pride and preferred to conserve some mystery.

Tore Renzetti, however, was charming, consistently courteous and respectful. Always entertaining, great sense of humour, amazing in bed and in the shower and in all the other locations he had seduced her. He was no innocent but there was nothing fake about him. He gave her gifts all the time. They couldn't go out without him buying her something he believed she lacked, whether it be a new watch, a bigger handbag or the pool lounger of her dreams.

But she didn't think that emotions came into their marriage at all for Tore. Which reduced her status to one of convenience, she acknowledged unhappily. He held her in his arms most nights, though. He was surprisingly cuddly and a fabulous father figure for Belle. He had barely worked since they'd arrived in Tuscany. He had made time for her. He gave both her and her daughter his full attention. A lot of women would kill for what he was already giving her in the husband stakes. Unluckily for her, she wanted love and longevity. She wanted him forever, no take-backsies, no divorce and he hadn't signed up for that. And she was the total idiot who had invited him into bed and ensured that they got much, much closer in every way!

'Have you ever been in love?' she had asked one night, lying entwined in his arms in the shelter of darkness, asking one of those questions women always want to ask.

'I thought I was when I was a teenager and it creeped me out,' he had admitted.

'Why did it repulse you?'

'Just think about it. Having to *trust* someone to that extent. Fortunately for me, she slept with someone else before I got in too deep,' he had explained. 'I dodged a bullet. I still see her around occasionally. She's already on her third marriage and she's been faithful to none of her lovers. At heart, she's reckless, changeable, disloyal and not my type at all.'

'But you must've met someone more appealing since then,' she had persisted.

'I didn't want to. I like my focus on work and if you have the kind of brain that focuses on a woman's flaws rather than her virtues, it's easy to avoid entanglements. I expect too much from people but at heart, I think I'm too cold and logical to fall in love. I mean, there's nothing logical about love.'

And she hadn't slept that night for ruminating on what he had told her, thinking of the fiery arguments they still had over silly things, of her own many flaws and the truth that she came with a dependent child. So she had suppressed her fears, had tried to lower her expectations and had attempted to just make hay while the sun still shone. Only now the sun was about to go down on their intimacy.

As they crossed the inner courtyard of the villa, Tabitha phoned her.

'Just thought I should say…' she began. 'You know that social worker in charge of your adoption thingy. Catriona? She's visited a couple of times, wanting to know where you were. I forgot to mention it. I told her you were on holiday on her first visit and she was happy enough with that but I had to be more honest the second time.'

'Why? What did you tell her?' Violet pressed worriedly as she paced and watched Tore carry Belle into the house.

'Well, obviously, I couldn't tell her the truth about the contract but I tried to be as honest as I could be,' Tabitha explained. 'I admitted that you'd got married and she was very taken aback that you hadn't informed them of your changed circumstances. I thought you were only waiting for the adoption order to be ratified by the court.'

Violet flinched. 'I am but this is my fault, *my* oversight. I didn't once think of how this marriage would affect my standing with social services.'

'I shouldn't think it'll be a problem. I mean, Tore's young and loaded, perfect daddy material. But Catriona said they would have to vet him as well and see your new home.'

'Vet him? Vet Tore?' Violet exclaimed in horror. 'I *can't* ask him to go through all those intrusive questions and interviews on my behalf!'

'Don't think you're going to have any choice,' Tabitha groaned with sympathy. 'Now that you're married to the guy, he has to be passed as a suitable parent, too. I'm sure he won't be difficult about it. The two of you are getting on like a house on fire, and going by the photos you've sent me he's clearly fond of Belle, so there shouldn't be a problem.'

Violet flinched and muttered uneasily, 'I don't expect so but I'll feel awful having to ask him because it's not like it's really any of his business when we're not staying together. I don't want him to feel obligated to do anything he doesn't want to do.'

And how could she ask him to adopt Belle with her when they would only be in his life for such a short time? It wouldn't even be fair to Belle to give her an adoptive father who would not be staying, she reflected wretchedly.

'Tore doesn't sound to me like a guy who ever does anything he doesn't *want* to do.'

'He agreed to marry when he didn't want to,' Violet protested defensively.

'You're getting so protective of him and you're such a worrywart,' her twin lamented. 'If he's halfway decent as you say he is, he's not going to want you to risk losing custody of Belle. I'm sure he'll help.'

Alfredo was hovering on the front steps awaiting the end of her phone conversation. As she returned the phone to her bag, he informed her that lunch was ready.

Tore was pacing the hall. Stella had taken Belle. He wondered if Violet realised how clear her speaking voice could be surrounded by stone walls. He had only caught a couple of phrases of her conversation. *When we're not staying together*, she had said. *I don't want him to feel obligated*. What didn't she want him to feel obligated about?

Dio mio, was she pregnant? It was wondrous how calm he felt at that prospect. The advent of another Belle didn't seem like the end of the world, yet that is how he would have reacted to such a possibility just weeks earlier. Even though he had taken no risks, protection was never fully guaranteed. But would Violet already know if she had conceived? Then he scolded himself for being unusually fanciful. They had only been together a month. He supposed it was possible that a woman would know early. He hoped she realised that if she was carrying his child, she would be going nowhere away from him any time soon. A faint smile softened the tense line of his mobile mouth. His grandparents would be ecstatic. Married young themselves and parents soon after, they could imagine nothing better at maturing a young man than the added responsibilities of marriage and fatherhood.

'Sorry about that,' Violet muttered as she joined him in the hall, looking shifty with her eyes averted and visibly uncomfortable. They walked out to the loggia to sit down for lunch. 'It was Tabitha.'

'Problems at the bakery?'

'Nothing important,' she answered dismissively, reckoning that she would leave the request about Belle until they had returned to London. That would be time enough, she reasoned unhappily.

A beautiful pasta salad was served. She was offered wine and demurred, having discovered that wine in the afternoon tended to give her a headache and simply make her sleepy.

But was it wrong of her to withhold from Tore what she had just learned about her adoption of Belle? Exactly how would she go about asking Tore if he would agree to being questioned as Belle's potential adoptive father? Tore was a particularly private and reserved man.

Yet, she could only blame herself for the issues that had arisen. Knowing that she was only waiting for the court to verify the social services' recommendation, she had relaxed and forgotten that she was still living under official scrutiny. Indisputably, the reality that she had now acquired a husband and moved house was relevant to her adoption case and she couldn't admit the truth. She couldn't admit that hers was merely a marriage on paper that would leave her richer but otherwise back where she had started out as a single parent with a small business. But surely, Tore wouldn't object to playing along and faking it as a husband and father for Belle's sake?

'You seem preoccupied,' Tore remarked.

'Leaving this place will be a wrench,' she admitted reluctantly for it was never easy to face leaving somewhere where you had enjoyed real happiness. Even if that happiness had been built on sand foundations? She ignored that warning, censorious voice in her head.

Tore had made them both very happy and she wouldn't deny that, even though it seemed that those fragile feelings of contentment couldn't possibly last.

'I have something to say, then,' Tore stated quietly, reckoning that lunch was already a bust in the mood she was in and deciding to press ahead with what he had always intended to tell her. 'This plan you have where we suddenly start living as strangers again won't work.'

'Why shouldn't it?' Violet pressed in sudden dismay, disconcerted and on the immediate edge of distress at the opening of that previously unmentioned topic. 'Why shouldn't it work?'

'Because everything has changed between us. We're not strangers anymore and we're certainly not friends in the normal sense of the word. We never were. It makes more sense to explore the connection that we have established now rather than try to change it into something else and turn the clock back,' Tore reasoned feelingly, green eyes alive with resolve and fierce energy.

Violet leapt upright. 'Go on, remind me that this is all my fault! I changed our arrangement first—'

Tore expelled his breath in an exasperated hiss. 'It's nobody's fault, Violet. What we've discovered together should be celebrated, not criminalised, not suddenly put on the forbidden list. We're both content and we're independent adults. What we do is our business. Why change anything? Especially something that will feel unnatural to both of us.'

'Only a few weeks ago, being polite to each other

and keeping our distance in every other way *wasn't* unnatural,' she reminded him stubbornly. 'We can get that vibe back if we work at it.'

'It's not what I want,' Tore admitted grimly. 'And maybe I'm not prepared to work to achieve what I don't want and don't believe in. There are two of us in this relationship. It's not only you. I've adapted to being a married man, a husband and a stepfather. Those are big concessions on my terms. But I am happy with the changes. I won't apologise, however, for the fact that I neither agree with nor *believe* in your current plan of action.'

'If I'd listened to you, we would never have got this close!' Violet exclaimed vehemently.

'But you were braver than me and possibly more insightful. If we hadn't made this a real marriage, we would've missed out on a great opportunity. As I see it, between us we've created a very successful relationship.' Tore compressed his lips on that note, lean, darkly handsome face shadowing, already convinced that he had said more than he should've done. 'We may have had an unconventional beginning but we've overcome that. So again, I ask you... Why would we change anything?'

Turmoil was eating Violet alive as she moved back into the villa. She hadn't expected Tore to put up a fight to maintain the status quo. She got his point that once again she was making a unilateral decision that affected him as well. But never had his cool, logical approach worked more against him than then. Violet really just needed him to put his arms round her and tell her that everything would be all right and that she didn't need to worry about anything. And yet, she knew he didn't have the power to make everything right. But for the first time, she grasped that Tore was more invested in their marriage than she had previously appreciated.

'Violet…' His dark, deep drawl halted her a few steps away and she turned her head back unwillingly. 'I caught a few words of your conversation with your sister on the phone. I heard you refer to the fact that our marriage was temporary and that you didn't want to put me under an obligation. All I could think then was that you might have fallen pregnant…'

Shaken and wide-eyed at that suggestion, Violet stared back at him and shook her head. 'No, I'm not pregnant. We've been careful—'

'Yes, but as you pointed out, careful isn't always enough. Are you sure?'

'Yes, I'm sure,' she said limply, thrown entirely by his suspicion but not ready as yet to open up another possible source of conflict until she had calmed down. And the one thing she wasn't in that moment was calm.

Tore looked disappointed at the news that she wasn't accidentally secretly pregnant. The more time she spent with him, the more she learned about him, she conceded wretchedly. He could've accepted an unplanned pregnancy, could've made the best of it, it seemed. Surely, that softness in him, that very acceptance, would make him more likely to agree to adopting Belle with her? She could only hope.

CHAPTER TEN

THE FIRST THING that struck Violet when she walked back into her rooms in Tore's massive London home was the silence and the knowledge that he was no longer nearby in the way she had grown accustomed to him being. He was on the other side of the house and he had mentioned that he had to check in with the London office, so had undoubtedly already gone out. Stella was chattering away to Tore's housekeeper about her plans to explore London, and Belle was muttering with excitement as she toddled across her old nursery to a reunion with familiar toys.

In fact, everyone was on a high over their return to London and she gave herself a mental kick. Buck up, straighten up, stop acting like the world is over because you had a difference of opinion with Tore. Had she been too hasty in telling him she wanted to go back to being platonic married strangers? Wasn't it a little too late in the day to make such a change? And what did it matter anyway when she was already madly in love with him? The damage was done. She had little time to consider her doubts once she headed over to the bakery to catch up with her sister.

'You've totally fallen for him!' Tabitha condemned

the minute Violet had brought her up-to-date. 'I suspected it when you were talking about him on the
phone but now you've thrown him out of the bedroom,
haven't even spent one night alone and you're already
miserable. Violet, this guy is planning to walk away
from you in just thirty months' time and he'll forget
that you're alive…wasn't that the deal? Have you forgotten that? How *could* you forget that?'

'I know the situation and I'm not miserable, really
I'm not,' Violet argued defensively.

'Put you and Belle first,' her exasperated twin encouraged. 'Regrettably, barring Tore from your bedroom may not have been the wisest move when you're
on the brink of asking him to adopt Belle with you. I
mean, things were great with the two of you while you
were in Italy but now you've chucked all that down the
drain…and I really don't understand why.'

'I was trying to protect myself.'

'Much good it's doing you. Anyway, you were a goner
for him from the start when you said he reminded you
of one of the Lord of the Rings' elves!' Tabitha began
to giggle. 'I bet you haven't told *him* that. He sounds
like such a serious type. In fact, I bet he'd be offended.'

'He's never going to know,' Violet swore, her face
burning. 'What about your baby daddy?'

Tabitha went rigid. 'Don't call him that! He's never
going to be my kid's dad. He's an obnoxious playboy
who thinks every woman is out to rip him off!'

'That's horrible,' Violet agreed. 'But you have to tell
him you're pregnant eventually, no matter how challenging it might be. He has legal rights.'

'I know that but he has to *know* there *is* a child to do anything about it.'

'Agreed but you're entitled to his financial support and you will need it. Also...' Violet hesitated before pressing on. 'You need to think about your child wanting to know who his father is when he's older, so it's best to bite the bullet now.'

'So practical, Violet,' Tabitha commented tongue-in-cheek. 'Unless you're throwing your billionaire out of your bed! That was *not* practical.'

Violet thought about that exchange over her solitary supper with Belle. With Tore at the table there would've been adult conversation, and Belle would not have dared to throw her toast off her tray. Belle had a healthy respect for Tore when he spoke in a certain tone. Violet just couldn't stop thinking about him. Other possible elements of her decision were currently crossing her troubled mind. Would Tore now take some other woman to bed? Could she expect him to stay celibate for the sake of a marriage that wasn't a true marriage?

Fidelity was nowhere mentioned in his side of the marriage contract although it was referred to in hers. Evidently, he and his legal team had been afraid that his bride might be some wild woman, engaging in affairs and causing scandals and potentially even producing a child that was not his. Every possibility had been explored and covered in that contract but there had not been a single reference to Tore staying faithful. All of a sudden that inequality infuriated her. Was he even now planning to go out and find another woman to satisfy his needs? Was he even at home?

Violet could not contain her curiosity and she slid quietly out of bed, determined to find out. She was unlikely to bump into any staff at midnight, so she didn't bother with a robe. She padded on bare feet down the long corridor that separated her wing of the house from his. She hadn't been in that wing before, hadn't been in the house long enough to stray there before they left London for Italy. Now she was on a quiet voyage of exploration in unfamiliar territory.

She found an office, no surprise there. A meeting room, various empty guest rooms and then she reached the very foot of the corridor where a single door awaited her. She wasted no time in slipping through that door because her curiosity, her search, had reached its peak and it was insatiable in its need to know where he was, what he was doing and who he might be doing it with.

A light illuminated the big bed and there he was, alone, working on a laptop, his phone in one hand in spite of the lateness of the hour. 'Violet...?'

He was naked apart from a pair of black boxers. He was totally relaxed, comfortable. He wasn't visibly missing her. She didn't know what she had expected to see or what visible signs of missing her he could've offered, but he looked happier than she felt and that could only be a source of annoyance. 'I just wondered where you were,' she said tightly.

Tore focused on his wife, who had made it clear that she was not a wife and not prepared to explore being his wife in reality, either. She was clad in a diaphanous lilac silk nightdress that clung to her sinuous curves in the most revealing way. 'Well, now you know,' he said ungenerously because he had been silently smouldering over her stubborn attitude. Every time he wondered what he would do about it, he was exasperated that his usual disciplined concentration was absent.

'Tell me,' she muttered daringly. 'Did you ever intend to be faithful in this marriage?'

'No,' Tore admitted without hesitation. 'But that changed for me the moment we consummated our marriage. I intended to be faithful then…at least until you changed the game today.'

'It's not a game. It was never a game for me,' Violet protested, disconcerted by his honesty, a shiver filtering through her body because he had the air-conditioning on and the nightdress provided no insulation whatsoever.

In a silent gesture, Tore flipped back the duvet in invitation.

'Definitely not a game,' she reiterated, goose bumps rising on her arms before she accepted the invitation and took a flying leap on to the bed, shooting below the duvet at speed.

'But you changed the rules and now I don't know where I am with you,' Tore imparted, setting his laptop and phone down on the cabinet by the bed.

'I thought you liked rules,' she mumbled.

'Not one that drives us apart.'

'Oh, for goodness' sake, switch the air-conditioning off before I turn into an icicle!' she launched back at him.

With a chuckle of appreciation, he stretched up a lean, muscular arm and switched it off and then pushed back the duvet to uncurl her coiled limbs and tug her gently into his arms. 'It's probably against the rules but I missed you and Belle at dinner. My home life was very colourless and flat until you came along.'

'Yes, you were just gasping to have a mini demon throwing toast at the table!' she framed, her entire body reeling in sensual shock from the sheer heat of his lean, powerful physique wrapping round her chilled body.

'Belle's still very young, still very much a baby, even though she's walking but she's incredibly independent for her age,' he commented with pride.

Warmth feathered through her heart as she recognised that pride. Tore was fond of her daughter and she could not credit that he would do anything to wreck the stability of Belle's life. Had she made a mountain out of a molehill in her eagerness to follow through on her conviction that they should sleep apart? It seemed to her at that moment that she had overreacted and had failed to consider how much closer they had become in recent weeks. In effect, she had shot herself in the foot, forcing a separation long before it was necessary and far too late to stifle the strong feelings she already had for him.

'You staying with me tonight, *mia lucciola*?' Tore murmured huskily, one giant hand spread across her curvy derriere as he scrutinised her delicate face, watching her smile up at him, revelling in the warmth of her, triumphant that she hadn't been able to stay away. 'Tomorrow, hopefully, we'll get the both of you moved into this wing. That will be a much more comfortable arrangement. No more divisions.'

'And you'll be totally faithful?' she checked.

His slashing, still-boyish grin lightened his lean, dark features. 'One hundred percent with you in my bed.'

'Do you trust me now?'

Tore frowned. 'More than I've ever trusted a woman.'

'And you're not going to complain when I get up in the early hours to go off and bake?'

'Aside of the fact that I start my working day at dawn as well, I do think we'll be discussing the potential in the hire of a competent baker to free you of that necessity on a daily basis. I'm not trying to take you out of the kitchen. But for you to be free to travel when necessary, you'll have to have a suitable stand-in ready,' Tore pointed out calmly, pulling her closer to make her maddeningly aware of the long, hard erection against her stomach, setting off all the little ripples of arousal and anticipatory thrills that such contact usually brought her.

And when she got up in the morning, Tore was in the best of moods because he was setting out on his working day as well and delighted to share a shower with her...at length, so that she almost ducked having breakfast with him because she was running late. With Stella looking after Belle, however, she would have more time to bake, she reminded herself while she got dressed on the other side of the house in her own suite of rooms. She hurried downstairs to the grand dining room on the ground floor where she had never eaten before and wandered in, suddenly self-conscious as the hovering employee by the table shot her a surprised glance.

Her cheeks coloured as she dropped into the chair to Tore's right, taking in his magnificence in a formal charcoal-grey suit and pale grey shirt and tie with a heady sensation of warmth blooming inside her chest. She decided to tell him about the question mark now hanging over Belle's adoption case and launched straight into an explanation. She had to move fast now that she was back in London. She needed to phone Catriona and apologise for her oversights and set up a meeting.

'Of course, it should've occurred to me that I needed to keep my circumstances updated and that a substantial change like getting married and moving house would be important and relevant.'

'By the way you spoke, I had assumed that the adoption had already been finalised,' Tore admitted, pouring her a fresh coffee.

'It's been months since my assessment was done, but there's a backlog in the family court and we're still awaiting a final court date for the case. I stopped worrying about it once I had the social workers' approval but that was rash of me,' Violet added ruefully. 'So now I need to get all my ducks in a row in a hurry and I can't do it without you.'

His brows pleated as he lounged back in his seat cradling his black coffee. *'Me?* What do I have to do with it?'

'Think about it, Tore.' Violet looked at him in surprise because she thought she had already explained the situation. 'As my husband, *you* have to adopt her *with* me for the application to continue. And that would entail you being interviewed about how you feel about Belle and becoming her father.'

'But I'm not about to become her father. To become her father you would have to pretend that you intend to stay married to me for good. To say otherwise I would have to lie, and I'm not prepared to do that,' Tore informed her with sudden bite.

Shock roared through Violet like an earthquake had shaken the ground beneath her off its sturdy foundations. She blinked in disbelief. She had been in no way prepared for his immediate refusal. She had simply assumed that he would agree to be added to the adoption application.

'You're not being reasonable, Tore,' she said in a small voice. 'It's not like I can admit that we got married to fulfil my grandfather's ambitions. We *have* to lie. We have to pretend it's a normal marriage…and right now, it *is* a normal marriage.'

Tore skated up an ebony brow. 'Is it? When you're going to walk away in three years? Yet, you're asking me to take responsibility for Belle's future. How could I do that? I won't *be* there. You could get tangled up with some thug who mistreats her and I won't be there to guarantee her safety. Those are serious facts, Violet. I refuse to take responsibility for a child I will not be in a position to protect.'

'I'm not going to get tangled up with some thug, for goodness' sake!' Violet objected in a strained undertone. 'I haven't even *had* a man in my life since Damien, and I'm not even sure he counts because we were really only friends who briefly assumed we could be something more.'

'I'm sure you'd be very aware of Belle's security at all times but occasionally adults make wrong choices as I discovered during my own childhood. I was abused because there was nobody mature or decent enough within that home to supervise my welfare. For me to take full responsibility for Belle, I would need to know that she would be in my life until she's a legal adult,' he completed grimly.

'And how am I supposed to accomplish that?' Violet asked, her voice breaking slightly in her distress, a giant sob forming in her throat and making it difficult to breathe. She felt like he had cleaved her very heart in two, and the pain of that hollow agony inside her slivered through her. She had never believed that Tore would just say no to her request. He liked Belle, he made an effort with Belle; she had even thought he might be starting to *love* her daughter. But without his support in the adoption application as her husband she might not be able to make Belle her daughter, after all. In fact, Belle might be taken away from her altogether and given to someone viewed as more suitable.

'On the other hand,' Tore mused, appalled by the pallor of Violet's face and the desperation in her eyes, but characteristically reluctant to embark on delicate negotiations without encouragement from the other party. 'Were you to declare that you *would* stay married to me until she's grown up, I could possibly adjust my conscience accordingly.'

'Whatever,' Violet mumbled, barely having heard him speak but automatically assuming he had said something intended to be soothing because whatever else Tore was, he was not a cruel man. He was a forthright male with strong convictions and she knew she would never get him to change his mind on her behalf. Dear heaven, what was she going to do now?

'I'll see you later,' Tore told her, more than a little disappointed by her failure to respond to that suggestion. Had he been too half-hearted? Or too enthusiastic? What he had proposed went so far beyond their marriage contract that it didn't even fall within the same territory. In fact, his words would appal his legal team, who were already aghast at the realisation that thanks to it bearing Tabitha's signature and not his actual wife's, his prenuptial agreement was worthless.

Violet tottered blindly out of the dining room and headed upstairs. What was she going to do? And then the answer, the *obvious* answer, came to her in a great upsetting surge. She could leave Tore and move back to her apartment. She could explain that the marriage had been an unfortunate mistake and then Belle's adoption case could proceed just as it was with her as a single parent. True, it would make her look a little foolish that her marriage had broken down within a month, but stranger things had happened and she wouldn't be the only woman who had fled their marriage in those first crucial weeks.

That huge decision made, Violet sat down and cried

her eyes out. Just the idea of walking away from Tore crucified her. She didn't want to do it, even if it would only be a temporary relocation. What if Tore didn't want her back after the adoption was finalised? What if he felt that they had already done enough to fulfil the original contract? And that in any case, she had been the partner to drop out of their agreement?

Pulling the ragged pieces of her wretched self together, she splashed her swollen eyes with cold water and asked the housekeeper for her cases. She packed, taking only her original clothes. Stella was taking Belle out to the zoo and she wasn't about to interfere with that treat. She would come back in the evening and collect Belle and all the baby stuff. She would have to talk to Tore then. She winced. It would be better by far to leave him a letter explaining her plan of action so that he could adapt to her sensible decision before she saw him again.

Their marriage? That contract? Well, hopefully, if Belle's adoption came through, she could return to him then. Would that be enough for him? Or would she find herself charged with breach of contract? She had plenty of fabulous jewellery now to hock should she require a good lawyer, she reminded herself. Really, Belle was the most important person in her world and she had to put her first.

Even above Tore? Tore would be furious. Hurt? Possibly. Betrayed? He would probably feel she had let him down badly and the idea of him believing that of her wounded her. She sat down at her laptop to write a letter and just let the words flow as she pointed out that it was easier to walk away from a sudden, mistaken marriage than risk losing custody of the little girl she already thought of as her daughter. But that, all things being equal, she would return to their marriage should the adoption be finalised in the near future. Would that satisfy him?

Tore had agonised all day about the answer he had given Violet on the adoption question. Rationally, he stood by that answer. He could not agree to parent Belle unless he could stay around to complete that job. Violet hadn't thought her naive expectations through. She had been very much shocked by his flat refusal, however. But why hadn't she latched on to the offer he had made for her to remain married to him? Her lack of reaction had bitten him deep. She could, at least, have discussed his proposal and given him an answer. Troubled, he left the office early.

His housekeeper informed him that Violet hadn't returned since leaving with her cases. *Cases?* Maybe she was disposing of some of her old clothes. Regardless, he was curious enough to stride through to her wing and walk through the empty rooms. Everything he had bought her still hung in the closets, the jewellery boxes left out in a seeming statement on the dresser and most noticeably, her wedding ring. Taken aback and losing colour, he uttered a curse, his chest suddenly uncomfortably tight and he breathed in fast and deep. She had walked out on him.

She was *gone*. He didn't like that, couldn't accept it. His hands clenched into fists; indeed, that wasn't an ending that he could handle. It wasn't what he wanted.

It hadn't been what he wanted for longer than he cared to admit. He had found something special with Violet, something he couldn't put into words but which he had never had with any other woman. Somehow, daily interaction with Violet had become crucial to his well-being. She made him happy, honest-to-God happy, and with the simplest of things. Her smile, her warmth, her infectious friendliness and honesty, her innocent willingness to trust in others in spite of her difficult childhood.

'Mr Renzetti?' his housekeeper said from the doorway. 'Will Mrs Renzetti be staying for dinner when she picks up the little girl at seven?'

'I don't know yet. I'll let you know,' Tore countered stiffly as he headed for his own room, struggling to get his head straight, his thoughts ordered, instead of taking off on wild tangents. She hadn't taken Belle yet. He clung to that fact. He would see Violet again, however briefly.

The envelope in the centre of the bed she had shared with him the night before stole his attention the moment he entered the room. He tore it open, unfurled the closely typed two sheets. He supposed it was good that she had so much to say. Hopeful? He didn't know. But the letter was very much Violet, telling him that absolutely everything was her fault from start to finish and that she wasn't betraying his trust. No, only trying to correct her status for the benefit of Belle's ongoing adoption and that she had every intention of returning to him as soon as possible to fulfil the contract.

Dio mio, the contract again when he couldn't care

less about that stupid contract, which had caused more trouble than it was worth. He had clung to the letter of the law in that contract and where had it gotten him? He should've told her that he loved her in Italy. He shouldn't have sat on the fence, too proud to say it first. He shouldn't have stuck to his moral convictions when it came to Belle's adoption application, either. He should have said yes just to free Violet from worry. He had left her alone all day to deal with that stress. Was it any wonder that his wife regarded pretending to be single again as the simplest solution to her predicament?

Tabitha set a mug of tea down beside her sister. 'So, you're fully on board with the leaving Tore bit even though it's breaking your heart?'

'I have to get over him some time! It's just happening sooner than I expected,' Violet muttered tightly.

'He's a monster for not being willing to do his bit for the adoption. I don't care about his convictions,' Tabitha said sharply. 'If he cares about you and Belle, he should've agreed to do it.'

'You can't expect that from a man who married me because of a stupid contract to acquire voting rights for his business,' Violet sighed miserably. 'He's not an emotional man.'

Tabitha hovered by the window and stared down. 'So, if I was to tell you that he's pacing the pavement down there carrying the biggest, most ridiculous bouquet of flowers I ever saw, you're not interested?'

'I beg your pardon?' Violet flew up and over to the window. 'Those are beautiful flowers!' she told her sister argumentatively.

'Right, I'll let him in and take over the counter downstairs so that the staff can clear up for closing,' Tabitha declared. 'I'm not going to stay up here and play gooseberry.'

Violet compressed her lips and glanced in the mirror, finger combing her hair to tidy it, pinching her cheeks because she looked colourless and miserable. Well, she *was* miserable. What had seemed so simple earlier that day was a lot tougher when push came to shove. She knew she had to make the sacrifice of leaving Tore for Belle's sake but being away from him, not knowing when or if she would ever be with him again, was a punishment.

Hearing his steps on the stairs, she went out to the tiny landing and collided with shimmeringly intense green eyes long before he reached the top step. She backed into the cosy sitting room. 'Did you read my letter?' she prompted anxiously.

'Yes. You don't look at all like your sister,' he remarked wryly as he handed her the flowers and she disappeared through a doorway into the tiny kitchenette to put them in water.

'I told you that. Before we talk about what you're doing here, I've always wondered why you didn't want to meet either of us before the wedding.'

'It made it too real. It personalised what I was determined would be a business-oriented alliance. After all, looks didn't come into it.'

'Agreed, but your lack of curiosity was weird.'

'I didn't expect to be attracted to you or end up in bed with you but you shook me up from the first moment,' Tore revealed. 'You were always taking me by surprise. You dealt with my relatives like a pro at the *castello*. I'm sorry I didn't give you more support. I took advantage of your good nature so that I could work. But I didn't do *any* work today. I was stuck stressing about the bad way we parted but I planned to sort that out once I got home…only you were gone.'

'You may not agree with what I'm trying to do here but you have to admit that it will simplify things.'

'How? It means I have to do without you and I'm not prepared to do that. Why didn't you accept the offer I made before we parted?' Tore demanded, seeing the tearstains on her cheeks and feeling encouraged by them. 'I realise that I didn't voice the suggestion in an emotional or romantic way, but if you didn't want to leave me for heaven only knows how long, why didn't you consider that as an option?'

'What offer did you make me before we parted?' Violet queried in confusion.

'That if you agree to stay with me until Belle grows up, I'll go through the adoption process for Belle with you,' he reiterated. 'Neither of us would be lying then.'

'You said that this morning? I didn't hear you! For goodness' sake, why would you say that? Why would you ask me to stay?'

'Why am I here now? You're being very slow on the uptake this evening, *mia lucciola*,' Tore groaned. 'I want you forever. I don't want to lose you or Belle in three years' time. I want to forget about rules and contracts and have a normal marriage with you.'

'Forever,' she repeated in emphasis.

'You get greedy when you fall in love with your wife. Even forever doesn't seem long enough. Let's say forever plus added time in interest,' he quipped, and reaching down he clasped her waist and lifted her, taking a seat with her across his lap. 'I love you. I think I started falling in love with you when you were screaming at me. You probably don't want to hear that but you were so passionate about your rights I was impressed and wildly turned on.'

'You love me? But how? You said you were too cold and logical.'

'You slid into my heart somehow. Don't ask me how it happened. You kept me off balance. You fascinated me. I wanted you all to myself. It was amazing when it was just the three of us at the villa. I feel so comfortable with you. I've never had that before with a woman.'

'Only because you wouldn't give any other woman a chance.'

'Trusting anyone that far was too difficult. My mother, whom I loved, disappeared between one day and the next,' he reminded her. 'My aunt was practically a stranger and my time with her was frightening and unstable. Then I experienced life with my grandparents, more change. They loved me and I loved them but as I matured, I understood that my late father had been a disappointment to them. He didn't fit and I was determined that I would and that I would be the perfect grandson because I owed them that for their care of me.'

'I don't think that's how they feel. They just love you, faults and all, the same way that I do. I'm not expecting perfect. I know you're prone to being a work-aholic and that you're very, very stubborn but I still love you. After all, if you can put up with me being hot-tempered and stubborn, why would I criticise you for what you can't help?'

'You don't but it doesn't matter. I'm convinced that we're meant to be…' Tore lifted her left hand and threaded her wedding ring back onto her finger and then he withdrew a small box from a pocket to extract a second ring. 'Engagement ring. To make us more of a conventional couple.'

Enchanted by the gesture, Violet squinted down at the glowing ruby ring on her finger. 'I made the no-sex rule because I thought it would protect me from getting hurt.'

'It was already too late by then. I was falling for you before we left the *castello* and our time at the villa sealed it into a done deal. I love Belle, too. I'm looking forward to us becoming a proper family and we'll just go through the adoption process for her like normal people *without* any fake breakups, lies or drama,' Tore assured her firmly. 'It'll be fine. I will be a great papa and any time you get a yen for another child, you only have to mention it.'

'Mention it?' she whispered. 'Are you serious?'

'As a heart attack. When I had that crazy suspicion that you might have conceived, I was disappointed when I realised I'd got it wrong. So, evidently you have to fall in love or have a Belle in your life before you want to reproduce,' Tore told her very seriously.

'Gosh, I love you!' Violet exclaimed, stretching up

to steal a kiss. Her mouth was thoroughly ravished by his hungry urgency. 'So what now?'

'We go home, have dinner, see Belle and go to bed. Tomorrow we sort out that adoption application and get it updated to reflect our current circumstances,' he told her, settling her upright between his spread thighs and smoothing her hair with tender, possessive fingers. 'And then the week after next—you having found and purchased a suitable ball gown—we will return to the villa to host the Summer Ball.'

'You have it all planned.'

'I *tried* to plan everything. But I didn't plan to fall in love with you. I didn't plan to be married and/or to want to stay married at the age of twenty-nine. I expected to marry in my forties but I couldn't possibly pass you up and hope to find you again at a later date,' Tore informed her cheerfully. 'And now we can get a dog for Belle. Everything is falling beautifully into place.'

'Yes, it is… I'm taking my flowers back with me,' she said sunnily, plucking them back out of the vase and stuffing the stems into a plastic bag. 'Flowers and a ring. You're getting romantic, Tore. Who would ever have dreamt?'

And then they went home and made love far into the night, both of them bolstered by a buoyant sense of happiness and the glory of having found each other.

EPILOGUE

Five years later

VIOLET WAS DAYDREAMING as she sat on the loggia at the villa. Most of her happiest memories were related to their Tuscan home. A year after their wedding, they had enjoyed a blessings ceremony staged in the villa chapel. She had worn the wedding dress of her dreams, pearl roses on her shoes and silk flowing round her. She had walked to the altar with her mother, Lucia, Tabitha acting as her maid of honour. It had been a glorious day and it had more than made up for the deficiencies of that first wedding of strangers, united only in misunderstanding.

Her mother's illness was currently in remission. The new drug had worked. Lucia had put on a little weight and freed of the strain of her disease, she had recovered her spirits. Soon after her return home to the UK, Violet's grandfather, Tomaso, had passed away during heart surgery. Lucia had been stunned to discover that in spite of all the years of estrangement, her father had not changed his will. She had duly inherited her childhood home and her father's entire estate. Now she lived there comfortably with her best friend and was within easy reach of London, enabling her to freely meet up with her daughters and her grandchildren for days out.

The bakery had turned into a small chain of four scattered across London, and Violet only baked at home for her family now. Tore had persuaded her to hire more people and expand once he realised how successful the business was. She loved running the bakeries but she did not miss those dawn starts. In fact, now that they spent most of their time in Italy and the children went to school there, she was less and less a hands-on boss but she was grateful to have the ability to spend more time with the children while they were still young.

'Mama…' a firm little voice said.

Violet looked up to see her daughter, Belle, coming up the steps towards her, a very pretty slight girl of almost six years old, who occasionally talked like a judgemental little old lady. 'Sofia got stuck up a tree…' she complained. 'You can't take her anywhere without her getting in trouble.'

Violet flew up out of her seat immediately. 'Where is she? In the woods?'

'Papa got her down and he hugged her because she was crying and then her and Enzo had a stupid fight. He wanted to be the one who climbed that tree and she beat him to it.'

'Your father's back early?' Smiling, her concern evaporating, Violet wandered to the top of the steps to watch out for her husband because he had been out of the country for a week on business.

Their twins, Sofia and Enzo, were four now. That pregnancy had been tough for Violet and it had taken a while for her to consider a second pregnancy. A lively team, the twins ran wild at the villa. Belle had never run wild in spite of encouragement. Belle liked everything just so and she was very feminine, preferring dresses to shorts or jeans. She hated to get dirty and had never climbed a tree in her life. She was a terrific reader, though, and she adored animals.

Sofia, in comparison, was a real little tomboy, who rarely sat still and who was more likely to get into mischief than her brother. Enzo was Tore to the life, a rule follower, very clever and thoughtful and always careful. Enzo, however, had inherited his father's silver gilt hair, which had delighted his mother.

All their kids adored Aldo and Matilde, who only lived half an hour away from them and were regular visitors. In Italy they enjoyed a large gregarious family circle and they always spent July at the *castello* where the children could play with their cousins and enjoy the beach. The children spoke Italian like natives while Violet was still stumbling a little in conversations in spite of the lessons she'd had.

Tore saw his wife awaiting him at the top of the steps. It was their fifth anniversary and his grandparents were on the way to pick up the children and give their parents a quiet weekend. Violet was wearing denim shorts and a bright white top and he started to smile. She was glowing like the firecracker she was. She looked amazing. Five years had whizzed by in the blink of an eye and Violet still sizzled him to the bone. She had set him free from his rule-following routine and he had eventually taken the hint and learned how to dance, although he was still a far-from-keen participant.

Tonight they were dining out in Siena at their favourite restaurant. Sofia shouted and started running as their great-grandparents' SUV purred up the drive. Violet called to bring the dogs, Fabio and Luna, back indoors and stop them from chasing the car. The labradoodles eventually obeyed but they were fairly laid-back about doing so until Tore shouted at them, whereupon they lowered their tails and slunk up on to the loggia.

'Why do they always listen to you and not me?' Violet demanded irritably.

'Because you have a soft voice…except when you're shouting at me,' Tore added with humour, his stunning green eyes glittering.

'That doesn't happen very often now,' she chided. 'I'm much calmer than I used to be.'

Tore tried not to grin. If Violet got any more laid-back she would be horizontal. There was a hiatus as his grandparents arrived and the kids and their luggage piled into the SUV and Aldo and Matilde drove off, everyone on board talking at the same time.

'Give me ten minutes for a shower,' Tore told her.

'I thought we could share it,' Violet murmured, stretching up to lace her hands round his neck.

'You do have the very best ideas, *mia lucciola*. It's been a very long week,' Tore commented as he shed his suit at speed, none of his usual tidy traits identifiable in that moment. 'I missed you.'

Violet hurtled into the shower ahead of him, shrieking when he splashed her.

'You're very lively for a birthday girl,' he remarked as he showered, water gushing down over his washboard abs.

Just looking at all that muscled, bronze perfection made her mouth run dry. As she sank down on the bench, he reached for her and tugged her up against him instead. He pushed her wet hair back from her brow and stared down at her animated face. 'It's time to make the big announcement,' he told her softly.

'You *can't* have guessed!'

'You haven't had a glass of wine in weeks,' he pointed out. 'I was waiting for you to tell me and you *didn't* so I began to worry that something was wrong.'

'No, no, nothing wrong,' she hastened to assure him. 'I was waiting for the results of the blood test. In six months we'll have another little boy and thankfully, it's a single pregnancy,' she imparted with a bewitching grin.

'That's wonderful news. You're saying that I've been worrying about nothing?' Tore demanded with a frown.

'That's what you do, which is why I didn't want to tell you until I knew absolutely everything about this pregnancy,' she reasoned. 'I planned to tell you over our meal tonight but a public place wouldn't feel right.'

'No, there are certain things we can't do in public unless we are very, very sure we're alone,' Tore purred, thinking of stolen idyllic moments in the woods or on picnics at the Calabrian farm.

He claimed her lips in a passionate kiss of affirmation as he stroked skilled hands over her wet curves, caressing tender flesh to make her squirm and moan until those little familiar sounds began to rise to a peak.

Only then did he bring her down on him, sleekly shifting her in one direction and then another so that the pleasure of his hungry possession sent her flying to the heights and tipped her over the edge.

In the restaurant, Tore surveyed his beautiful wife, clad in something red, short and elegant, appreciating the flame in her flushed cheeks and bright eyes in the candlelight. His woman, his wife, the mother of his children, and his heart swelled with happiness that he had found her and had the sense to hang on to her. 'I love you very much, *mia lucciola*,' he said thickly, covering her slender hand with his own.

'And I love you,' she whispered with her heart in her eyes as she revelled in the simple pleasure of being with him again.

* * * * *

If you couldn't put
Unveiling the Wrong Bride *down,*
then be sure to check out the next instalment in the
Billion-Dollar Bride Swap duet, coming soon!
And why not try these other stories
by Lynne Graham?

Baby Worth Billions
Greek's Shotgun Wedding
Greek's One-Night Babies
His Royal Bride Replacement
Shock Greek Heir

Available now!

SECRETLY PREGNANT PRINCESS

LORRAINE HALL

MILLS & BOON

For the protectors.

CHAPTER ONE

PRINCESS EVELYNE LUCIA MARTINA LIDIA had been summoned to her father's office often in her almost twenty-four years. It was *never* a good thing.

Still, today, she was lighter than usual. Because tonight, her brother was to be married. And a royal wedding for the heir meant a respite for Evelyne. Whatever complaints her father levied against her this morning, whatever punishments for petty infractions about to be doled out, they were small prices to pay for a little bit of freedom.

It wouldn't last forever. No doubt Father would be back to scheming her into the marriage mart soon enough—but Alexandre's wedding, and hopefully a royal baby soon after, should take the heat off for at least a year.

Within a years' time, she could convince Jordi to either stand up to her father or run away with her. He loved her. Said so all the time. As a royal aide, she knew he had a deep fear of upsetting her father, and who could blame him? King Enzo was a volatile, violent, *evil* man.

But with enough time, Evelyne was sure…she was *sure* she could convince Jordi to be as brave as she was willing to be.

For love, she thought dreamily.

But all dreams died when walking into King Enzo's grand office. Luxurious, gleaming gold that always gave her a headache, and her father always dressed in some uniform or another. He'd never actually trained or served in the Alis military, but he liked to stomp around in his role as *leader* as though he had.

Mostly, it was to intimidate. Such was Enzo's way. No one loved or respected the king, his children included. He was a mean, petty man full of spite, hate, and obsessed with retribution. Evelyne did not remember her mother as she'd been told the queen died in childbirth, but Evelyne wouldn't have been surprised to find Enzo had killed her.

He was that horrible. And on those occasions he beat her—something she knew her brother did his level best to stop—she could see it in his eyes. The fact was he *would* kill, given the right opportunity. Evelyne would have run away long ago, but her father was powerful, and his little spies were scattered across their small country. He ruled with the iron fist of a dictator, and everyone fell into line. Even her.

For now, she told herself.

All who existed in their little country waited for the day that King Enzo would die, and Prince Alexandre would take the throne. There was no doubt in Evelyne's mind that Alexandre was the best man in the world, and everything would be all right once her brother was the king.

Whether it be true or not didn't matter. What mattered was hope.

But for this morning, as she walked into her father's office, she found her hope a little unsteady. Because yes, her father was there in his usual military uniform with his usual smug expression on his face, but Alexandre was here as well. He was not yet dressed for his wedding, nor did he wear an expression fit for a soon-to-be-groom. His mouth was in a grim line, his dark eyes flat.

She knew he did not love his fiancée. He was doing his duty. *That* was Alexandre. She might have hated him for being so good, so perfect, but in doing his duty, he often protected *her* from whatever plans their father had for her.

Still, she felt sorry for Ines, because it was unclear whether the soon-to-be-bride believed her marriage into the Lidia royal family was one based on money and power, or one based on love.

There was no love in this kingdom as long as Evelyne's father ruled.

Father glanced at the large watch on his wrist. "I summoned you ten minutes ago, child."

She didn't point out that the palace was huge, that it took *time* to get from one end of it to the other. She'd learned her lesson about arguing with him as a young girl.

Eventually.

"My apologies, sir." She gave a regal curtsey. Mostly for Alexandre's benefit. Because he was here and it was his wedding day, and she knew her father was just *itching* to punish her in some way to make Alexandre's day even more miserable.

Father eyed her, which would have been enough for the warning alarms in her head to sound, but then he eyed Alexandre, and smiled.

"On this happy day where Alexandre submits to his duty and marries, I would like to inform you that you will soon follow."

Evelyne did not allow herself to react outwardly. She kept her expression placid and bland. She did not look Alexandre's way like she wanted to. She didn't even dare clasp her hands together or demand to know what he meant. She stood, settled into her regal bearing and waited for the bomb to drop.

"I have long sought the right man for you to marry, Evelyne. It has been quite the ordeal since you prefer to be so…rebellious."

Evelyne couldn't remember the last time she'd *rebelled* against him, unless he knew about Jordi. Which made her cold all the way through.

"He must be strong, of course. Powerful. Someone worthy of being the father of royal children, but someone who would not simply do whatever *you* told him to do." Father came around to rest a hip on his desk. He surveyed her with analyzing eyes. "Someone unafraid to use whatever methods might keep you in line."

Might. In line. This time Evelyne could not resist looking back at her brother. Who stood exactly as he had been, but his expression had moved far closer to fury than it had been.

"General Sergi Vinyes has expressed an interest in you, my dear."

If she thought she'd been cold before, now her blood was nothing but ice. She couldn't breathe. General Sergi Vinyes was a monster, as bad as her father if not worse. She knew she could not say that to her father, but she also couldn't hold her tongue completely.

"He's more than twice my age, Father." And known for his brutal tactics on the military fields—not with enemies, mind you. Because despite Enzo's blood lust, he had not engaged in a full-on war *yet*. The general was known for his cruelty with his *own men*.

"What of it? I was more than twice your mother's age when we married." He smiled as if this was a positive, something to brag about.

Evelyne wanted to retch.

"Father," Alex said in that calm, firm voice of his that allowed Evelyne to think there was some hope of getting out of this. "I am getting married tonight. And, with any luck, there will be a royal baby announced by next year. There is no need to rush Evelyne into marriage. She is young, and it is best to spread the pomp and circumstance out a bit, don't you think?"

"She will accept Sergi's proposal when it is offered. End of story."

He turned his back on both of them, a sign of dismissal. But Evelyne...

"I will not marry him." Could not. Would not. There was no arguing with her father, but she could not marry the violent general twice her age.

Very slowly, Father turned to look at her with that icy blue gaze of his. She felt Alexandre come to stand behind her, but she knew... Even two against one they would not win.

"You will," Father said very quietly. "It is not your decision to make."

Alexandre put his hand on her shoulder. "Evelyne, let this rest for now," he murmured in her ear.

"I will kill myself before I marry him." And she meant it. She would not suffer through that. It was bad enough the way her father treated her, the punishments she was subjected to. She would not be bartered off into even more violence.

"Ah, Evelyne." Father tsked. "You will not have the chance."

She saw it so clearly. She would not have the chance.

She thought she'd been about to experience some modicum of freedom, and instead she was sentenced—far earlier than expected—to an even worse jail than the one she'd imagined.

No. No, she wouldn't take it. She *wouldn't*. She turned on a heel and ran.

She ignored Alexandre calling her name. She had to find Jordi. He was her only hope. And she still had hope. They would run away together. He would take her away. France. Spain. The end of the *world*, she didn't care. Just away.

Since Jordi was one of Alexandre's aides, he was quite busy with wedding preparations. But that meant Evelyne knew exactly where to find him. With just hours before the wedding, he would be in the ceremony hall, dealing with last minute details.

She ran down hallways, upstairs, and when at last she found him in the ballroom double-checking seating assignments, she ran right to him, grabbed his arm. "Jordi."

"Evelyne, calm down." He gave her a scowl—she'd called it handsome on more than one occasion, perhaps perversely enjoying his occasional disapproval.

Because sometimes he did not approve or agree, but he *loved* her just the same. *Regardless.* She did not have to be anyone but herself with Jordi.

"Jordi," she repeated, breathless from running. "Father has insisted I accept a proposal from General Vinyes. We must run away! We'll run away together. It's the only way."

Jordi looked at her like she was speaking in tongues, but he patted her hand. "Calm down, Evelyne."

"Calm down? Are you listening to me? General Vinyes. I cannot marry him. We must leave the palace at once."

"Your brother's wedding…"

"That is why we must go now. Alexandre will understand. Come." She tugged on his arm, but he did not budge.

"Evelyne… I cannot go against your father. He is a *king*. Do you know what he'll do to me?"

"That's why we'll run away." Panic had big, heavy wings now, beating against her chest. Why wasn't he rushing to help her? Why wasn't he rushing to agree? Why was he looking down at her with something close to pity?

"Don't you understand?" she implored him. "He won't change his mind. We must…" It dawned on her then. "You were never going to marry me."

"Evelyne, come now."

Which was neither agreement nor rebuttal. Which made her realize that all the plans they'd made had been…hers. And he'd never disagreed with her, never told her she was fanciful or in the wrong.

But he never agreed. Never supported. Never *acted* to make any of her dreams come true.

Because he'd always known. She saw it so clearly now, in this terrible moment where her future was turning to darkness. *She'd* let herself build a fantasy on him. *He'd* let her.

But fantasy was all it was.

Fine enough to risk the king's wrath when he got a princess sneaking into his bed out of the deal, but not enough to actually…*do* something.

"You said you loved me." That he *had* said.

And it was a lie.

"Let us not make a scene at your brother's wedding," Jordi said, patting the hand that held on to him. When the wedding wasn't set to start for another few hours.

She looked at him, his handsome face. Those green eyes she'd been so taken with that refused to meet her gaze. The way he held himself, leaning slightly back as if he was afraid she might transfer a sickness to him.

The sickness of being a Lidia.

Something inside her broke. Whatever youthful naïveté she'd managed to hold on to in this place. Whatever belief she'd had that Jordi might have seen her and loved her, was gone, and with it…all her hopes for a future out of her father's influence.

She heard her name, turned to see two of her father's guards striding toward her. Because she would not be given a moment of freedom any longer, not after threatening to kill herself. So now it was all over.

Hope was dead.

Gabriel Marti did not relish spending time in Alis. He found the small, military-obsessed country stifling. His father had been born here, had been a diplomat from Alis to Italy when Gabriel had been born, but had fallen in love in Italy. Though Gabriel had spent his very early years in Alis, his father had moved them to his mother's home country before King Enzo had gotten too obsessed with might and violence and canceled all diplomacy to other countries.

He'd gotten them out just in time too. Not long after Gabriel had turned eight, King Enzo had shut down the borders and kept all citizens prisoners, essentially. Father would often lament that Enzo was a simple man who had followed the simple adage—absolute power corrupts absolutely.

Gabriel would not visit at all, but Prince Alexandre Lidia had been his best friend since he could remember. First here at the palace, and then at the boarding school his parents had allowed him to attend so that he and Alex could continue their friendship.

Gabriel owed Alex much, his entire life, really. So he'd spent the past week at the Lidia palace preparing for the royal wedding where he would stand up for his friend.

Besides, Gabriel had long ago learned that finding *humor* in a complicated situation was far better than getting sour about it, taking it too seriously, and then traveling the path toward ruin.

Sometimes he worried that visits to Alis would end with the king finding some way to keep him here. One never knew with King Enzo, and since Gabriel had built himself up into an independent, wealthy businessman, he knew the king had *some* interest in him, claiming him to Alis in some way.

But so far, he had outwitted all the king's attempts to keep him here and claim him as an Alis citizen. Gabriel was confident in his skills...but not so arrogant to ever let his guard down.

This trip, the king had been surprisingly hands-off. Gabriel hoped it was because he was busy and wrapped up in the wedding, but he still didn't let his guard down. All throughout the ceremony, and into the reception, he kept himself in a group at all times.

And since he valued enjoyment and having a good time no matter the circumstances, mostly the groups were made up of beautiful, glittering women.

Until Alexandre came up to him and handed him a glass of wine. The smile was fake. No matter how good Alexandre was at being stoic, Gabriel had known him long enough so that he knew how to read him. He also knew that if Alex was moving him toward a shadowy corner, away from the flirtatious royals, debutants, and so on, it was for good reason.

"I need you to do me a favor," Alex said, his voice low and intense. His gaze tracked around the room. Gabriel noted the king was currently talking to the bride and her parents. Occupied. But Alex kept his dark gaze on his father.

"On your wedding night? Shouldn't you be more concerned with your new bride?"

Alex's gaze moved to Ines. His expression seemed to grow more grim, if possible. Gabriel knew there was no great love match there. If anything, Alex and Ines tolerated each other for the greater good.

Gabriel thought it was a pity. He wasn't sure he believed in something as deep and abiding as soul mates. Such depth of feeling would be dangerous, no doubt. But he had spent his childhood in the warmth of his parents' good marriage and figured a bad one would be rather soul sucking.

Ines was a pretty thing, but…fragile seeming, and the huge white confection of a dress did little to dispel that aura. She seemed the kind of fragile that would never survive life in the Lidia palace.

Oh, Alexandre was a good man who would try to protect her, because nothing survived here without Alexandre's protection. But Gabriel had his doubts that even Alex could save Ines from the life she was about to lead.

"Evelyne," Alex said, mentioning his sister. "You must use one of your escape routes and take her away."

Gabriel choked a bit on the drink he'd taken. He coughed, cleared his throat. "Away?" he croaked.

"Without anyone knowing where. Including myself."

"Alex…" This was a great task. One with immense meaning. And great risk to Gabriel.

"My father has promised her to General Sergi Vinyes."

Gabriel looked across the ballroom to the woman in question. Evelyne had no aura of fragility like Ines. She was bright and vibrant, a shining beauty. He had often wondered how she maintained it in a place such as this, with a father such as hers.

Evelyne was another reason Gabriel did not care for spending time in Alis these days. As she'd grown into a beautiful young woman, she'd become a temptation. For some time, Gabriel had made certain to indulge *all* his temptations.

But Evelyne was one that reminded him of the adolescent he'd been—full of rage and obsession. Alex had saved him from that, so he could not go back to it. Certainly not because of his little sister.

Like every other sane person in this palace, he owed Alexandre too much to fool around with the prince's sister.

But no one deserved General Vinyes. Gabriel didn't even know the man, spent very little time in Alis, and still the military man's reputation for blood lust, revenge, and fury was something well known across Europe. Something that kept many countries from invading this small, belligerent one.

So no, no one deserved the general. Certainly not a young, vibrant princess as beautiful as Evelyne.

Tonight she was dressed in a glittering green dress that didn't match the wedding colors but complemented them. The garment skimmed along her curves, a sensuous delight Gabriel knew better than to allow himself to notice. Her hair—somewhere between a honeyed blond and a shiny chestnut—was pulled back in an elaborate twist. Her lips were painted a dark, purplish red that would have short-circuited his brain if he allowed his vision to linger there.

Instead, he noted the two serious-looking guards who flanked her, both armed.

"Get her away from the guards without causing suspicion," Alex was saying fervently. "Get her out of here. Take her somewhere she won't be found. If possible, on a plane that can't be tracked to either of us. Tonight. Then set her up with a new life. While my father is distracted and thinks I've no time to plan. I will pay you back when I am able. It is too much to ask, I know this, but I must ask it anyway. She cannot be married to that monster."

In any other situation, Gabriel might have led with a joke,

with the aura of casual nonchalance, but not with Alex. Not with the one man in the world he allowed himself to owe.

"There is no ask too big, Alex," he said, even knowing this *was* the biggest ask for a wide variety of reasons. "You once saved my life," Gabriel reminded him.

Alex sighed impatiently as he often did when Gabriel brought it up. If Alexandre had faults, his stark refusal to admit he was near saint levels of *good* was one of them.

Gabriel looked at Evelyne and the guards once more. He'd have no trouble getting her out of the palace—he and Alex had studied and planned escape routes for nearly two decades now. And thanks to that, Gabriel's entire personal fortune was built on understanding and implementing security for the well-connected wealthy, the royal.

And since it was, he knew how to get around it, especially since he'd designed and implemented much of the palace and country's security himself.

But the guards… They were under King Enzo's command and King Enzo's command alone. Getting around them would take some doing. Not that Gabriel had any doubts he could accomplish it, but it would require time with Evelyne. In that dress. "Have you told Evelyne of your plan?" he asked, his mind already imagining and rejecting ideas.

"No, I'm afraid she'll…do something unwise if I give her warning. You must simply whisk her away. You can tell her my plan once she's on a plane. Safe from the king."

They both looked at the king across the room, holding court. Gabriel was well acquainted with evil—the different shapes and sizes of it that existed within men. So often it came cloaked in power, influence. So often it hurt the glittering innocents like Evelyne. He had found that even power and money could not always protect a woman in this cruel world.

King Enzo knew how to wield it all. As General Vinyes would.

No, he could not allow such to be wielded against Evelyne, both for Alex and for the princess herself.

"I trust you, Gabriel. With my sister's safety."

And because Alexandre had once saved him from the evil he had been close to succumbing to those years ago, Gabriel nodded, now determined.

He would help Evelyne, regardless of personal sacrifice, and honor the debt he owed her brother.

And he would certainly keep his hands to himself while he did it.

CHAPTER TWO

EVELYNE WAS NOT much of a drinker, but tonight she set herself to the task. Hope was gone, why *not* make a scene? If her father punished her, so be it. Before today, she'd had some vague hope that *eventually* the king would die of bitterness and old age.

But now she had two captors lined up. Even with the general being more than twenty years older than her, hoping for *two* men's death in order to be free was too great a weight to hold.

What was the point of anything now?

Father and General Vinyes would keep her from even the escape of death. She had no doubt they could, based on how close two of her father's guards stayed to her throughout the afternoon, ceremony and now reception. So far, her only respite had been to use the restroom, and they'd been waiting for her right outside when she was done.

Any room with *windows*, they followed her into. Like she'd fling herself from one given the chance.

But the worst part was she didn't *want* to die. She simply didn't want to suffer anymore. Was that so wrong?

She downed her third glass of champagne, and since the guards didn't stop her from doing such, she went over to the bar to procure her fourth. She'd ask for something harder, but she was afraid they'd stop her. So she'd settle for drinking as much champagne on an empty stomach as humanly possible.

She could already feel a pleasant fizzing sensation in her mind, in her body. She felt a little unsteady and *liked* it.

It was the only thing she liked. The guards, she knew, were a hint of what was to come, and it made everything… horrible. Because while she'd spent some twenty years devising ways around her father's punishments—mental and physical—this seemed to be the last unsurmountable challenge to finding an even somewhat pleasant life amid her royal shackles.

"Good evening, Evelyne."

The voice was familiar, but she was surprised to find a hand on her elbow to go with it. Gabriel Marti *never* touched her. Her brother's best friend tended to avoid her. If he could not, he often treated her like an amusing but spoiled child.

It grated, and he knew it. She had no doubt that's why he did it. He was the kind of man who read a room and behaved accordingly. Sometimes she wanted to hate him.

But sometimes, she could admit, she wanted to throw herself at him. Handsome and competent, people *laughed* when they were with Gabriel. Gabriel himself smiled and charmed.

There was none of that in the palace when he wasn't around.

So she could admit surprise, and a flutter of interest, at his large hand on her elbow, a warm, steady strength and counterpoint to all the upheaval inside her.

Saying nothing else, he expertly navigated her away from the bar before she could get that next glass of champagne—smart move—and toward one of the terrace doors.

"It was a lovely wedding," he said, his voice low and pleasant in her ear.

"It was." She glanced over her shoulder to where Alexandre stood with his bride while they spoke to a couple Evelyne didn't recognize. "I hope they can be happy." Someone should be. Maybe Alexandre didn't love Ines, but if they could find some *solace* in each other, maybe...

Gabriel opened a terrace door, but before he ushered her out into the glittering evening, he smiled at the guards who had fallen into step behind them. "I will keep an eye on her for a bit, gentleman. The prince's orders." Then he led her outside.

Onto the terrace, but he didn't stop there. He kept pulling her along, down the grand staircase and into the gardens that were lit with fairy lights and candlelight and little bonfires so guests could enjoy the grounds despite the chill in the air.

"They're still following us," Evelyne pointed out. She would never be free. Never, ever, *ever*. Tears filled her eyes, but she refused to cry again. She'd had a nice jag over Jordi. Now...

Now what?

"Yes, but they've given us more space. There's a lot we can do with more space."

She glanced up at him. He didn't *deliver* it like innuendo, but she had to admit that's where her mind flitted.

The alcohol probably. And the fact he was outrageously handsome. So tall, his dark hair swept back in a careless kind of style that somehow felt both casual and perfectly suited for a royal wedding. His eyes were a kind of hazel, she supposed, a fascinating array of greens and browns with a hint of blue. His suit was dark, elegantly tailored, but simple when compared to Alexandre's royal costume for the wedding.

This close, she could smell expensive aftershave, champagne and the hint of something else, smoky almost. Intriguing.

And it was nice, to be intrigued, to notice all these things, rather than drown in her own misery.

Gabriel moved her through the maze of pathways, arm in arm, talking lightly of the weather, of Alex, of Ines. The guards kept their distance, one even peeled off and lit a cigarette. They must trust Gabriel to keep her in line or keep her from hurtling herself onto the nearest sharp object.

She considered if *she* trusted the charming, roguish Gabriel. He and Alexandre had been friends since they were boys, and so Evelyne had always known Gabriel in a distant kind of way. She knew Alexandre trusted Gabriel implicitly, though they were as different as night and day. A point in Gabriel's favor.

She had gone through phases of fascination with him, but she hadn't seen him in Alis for at least a year if not longer, and all her male infatuation had been on Jordi in that time.

Jordi. Had he ever loved her? Would anyone ever love her? And would she even care if there wasn't marriage to a sadistic general on the other side of that?

She hated that she wasn't sure. That it felt now like she'd simply convinced herself to love Jordi. Because it had been a choice she could make, a hope she could have. Was it about wanting *something*? Or was it about wanting *Jordi*?

She hated the answer almost as much as she hated him rejecting running away with her.

"Does Alexandre love Ines?" Evelyne asked abruptly, because she assumed Gabriel would know. Maybe he wouldn't tell her, but he would know.

Gabriel did not answer right away. He pulled her around another corner of shrubbery, under an arbor that somehow smelled of spring though winter was on its way.

"It is not something he has spoken of, one way or another," he said at length.

Evelyne was not sure if he sounded distracted because he was or because he was trying to lie. Though a nonanswer was hardly a lie.

"I hope he does. At least a little bit. I hope she can be a bright spot."

"I hope so too."

She looked up at him then, surprised to find that his voice sounded…at least somewhat earnest. But she shouldn't be surprised. If there was one thing she knew, it was that Alexandre and Gabriel cared for one another like brothers. She'd always thought that Gabriel might be the sole person in the world who knew Alexandre's inner troubles—because he made sure their father didn't, and he didn't want to worry Evelyne with them.

It was dark where they were now. She couldn't make out Gabriel's expression at all, but his hand was still hooked in her arm. He stopped their forward progress, so they stood in the dark, the only sound the rustle of the breeze and their own breathing for a few moments.

Everything suddenly felt odd and tense, when Gabriel was usually the life of the party. Not serious and silent like her brother.

"Gabriel—"

"Shh." His hand curled around hers so that they were *holding hands*.

What on earth was going on?

"Come," he said, his voice low and sensual in her ear. "We must hurry now."

Hurry?

He pulled her along, and she had to all but jog in the painful heels to keep up with him, because for a moment she didn't know what else to do but obey. Maybe she was just too used to obeying.

When he finally came to a stop, it was at a car. She blinked at it, even as he dropped her hand and opened the passenger door and gestured for her to get in. When she didn't move, he crossed back to her and pulled her along.

"Get in the car, Evelyne."

It felt suddenly…threatening or sinister. Why did he want to get her into a car? What was this about? She pulled at his hold, but he did not let her go.

Twin but opposite feelings fluttered low in her stomach. A seed of fear, a sparkle of interest. But since hope was dead, she figured she should listen to the fear. When had she ever been able to trust a man who wasn't her brother anyway? Men, it seemed, were all the same. Maybe even Alexandre was underneath it all, and she only didn't see it because she was his sister.

"Unhand me, Gabriel," she ordered.

He did not. "Do as you're told, Evelyne," he said in a quiet, authoritative tone she'd never once heard from Gabriel.

She lifted her chin, stopped trying to pull her hand from his grasp, and used all her royal training to sound threatening. "My brother will kill you if you take advantage of me."

Gabriel muttered something in Italian, though she couldn't make it out. It reminded her that while he was *from* Alis, he had spent much of his adolescence and all of his adult life in Italy. Free from Alis and her father.

Free.

And friends with her brother, who she had no reason to doubt. No reason to distrust, male or not. Alexandre had been nothing but a protector in every sense of the word, and it was a sad state of affairs indeed if she let Father, the general and *Jordi* change her sturdy belief in her brother.

"I am not taking advantage of you," he ground out, though he did not loosen his grip. "If you have any sense at all, you'll get in the car."

He glared down at her in the dim light of the palace garage.

He was really quite handsome, particularly in a scowl, which she wasn't sure she'd ever seen on him. It heightened his angular features, did interesting things to his mouth.

Before Jordi, she'd tried her hand at flirting with Gabriel on occasion. He was so *tall*. And he was a man who smiled. No one in the palace ever smiled. Not a real smile.

She thought Gabriel Marti might be the only man she'd ever met who was actually *happy*.

He was not happy now, and she didn't understand why, or what he was doing. Why was he trying to get her in a car? She looked around. No guards. No one watching. If Gabriel could actually get her off the palace property, she could...

She had no idea, but she got in the car all the same on that little spurt of hope that maybe, just maybe, on the other side of this lay freedom. One little sparkle of hope, that Gabriel might in fact be like her brother, might in fact do something that allowed her the freedom she was desperate for.

Gabriel climbed into the driver's seat. He pushed a button and the car started—quietly, almost silently. Then, he began to drive. Toward the palace exit. She looked behind them.

Just twinkling lights surrounded by darkness. The shining lights of the palace getting dimmer and dimmer. No headlights. No shadowy guards dashing after them.

She was afraid to hope. Hope was dead. Except Gabriel was fanning a little ember back to life. "We're escaping?"

"Yes. To a new life, Evelyne. Courtesy of your brother. So if you'd stop arguing with me at every turn and behave, perhaps we could actually save you."

He drove without being followed. It was a positive, but not certain freedom. Not just yet.

He couldn't go to the royal airport without being found out, but if he could get across the border into France, there was a small regional airport not far. His connections outside of Alis were legion, so he already had a plane waiting for them that could not be traced to him or Alexandre.

But he had to make that border crossing first, something that would have been fine if he didn't have a princess in tow. Luckily, he'd always had a backup plan in case King Enzo had decided to try to keep him in the country, or if Alex needed a quick escape. And it had started years ago, when Alex had convinced King Enzo to hire Gabriel's fledgling company to design the wall around the country and some of its security features.

The argument had been that with a novice security design and logistics company like Gabriel's, an Alis native, the king would be wholly in control, with no competing clients to take away focus.

It had been true at the time. And it had given Gabriel the opportunity to design in some…fail-safes.

Maintaining a casual and unsuspicious speed, Gabriel pulled off onto the little-known dirt road that would take him up beyond the border checkpoints. Because there was a point up here where no one knew that Gabriel would be able to get through, car, princess and all, no border checks necessary.

"Gabriel, where are we going?"

"Don't you trust me, *principessa*?"

She sighed heavily. "Alex trusts you, so I will endeavor to, but how are we going to leave Alis if we are just following the border? We will need to go through border patrol, and they will never let me through. Even if Father isn't aware I've run away yet, they won't let me through."

"I have my ways. Relax."

She laughed. Bitterly. "Yes, it's been quite a relaxing day."

He was not sure, despite her upbringing, he'd ever heard *bitterness* from Evelyne. It must have been a family trait, because Alexandre was rarely bitter either. Stern, stoic, determined, but not bitter.

Evelyne was usually cheerful, bubbly, full of…life or hope or something. It was easy to be drawn to Evelyne.

Which was why he needed to get her situated somewhere quickly—so he could resume his distance over being *drawn*. She had all the marks of someone who could pull him under, and he would never be pulled under again.

He took an almost unmarked pathway into snow and coaxed the car toward the wall.

Evelyne shifted in her seat, leaning forward, squinting at the wall the headlights of his car illuminated.

"Wait here."

He got out of the car, strode to the wall. With the flashlight of his phone, it only took a minute or two to find the hidden control panel. Alex was lucky Gabriel traveled with a screwdriver on his key chain. Or he was lucky. Or Evelyne was.

He unscrewed the necessary components, hit the correct order of buttons, then replaced the cover and screwed it tight. There was an easily pushed button on the other side to close it.

He heard the engine inside engage, though it rattled a bit. It hadn't been used since Gabriel had tested it when he'd first installed it himself all those years ago. Hopefully it still worked.

He got back into the car, rubbing his hands against the cold.

"What are we going to do?" Evelyne demanded. "Drive through the…" She trailed off as the motorized entryway he'd designed began to move, open. With enough space he would be able to drive the car right through.

The terrain would be rough on the other side, but it would get them into France undetected.

Evelyne was uncharacteristically silent as he drove through the opening in the wall, stopping the car, then getting out to push the button that would close it. Even when he started driving again after waiting for the door to close— this time with no road or path—she didn't say a word.

But he could all but *hear* the wheels turning in her head.

"Does Alexandre know about that?" she asked once he'd finally maneuvered the car back onto a road—this time on French soil.

"In a way."

"What does *that* mean?"

"He knows I designed some…escape routes into the wall, should they ever be needed. But to protect himself, and no doubt me, he doesn't know exactly where they are. I would of course give him the information should he request it. Instead, he tasked me with getting you out undetected, so here we are."

She said nothing else, all the way to the airport. He supposed she was working through the implications of what escape really meant. Not just a vacation or a lark, but something a little bit dangerous, and a lot life-changing.

Her father was a vindictive man, and she'd never lived anywhere but the palace. Though Alexandre had been sent to boarding school and royal training throughout Europe, Evelyne had been educated in the palace under her father's patriarchal views that a woman did not need worldly experience.

Gabriel arrived at the airport and parked the car where his associate had instructed—an associate who was not supposed to own or operate said plane, so certainly wouldn't go telling anyone that Gabriel had borrowed it.

In the hangar, Gabriel parked out of the way of the plane, turned off the car engine, then got out. Evelyne did not wait for him to come open her door. She got out of the car and eyed the plane.

"I suppose we will need to wait for daylight to fly."

"Not necessarily. What we *will* need to wait for is me to return to the castle."

She whirled to face him. "What?"

"Only briefly. To make an appearance so no one suspects *I* am the one who absconded with you as I was the last one seen with you. I'll drop a word to the guards that you voluntarily left with a shadowy figure. And I was distracted by another young lady. Something along those lines." He flashed her a grin. "Easy enough to be believed."

Evelyne's eyebrows drew together as she thought this over. Then her eyes narrowed.

"Tell them it was Jordi Ferriz. Not a shadowy figure. An aide."

He found her fervor suspicious. "That would put a target on this Jordi's back."

She lifted a regal chin. "Good."

Ah, some sort of…lovers' tiff, he thought. He did not know this aide named Jordi, but he did know something about revenge. And what it did to you. "Vengeance is a dangerous game, *principessa*."

She lifted a bare shoulder, and Gabriel might have been frustrated with her, except he was too distracted by *her*.

The dress was a torture device, Gabriel was quite certain. It skimmed every curve, something about the green color seemed to gild her skin with gold. A gold that reflected in little flecks in her dark eyes.

And he did not have any clothes for her to change into on the plane. He couldn't risk grabbing something of hers at the palace to bring back. He wouldn't be there long, with any luck. Just a quick appearance, a word to the guards, then off again.

"Get on the plane. Wait for me there. I will be back in under an hour." Hopefully.

She met his gaze. There was trepidation there, but she nodded and allowed herself to be helped up into the plane.

She hesitated at the top of the stairs. "Gabriel… Are you sure…" But she didn't finish that sentence.

"Would you rather return to the palace, Evelyne?"

She immediately shook her head. "No, I cannot stay. I cannot marry the general."

"No, you can't. Your brother agrees. So we will find a new life for you."

"What about Alexandre?"

"Alex is the only one who has any hope of surviving your father's reign, especially after marrying Ines. I think he knows this as well as you and I do."

Evelyne let out a shaky sigh. Gabriel took it as agreement and turned to leave, but Evelyne reached out, her slim hand curling around his hand.

"What if Father punishes Alexandre? What if…?"

"He won't," Gabriel said with more force than he actually believed, but she needed reassurance, and he supposed he did as well. "First, your father needs his son, his heir. If he didn't, Alex would have been punished with much worse long ago. Second, Alex will not know where you are, just that I have taken you somewhere safe. There will be no evidence connecting you to him, so while your father could *decide* to blame him, he can't prove it. He won't want to prove it. He'll probably make up some boogeyman who stole you. Send General Vinyes on a wild-goose chase."

"I suppose you're right." She chewed on her bottom lip, a distracting and brain-draining move that distracted him enough to meet her golden gaze. "What if he punishes *you*?" she asked, eyes worried, voice soft. "What if the chase is General Vinyes to us?"

"Do you underestimate me, Evelyne?" he quipped, but her eyes were wide and shiny as she studied him.

He had never seen Evelyne look vulnerable. He knew, from Alex, that the king was especially hard on her, but Alex had always been vague about what that meant. And Evelyne never seemed to be troubled. Sociable, confident, cheeky even.

He saw the troubled in her now.

"Everything will be all right," he assured her, with an odd gentleness from himself he did not quite recognize. "You have my word."

So he left her there, determined to see his word through.

CHAPTER THREE

EVELYNE WAITED FOR Gabriel's return, trying not to fret and failing. Her father *was* a vindictive man, and even if Gabriel somehow managed to pull this off, Father would look for someone to blame.

Who would be harmed because of it? Perhaps it had been vindictive and petty to want to name Jordi. Maybe she was more like her father than she'd want to admit. She almost hoped Gabriel would ignore her there.

Almost.

Unfortunately, the only other option to this one would be to return to the castle and marry a man as evil as her father.

Impossible. She had to take the freedom Alexandre had arranged for her.

That Gabriel would put himself in the line of fire for her—no, not *her*, for Alex—was a surprise. And now she was curious just what would indebt the man to her brother so much. She was quite sure Gabriel had built his own wealth and success with no help from Alex.

But surely just being good friends wouldn't be enough for Gabriel to risk life and limb to do all *this*. And surely her brother would not have asked it of Gabriel if there was not something…more to this.

But what? She couldn't even come up with an idea.

She did not have her phone. She did not have a jacket.

She had nothing except this dress suitable for a princess at a royal wedding, heels that felt too tight and painful to put back on and the sloshing feeling of nothing but champagne being in her stomach.

And Gabriel was going to be gone for at least an hour.

She dozed. Probably ill-advisedly considering she was alone in a strange plane in a deserted hangar, but the events of the day had just completely sapped her energy, and the low-level nausea wasn't helping. So she reclined back in the comfortable plane seat and slept.

When she opened her eyes, not quite remembering that she'd fallen asleep and certainly not sure how long she'd been out, she was not alone anymore.

She might have startled at direct hazel eyes clearly having been watching her, but there was something very centering about Gabriel. Like an anchor amid this very strange and unexpected storm.

He moved toward her. "Here." He handed her a bag. "Just things I could pick up along the way. Some guests of the palace will wonder where their things went, but I'm certain they'll get over it."

Evelyne shook her sleep-and champagne-foggy mind and unzipped the bag. She pulled out a man's coat—too small to be Gabriel's. Some kind of faux fur shawl. A pair of slippers—she was so excited about those she immediately shoved them onto her feet.

She let out a sigh of relief.

"Now, eat while I prepare to take off." This time, he set a kind of bakery box in her lap. She opened it, saw an array of bits and pieces from the wedding meal and reception food.

Her stomach sloshed in protest. "I don't feel so well."

"Eat," he insisted. "That will help." He turned, walking up the aisle toward the cockpit of the plane.

"Where are you going?"

He glanced over his shoulder at her. His hair was more disheveled now, and he'd lost the suit jacket somewhere along the way. His smile was rakish. "Someone needs to fly this, don't they?"

"And that someone is *you*?" She gripped the bakery box and leaned forward. "Gabriel, please don't tell me you're one of those men who thinks he can fly a plane simply because you're good with machines."

His mouth curved in amusement. "It might be enjoyable to let you think that, but no, Evelyne. I have a license and everything. I imagine there is *much* about me that would surprise you. Now eat." He nodded at the box in her lap then disappeared into the cockpit.

He could fly a plane. There was indeed much about Gabriel that would no doubt surprise her. Everything about this night would be included in that list.

She was used to taking orders, so she felt compelled to do as she was told. She surveyed the offerings of the bakery box.

A few of the puff pastry appetizers that weren't too appetizing this many hours on. Two rolls. And most importantly, a piece of wedding cake, wrapped up to protect the frosting.

She ate that first, though it probably wasn't her best choice. Still, she'd been dreaming about this cake all week. Ines had impeccable taste in baked goods. Once she was satisfied on a taste level, she forced herself to eat the rest.

The plane lurched, and so did the food in her stomach, but she closed her eyes and breathed through it. The nausea *and* the knowledge that Gabriel was the one taxiing the plane out of the hangar. Onto a runway.

The sun was peeking over the horizon, painting the sky in blush pinks and oranges. Evelyne decided to take it as a good omen. As hope.

Hope was back. Freedom was here.

That spurt of joy was fleeting as they traveled. It would seem she'd doze off just as they arrived somewhere new and switched planes. At one point, they even had a private room on a railcar. Gabriel had presented her with a large meal there, and a shopping bag. Inside were silly tourist clothes— but anything was better than someone else's coat and the godforsaken royal dress. The best part were the sneakers—a step up from the slippers she'd been schlepping around in.

When they boarded yet another private plane, Gabriel once again in the pilot's seat, she was perilously close to crying. She didn't know how many hours, *days* it had been. She'd wanted escape, but she wasn't sure how much she had left in her. Which no doubt made her weak.

"This will be the last one," he told her gently. "We will have a bit of a drive once we land, but this is the last flight."

Evelyne seated herself in the copilot's seat. "Where are we going?"

He looked at all the dials and whatnot, didn't even spare her a glance. "The States. A new continent seems safest."

A new continent. A new life. Away from everything she'd ever known. The palace, her father. She was free… But at the cost of everything. Including… Alexandre. Would she ever see him again?

The thought brought a stab of pain, and tears to her eyes she was afraid she wouldn't be able to fight if she stayed in that thought. "I know nothing about America," she said instead of, *will I ever see Alex again?* She was afraid if she voiced that, she might fall apart completely.

"You know how to speak English. That should be enough."

Evelyne did not know *how* speaking the language would be enough. It had been one thing to insist Jordi run away with her, it was something altogether different to actually think about the practicalities of what running away meant.

She had been raised a princess in a small, isolated country. While she had suffered monstrous punishments at the hand of her father, she had also been waited on and pampered in other ways.

What would she do in America? How would she survive without Alexandre's protection and guidance? It seemed unsurmountable.

And still, this horrible, terrifying unsurmountable was better than marrying the general. *Everything* was better than that, and she reminded herself of this again and again while Gabriel once again guided a small plane into the sky, taking her far away from the monsters that had stalked her pampered life.

Maybe somewhere between the two extremes lay a life worth living.

Gabriel was glad she was sleeping, even if he was concerned about the amount she'd done since this whole thing started two days ago now. She'd had a traumatic event. Sleep was good. He wished she'd eat more. Once he got her settled, he'd insist upon it.

He drove up the curving driveway to the home he'd procured for her. He'd had to pull some considerable strings to get a house off the market with no connection to him, but the thing about designing and implementing security systems for the rich and powerful was that he had just the kind of connections that could keep things...*off the books*.

He'd considered going small, rustic. Some tiny, rural town no one would ever expect to find a princess in, but Evelyne would not know how to survive *rustic*, and he doubted very much she could fit in *with* rustic. Since Gabriel could not yet afford to risk hiring staff for her that might wonder who the regal beauty was, he thought procuring something she was better used to was the better bet.

So he'd gone with the grand *and* isolated. The rugged Maine coast boasted some beautiful homes, spread out and situated far away from any metropolitan center. The mansion he had procured for her stood on a sea cliff overlooking the crashing Atlantic. He could not staff it yet, until he found someone trustworthy and who had no chance of discovering who Evelyne really was. So she would be all by herself in all that space.

She would no doubt not find this ideal, but escape—even well-funded escape—did not always get to be ideal.

He turned the vehicle off, and this must have woken her, because she blinked her eyes open, straightened in the seat, gazing out the windshield at the grand house spread out before them, the ocean in the distance.

"Welcome home, Evelyne."

She didn't say anything, so he got out of the car and skirted the hood to open her door for her. He even helped her out. Her gaze stayed glued to the ocean beyond the house.

"Gabriel…" Her eyes were wide. "This is… Is this yours?"

"No, it is Francesco Marino's. He's an eccentric Italian billionaire—a false identity I have used before when needed. Now he has a young wife, Lina, and they have hermited themselves away in America to enjoy their newly found wedded bliss." He made a grand sweeping gesture to encompass the house and sea.

He enjoyed the stories, creating them, implementing them. In his business, it paid to have an identity or two that had no connection to who he really was. Both for himself and sometimes his clients.

"Locals will occasionally catch a glimpse of one of them on the balconies," he continued. "But never in town. The nearest town could never meet their extravagant needs anyhow."

"But… Even with these fake identities, you bought this, you paid for it, you…"

"Have no worries, Evelyne, I can certainly afford it," he said dryly. "And a land holding, even under a fake identity, is never a bad thing to have."

"It's so big. It's so…much." She shook her head. "Are you to stay with me?" she asked.

"Not for long. It is too dangerous. I must return to Italy and work as soon as possible, before King Enzo starts concerning himself with my whereabouts. But I will stay long enough to get you settled, under the guise of being out of contact range on a job in Moscow. Now, you are not to have any contact with Alexandre, or anyone back in Alis, but either of you can contact *me* and I will act as careful conduit. But I would relegate this only to emergencies, Evelyne. This is very delicate." He began to lead her toward the house. "I will visit on occasion, to take care of whatever necessities arise, but it must be done carefully, so it will be infrequent. Eventually, we will hire you some staff, but for now, you will have to make do on your own."

He pulled the key he'd procured in New York from his pocket, unlocked the front door and gestured her inside.

She stepped in, a bit like someone suffering some kind of shock. Like she didn't quite know how to put one foot in front of the other.

"It is yours, essentially, for the time being. As long as your father searches for you, it will be your home and refuge."

She turned in a circle in the soaring foyer, white and

a bit bland. The whole house was rather commercial and bland feeling.

Evelyne's dark, gold-flecked gaze met his. "Why are you doing this? I know you and Alex are friends, best friends, but this is…above and beyond friendship."

He considered just what to tell her. This *was* above and beyond, and while he liked to think of himself as a good man, now that Alex had put him on that path, he would not have gone to *such* lengths for anyone else. Though he liked to think he would have gone to *some* lengths to help a young woman escape what would no doubt become an abusive situation.

Still, the truth of his bond with Alexandre, the truth of *him*, was not something he shared with anyone. But there was a way of phrasing anything that left people thinking they knew the answer to something, even if they didn't.

It was how he'd lived his adult life, skating the surface of any real connections. Anything that might threaten to pull him under again.

"Years ago, I almost made a very grave mistake," Gabriel said conversationally, walking through the foyer and into one of the sitting rooms, knowing she'd follow. The furniture here was almost cozy, though still too much white to be a welcoming room. "One that would have ended my life— literally or figuratively, one way or another. Your brother was the one who stopped me. He saved me—and had to fight tooth and nail to do it—and I owe him for this."

"So this is your payment?" she asked carefully.

"It is my thank-you gift." He corrected her, because friendship did not require payment, to his way of thinking. He gestured at the window, which was the entire length of the wall. It looked out over the crashing ocean below.

Evelyne stepped to the glass. The cloudy light gave her

an ethereal glow, even with the silly sweatsuit emblazoned with mountains and *Interlaken* in looping script. She would need a wardrobe, a way to get groceries without being seen, little things like that to keep her well the next few weeks while he made sure nothing connected him to her disappearance or her to Maine.

She all but pressed her nose to the window, clearly delighted by the view. Which gave him a satisfaction he did not wish to think too deeply on.

"Sometimes I wonder if he's really as good as he seems to me. Can anyone be that saintly?"

There could only be one *he* she was referring to. "Sometimes I wonder this myself. He has always seemed…otherworldly, almost, in his determination to the right thing. If he was a terrible man, like your father, I could understand it. His *right thing* wouldn't be right at all, if he was like the king. But he understands real right, and insists it be done. I do not know how, but he *is* good."

"I think it must have come from my mother," she said quietly. "He was almost eight years old when she died. He remembers her. She must have taught him." Evelyne looked back at him as if hoping he could confirm this.

But he could not. While Gabriel remembered their mother in a vague kind of way, he had moved away from Alis about a year before the queen had died. On top of that, there were subjects Alexandre never broached. No matter what.

His mother was one of them.

"Well, I do not know how to thank you, Gabriel. Even if you've done this for Alex, you have taken great pains to do something that will benefit me." She reached out, took his hands in hers and gave them a squeeze. It was a very royal move, but the warmth of her small hands, the warmth of her words…they had an effect on him, royal or no.

The gold in her eyes, the fervency in her voice seemed to spread a heating warmth through him. That alluring temptation he had little experience resisting, because what temptation couldn't he indulge in?

Her. Her. Her.

"You have saved me," she said, her voice rough. "I owe you everything."

Uncomfortable with a great many things, he pulled his hands from hers, stepped back. "I do not require thanks. Come, let us see what we can scrounge up to eat." He turned on a heel and walked out of the living room in search of the kitchen. He had seen the floor plan of the house, so he had a vague idea where everything was.

Another thing he would do with the days he could afford to stay was ensure her security system was state of the art. The best Marti Systems had to offer.

While he kept her from touching him, even so generically, ever again.

The kitchen was big. Everything seemed commercial grade. Still with that almost corporate feeling. Perhaps once some time passed, he could have it redecorated, give the place some warmth for her.

"I'm afraid all this will be lost on me," Evelyne said, peering down at the stainless-steel gas stove. "Father often punished me with cleaning tasks, but I was never much allowed in the kitchens. I'm not even sure I know how to make toast."

"Lucky for you, the internet is a trove of information that can teach you. Definitely how to make toast. I have already had the fridge and pantry stocked for you prior to our arrival, and we'll set up recurring grocery deliveries in some way before I leave."

"I don't have my phone, my computer..." She looked

around, clearly a bit overwhelmed by everything, and understandably so. "I don't have anything."

"It'll all be taken care of before I leave."

"Leave." She wrinkled her nose, but she turned away from him so he only caught the hint of her profile. "What will I do in this big house all by myself?" she asked, hugging her arms around herself.

"Stay out of sight. Live a quiet, private life. Learn to cook, perhaps." He shrugged. "That is up to you, how you spend your time. Such is freedom."

"How novel." She delivered the quip with a hint of humor, a hint of self-deprecating sarcasm. "I am not sure anything of importance has ever been up to me. I am not sure I know how to…handle things being up to me."

"Freedom always comes with a bit of a price and learning curve, I fear."

She nodded, straightened her shoulders. She looked older than she had. Not quite duller, but not as *shiny* was the only word he could think of.

"Well, I'm ready to pay it," she said resolutely.

He felt strangely proud and figured it best if he didn't linger on that feeling.

CHAPTER FOUR

THE DAY EVELYNE dreaded had come. After just three days of getting her settled, Gabriel would leave her here. Alone.

She *almost* loved the house. It was beautiful, if a little overly white and almost sterile feeling inside, but she absolutely loved standing on the balconies, terraces and porches watching the sea's fascinating dance. Sometimes the lull of calm waves against the rock, sometimes angry slaps, sometimes chaotic whirls. It made up for the bad decorating.

She would have loved the house itself, she thought, if it was full of people—like the palace had been. But the echoing emptiness of it at night—with Gabriel the entire length of the home away—left her uneasy and...sad.

Sadness was silly, she knew. She had escaped her father and General Vinyes. This was cause for constant happiness and celebration. She should be *ecstatic*.

But really, she'd traded one prison for another. Gabriel even warned her against taking walks just yet. And now he was leaving her alone and with instructions to stay inside.

This prison was *better* of course. No one would beat her or ridicule her or force her to marry a man who would also no doubt beat and ridicule her, but it was still...forced solitary confinement—even if the confinement was elegant and luxurious.

Gabriel must have read her distress over that—he was

good at *reading* the room. Or just her. And not in the way her father or even Alexandre was. Though she hated to draw comparisons between her father and brother, they both had a way of understanding her in order to *maneuver* her into whatever they wanted.

But what Alex wanted was for the greater good, so that was not so bad. What her father wanted was always to prove his power, his dominance, so that *was* bad.

But Gabriel seemed to read her in order to…understand. And now, he assuaged her concerns. Or tried to.

"Eventually, we will ease your way into a less isolated life," he was saying while she watched him fiddle with a computer—*her* computer now. He'd gotten all sorts of things in place over the past three days. A computer, a phone, an entire security system controlled by both. "Once the talk of your disappearance dies down, once your father finds some different vengeance plot to follow, and with some slight physical details shifted, you may eventually lead a very normal life."

May. Eventually. She tried not to be depressed by those words—she was safe from both her father *and* the general, after all. She was *lucky*.

She would teach herself to cook. She would watch the ocean. Maybe at some point she could buy some paint, some new furniture, bring life to this place's interior.

And she would do all of these things without being manipulated, ridiculed or beaten. Ever again.

"Grocery delivery is set up, just as I showed you, without any personal contact. I have left you a document full of instructions for the security system. It should answer any query. You are not to contact me unless it is a dire emergency."

She nodded, not trusting her voice. She didn't want him

to go. She'd come to realize she enjoyed his company. He was charming, funny, and that bright smile was like sunlight after years in shadows.

And in Gabriel, she saw everything Jordi had let her believe about him that hadn't been true at all. Gabriel saw things through. He had no fear. He had *risked* for her. Well, for Alexandre.

She could trust Gabriel to protect her, just as Alexandre had always protected her. Even if he left. He had done *all* this, at great risk to himself. Regardless of the reason, he was brave. Strong. Admirable.

She would miss him. Desperately.

Gabriel studied her. Saw through her, she could tell. "I will come back to check on you in a few weeks," he said gently.

She felt as though she might cry. Or fall down at his feet and beg him to stay. She *refused* to do either. At least in front of him, but it didn't stop her from being a little bit pathetic. "Do you promise?"

"You have a state-of-the-art security system in place if you are worried about safety. I will make certain no one from Alis finds you. I promise you, just as I promised your brother."

"I'm not afraid. Not like that. I just…" She looked around the room. "It will all just be so empty. I have never really been alone before. Not like this."

"Then enjoy it, Evelyne." He gave her shoulder a brotherly kind of pat. "I'll be back in a few weeks. You have my word."

And he kept it. Every few weeks, Gabriel would appear with no notice. Usually in the dead of night. She would get a little notification on her phone, waking her up, and she would let him in the back door.

In the shadows of those nights, Evelyne felt her heart race. The sound of his voice would drift along her skin like a delicious secret. The scent of him would find itself in little spaces around her house, and even though he stayed in a bedroom on the other side of the house, she slept easier every night he was here.

The first trip he arrived with hair bleach, which she hadn't been able to bring herself to use. She didn't think she was *vain*, but she liked her hair the way it was, and if she wasn't leaving the house, what was the point of changing her appearance?

He had *laughed* at her, but not in a mean way. As though he was just amused by her.

"Well, keep it around, for the future."

She spent the weeks in between his appearances trying to keep herself entertained. Gabriel had suggested she enjoy some alone time, and while she enjoyed being able to do whatever she wished around the house whenever she wished, it was still a very small life.

And she missed people. She missed Alexandre. How was Ines settling into the palace? Would they be introducing a baby soon? A baby she'd never get to meet?

Thoughts like that made her incredibly sad, or would start a spiral of thoughts… Was her father mistreating Ines? Would he mistreat a grandchild? Especially if Alexandre and Ines ended up having a girl?

Or was he so obsessed with her disappearance—something that would no doubt haunt him as a symbol of his lack of power—that eventually he'd track her down and find her?

But every time she got to *that* thought, she reminded herself to breathe. If there was anyone in this world she thought could keep her safe and hidden from her father, it was Gabriel.

So in the weeks between his visits, she threw herself into whatever projects she could think of. Mostly, she worked on teaching herself to cook, via those internet videos Gabriel had suggested. She tried to not think of the palace, of Alis. Instead, she simply tried to survive.

When Gabriel appeared next, almost two full months from their escape, she had a meal all planned out. She put it together while he locked himself in one of the office rooms and talked to someone on the phone in a language she didn't know.

She had spent weeks upon weeks watching cooking videos, and while there'd been a few fails along the way, she was starting to get the hang of it. She was proud of the meal she'd made Gabriel, and the pretty little dining room scene she'd created—complete with flower arrangement and candlelight.

She was even more proud when he strode into the dining room and stopped short, like he couldn't quite believe what he saw.

He blinked once, then carefully swept that surprised expression away. He smiled. "Look at you. I suppose you can teach an old dog new tricks."

She rolled her eyes at the idea of being *old*. "It's fun." She thought of the pile of dishes in the kitchen sink that would be her responsibility and hers alone. "Sort of."

She'd set the table family style, with plates set next to each other so he couldn't try to sit all the way down the table like he had last time. She hated the huge, ugly, black, shiny table so she'd scrounged up an elaborate silk tablecloth. Still not to her tastes, but better than *black*.

Gabriel took his seat, and she took the one next to him. She watched him with a growing fascination. He did not treat her like he treated other women. She was pretty sure she'd seen him harmlessly *flirt* with anyone from the age of five to ninety-five. It was just *him*, and the way he moved through a crowd. Charming, happy, easy.

Except with her. He kept himself a little…tense, a little…closed off. Not that he wasn't charming, exactly, but he was…stiffer, she supposed.

Evelyne had spent an inordinate time deciding what that meant. What else did she have to do? Learning to cook and cleaning up after didn't take up full weeks at a time.

"I think I should like some paint," she told Gabriel, as he usually restocked anything she needed on his little visits. "Some new furniture. I'd like to make some of these rooms at least a little but more…cozy."

"Write me out a detailed list. We'll figure it out."

She smiled. "You're too good to me."

His smile was…tight. She studied it now, then picked up the glass of wine she'd already poured, sipped. He gave it a fleeting glance, before his eyes moved to his own untouched glass, then his plate.

"Is something wrong?" she asked. She didn't think there was, and she also knew he wouldn't tell her if there was, but she wanted…something. A reaction? A blip? To be able to read this way he dealt with her.

"Everything is going according to plan," he said. "Your father has told the press that he has a 'suspect' in your disappearance."

"Who?" Evelyne demanded, setting the wineglass down a bit too hard. Worry spiraled through her. Did Father suspect Alexandre? Gabriel?

Gabriel lifted a shoulder, cutting through the chicken in a lemon cream sauce. "He's keeping it quite tight-lipped, which makes me believe it's a story to save face. If he has *no* idea what happened to you, he looks like a fool." He took a bite, nodded approvingly. "So he's invented this 'suspect.' With any luck, he'll invent a story that makes everyone think you're dead."

How odd for that to be counted as luck.

She looked down at her plate, poked at the chicken as dread and the deflation of any wisp of happiness took up residence in her stomach. "He'll never stop looking for me." She knew this deep in her bones. The idea of her somehow tricking him, escaping him would not be one he'd ever get over. Gabriel would and could protect her, she had no doubts.

But would it require her to live like this always?

"No," Gabriel agreed in that easy way of his. "But I think he might tell the country you were murdered. He hasn't yet, but it's a rumbling. He'll keep looking, since he knows you weren't, and it'll never sit right with him that you escaped, but if he's the only one looking... It makes things easier for us."

He lifted his hand, and for a moment, she thought he'd put it over hers. Instead, he reached for his wine. Took a drink.

A very large drink. What was that about?

She watched him eat, thought about it as he easily led the conversation around to a wide variety of topics. It was not a surprise, exactly, that he was so intelligent, so well-versed in so many things. He was a wealthy, privileged man.

But he spoke to her...like an equal. She hadn't fully realized how rare that was until this moment. Her brother had a...paternal way of dealing with her, which she'd never minded overmuch. He had been her protector for her whole life, and she had certainly spent a lot of time wishing *he* was her father.

The staff treated her in much the same way, even the well-meaning ones who were simply scared of her father, not loyal to him in that way. Her life had always been an odd extreme of privilege and punishment.

But the way Gabriel asked questions about what she knew, what she thought, made her realize that even Jordi had treated her a bit like a child who couldn't possibly have opinions of her own.

The thought depressed her. It spoke to desperation, she supposed, that she'd believed his seduction had been love, simply because he had given her any attention.

Gabriel nudged her plate. "You need to eat, Evelyne."

"You are the only one who has ever concerned themselves with if I do not eat."

"I'm sure that isn't true."

"I'm sure you'd be wrong," she muttered, poking the chicken with her fork, then forgoing the food for another sip of wine. She studied him, didn't bother to hide it through sideways glances or anything else.

"Father used to punish me if I ate too much," she said conversationally. She supposed she had to admit that some of her food issues stemmed from trauma right there. "Or if I did not like something I was supposed to. Or if I made a mess of things. A princess should eat small portions and do it prettily," she recited.

She looked up, vaguely amused at how *silly* it all seemed, but the expression on Gabriel's face was not what she expected. She had not been sure what to expect, but certainly not *rage*.

She swallowed, surprised that the fury she saw there did not frighten her, did not remind her of being in her father's office, but instead seemed to hit her bloodstream like alcohol—a burning, freeing, *fizzing* wave of what could only be termed as desire.

That someone might actually be…angry on her behalf.

Not because they were related, but because it had...harmed her. She knew that everything Gabriel did was because Alexandre was his friend, but being *angry* on her behalf was something...else.

Something about *her*.

"Your father is a scourge," Gabriel said darkly, but she saw the way he was fighting back the severity of his reaction. He breathed carefully, unclenched the hand that had balled up into a fist.

He was a fascinating man, so many little pockets of emotion and reaction. So different from her brother, whose stoicism bordered on a total lack of personality.

It made her wonder. She understood that so much of what Gabriel had done was a thank you to Alexandre, but she still existed. She breathed. She was involved.

And he was angry at her father on her behalf.

"What do you think of me, Gabriel?"

He raised an eyebrow, took a sip of his wine before responding. "That is a leading question."

"Indeed. Answer it anyway."

His mouth curved, ever so slightly. "You are not a princess here, Evelyne. And I am not your subject to order about."

"Well, you are wrong on half of that," she replied, grinning at him in humor. "America and fake identities or not, I am *always* a princess."

That curve of his mouth turned into a full-blown smile in return, the rage and anger gone. This had a similar effect though, a beautiful fluttering in her chest, spreading warmth through her body. Like a...blooming.

"Fair enough, *principessa*. What do I think of you?" He speared a piece of chicken with his fork. "You are impressive, Evelyne. This is delicious, and while you might have had ample time to teach yourself how to cook, not everyone would use their time wisely."

It surprised her, how easily the compliment was delivered. She hesitated, shifted in her seat, not quite sure what to do with *praise*. "Well. I have also spent a lot of time staring off into the ocean."

He shrugged. "Understandable. You have withstood having to leave everything you've ever known behind and exist mostly alone. The surroundings are nice, no doubt, but that doesn't make the process easy. But you have spine. Underneath that sparkle and personality. You have your brother's strength, or you would not have survived your father."

For a moment, she was rendered completely speechless. Compliments were not something she was used to, aside from ones about her looks. Anything complimenting her *spine* or *strength* was completely foreign and…wonderful.

He must have sensed something of the enormity of her reaction, because he frowned, then shifted in his seat. Almost as though confident, carefree Gabriel Marti was *uncomfortable*.

"Eat three more bites," he ordered, like a parent would to a child. "Then I will help you clean up your mess."

She thought to argue with him, but eating the somewhat insulting *three more* bites like she was a child and having him help clean up kept them close.

So she ate a little bit of her chicken while he cleared his plate. This filled her with satisfaction too. He would not clear his plate if the food was horrible, even to assuage her ego. Gabriel was *nice* to her because of Alexandre, but she did not think he cared all that much about her *ego*.

He cleared the table with her, then moved to the sink. This was something she had come to the house knowing how to do. One of her punishments as a child for her many infractions at the dinner table had been to wash all the dishes for the palace. By hand.

Some of the women in the kitchens had been kind to her, taught her how to take care of her hands, had tried to carefully help her, but since everyone was afraid of King Enzo they had not done her work for her.

"I'll wash, you can dry," she told Gabriel.

"Do you know what this contraption is right here?" he asked, amused, pointing at the dishwasher.

She batted her eyelashes at him. "I thought it was a paper shredder."

"Funny."

Since she *did* know what it was for, and in fact how to use it—she'd even read the manual she'd found in the kitchen drawer to be sure—she handed him a dish towel. "You are meant to handwash these pans, and the knives. The kind women in the kitchens of the palace taught me this. Then, since I already have to do that, I handwash the rest. It's just me. Or me and you, so convenience doesn't really have much of a place here. It gives me something to do."

If he had a reaction to that, she couldn't read it. "Very well." He unbuttoned the cuffs of his shirt, pushed the sleeves up to the elbow.

Evelyne found her gaze trapped there for a moment. She studied the muscular forearms, wondered how he kept in such good shape. Was he some kind of gym rat? His hands spoke of…some kind of physical work. Though his watch was expensive, he had the slash of a faded scar over the back of his left hand.

Would his hands be rough then? What would it feel like to be touched by hands that had seen work outside typing up missives and handling phone calls in the palace? She'd

only ever been with Jordi, and not often. It had been…
pleasant enough, though she thought most of the enjoyment came from doing something she wasn't supposed to
be doing under her father's nose.

Perhaps for both of them.

Gabriel, on the other hand, didn't strike her as a man
who concerned himself with what he was *allowed*. Didn't
her entire escape prove that? Not many would go against
King Enzo's wishes.

But he had. For Alexandre, yes, but because he was a
brave man, a strong man, a smart man.

A handsome man who she knew only in relation to her
brother. But he was a good man, or Alexandre would not be
friends with him—no matter what stories Gabriel had about
being saved by Alex. He was a good man, or he would not
have risked so much to bring her here.

She did not know very many good men. If not for Alexandre, she would know none, believe in none.

But she believed in Gabriel. She believed that she could
feel freedom and hope in his arms. Because if she could
convince him to touch her, kiss her, be with her, that would
be for *her*. Not to endure something. Not to save her.

No, it would simply be something to enjoy.

Would he be appalled by her thoughts? Amused? Or was
his behavior at dinner, and a few other times over the course
of all this, a sign that he might have thoughts along the
same lines?

He thought her *strong*.

She wanted him to show her strength. She wanted him
to show her a million things. She wanted to feel alive, and
independent and *free*. She hadn't yet. As much as this was
better than the palace, a life being promised to General
Vinyes, it had yet to feel like real, true freedom.

He would feel that way. But how could she make that happen?

There was a moment, brief and exciting, where she handed him a wet pan. He lifted his gaze, and it met hers. He *must* have realized what was in her gaze—heat, interest, want. And he did not immediately look away or rebuff any of these things.

No, she saw each and every one of those in his own gaze, before he blinked them away.

And made his excuses to leave.

But Evelyne was beginning to formulate a plan. One that involved more than just *gazes* meeting.

CHAPTER FIVE

GABRIEL HAD PLANNED on staying three nights this trip. After that moment in his kitchen, he had his concerns about such a long stay.

Perhaps he should cut it short, just as he'd cut short helping her with kitchen cleanup. He'd leave in the morning with an excuse he'd gotten called away on business.

Cowardly. He was currently lying in a bed an entire length of the house away from where she would be lying in her own bed, arguing with himself over which was worse— a cowardly escape or an impossible temptation.

Would she be thinking of him as he thought of her?

She looked beautiful in candlelight. She looked beautiful in all lights. Her interest or curiosity or, he supposed, *both* wasn't lost on him. And in every under-the-lashes or sideway glance was a potential land mine.

He was not immune—could not seem to find the reserves to *be* immune. Not to Evelyne.

The straight-on look over dishes this evening was more than any land mine. He had seen stark invitation in her eyes, and he wanted to accept. The claws of need had insisted upon it.

Only a strength born of learning of his own potential to destroy gave him the strength to rip those claws out. He had learned that anything deeper than superficial interest could lead him to the depths of violence and loss of control. Something he could never afford again, especially around someone who had already suffered violence.

He could not touch Evelyne. The obsession would become untenable. It was already too much. He thought of her constantly when he was away. He found every new layer he discovered about her fascinating. Every time he planned his clandestine returns, he was filled with brand-new energy. Anticipation.

He wanted to see her smile, to hear her laugh, to inhale the subtle floral scent that followed her around every room. He wanted. Period. A want that had gotten too large in his mind.

He took some solace in the fact that his obsession with Evelyne hadn't affected his work, but it *had* affected his social life. He had not enjoyed going out since he'd brought her here. Had not been with a woman since he'd gone to Alexandre's wedding. All the surfaces he'd skated across no longer held any distraction for him.

Pathetic. He needed to fix that before he made a larger mistake. Here. With *her*.

He had known she had spine and strength—to come out of a childhood raised by King Enzo and retain any sparkle took an immense capacity for both. And yes, she had Alex to cushion some of her blows, but not all.

But for some years he had kept his distance because he knew that the combination of her was a temptation not just in terms of sex—but in terms of this, the dangerous claws of obsessive *want*. She was beautiful and alluring, but beyond that she was complex, intriguing, intelligent, with some added extra dash of something he could only describe as *fun*.

He got out of bed, frustrated that over ten years of learn-

ing how to be a different man seemed to crumble in the face
of one woman.

There were threats against her, and he would save her
from all of them. Protect her from anything that might touch
her.

And he knew that in the depths of this obsession, it could
lead him to kill. *That* was inside him. No better than King
Enzo, really, except he knew he had to control it.

The room had French doors that led out to a balcony that
looked out over the sea, so he opened them and stepped out.

The cold, whipping air and the salty tang of sea hit him
like a blow—a welcome one tonight. The little tempest that
raged out there felt like solace against his bare skin.

He understood her loneliness. There was something exhilarating and wonderful about the thrashing sea below, but
it served as a reminder to him how different her new life
was. How he'd plopped her here, yes, to save her, but alone
with no one to talk to and with nothing to do but learn how
to haunt a house.

She was too skinny. Too…fragile seeming yet. She
wouldn't crumble, she had too much spine for that, but she
wasn't *thriving*. He told himself that wanting her to thrive
was for Alex and Alex alone, but he knew better.

The thought of her being punished for *eating too much*—
in a *palace*—boiled his blood. Knowing some of the details
of the way King Enzo had abused her—and he had no doubt
that only scratched the surface—enraged him.

He had once been enraged on behalf of a woman. And
his obsession had led him to a violent outburst that would
have resulted in another man's death. Would have, if not
for Alexandre.

All these years later, that fire still burned within him—

twined with the relief he had been saved from the dangerous poison that had held him in its grip.

He had never allowed himself to dance near that flame again. He skated along, not letting himself get hooked into all that could devolve into the desire to destroy.

But he didn't have a choice now. He'd been named Evelyne's savior, her protector. Just like he'd once named himself a young woman's protector.

He could not sink into those old depths of disaster, but he had yet to figure out a way to extricate himself from this, the *flame* of all Evelyne was.

You don't want to.

He'd seen desire in her eyes, the heat of chemistry. He'd felt it echo through him, a bit like a bomb detonating. Just as he'd known might happen. *Would* happen.

He had learned how to handle his…appetites, desires. It was easy now, to keep the *personal* out of any sexual encounter. Enjoy it for what it was. *Enjoy* had become the cornerstone of his life. A surface level amusement with everything. Nothing mattered enough to obsess over. Nothing mattered enough to fan the fire of vengeance that lived in him—a seed of disaster always searching for a little bit of water and sun.

Nothing could be *surface* with Evelyne. Everything about her was personal. Deeper. A constant, dangerous pitfall. Because he remembered all the times she'd attempted to flirt with him in the past.

All the times he'd been tempted to fall for her alluring smiles and sparkling wit. He'd known then, even as a young man, to keep his distance from Alex's enticing sister.

She would be a vine that grew and choked out all reason and restraint.

He *knew* this, deep in his bones.

He breathed in the cold air, hoping it would somehow cool him. But he stood, shirtless and vibrating, heated all the way through.

He heard a noise somewhere underneath the roar of surf and wind. A kind of *squeak*. He looked toward where he thought it might have come from.

And then there she was, illuminated in a warm cast of light. As though his traitorous thoughts had conjured her, there on the terrace down the way. It was not her room she stepped out of. He did not know what room housed those terrace doors, but not her bedroom, even though she was dressed for bed.

Because she was far closer than a full house-length away.

She wore a robe, but it was open, revealing a brief, silky nightgown. The breeze fluttered over the fabrics.

He knew it was silk because he'd had to handle procuring her wardrobe himself. He'd handled every inch of her life these past few months himself. Because no one but him could know she was here.

And he *liked* it. He had been avoiding accepting that realization, but he could not push it away in this moment.

He liked being her only point of contact. He *liked* being her savior, and he damn well *liked* the way she looked at him.

Even when he shouldn't. What did that make him? No better than the controlling, abusive men in her life thus far. She deserved better than that, but he did not know how to give it to her.

He saw her mouth move but could not hear what she said over the sound of ocean and wind and storm. When he shook his head in signal he could not hear her, she held up a finger, then disappeared.

The storm outside echoed in him. It was not a good-night gesture. It was a *hold on* gesture.

And he had nothing to hold on to when he heard the door behind him open. He turned slowly to watch her enter his bedroom. She moved through the room, her robe still open, the nightgown brief and flirting with her golden thighs. Her feet were bare, her hair down and wild around her shoulders.

She looked more nymph or siren or something from some old painting. Dangerous, seductive, a cautionary tale. He knew all the cautions, wanted to heed them, and yet…

"What are you doing up?" she asked conversationally as she went to stand next to him on the balcony.

Her robe was still undone, and the nightgown she wore dipped low, offering a tantalizing glimpse at the perfection of the tops of her breasts. She would be soft, fragrant and responsive, because while he didn't think she was here for seduction *alone*, she knew what she was doing.

What she was after.

He forced himself to look away from the sweet, golden temptation of her skin and stared out at the ocean, focusing on her words, not her intent. What was he doing up? Wondering how he'd gotten himself into this mess where she became the sole center of all his thoughts, wants, desires.

Like he was eighteen years old. Obsessed, and righteous with it. A woman's sole protector from those who would hurt her. It *should* be noble, until a man used it as an excuse to hurt. To be violent himself. To follow that violence to its natural conclusion.

As Gabriel once had, to *almost* disastrous results.

But he could not verbalize this to Evelyne.

She sighed, an awed, satisfied kind of sound. "Isn't it beautiful?" she murmured, leaning against the railing. "I never knew how much I would love living next to the ocean, especially since it's hardly some tropical paradise, but it's better somehow than sun and blue. It's moody. Brooding. I think I even enjoy the cold." She smiled up at him, a goddess among mortals. "You made an excellent choice."

The curve of her mouth beckoned him. Lush and soft. The wind tangled in her hair, fluttering a scent of florals and sea around him like some kind of potion meant to tempt him. She would be a dream come to life if he pressed his mouth to hers.

She would be his end if he did not extricate himself from *this*.

"I have to leave," he told her, the words coming from some strange place of panic he didn't recognize. He had never panicked. He had plotted, he had acted. He had been in some…dangerous situations here and there for his job when dealing with people who were not altogether on the up and up.

Never once had he panicked.

But he recognized this need and its potential to turn him into what he'd been at eighteen. Obsessive, vengeful and *wrong*. No better than King Enzo with his manipulations and violence.

"Why?" she asked.

"I've been called away to work."

"Have you?" she murmured, her mouth curved into a smile.

Like she didn't believe him. Like she saw through him.

When certainly neither should be nor *could* be true.

He pushed off the balcony and moved back into his room. Never in his life had he *lied* to a woman about his reasons for leaving, probably because never in his life had he had to *run* from a woman. In any other situation, he would be sure he was made of sterner stuff.

But she tempted him, and she was the one temptation he could not allow. The one temptation that could never surface.

He found his bag—thankfully mostly packed—and tossed it on the bed. "I should be gone closer to a month this time." Perhaps longer, but he didn't need to say that. He put his laptop that sat on the desk into his bag. He'd leave his toiletries—there was nothing in the bathroom he could not replace once safely home in Milan. Perhaps he'd go to his other estate in Sydney. Surely that was as far away from Maine as he could be. He would find a woman. He would remind himself that what had taken over his mind was simply temporary.

That he was stronger than it.

He made a move to shoulder his bag, then realized somewhat belatedly that he was not wearing a shirt. Yes, he would need a shirt. And shoes. He set the bag down, but there was a problem.

Both shirt and shoes were on the other side of *her*, unless he crawled over his own bed.

He would not *crawl*.

So he stood there.

She stood in his way. Purposefully, he knew.

Her gaze roamed his face, like a tentative, explorative caress. He should have stopped it, sidestepped her. Instead, he stood frozen as she moved closer, gracefully, a bit like a ghost. A ghost that haunted, that played with his mind, because he did not move out of her reach.

He held himself perfectly still as she reached up, with those slim, elegant, princess hands to touch his face. Her fingertips danced across his cheeks. Her eyes were luminescent, her lips pink and lush. She studied his face like it was a marvel.

"Gabriel," she murmured, his name shaped by her lips causing a bolt of lust to obliterate the recriminations he tried to hold on to. "You do not need to leave. I do not want you to leave."

She moved to her toes. He reached out to stop her, to push her back down on her heels, to move her out of his way so he could walk around her.

Instead, his hands found purchase on her hips and stayed there, the soft fabric a whispered promise against his palms. *Her skin would feel even better.*

Perhaps that thought, and the attempt to fight it, distracted him, because it gave her the chance to brush her lips across his. The low beat of need held him in his grip. It was shame that he had not had the fortitude to stop this before he had been given a chance to linger.

But linger he did, in this half-kiss. Gentle, almost nothing pressure, even as his grip on her hips tightened, bringing her up closer, plastered against him. He could feel the weight of her breasts, the shuddery intake of breath. The way his own body turned to painful, hardened *need*.

She smelled like something fresh and new. Spring and promise. It would haunt him the rest of his life, he had no doubt. And if he got a taste of her...

No, it would be a step too far. A step he could not take back.

So he had to put a stop to it. Now. He set her back on her heels, ignored the ringing in his ears, that pulling, incessant need that he knew too well led him to dangerous places.

He focused all his energy on making sure his voice sounded like a scolding schoolteacher, though his breath felt ragged in his lungs. "That was uncalled for, Evelyne."

"Uncalled for," she echoed. Her color was high, her golden eyes dreamy, her hands on his shoulders. The scent of her, the faint taste of her lingered, fogging up his brain for a moment before he had the good sense to step back, away from her grip on him.

She touched her fingers to her lips, still looking at him. He had a very disconcerting *upended* feeling. For most of his life—even when he'd been traveling down the wrong path—he had always felt in control. It wasn't loss of *control*. It was letting base urges win. He would have succeeded in murdering that man, if Alexandre had not waded in and pulled him off. If Alex had not said the words that got through the haze of violence and revenge.

You are not like my father, Gabriel. I will not let you fall down that path.

So he had never once let himself follow the path of obsession again. These days, he remained one step ahead of anyone who might lure him below that surface. He was intelligent, privileged and quick.

But he was not one step ahead of her. Not even close. If he'd listened to his instincts instead of believing he had a handle on the situation, he would have been gone long before now.

So he had to use whatever tools he had to stop this. Now. Cruelty seemed the only way, much as he loathed to treat her badly. It was for the best. "A little hero worship is natural."

She held his gaze, not getting haughty or even narrowing her eyes at him as he'd expected. As he'd *hoped*. Instead, she *smiled*. "Then why won't you let me worship?"

That had more than just his throat tightening. He could not find his voice for a throbbing, portentous moment. When he did find it, the sound was rough, pained. "Evelyne, I do not know what you think is happening…"

"Well, apparently nothing is happening. Though I don't see why." She gestured at him. "You aren't…uninterested."

Uninterested. If only he could even conjure the meaning of the word in this moment.

"Do you remember what you told me that night I broke you out of the palace?" he demanded.

Her eyebrows drew together, as if thinking back and coming up empty.

"You told me, in that haughty princess way of yours, that your brother would kill me if I took advantage of you." And he did not believe this exactly—because Alexandre was good and right and had once stopped *him* from killing a man—but there were dungeons in Alis, among other punishments.

She reached out, slid her palms up his chest before he stepped away. "You wouldn't be taking advantage. Have I not made that clear?"

He caught her hands by her wrists. Slim, her pulse skittering under the weight of his fingers.

For a moment, he forgot himself. He thought only of the feel of her hands against his skin. And he held them in his own. He could put her hands exactly where he pleased. He could...

"You're bored," he said, forcing his voice to be commanding and cold. Forcing himself to believe the words he said. "You're lonely. I'm not your plaything."

She looked up at him, head cocked, the gold of her eyes glowing like a hypnotist's pendant. "Why not?"

He thought he should be outraged by how flippant she was being. Instead, he was aroused. Tempted. If she wanted to play...

"I'm not a virgin, you know," she continued, turning her hands in his grip so that her fingers trailed along the underside of his jaw. "I can be your plaything right back. Perhaps

I am lonely and bored. What would be so wrong with…entertaining each other?"

Entertaining each other. It brought to mind a million scenarios, but he did not let his mind settle on one. He thought of another time, when the obsessive want for a woman had obliterated all else. And his only savior had been…

"Your brother."

"Is a continent away," she said, as if every excuse of his was *nothing*.

He could not let himself be fooled. But by God he wanted to be. The *want* of it all beat in him, loud and tight as any drum.

"I cannot contact him," she continued, her gaze watching where her fingers touched his jaw. "And he cannot contact me. If you feel so certain he would be…disapproving, he would not have to know. No one, in fact, would have to know." Her gaze met his. Direct. Seductive. "But us."

For a moment, his grip tightened. For a moment, he thought giving in was all he had in him.

But this was Evelyne, and he had promised to save her. Truly save her. Not sink her into his darkness like he once had another young woman. Not become a monster like the father he'd saved Evelyne from.

You are a monster, Gabriel. That old voice. That old reminder.

Yes, he could be. But he would not be.

He dropped her hands and whirled away, furious with how she had somehow turned all his normal protections on their head. "Have you thrown yourself at anyone who shows you a modicum of attention?" he demanded of her.

He knew how to be mean. He knew how to cut an unwanted pass off at the source. He knew how to accomplish all these things. To keep that surface level. To never allow anything deeper.

For her *own good.*

Why didn't they seem to work on her?

No one would have to know. But us.

He found his shirt, jerked it on. Everything inside him was a hard, tense ball. "I'll be back in a month or so."

"It was about a month just five minutes ago. Now it is a month *or so?*"

He shouldered his bag, gave her a cold look. "Behave, Evelyne." He moved past her, almost to the door.

"Run away, then."

He stopped, midstride, turned in utter shock. "What did you say?"

"I said, *run away, then,*" she replied, enunciating each word carefully. A bright, glittering challenge. She even lifted her chin.

He moved for her then, swift and furious, and held himself back with his last shred of strength. He towered over her, desperate to put his mouth on her neck where her pulse fluttered. On her breasts, right where he could see the outline of her hardened nipples through the fabric of her nightgown.

Instead, he kept his voice cool and cutting. "If I fell for your sad attempts at seduction, it would be *you* who would be wanting to run away. Except it would be too late for you. You're a sheltered, pampered *child,* and you know nothing of the real world, or a *man's* wants."

She didn't drop her gaze. Color didn't even bloom on her cheeks. She raised a regal eyebrow.

"You forget, Gabriel, where I grew up. I may be lacking in education, the ability to cook or take care of myself in a country under a fake name. Perhaps you are even right about a *man's wants* and how little I know of them, but I know how to handle angry men. I know what *really* drives them, and you aren't angry at me."

"No?"

"You're angry at yourself, because you want me too."

He stood there, breathing through the truth. There was no way to win this fight. He recognized that, just as Alex had once taught him that sometimes you could not advance, advance, advance. Sometimes you had to have the where-withal to separate from your feelings and retreat.

"Goodbye, *principessa*," he said, and then he left her.

Not sure he'd ever return.

CHAPTER SIX

EVELYNE CLUNG TO the belief that Gabriel would return, did not allow the fear he wouldn't to take root.

Perhaps he wished to never have her throw herself at him again, but he wouldn't leave her without a way to survive. If he was so worried about what Alexandre would think about *seduction*, then he'd certainly be too indebted to Alex to leave her to fend for herself *forever*.

And more… He was too good of a man to let that be how he abandoned her. He had brought her here because of Alex, but he had not sat at dinners with her, listened to her, had actual conversations with her for *Alex*. He had not procured her paint and such for the house for *Alex*. That had been for *her*.

There was something more between them than just her brother, than just him saving her.

She told herself that for three long weeks. Long weeks where she spent an inordinate amount of time thinking about that night. About the way his mouth had shaped to hers. Brief, far too brief, but he *had* kissed her back. His grip on her wrists had done more in a few seconds than grappling with Jordi in the dark completely naked had *ever* done.

Which had given her some pause, as she recounted the moments over these weeks. Maybe she *was* a child. She thought not being a virgin meant something, but everything in that kiss, those few, minor touches with Gabriel in his bedroom had been something…far different than what *she'd* experienced.

It was like a whole dark, promising world she didn't fully know about.

But wanted to. And he had not been unmoved. She was not *imagining* anything. She had felt his want throb between them—in his gaze, in his anger. And when she'd told him that he was only angry at himself for wanting her, she had hit the mark. She *knew* it.

He had been cold and cutting, but she had seen underneath that. Just like she'd said—she knew all about angry men.

Besides, he hadn't really given a good reason for nothing to happen between them. He'd never said: *Evelyne, I do not want you*. No, he had brought up her brother, made snide remarks about her.

But he had not denied that an interesting and complicated heat erupted between them.

Sometimes, she touched herself and thought of him, and she was quite determined if—no, *when*—he returned, she would tell him so. Watch his reaction. She could picture it. He would get that pinched look about his mouth, but his nostrils would flare, his eyes would heat and his hands would curl into fists as if he could fight away his attraction to her.

She smiled to herself, because he couldn't. He wouldn't have run away if he could.

Almost exactly a month after their kiss, three months into her life here on the Maine coast, Gabriel returned.

For the first time, he did not wait until nightfall. He appeared at the front door one late dreary afternoon. He carried enough bags that excitement and joy twined with troublesome hope so that her heart actually trembled.

Did he intend to stay for some time? Was it possible she wouldn't be quite so lonely anymore? Was it possible he had dealt with whatever…reservations he might have about her to want to explore this thing between them?

"What is all this?" she asked as he carried it all inside and dropped the bags and one box on the floor in the sitting room. She had repainted this room, switched out some of the furniture. It still wasn't perfect, but with one entire wall a window out to the sea, she was determined to keep working at it until she was satisfied. So she could sit in here and enjoy the beauty of the world outside.

"Supplies," he said, the word clipped. "We will go through them, and I will put them where you'd like, but I only have a few hours."

She blinked, some of her hope deflating, though a seed of it stubbornly held on. Surely he didn't mean… "A few hours?"

"I have a plane to catch at three."

This made no sense. He was here with all these things, and he was leaving in a few hours? On a plane? "To where?"

He did not answer her question. Instead, he opened one of the bags he'd brought. "These are contacts that will change the color of your eyes. The instructions for how to wear them are on the box, or I'm sure you can find some instructional videos to help learn if that's necessary."

"Change the color of my eyes, but…why?"

"If you dye your hair as I've suggested multiple times, wear these color contacts and dress to hide your figure, you may enter society here. You will use the fake name and backstory I gave you. You should be able to take care of yourself just fine without these risky visits. I have brought you a car. You can drive, can't you? I have obtained you an American license that no one will be able to question."

It fully dawned on her. This was not a visit. This was not going back to the way things were or moving forward on a new path. Together. "You're leaving me," she said as he crushed all that horrible hope, causing a river of pain. "For good."

He did not look at her. He looked at all he'd brought. His words were formal and final. "It is for the best."

She would never see him again. She would never see anyone she knew again, or at least until she was very old. She would be wholly alone in this world for so long as her father drew breath. Tears filled her eyes, but she blinked them back out of habit.

She looked at him, refusing to meet her gaze. No. Just…*no*. She would not let him cast her off. Not easily. "Who's best?"

He still didn't look at her. "You *can* drive, can't you? I thought I remembered Alexandre making sure of it," he asked again instead.

"Yes, I can drive," she retorted, irritation and panic mounting in equal measure. "Though I suppose I haven't done it on the side of the road that they do here."

"You'll pick it up. Town isn't far."

Town isn't far. This was beyond anything she had considered, and her brain was struggling to catch up. She had spent the past month alone and now he was cutting off what little joy, what little connection she had.

All her hope. Again.

"What if… What if something happens?"

"Should you have an emergency, you can of course still contact me, but I cannot continue to live my life if I am continually popping in to keep you going every few weeks. I have work, Evelyne. A life."

"Other women?" she demanded, and didn't care if she sounded a bit like a harpy. She wanted to harp.

He gave her a sharp, disapproving look. *Finally.* "There are not *other women.* There are women. Because the word *other* suggests there is a woman in my life. And there is not. You are like…a ward. At best."

"At best." She laughed, bitterly she knew. *There are women.* Oh, she wanted to *hurt* him. She shook with rage, and she was self-aware enough to know underneath the rage was fear, but she was so tired of being afraid.

"All the boxes and bags are labeled. It should be everything you need. You have a driver's license, a passport, credit cards. Everything you could possibly need to be Lina Marino."

She tried so hard to fight back the tears, to focus on the anger, but this was so gutting. She had survived these past three months on his visits. And maybe she had been in some denial. Denial that this would be forever.

Now he was describing a forever in which she couldn't even be *herself.* She had to pretend to be some Italian billionaire's wife. Not even *this* Italian billionaire's wife.

She was free from abuse, but not *free.* She was utterly alone, and she could not even be herself. When he was here was the only time she could even begin to experience what *herself* meant. How would she discover who she really was now?

The first tear fell, and she quickly dashed it away with the back of her hand. "Is this really necessary?" she croaked out. "Couldn't you have just made me promise not to kiss you?"

He got very stiff then. "This isn't about that."

Fury leaped at that, twining in with the sadness, disappointment and fear. She looked up at him now, eyes narrowed. She settled on the fury, held on to it, nurtured it. She wanted *that* above tears. She wanted to *hurt* him as he was hurting her.

Fair? No. But none of this was *fair*. And if it wasn't, if nothing could be, if even in escape she could not have any sort of freedom, then why be fair? Or rational? Or anything other than *furious*?

"No, Gabriel, you do not get to pretend. You are punishing me because I had the *audacity* to suggest we might enjoy each other."

"It is not punishment," he returned flatly. But she saw something in his eyes. A kind of softening. Which did not make her feel better. It somehow made her madder. That he could be soft, that he could be *interested*, that he could be so many things when it came to her and want to cut them all off.

"I am not *punishing* you, Evelyne," he said with that infuriating gentleness.

"You are. You're leaving me *alone*. Forever."

Gabriel thought he could fight anything. He'd *prepared* to fight anything, even a bit of hysteria, but the tear that tracked down her cheek sorely tested that preparedness. Because it wasn't hysteria. There was a bone-deep sadness in her, even underneath this new flash of temper.

She had been cut off from all she knew, and he was her only anchor. But he could not safely continue to be this for her. She might be upset, but he was doing her a favor.

If she got under the surface any deeper than she already was, he would only make her miserable. He would only be shades of her father. Even if he never laid a hand on *her*, he would not be the man she thought.

He could not be the man she needed. Calm, rational, in control.

"If you wear the disguise, you can meet people. Make

friends. Make a life here." He tried to keep his voice from softening. "It will not be so bad."

"But it will all be a lie." She dashed another tear off her cheek, but another spilled over and she left it there to trail down the soft gold of her skin. "No one will really know me. I cannot ever be *me*."

He could not let that truth change his course. "It was never permanent, Evelyne. Me visiting you. You must make your own life."

She shook her head. "Of course. What I want has never mattered. Why would I think that would start now simply because you saved me from marrying the general? It's all the same to the likes of you."

"The likes of *me*?" He thought of everything he'd done for her—not just Alex, but for *her*. Frustration wound deep with a nagging guilt that irritated him. He had nothing to be guilty for. Not when it came to *her*. He was doing this *for* her, so he would *not* be the *likes of* anyone who'd hurt her. "I would suggest you don't lump me in with your *likes of*, if they include your father and the general."

"Why not? Rich, powerful men who see women as nothing but pawns. Move me about the country. Leave me alone. Cut me off from everything I know—for my own good. Yes, I know. And I am grateful. But when do I get to choose for once? I didn't even choose this damn house."

"Leave it then. Find a new one. Do something else, if you want to be a child throwing a tantrum."

Her eyes widened then, got a little wild. He surveyed her warily.

"Would you like to see a tantrum?" she asked very quietly. The kind of quiet that was never safe for anyone. "I think I *will* throw a tantrum. I've never been allowed. If I cried, I was sent to the kitchens. If I yelled, I was beaten until I apologized. If I rebelled…" She shook her head. The tears didn't just *trickle* now, they poured out.

But she didn't sob. No, there was as much anger as hurt in her expression and her tears.

And it was too easy to imagine what she spoke of. King Enzo's fists and her delicate build. If anything tested his resolve, it was that. "Evelyne."

She whirled away from him, kicked over the box. The contents clattered around, but didn't spill out. That clearly didn't satisfy her, so she gave it another kick. When that did little more than clatter around again, she marched over to a little decorative shelf—new since the last time he'd been here. On it she'd arranged some colorful bits of shells and glass and tiny vases. She picked one of the vases up, hurled it across the room, where it crashed against the wall, glass splintering.

"How is that for childish?" she demanded. "Perhaps now that you're leaving me alone, I will just *always* act like a child. Perhaps now that you're abandoning me after I was forced to leave everything I've ever known, *that* is what I will lean into. Perhaps *childish* is who I am, Gabriel."

Her breath was heaving, her eyes wide and wild. He wanted to find himself disparaging of her behavior, but it was hard not to understand. Yes, he had saved her—something he accepted knowing he'd enjoyed it too much, knowing the dangers of *saving*, but it's not like being removed from a threat and being plunked down in the middle of luxury meant she couldn't be *angry* that choice and hope had been stripped from her.

He had known she could be mad, but he'd assumed she'd handle it with icy, royal dignity. Some pithy remarks. *Maybe* he'd anticipated some tears. But not this wild, immature undoing.

Certainly not his reaction to it. Fascinated, aroused. She was usually so poised. Even when they'd been sneaking out of Alis, hopping from plane to train and back again, she'd kept up that regal princess-like behavior, wilted—yes, but held together. Even when she'd come to his room in her skimpy nightgown, tempting him, attempting to seduce him, she had maintained her control.

Now it was gone. She was the ocean, crashing against the rocks, furious and glorious all at once.

She grabbed another tiny vase, hurled it against the wall again. This one did not shatter, but it dented the wall, fell to the floor with a *thud*. "You get to choose to leave me. You get to choose to reject me. What do I get to choose? Nothing. Not even you."

He watched her eyes track to the last vase, and then the giant window. "But if you're abandoning me, you have no say in what I choose." She said this with an almost eerie kind of calm after the outburst directly before it.

She reached for that vase, her eyes on the window. He wasn't sure it would do damage against the thick glass, but he wasn't about to let her find out. He crossed the room and took her by the arms. He gave her a gentle shake.

"Enough," he ordered, but he kept his grip on her arms so she could not fight him or try to destroy more. "Stop this now."

She tossed her hair back, chin darted up to stare him down, even though she was nearly a foot shorter than him.

"What are you going to do if I don't stop? Beat me?" she demanded.

But touching her was such a curse. He could think of nothing but the kiss they'd shared. The way she felt against his body. He couldn't even fully absorb her words, because he was lost in the golden threads in her eyes.

Even amid this wild tempest her scent was something sweet and delicate. For a month that scent had been at the edges of his life. There had been times he'd find himself distracted by it, look around whatever room he was in expecting to see her.

"You haunt me." He said the words as if he'd been cracked open and they'd simply fallen out. Against his will. Against his everything.

Some of that fury in her expression faded, but the chin didn't go down, the tension in her muscles didn't relax. She held his gaze, defiant. "Good."

Good, she said. *Good* as if any of this was *good*.

He knew what he had to do. Release her. Walk out of this house. Never, *ever* return no matter what Alexandre asked of him.

There was still a way out. Just disentangle himself. Walk right out the door. Resist this one more time and then he would never, ever allow this temptation in his life again.

She bent her arms, and he did not let her go, but he did not stop what she was doing. Which was reaching up to her shoulders and pulling the straps of her dress down. Nothing could happen if he did not let her arms go. The straps would be stuck. She could not make this happen.

He dropped his hands. The dress fell. There was nothing particularly alluring about the underwear she wore under it. Serviceable cotton, he supposed.

But there was *everything* alluring about the woman who stood before him. Her hair, glinting honey in the cascading afternoon light, wild around her shoulders. The pale golden expanse of her skin. She leaned back against the wall behind her as if in offering to him.

Even as his body raged with want, he catalogued every

beautiful feature. He thought he could have spent his entire day just looking at her.

But Evelyne had other plans.

"Touch me." She reached out, took his hand. "Feel how much I want you."

Madness. Obsession. Danger that would obliterate everything he'd built. Some echoing voice in the back of his head told him to stop. This was the last step before stopping was not an option.

But he did not pull his hand away. He let her draw him to the apex of her thighs. He cupped her there, half convinced there was still some exit route behind this.

Her sigh, her gasp, the hot, needy heat of her as she moved against him, whimpering, proved that thought wrong.

And all exit routes were gone. There was only her. There was only this. He moved the flimsy underwear out of his way, teased her with his hand while the other tugged at the strap of her bra. All the while watching her eyes, the way they swam into nothing but golden heat. The way her lips parted, her breath panted, moaned.

He pulled the bra fabric away, then fixed his mouth to one tight nipple. She cried out, tensing around him, tangling her hands in his hair. Vibrating through the climax he felt ripple through her, while his body raged with unspent want.

She tugged his hair so he looked up at her. She met his gaze, her eyes cloudy with desire, but direct and fierce. So damn fierce. "I'm choosing this. You're choosing this. Take me, Gabriel. Before you leave me, my God, take me."

Whatever last grasp on control he had was obliterated. *Leave.* He had to leave, but by God, he had to have her first. Just as she said.

He jerked the bra all the way down, and she laughed in

breathless excitement. He didn't bother to finesse her underwear off, just ripped it out of the way.

Then his mouth was on hers. Nothing holding him back. Only that desperate want that would be his undoing and his end. He tasted, devoured, glutted himself on the hot, delicious contours of her mouth.

She fumbled with his clothes, unbuttoning maybe two buttons before she just yanked, sending buttons flying. Then her small, slender hands were on his bare skin and he growled into her mouth, plunging his fingers into the wet, willing heat of her once more.

She moaned, wild and free. There was no timidity. Just giving. Just that same wild storm—heat and a loss of control and the desperate pull to destroy.

She would destroy him, he had no doubt, and with her body bared to him, golden and beautiful, he reveled in the destruction, in her. His hands roamed her body, tending to fires until she begged, pleaded, arched.

She worked to undo his pants, until he shoved her hands away and freed the painfully desperate erection himself. Then he lowered her onto the plush carpet beneath them, and in the same move entered the welcome heat of Evelyne. She came apart around him in one quick thrust, a glorious scream of pleasure as she pushed against him.

He gritted his teeth against the swamp of pleasure. Too much and not enough. He needed more. So much more. All. *All, all, all.*

He moved inside her and she moved with him. She chanted his name, and she dug her fingers into his shoulders, demanding more. Demanding that *all*.

It was a storm. Perhaps it would destroy, but in the throes of it, Gabriel only felt the power, the pleasure. The rightness of plunging into her, again and again and again.

She moved against him, a wild, wanton mythical creature, too beautiful to believe she existed. She consumed him, until he felt like he was but a wave, crashing again and again against the rocky surf himself. Maybe they were nothing but wind and sea, crashing against each other, never meant to do anything but.

And he crashed into her one last time, a glorious release of everything. Disaster. Absolute glorious disaster.

When he could see again, he looked down at her. Her smile was smug and her eyes half closed, like she would just drift away into sleep, here on the living room floor in the middle of the afternoon.

But it was not over. It could not be over, because once it was…

He refused to think past that. He swept her up into his arms. He did not recognize what fueled him, what moved through him with her warm body tucked against his. It had a different tenor to everything he'd felt before, and yet he knew it was just as—if not more—destructive. It would be obsession, it would be vengeance, it would destroy.

In the moment, he wanted all that destruction. He carried her upstairs and all the way to her room. He laid her on her bed, and nothing about the smug satisfaction on her face changed him. She regarded him under dark lashes.

He stood on the side of the bed, rational thought trying to get its grip on him again. But she had other plans.

"Do you want to know what I did while you weren't here?" she asked him, sultry and full of promise, her intent whispering through his brain so that all the warnings went silent.

She lay naked on her bed, stretched out and magical. Maybe she was a witch casting a spell on him. The spell was better than anything he'd ever experienced.

"I touched myself and wished it was you."

His body hardened again, so easily, so powerfully. He *throbbed* with need. But he didn't touch. He didn't lower himself to her once more. He met her gaze. "Show me," he ordered.

Her mouth curved. "I dreamed of that too." She trailed one hand down her body, cupping her own breast with the other. She did everything to her own body he wanted to do with his own hands, but he watched instead, hardening as she brought herself to a glorious, crashing climax.

Her gaze met his as her breathing came in quick bursts. "You're better."

He had no response to that. To her. Nothing in words anyway.

He gripped her leg, pulled her to the edge of the bed, spread her legs wide so that he could see the glorious heart of her. He waited there, watched the color rise in her cheeks, spread over her breasts. And still he waited, drawing out the moment, the anticipation.

"Gabriel," she whispered finally.

And then he positioned himself at her entrance but then waited again. As she tried to move against him, wriggle closer. "I like watching you so desperate, *principessa*."

She huffed out a sound, frustration or amusement or both. "I would think you might like watching me come apart."

"That too. I like it all." He moved slowly. Drawing out the anticipation and pleasure. She was begging long before he was fully inside her, and even as his body demanded more, he stretched it out. Denied them both what they sought.

"Gabriel. Now." It was not an order. It was a plea. But she spread her arms wide, arched her body, taking him even deeper. "*Now*," she repeated.

And then something broke. Him. Both of them. Everything went wild and uncontrolled. Her screams, his demands, echoing through the house. The desperate sounds of bodies meeting. And her scent, still sweet and everywhere.

He felt her fall over that sensual cliff over and over again before he could no longer deny himself. He emptied himself into her on a primal growl of triumph.

Yes, this. Her, always her. His.

At some point, night had fallen, and they had dozed, sated and perhaps mind numbed by all they'd found in each other.

When he woke, it was pitch-black, and Evelyne was curled up next to him, fast asleep, like that was exactly where she belonged.

His heart cracked, but he had been down this road before. Maybe it felt different, but it would be the same obsession, the same madness. It would drive him to places he could not allow himself to go.

It would drive him to places she did not deserve to witness.

Didn't all of this prove it? He should have never crossed this line. It was a betrayal of what Alexandre had asked of him, and it was a betrayal of all the promises he'd made to himself when he'd gotten his life back.

Even as need tried to find its way into his bloodstream once more at the feel of her warm body pressed to his, he felt cold. He could see it all clearly now. He slipped out of bed. She didn't stir.

Had he known this would happen all along? Had he *hoped* this would happen all along? He watched her sleeping form and accepted that, yes, if he'd truly wanted to stop this—he would have never returned after that kiss. He would have handled all of this from afar.

But he'd returned. He'd needed to see her one last time.

More though, he'd wanted just this. Her. And because he was weak, he had taken it. A mistake, but a fixable one.

He left her sleeping.

With no plans to ever return.

Evelyne had awoken to night outside her window and the unsurprising truth that Gabriel was gone.

Truly gone. He had left her. She knew he would not come back now. There was no doubt in her mind. Whatever he had allowed between them he viewed as an unfixable mistake. The heat, the passion, the glorious pleasure of it all was wrong in his mind. For whatever reason.

Evelyne sighed. She didn't cry then—tears would come later as she sought to live someone else's life. As she came to certain realizations. In this moment, she made a promise to herself.

She would make the best of what came next. She would live as Lina Marino. She *would* drive to town and make friends and build a life. Maybe it would be a lie, but it would be *her* lie.

So a few months later, when it finally occurred to her that the lethargy, the nausea, the tears that finally did come and didn't want to stop was a sign that she might be pregnant, she did not ring the emergency number Gabriel had given her. She did not contact him.

She calmly put the color-changing contacts in—though she refused to dye her hair—and drove herself to the store in town, purchased a pregnancy test, figured out the self-checkout so no one in the village she'd come to know would see and took it home.

When the test was positive, she still did not call Gabriel.

No, he had left her. And this was no emergency. This was her life, and she got to live it as she saw fit.

So she would do this on her own.

CHAPTER SEVEN

GABRIEL DID NOT go back. He was proud of himself for that. Because there were a few times over the course of the next six months that he had gotten close to breaking. Once, he'd even arranged for a plane.

He would have gotten on it, with no clear intention but to see her again, get his hands on her again, but he'd received an email from Alexandre that day about some party in Alis he wanted Gabriel to attend.

Gabriel had canceled the plane immediately, gone to the insufferable party and thought of Evelyne the whole time.

But he knew what would happen if he ever went back to her. He would not be able to resist. Because separation had not dulled this obsession. He thought of her, dreamed of her, cursed her.

Wanted her with every breath, like she had become the very air he needed to survive. It was insanity, this warped thing inside him. Because he could think of nothing, feel nothing, want nothing but her.

He would not allow it to tear him apart a second time. Perhaps it felt different from before. He thought more of *her* than avenging her.

But at its heart it was the same, so what did it matter?

When his phone rang one night as he tried to convince himself to go out, find a woman, he saw the screen read

Alexandre and he answered it, teeth gritted. He felt an immeasurable guilt every time he spoke to his friend that did not go away with time or separation from Evelyne.

"Alex."

"You must come at once," Alexandre said with no preamble. "And I cannot explain until you get here."

So, quite against his will, Gabriel flew to Alis that very night, because Alexandre had not sounded himself, and it worried Gabriel. He arrived in the dead of night, and it was Alex himself who let him into the palace.

The prince *never* answered the palace doors.

"What is it?" Gabriel demanded on a hushed whisper—the dark, silent halls around them seemed to demand it. Everything felt wrong, but Alex vibrated with a strange kind of energy.

He leaned in close. "My father is dead," he whispered.

Gabriel wasn't sure he understood the words. "I beg your pardon?"

"We have not made it public yet. The doctors thought they'd be able to save him at the eleventh hour, but he took his last breath right before I called you. I have much to do. A million arrangements to make." He raked a hand through his hair, an almost never seen movement of being overwhelmed from the pri—the *king*.

Because the old king was dead. Enzo was…dead. It felt impossible, but Gabriel knew he had to be more than shocked. Alexandre had called him for a reason. For help. He would jump to do whatever Alex required.

"What can I do?"

Alex turned to him as if he just remembered he'd been the one to call him here. "You must bring Evelyne home."

Ice slid through Gabriel's veins. Evelyne. Home. He had to clear his throat to speak. "I'll send for her."

"No. No, you must fetch her. This is delicate. I have taken the oath, but until the coronation happens, things are very complicated. Especially with the general. I want her here for the coronation, but I do not want it to be publicized. Not yet. You must go get her and bring her here without anyone in the palace knowing. Ensure she is safe. We will not make the announcement until she is here."

"Are you certain…" Gabriel wasn't sure what he meant to ask, so he only trailed off, not sure how to proceed.

Alex laughed. Not a joyful sound, but not a bitter one. Just a kind of wondering. "He just…keeled over in front of me after dinner."

Gabriel said nothing, let Alex talk. Clearly he needed to say it, accept it.

"He was talking to me, muttering about some slight handed to him by some diplomat. He was planning a war." Alexandre shook his head. "And then he put a hand to his head, complained of a headache and just…crumpled. The doctors believe it was a stroke." Alex looked around the darkened entryway as if seeing it for the first time. "He is truly dead, Gabriel. I saw it for myself. A stroke."

"A stroke of luck, perhaps."

"I suppose," Alex agreed. He was looking into the dark shadows of the hall. His voice was very quiet, very tortured when he spoke. "He lay there, Gabriel, and I did not want to call for help."

"And why should you?" Gabriel returned, knowing his friend needed assurance, comfort, even as Gabriel's mind whirled with thoughts of Evelyne. "But you did call for help. There were doctors. So there is nothing to concern yourself over," he said fiercely, because he could see Alex doubting himself and it would not do.

One of them was a good person, and one of them was not. Alex would always be the good. Gabriel…never now.

"I suppose." Alexandre shook his head, as if to scatter unwanted thoughts. His gaze zeroed in on Gabriel again. "You must bring Evelyne safely home, Gabriel. As quickly as possible. I want my family together. To usher in a new era for Alis. A good one."

Good. God, Gabriel hoped so, but first he had to face Evelyne.

What he had done.

And would no doubt want to do again.

Evelyne was humming to herself as she turned into the drive. Her monthly appointment with Dr. Stevens had gone well. She liked the doctor, even if he was a bit elderly. He was sweet and kind and asked no probing questions about the missing father of her baby—unlike some of the nosier ladies at the general store who wondered aloud why they never saw her husband.

Dr. Stevens answered all her questions with a calm patience that soothed her. He was like a father—or perhaps grandfather—figure. And when he gave her advice, she listened. Like when he'd told her to stop reading about pregnancy online—her anxiety had calmed quite a bit since she'd done so.

She found she fit in better with the elderly population of Bay's Point. She did not know how to relate to people her own age, though she had tried. It wasn't just that she was a princess, or had been raised so differently from the younger people of town, it was that she was pregnant, and alone, and, probably since everyone thought her incredibly wealthy, they viewed her as an oddity. Not a potential friend.

But the older people of the town seemed hell-bent on

making sure she was hardly the oddest thing *they'd* ever beheld, and there was a great comfort in that.

"Maybe I do not have any young friends yet," she said, talking to her baby bump as she often did. "But we do have *friends*, and they will be very helpful when you arrive, I have no doubt. You'll have better honorary grandparents than your actual grandfather, that is for certain. And then, perhaps when you are in school, there will be other children's parents to befriend. Maybe by then, I won't be so odd."

It was a comforting thought, if a bit of a stretch. But kindergarten in the States started at five. She could enroll in a preschool before that. It *felt* a million years away, but she was assured by anyone she talked to that the years would fly by.

And she would have a baby. A child. "You will be the light of my life," she murmured as she drove up the winding drive to her house. There would be no cruelty. No punishments. There would be only love.

She reminded herself of that any time she considered calling Gabriel's emergency number. That her baby would be wanted and loved and feel nothing but *joy*. Maybe Gabriel would not reject a baby as he had rejected *her*, but Evelyne refused to take that chance.

Still, it left an ache in her heart. For him. For home. For family.

"And maybe someday, when it is safe, I will be able to take you to Alis and show you your birthright."

She thought of her home, her brother. Would Ines be pregnant yet? The only reason for Alexandre to get married was to produce an heir. Would they have children around the same time and never know it?

She shook that depressing thought away. "Only happy thoughts," she told them both cheerfully.

But the attempt at cheer was immediately threatened by an unfamiliar car parked in her driveway and the worry that fluttered in her chest at all the possibilities.

But then she saw the man on her doorstep. He was not unfamiliar.

She sat in the driver's seat, simply staring at him. Maybe in those first few weeks she had allowed herself the tiniest seed of hope that Gabriel might return, but once she had come to accept she was pregnant, she had not allowed herself errant thoughts of his return.

She did not need him and his rejections, and neither did their baby.

But there he was. Looking as handsome as ever. Visions of their night together tried to take up residence in her brain, but she shoved them away. For many reasons, but the most important one was the child of theirs she was growing.

Some small part of her wanted to get out, dash to him, throw herself at him and tell him everything. Beg forgiveness. Beg him to love her, take her, care for them.

And that was so sad and desperate she stayed where she was. She had to figure out a way to get rid of him without him seeing. She didn't know what his reaction would be, and he'd *left*. Never checked in on her.

So his reaction did not matter.

But she could hardly just ignore him. He was *right there*, staring at her as he came down the stairs and toward her car.

Handsome. So *stern*. She did not understand what about *her* brought out the stern and tortured in him when what appealed to her was his charm and light with everyone else.

Tentatively she rolled down her window. "I do not recall

issuing you an invitation." He did not need to know about the gift he'd left her with.

Not until she knew why he was here anyway.

"We do not have time for childishness, Evelyne. Get out of the car. Pack a bag. You must come with me."

Childishness. So disdainful, so demanding. After the way he'd left her. "Why should I?" she returned archly.

He studied her face in return, and her heart trembled. He was so serious, and clearly here against his will. This was definitely not reconciliation, so it had to mean something was *wrong.* "Is it Alexandre? Is something wrong?"

"Alex is fine. It is your father. He suffered a stroke."

"A stroke." She couldn't imagine it. The hearty, powerful, untouchable King Enzo Lidia...suffering a stroke.

"He is dead, Evelyne." Gabriel moved closer to the car. "You may return home. For good."

Evelyne tried to absorb those words, but they refused to penetrate. Dead. Return home. Dead.

Dead. Her father, her own personal demon, was dead. Just...gone. In the blink of an eye. And she could go *home.*

"Get out of the car so we may have a real discussion," Gabriel ordered. "And get you back to Alis."

Home. Dead. It was all so much to wrap her head around, and he was right. She couldn't just sit in this car and wait for him to go away, even though she needed more time to figure this out.

He thought he would take her *home.*

She looked up at the beautiful house she'd tried to accept was hers forever. She had spent time forcing herself to think of this place as the place she would raise her child. And there *were* so many things she'd learned to like about this place, this house.

But particularly since becoming pregnant she had *ached*

for home. For her brother. For the familiar. She *liked* her friends here, but it was not the same. She had known she couldn't go back, would never subject her child to an Alis ruled by King Enzo, so she'd tried to accept that.

But what about an Alis ruled by King Alexandre? It was almost unfathomable in all the positive possibility.

She looked at Gabriel, who studied her with his dark eyebrows drawn together. Perhaps she should refuse. Perhaps that was her only choice to keep her child a secret.

But why should she now if there was no King Enzo?

Because he *left you*.

Which felt a bit childish now that there was more at play. She had to figure out how to work through it somehow. Sitting in this car wasn't that. So she picked up her purse, her jacket. She tried to arrange them all in front of her so that she could hide the bump. It wasn't unwieldy just yet, but it was getting there.

Carefully, angling her body just so, she got out of the car. She didn't bother to look at Gabriel. "This feels like some kind of…trick."

"It is no trick. The king died yesterday. Alexandre has tasked me with bringing you back home before the announcement is made to the kingdom and then the world. He wants you at the coronation."

Coronation. "Alexandre will be king." She wasn't sure she'd ever be used to it, so sure it would not happen until they were both old themselves. "He will…" Tears filled her eyes. Not just hormones. A relief from a tension she hadn't known she carried. It fully hit her now, with Alex in charge, he would not be in danger from her father's vicious whims. With Alex in charge, everything changed. Decades before she'd thought that possible.

But in her emotion, her *elation* and relief, she didn't hold the bag and coat just as she should. She saw Gabriel's eyes widen. She tried to recover, but it was too late. He'd seen.

He pointed at her—at her stomach. "What is that?" Gabriel demanded.

She had dreamed of this in her weaker moments. Telling him that he was to be a father. In her fantasies, she was calm, casual, disdainful almost. She did not give him the satisfaction of thinking that she needed him, wanted him, or was afraid of being alone.

She was determined to make fantasy a reality.

So she beamed at him, made sure she sounded cheerful. "In the States they call it a baby bump." She ran her hands over the roundness, moved to give him a profile view. Refused to let the nerves fluttering through her show—she'd had ample practice at hiding those. "Isn't that cute?"

He said nothing. Didn't move. She wasn't sure he breathed.

When he finally moved, it was with clear-cut precision. "Explain yourself," he said quietly, dangerously.

She chose to maintain her flippancy. "Is it not self-explanatory, Gabriel? I am pregnant."

"By whom?"

She startled a bit at that. She'd *assumed* he'd jump to the natural conclusion. Did he really think she'd just…immediately hopped into some townsperson's bed after him?

It ached, almost as bad as him leaving her. That he'd think so little of her. She refused to even acknowledge the question. "I will need some time to pack." She started to walk up to the porch, but he caught up with her.

She expected him to take her by the arm, but he stood in front of her blocking her bodily. Like he was afraid to touch her.

She almost hoped he was.

He pointed at her stomach again. "Evelyne… Is that baby mine?"

He was so *good* at poking at her temper. She used her purse to slap him across the chest. "Of course it's yours, you asshole." And with that, she pushed past him and stormed inside.

CHAPTER EIGHT

GABRIEL STOOD IN a bright sunshiny end-of-summer day in Maine in *America*, winded.

Of course it's yours.

It couldn't be. None of this could *be*.

Not because it was impossible—in his lack of control he had not used protection, a fact he remembered all too clearly *now*. It was impossible because he did not know how to move forward. When he *always* knew how. He had made mistakes before, but none had cut him off at his knees leaving him reeling and absolutely uncertain how to…exist.

Even losing his control and sleeping with Evelyne had left him with a clear course of action. *Leave. Never return.*

He could not leave now. He could not take her back to Alis in her condition.

What had he done? And what the hell could be done *about* it?

Of course it's yours.

A child. A *child*. He had left her six months ago and she'd carried a *child*—his child—all this time and…

And not told him. She had kept this a secret from him. If the king had not died… She might never have told him. A child would be alive, breathing, growing and he would not have known.

It was enough of a glimmer of something to *do* that he

stormed inside after her. He found her in the kitchen, humming as she put together a sandwich. Happy as you please, and definitely not packing as she'd claimed.

"You had my contact information," he blurted out.

"I did," she agreed. She took a big bite of the sandwich, looked at him with a careless smile. "I chose not to use it."

He opened his mouth, surely to say something intelligent and cutting. All that came out was some kind of pained grunt.

"You left, Gabriel. You made your feelings clear. You wanted nothing to do with me."

"You is not the same as *our child*." He did not like those words, could not fully engage with *child*. He had to think of this as a problem to solve or he might be forced to...*feel*.

There was a moment she held herself *very* still. Whatever reaction she had to the somewhat insensitive words was hidden in that stillness. She carefully set the sandwich down on the plate in front of her.

"Our." She laughed—it wasn't bitter, but it wasn't happy. "*Our.* How would there be an *our* anything, when you won't even deal with me? You run away."

The characterization of what he'd done—when what he'd done was *save them both*—still grated. "The last time I checked, people who run away did not leave their *contact information*."

She had the gall to roll her eyes. "You made it clear you wanted nothing to do with me. I mean, aside from sex. You seemed to enjoy that quite a bit."

"As did you, *principessa*." Which was neither here nor there, and certainly not the *point*.

She made a low, satisfied kind of sound that went straight to his loins with an arrow sharp intensity.

"How did you plan to explain this?" he demanded, so as not to think about his physical reaction to her.

"I didn't," she returned. She sighed in a way that made it clear she had had *months* to deal with this while he had only had *minutes* so far. "I would have kept him a secret forever," she said, and clearly meant it. She settled a hand over her burgeoning belly with a gentleness that thundered through him in ways he couldn't parse.

But he could not even be hurt by her *forever* because...

"Him." She would have kept *him* a secret forever. A boy. A son. No... He couldn't...

She was quiet for a long moment, almost looking sad. "Yes. Congratulations, it's a boy." She lifted her chin, finding her haughty. "I will *not* be naming him after you."

Naming... A boy to be named. His boy. His *son*. All Gabriel seemed to hear now was a high-pitched whistle in his ears.

"Do you need a paper bag?" Evelyne asked. When he stared over at her in confusion, she shrugged. "I saw this funny old TV show where someone hyperventilated into a paper bag."

"I am not hyperventilating," he ground out.

"Close."

"Evelyne, this is a mist—"

"Do not finish that sentence," she said fiercely, skirting the counter and stalking toward him. "I will not have anything bad said about my child. *Ever*. He will be loved and treated with kindness. Always. And he will never, ever, not *once* be made to feel as though he was a mistake. He will never be a mistake to me, no matter how you feel about it."

Gabriel wanted to tell her it was impossible to ensure a child was *always* treated with love and kindness, but she looked so fierce, with her arm curved around her belly. In a strange, blinding moment he knew she would be a good mother. She would protect the child—their child—in all the ways she had not been protected *and* all the ways she had.

And what would he be?

A father. He did not know how to wrap his head around this. His life had been nothing but skating the surface of anything so important as *fatherhood* since he'd been eighteen. Only Evelyne had taken him back under dangerous old waters.

The things he would do for her without a second thought, the violence he would enact throughout the world to keep her safe. Perhaps he would never turn it on her, on their child, but he had the potential to be an echo of King Enzo all the same. A *reminder*.

What would a child do to him? What would that kind of love and devotion create inside him?

It was terrifying. Overwhelming. He needed to somehow keep this…separate.

Why was she always overwhelming him when he had *learned* for years to fight against anything that might wave over him and crush him?

But he looked at her and felt endlessly crushed. Not just by this *child*.

How could she be more beautiful than when he'd left her? How could the obsession run so deep that cold turkey had not staved off this destructive need? She was *pregnant*, ripe with child, and he wanted to touch every inch of her, hear her pant his name again.

Which was no doubt incredibly inappropriate. Obsession and destructive need. He could not be destructive with a child's life at stake. He needed to focus on the practicalities. On what must be done.

Not *her*.

"I have a plane waiting, Evelyne. If there is anything you want or need, I will collect it for you. But we must hurry."

She cocked her head, studying him. He couldn't possibly read her mind. Didn't want to, at *all*.

"I can get my own things. Pregnancy is not fragility." But she did not make a move to get her things. She continued to study him and went back to eating her sandwich. When she finally spoke, the question was one that he was trying to avoid thinking about.

"What do you think Alexandre will say?"

Gabriel could not begin to guess. There would be no approval, no celebrations, certainly, even if he somehow fixed this so Alexandre did not know about the six-month abandonment. Alex would not *approve*.

So Gabriel had to find some way to ensure it. Practicalities. Legalities. He was good at both these things. They were part of his job. How could he use his expertise to make this all right?

The only way Alexandre would even begin to accept this were if certain…legalities were in place. It was not what Gabriel wanted, but he would have to make it work somehow.

Without destroying them all.

"If we take the personal out of it, you are the princess. A baby out of wedlock will be frowned upon," he said, knowing he sounded stiff and not being able to do anything about it. "Not just by Alexandre, but by the kingdom as a whole."

"Are you suggesting we marry, Gabriel?"

She said it like a joke.

It wasn't a joke. "I am not suggesting. I am stating that we will be married, Evelyne. Now, in fact. Before we return to Alis."

Evelyne stood stock-still, watching him as he moved into action. He disappeared and returned with a laptop bag. He pulled out the computer, sat at her kitchen table and began to…work.

Marry. Gabriel. She should be appalled, she knew. He wasn't marrying her out of anything but a sense of duty or whatever to Alexandre. He did not *like* her, and she needed to really accept that. She did not want her child growing up knowing his father did not like his mother. A forced marriage certainly wasn't going to make that fixable.

"Gabriel. Alis might be a bit old-fashioned and traditional, but perhaps this is an opportunity to usher in some modern ideas. Like, I don't know, not making each other miserable with a marriage neither of us want."

It was a lie. She did kind of want it. Because she liked *him*. But that was pathetic, and even if *she* didn't mind being a bit pathetic here and there, she now had a child to concern herself with.

She would not be pathetic for him. She would be strong and right and true. She would be an example of love and… and goodness. No matter the effort it took.

Gabriel looked at her, eyebrow raised in cool disdain. "Do you really think the time around your brother's coronation is the time to introduce *modern* ideas? Particularly when you have an entire army moving from a war-hungry king to one who will promote peace, and well they all know it."

Fear gripped her. She'd thought the danger died with her father, but… "Do you think he's in danger?"

"No," Gabriel said, with a certainty that eased some of her concerns. "Alex knows how to handle things. I'm only saying, I will not be adding to the things he has to handle. Any more than I already have."

Right. Because she did not just get to go *home*. She had to bring home a complication. She rubbed the swell of her stomach, chewing on her bottom lip. Should she take her child back to Alis with all this hanging over them?

But she thought of Alexandre. Of the palace. Of *home*. Even if her father had made her childhood hell, there was so much she yearned for back in the place she'd been raised. She wanted her son to have family. She wanted her son to have…

She studied Gabriel. She had not allowed herself to consider him as a father. As *the* father. She had spent considerable time just focusing on her and the baby. What she had, not what she wanted.

Now he was here. He was taking her home. He was talking about *marriage*. And it wouldn't be the kind of marriage she wanted, she knew that, but what if…

She shook her head. No. She couldn't introduce fantasies she'd avoided for six months just because he was here. She moved over to him though, peered over his shoulder at what he was working on.

It took her a while of watching him to fully understand what was happening. He was…working to forge some kind of marriage record.

For six months ago. As though they had married *first*. A legitimate child under law. She wrinkled her nose, trying to work through how she felt about it. An unnecessary lie— she would *never* allow her son to feel *illegitimate* just because of how he'd been conceived. But this was something that would make Alexandre's life easier. And probably her son's, if she was being realistic.

But there was something under the practicalities. The war of truth and best choices.

"Ah, so we are not *actually* getting married." She refused to sound disappointed. She was *amused*. Damn it.

"There may be no ceremony, the date might be fudged,

but it will be *actually* for all intents and purposes," he replied, without looking up at her. "From here on out."

It wasn't romance at all, and still her heart fluttered. They would be married. *From here on out.* And what did that mean to him?

"We will be husband and wife to everyone who knows us," he said, returning to his all-important computer.

"Will you share my bed then?"

His fingers fumbled on the keys, but he did not look at her. "That is hardly a concern right now."

"It is one of my concerns."

"You have a one-track mind," he muttered, typing away again.

"No, it has many tracks, actually. Some more enjoyable than others. For instance, I like to wonder what he'll look like, or plan the nursery, rather than read, think or *imagine* labor." She shuddered at the thought. There were so many worries, and she'd had to step away from them or get lost in them.

But there was one inevitability. This baby would come out of her one way or another. And the bigger he got, the bigger she got, the more impossible and inevitable it seemed.

She thought she could endure that inevitable if she was home. If she had the familiar, without her father's overbearing evil.

She thought—and knew it was wrong to think it—if she had Gabriel by her side to be her husband and this child's father, she might endure it just fine. Even if he didn't love her or like her.

Haven't you had enough of that in your life?

But Gabriel, for all his faults, was not her father. He was not *cruel.* His dedication to Alexandre no doubt meant he would be dedicated to their child.

Didn't it?

"We have not discussed what kind of father you will be. You can forge whatever documents you wish, tell Alexandre we are married, but these are…small details. The most important thing is this child."

She wasn't sure his expression was one of hurt. No, it was more…arrested. "I have a very good father. A very good example to follow."

"That makes one of us. What made him good?"

Gabriel blinked as if he did not know what to do with the question. "I suppose… He was a good man, who balanced his own needs with the needs of his family's. I assume my parents love one another, but I think just as important, I never doubted my father's respect for my mother."

"So you will have to work on that then."

He regarded her with a mix of emotion in his gaze that she could not quite make out. It was serious, weighty, but she did not know what it *meant*.

"And he did not leave us in Alis to become a pawn of the king," Gabriel continued, without addressing her comment.

"The dead king," Evelyne said, because she was still having trouble believing it's true. "My father is dead and I am free."

He glanced at her then, specifically at her belly. "You're pregnant, not free."

She didn't wish to engage with that, so she wafted away from him. "So the plan is to waltz into the castle. Hello, Alexandre. Allow me to kiss the ring, Your Majesty. Oh, by the by, I married your best friend. Baby on the way." She patted her belly to emphasize.

Gabriel was scowling now. "If that's the way you want to characterize it."

She did, because it felt silly that way. Not scary. Would

Alexandre be disappointed in her? Would this baby… It suddenly dawned on her, if she was going back that meant…

"Is there another royal baby on the way?" she asked Gabriel suddenly.

He regarded her with a puzzled frown. "Not that I've been told. Why?"

Evelyne chewed on her bottom lip, a new trickle of worry jittering through her. "Do you not know the Alis law about heirs?"

"You'll be shocked to know I have not studied the line of the Alis throne."

She had been given no choice and had never given it much thought because of course Alex would be first.

But he wasn't. "The firstborn of the king's children is the heir. It does not matter who the parent is. Alex will be king as long as he chooses, of course, but then…"

"You're saying our child will be the *heir*? That we have… usurped that from Alexandre's future child?"

"I do not think Alex will mind overmuch." She really didn't, but it felt good to say out loud. "I do not think being an heir served him enough to care about that. Though he might wish he hadn't capitulated to father and married. I quite like Ines, and maybe he does too, but it is certainly not love."

"She has made him a good wife. He has said so."

"Ah, romance *does* exist," she said sarcastically.

He did not engage with that. He closed his laptop and stood. "Now that we are married for all intents and purposes, it is time to go, Evelyne. It should all be settled by the time we land. If there is anything you want, I will send for it once we arrive in Alis. Alexandre will not relax until you are home, safe and sound."

"Even if I'm pregnant? And his best friend is the father? And, oh yes, we're married. Very relaxing thoughts."

"Perhaps relax is not the right word," Gabriel muttered. "But we must go anyway."

So Evelyne allowed herself to be led out to the car, away from the house she'd tried to make her own, tried to love. Away from the ocean and its comforting power.

And started the journey back home.

CHAPTER NINE

GABRIEL DID NOT believe in *anxiety*. He was not a man who allowed himself to worry. He dealt with. He acted.

But the tight band around his lungs as they drove up to the palace under the cloak of night was *something*, and he could not seem to work his way through it.

He felt Evelyne's hand curl over his, squeeze. He was horrified she might see the worry in him, but when he glanced over at her, he realized it was she who was worried. She watched the palace get closer with wide eyes and clear distress.

But when the car pulled to a stop at one of the private, side entrances, she let out a slow breath and smiled over at him.

"Thank you for bringing me home."

How could she undo him so simply? To thank him for something he wasn't even doing *for* her. He was doing it for Alexandre. If it had been up to him…

Gabriel said nothing and got out of the car, but he skirted the hood and made it to her door before she managed to open it. He did so, then braced himself for impact and offered his hand to help her out.

She took it, and he was grateful that in the dark he could not make out the expression on her face. Or he might be inclined to keep her hand in his. He might be inclined to hold her close and assure her everything would be okay. Instead, he broke the contact.

Except, it was dark out here, and he worried that in her condition she might trip over something or… Cursing his life choices, he tucked her arm into his so he could guide her. "I will come back and get our things later," he told her quietly. The door had been left unlocked for him, so he pushed it open and ushered her inside.

Much like when he'd arrived the night of the king's—the *former* king's—death, the palace was dark. Gabriel led Evelyne through the dark hall, keeping her arm in his, until they reached the king's wing.

Alex had instructed them to meet him in his private library, so that was where Gabriel lead Evelyne. The warmth of light from the doorway cascaded out into the hall, and Evelyne's pace increased when she saw it, their arms disconnecting.

Gabriel told himself it was relief that coursed through him. Certainly not regret.

She made it to the door before he did, and stopped there, taking in whatever sight was before her. Gabriel couldn't help but watch her face. The excitement, the joy, the relief, the *love*.

It roiled around inside him like a sickness, but he forced himself to continue forward. To step into the library with her.

Alex was pushing himself out of a chair. He set down the book he'd been reading, his eyes on Evelyne.

"Evelyne." Alexandre moved toward her with a genuine smile on his face. A rare thing for a very careful and private prince.

King, Gabriel corrected himself. Alexandre the *king*.

Evelyne's expression bloomed, and tears filled her eyes. She moved for him too. They embraced tightly, and said nothing, but the way they held on to each other spoke volumes.

Gabriel had understood that they worried about each other, but he had not realized perhaps how much that separation and worry for the other had weighed on each of them. How much they had simply missed each other. Though Alexandre had spent many years at boarding school with Gabriel, it was no doubt the siblings had long since relied on each other to be safe places in their father's awful kingdom.

They had both done some excellent acting over the past nine months to pretend as though the separation had not been as soul crushing as it had been for them.

It eased something inside Gabriel to see them together. To see them happy. A relief, his own version of joy, and feelings deep enough to cause him even more worry. This was not the surface level he needed to operate with.

Until Alexandre moved back from Evelyne with a frown on his face. He looked down, and while the coat she wore hid much of her shape, no doubt the tight hug gave away what lay beneath. "What…"

"Surprise," Evelyne said cheerfully. She shrugged out of the coat she'd been wearing that had somewhat hidden her baby bump. She turned to Gabriel and handed him the coat. The worry and nerves he'd seen in her eyes on the drive in were nowhere to be seen now. Gabriel knew it was an act, but it was a hell of an act.

"Evelyne…" Alex was shaking his head. "What…"

"I know it's a surprise, but I hope not an unhappy one." She patted her belly. "I am happy, and I think that should be taken into account. I know how much you respect Gabriel. We only kept it a secret because of Father. And now he's gone, so now we don't have to. You're happy for us, aren't you?"

"Happy…" Alexandre's eyes moved from Evelyne's stomach to Gabriel. "You…"

Evelyne moved over to Gabriel, slid her arms around his waist, looked up at him lovingly.

An act, he reminded himself when the warmth of the gold in her eyes shuddered through him like a promise.

"Gabriel saved me. Not just from this place and the general, but my sanity when I was alone and homesick. He was so kind and understanding and…caring. Which, as you know, was in short supply around here."

"Evelyne, I don't understand," Alexandre said, moving his gaze from Gabriel to his sister.

But she kept chattering on, inventing this phony love story. "I've always had a kind of crush on him, but this allowed us time to really get to know one another as people, as adults, and why… I just couldn't help but fall for him." She patted Gabriel's chest, grinned at Alex as though everyone was just as happy as she was pretending to be. Instead of shell-shocked on his way to fury—which was what Gabriel thought Alex was.

"I'm sure you can't blame me for that. You know what a good man Gabriel is. And well, I happen to think I'm a bit of a catch myself," she quipped.

Gabriel could not bring himself to look at Alex. His gaze was caught on Evelyne's hand on his chest.

He needed to get her a ring. And since that felt like something blatant he should have thought of, his only option was to cover her hand on his chest with his own. Hide his failing until he had a reason for it.

"It wasn't that we wanted to get married without you. It was just…we wanted that commitment. That promise to one another." Evelyne beamed up at him. It was *almost* too much. *Almost* amusing. He *almost* found himself smiling back down at her. "We certainly couldn't wait—or thought we couldn't—for Father to die. So we married, and now we are expecting."

"Married. Expecting…" Alexandre said these words like he didn't quite understand the meaning of them.

"I'm sorry if that ruins your…procreation plans," Evelyne said, looking at Alexandre now. "It was not exactly planned. We got carried away on the wedding night… Well, you don't need to hear *that*. I only mean to say, I don't wish you to be angry with us."

"Of…of course not." Alexandre cleared his throat. "Surprised, but not angry. Perhaps without the pressure, Ines will… Never mind." He raked a hand through his hair, reminding Gabriel of the night King Enzo had died. "You must be exhausted," Alex finally said, his voice sounding a little rough. "We can… Let us get some sleep, deal with everything…in the morning."

"Alex…" Evelyne crossed to him then. Before she could say anything, Alex put his arm around her shoulders.

"I am happy for you, Evelyne. Very happy. It has just been…a lot of change in a short period of time. We will get through it, but I think it's best if we all get some sleep tonight."

Evelyne nodded. "All right. Yes. I'm…so happy you're king now." Gabriel watched her swallow. *This* emotion was not put on, even if her story was.

Then her gaze tracked to his. "Gabriel has taken such good care of me."

Which was a *lie*. He had left her alone for six months. Pregnant. She held some blame for that—she *could* have told him. But he still felt the guilt sting.

"But I'm so happy to be home," she continued.

"A joy only equal to mine, Ev. Get some rest now. I… I should go tell Ines you are home." His eyes darted to her stomach, then to Gabriel. "We'll have a nice family breakfast in the morning. The…four of us."

Alex crossed the room to Gabriel before Evelyne moved. "Congratulations, brother." And Gabriel might have been fooled into believing there was an actual congratulations behind that, but Alex didn't stop there.

He spoke the rest quietly, possibly so that only Gabriel himself could hear. "We will talk in the morning. *Before* breakfast. Alone."

And he did not sound like a man talking to his friend.

He sounded like a king ordering his subject.

Evelyne walked to her room in silence. She didn't know what to say, and it was so dark and quiet in the hallways. She was exhausted, and a little hungry. She didn't have the energy to ask for something to be sent up, but she did have some snacks in her purse.

She yawned as Gabriel opened her old bedroom door. How funny to have Gabriel in her old room. It felt like her previous life had belonged to a different person. The thought of poor, cowardly Jordi almost made her laugh.

Gabriel was a great many things, perhaps even a coward when it came to *her*, but she had no doubt he'd stand up to any threat for her and her child. He wouldn't run away or stand down to a threat. Even if he didn't love her.

He was here, wasn't he?

She stopped short a few steps into the room. Everything looked…exactly the same. She turned a slow circle. A picture of Alexandre and their mother still sat on her bureau. The linens on the bed were the same she'd picked out when she'd been sixteen—pink and frilly, befitting a princess. Everything in this room spoke of a life of ease and luxury and royalty.

She supposed that had been purposeful. Some of the staff knew how her father treated his children, but he also kept much of it under wraps. This had all just been a veneer over the horrible truth.

And still, she'd *loved* the pink, the ruffles, the picture of the mother she'd never known. Much of the decor didn't fit who she was anymore, but it still felt familiar and like home.

Home. Except with none of the old fears. Because her father was dead. Every shackle, every abuse she'd suffered here was just gone.

Evelyne did not know how to fully absorb it just yet.

"What is wrong?" Gabriel asked when she just stood there.

"Nothing." Evelyne blinked back some tears, no doubt aided by the hormonal parade going on inside her. "I just assumed… I assumed Father might wipe any sign of me out, but everything is still here. Untouched, almost."

"No doubt Alexandre's doing."

"No doubt," she agreed, finally moving forward. Alexandre. She thought she'd done a pretty good job of smoothing over a lot of unexpected information, but… "He didn't seem happy," she murmured, wandering over to the cushioned window seat. Though it was dark outside, she could picture the gardens in her mind.

"Did you expect him to be?"

"I suppose not."

"He was happy to see you, Evelyne."

She inhaled deeply. Yes. Perhaps he'd been a little off-kilter, but there *had* been so many changes, and he was no doubt bearing the brunt of them. Well, now that she was back perhaps she could take on some responsibility, ease some of his.

She turned to face Gabriel. To deal with the fact it wasn't just her same old room, it wasn't just Alex, Gabriel was in her life now. Permanently, more or less.

She studied his expression. Guarded. Stiff. He didn't want to be here, but he was. What did she do with that?

A childhood of abuse, coupled with a brother who did everything he could to protect her from what parts of the abuse he knew about, had taught her that her only option was to roll with the punches.

She thought she'd done a pretty good job, through the past nine months of her escape and exile. And something about this pregnancy had supported the one truth she'd held on to to get her through the tough times.

Yes, there were *always* tough times, things to endure. But there was also always goodness and hope and something lovely on the horizon. Life was peaks and valleys of good and bad—sometimes all at the same time.

So it was imperative to reach out and relish in the good, hold on to it while it was there. She could be offended by Gabriel, she could be mad at him, she could bemoan the fact he didn't love her.

Or she could just enjoy him. Take what good there was in this situation and let that outweigh the bad.

She studied the handsome man in her bedroom, who she was now technically married to even though they'd said no vows. Perhaps that was not *good* as a whole, but there were parts of good to be found within this situation.

"I suppose you will have to share a bed with me, whether you want to or not," Evelyne said, trying for innocent, no doubt sounding smug. "If you want Alex to believe my little story."

"And what a story it was," he muttered. He ripped his tie off and tossed it on the chair. Frustration was at a boiling point, she could tell. And perhaps it was her great tragedy that she *liked* his boiling point. She *loved* when he lost control.

It was like seeing under a very shiny surface. Oh, she'd enjoyed his smiles and charm. The innate ease of friendliness he'd moved about the palace with *before*, but seeing the explosions underneath had revealed a much more interesting and alluring man.

Or you're just really messed up.

He undid the top button of his shirt like he was feeling a bit...strangled.

"Let me help," she said, moving over to him. She reached up to the second button and undid it before he grabbed her wrists and stopped her forward progress.

"We will not be doing this again," he told her darkly, stepping away from her and letting her wrists go.

She sighed. Would she always be throwing herself at him? Maybe. And maybe she should find some sort of shame over that, but for all her exhaustion, there was something else winding its way through her body, and she wanted him to take care of it.

Six months she had done her level best not to think of him, what he'd brought out in her, what they'd brought out in each other. But he was here now.

She smoothed her hands up his chest, just as she had done the first time she'd thrown herself at him. Would it ever get old? Would it ever start to be embarrassing?

Or was the sex just *that* good?

For both of them. Whatever his reservations about her, they were not their physical compatibility.

She still remembered the exact growled tenor of when he'd said she *haunted* him.

Had he thought of her in such ways these past six months? She hoped it tortured him, the thought of their night together.

But not enough to withhold the same now.

"Why not? We are married. You said so yourself. We are *actually* married and will function as such. I will not tolerate affairs, so I suppose you shall have to settle for me if you're expecting to enjoy more than your hand."

He scowled at her, but she saw the sparks of heat. Of want. Whatever he thought of her as a person, there was no denying they had chemistry.

A good. A good she wanted to enjoy.

"If you're worried about the baby, it is perfectly safe. Every book I read said so with annoying clarity." She moved to him again, this time putting her palms on his chest like she had the first time she'd kissed him. "Like a constant reminder I *could* be having sex with you and wasn't. Because you weren't there."

He looked down at her, his expression stoic and unmoved. But his body wasn't.

"What do you think is happening here?" he demanded.

"We are married. I like the way you make me feel. I like *you*. I don't know why you hate me so much, but I know you enjoy my body."

His scowl deepened, if that was even possible. "I do not hate you."

"You do a marvelous impression of dislike then."

"Dislike." He said the word with such disdain. "If only I disliked you, Evelyne."

She cocked her head. He sounded so *tortured* and she didn't understand. "I think if you liked me, you wouldn't be so dismayed to find yourself here." And still she moved her hands up his chest, around his neck, pressing her body against him—though that was quite a different experience with a baby bump between them.

"It must be nice to have such a simplistic view of things. Like. Dislike. Black. White."

She wondered if it was a flaw in herself that she found his disdain so funny. "All right. I have a simplistic view, what with this simplistic life I've been given." She gestured around her. She didn't need sarcasm to do the hefty lifting here. The palace itself would have been a complication even if her father had been given a heart.

Nothing was ever simplistic, but maybe that's why she did not get hung up in the complexities. They simply were.

"What is your complex view of the situation, Gabriel? Enlighten me."

"You are a smart, vibrant young woman." She thought he made a kind of move to remove her arms from his neck, but it was almost like he was afraid to touch her, even though she was touching him. "Your resourcefulness has been incredibly impressive. You're even funny, when you aren't trying to torture me. I have no reason to dislike you. Except for the torture, I suppose."

I have no reason to dislike you. It wasn't poetry, and yet she felt her poor romantic heart softening. He'd called her impressive. "Then why do you *behave* as though you dislike me?"

"Have you ever considered something darker and far more volatile?" he demanded. "Has it ever occurred to you that my obsession with you is unhealthy and that your insistence we act on it makes an already difficult situation untenable?"

He sounded so—the word he used—tortured. It made very little sense to her, but she liked the explanation. If it were true.

"You're obsessed with me?" She eyed him critically. She didn't know how leaving her for six months was obsession, but if that's what he claimed...maybe she'd claim it as well. "Though a six-month disappearance doesn't quite support that theory, I rather like the idea."

He shook his head as if despairing of her. "You won't," he said darkly.

"Perhaps I should be the one to judge." She moved to her toes, managed to angle herself enough to press her mouth to his. She wanted obsession. That all-encompassing need and pleasure she'd found in his arms back in Maine.

She wanted *him*. Here in her old life that would soon become her new life. With him and their baby. So *many* complexities. But what else was new?

He kissed her back in spite of himself, she knew. That it was physical reaction, not choice. Because he kept his hands off her, like he thought he could avoid this if he only kept his hands away from her body.

She pulled her mouth from his, scowled at him. "Oh, touch me, Gabriel. It is what we both want."

As if he'd been waiting for a command—and God knew he was not waiting to be told what to do, since he *couldn't* be told what to do—the leash on all he held back broke.

His hands were reverent, and it send waves of warmth and need through her. It was different, because her body was different. Because they were married. Because they were home. Because nothing had actually been settled, but he couldn't run away this time.

She wouldn't let him. Alex wouldn't let him, and actually, she didn't think he'd let himself. He would feel too responsible for the baby she carried now that he knew about his existence.

And so while the tensions he tightened inside her were the same, it was not the storm crashing between them. It was not anger and fear, and maybe that word he used—obsession. It was something deeper.

They were in it now. No way out. So they sank into the ocean that took them over. Onto the pretty pink bed, ridding each other of their clothes, until they were skin to skin, body to body.

His mouth tasted, his hands tormented in all the best ways. His body was a thing of glory—muscled and masculine. She roamed him with her hands, with her mouth, as he returned the favor.

When he moved her on top of him, seated deep inside, she looked down at him and felt like the ocean herself. A powerful, undulating storm that would not be satisfied until she'd crashed to shore over and over and over again.

And his gaze, stark and hungry, a powerful magnet. She moved against him, and they watched each other as the tension grew, coiled, and hers…exploded. He sat up, holding her in his lap, still deep inside her, and pushed her up, up, up again. Closer and closer to one more shuddering release.

She held on to him, whispered his name, reveled in the physical glory. She bit his shoulder, and he growled as his grip tightened, as his body tightened and then thrust one last time, pulling her down tight on top of him so that she catapulted one last time into that vibrating ocean of pleasure he always gave her.

Life was not simple, no, but it was so simple to give herself over to him, to enjoy him, to be with him just like this.

And when he did not immediately lecture her or get out of her bed, she smiled and curled into him. Perhaps he did not want to be.

But he was hers now. She cuddled in closer, rested one hand over her belly.

Theirs.

CHAPTER TEN

GABRIEL WAS NOT surprised to be summoned to Alexandre's office before the sun was up the next morning. He was already out of bed, watching Evelyne sleep, when the tap at the door came.

He could not come to grips with his next steps. So much of what she said made sense—they enjoyed each other, they were married, she was already pregnant, why not have sex? Why not share this bed and this room and behave in all the ways a married couple expecting their first child should?

But he knew the answer. Because he could not trust himself. The darkness of this obsession would only sink deeper and deeper until it damaged *something*. He didn't know what yet, but it didn't matter. The fact she even threatened the surface way he'd moved through life proved to him he could not be trusted.

But there was a child now. An undeniable fact. Staying away from her was not the answer, but what the hell was?

He had to find a way to…fix it. But he had time. He had three months to figure out how to navigate this before their child arrived. That was his deadline.

He would never remind her of her father. He would never give his child a reason to fear. There had to be some alternative.

When Gabriel walked into Alexandre's office, he found

him seated behind the desk waiting for him. He had not taken over King Enzo's gilt, over-the-top office, but had instead continued to use his own. Minimalist and stark, no doubt in direct response to his father.

Still, this was not a welcoming environment. Gabriel was not surprised there was no evidence of any place for him to sit.

This was to be an interrogation. One he undoubtedly deserved.

"Good morning, Your Majesty." Gabriel greeted Alexandre with as much royal reverence as a man who did not particularly believe in kings could manage, even for his best friend.

Alex did not return the greeting. "Please explain to me how you have come to be secretly married to my sister. How she is *with child*, and how I clearly would not have been privy to either piece of information if my father had not died unexpectedly and I demanded you bring her home."

Gabriel had to work not to scowl, because it reminded him that *he* would also not have known if not for that. And blame or anger or hurt had no place inside him if he was to make the appropriate plans for Evelyne and their child.

"Perhaps we should toast to Enzo's gift to us?"

"Answer me, Gabriel."

Gabriel didn't sigh, though he wanted to. He stood, hands clasped behind his back, searching for some explanation that was the truth because he did not wish to lie to Alexandre. But there were certain lies that must be told.

"Evelyne and I…" He struggled against the need to rub his hands over his face. *Evelyne and I.* Parents. Married. "She is an intelligent, witty, beautiful woman, and while I certainly didn't expect to…be so taken with her, it became undeniable."

"She may be all those things, but you took her away at my bequest—young, alone in a strange place, bereft, and dependent wholly on you."

Because those things were all technically correct, except maybe the bereft part, and yet didn't take into account the *scope* of Evelyne and all she was capable of, Gabriel stiffened. "I do not take advantage of women, if that's what you're accusing me of. I would never take advantage of Evelyne. Perhaps she is stronger than you give her credit for."

"You do not take advantage of women, agreed, but ever since…" Alexandre let the silence stretch out between them. Long and meaningful. Meant to be heavy and perhaps even a little cruel. A reminder of Gia, and what he'd been willing to do to save her.

Gabriel could not deny he deserved the stark reminder.

"You have not been serious about anyone since then," Alexandre continued. "I'm not sure you've been serious about anything, except maybe your work and even then, there's a certain casualness to your success there. And now you have married and impregnated my sister, two very serious and permanent steps. You can understand my concern."

"Yes, I can. It…was not planned. It came as a surprise, these…feelings for her." He sought to find some fine line of truth inside the lie, sought to not wince at the word *feelings*. He had to walk this line, between convincing Alexandre he could handle this without diving into obsession and violence, but that he was also not *flippant* about the situation, or Evelyne. "I tried to maintain a certain superficial distance, but it became impossible. She is…unique. It pains me not to give her what she wishes." Truth enough.

"And what do you wish, Gabriel?"

Hell if he knew. But he met Alex's hard gaze. "I shall endeavor to make them both happy."

"Endeavor," Alexandre scoffed. "Such a bland word."

"What would you prefer?"

"Ensure."

"Very well, I will ensure they are both happy." He did not know how he could possibly ensure such a thing, but he supposed he had no choice now.

Alexandre narrowed his eyes, studied Gabriel with that quiet, stoic intensity he had employed even as a boy. Like he'd been born with such abilities. Born to be a king.

"You are my best friend. I respect the man you have built yourself into. And while I know *you* do, I do not hold your youthful indiscretions and Gia's influence against you. We all have crises of self and fate, particularly at eighteen. It is not the crises that define us, but the choices we make in the face of them."

Gabriel felt as though he was a young man getting a lecture from a much older person. Perhaps his own father. Someone he'd *also* have to tell about this, but he wasn't ready to consider his parents just yet.

"My sister is now the mother of the future monarch. Your life will change. You did not know that going in. You thought, like I did I would imagine, that my father would hold on to life and the crown for quite some time. But these facts change things."

"I am aware."

"Are you?" Alexandre replied, quite royally. He stood now but stayed behind his desk. "You will be given a title. We will have a royal wedding ceremony of some sort. Your child will be the future king or queen of Alis."

It was…too much. Too many things to fully engage with. He wanted none of those things, but he could hardly deny them. The child existed. He would be an heir. *He* would be… "Future king. It is…a boy."

"A boy," Alex repeated.

And they stood there staring at each other, that fact between them, both perhaps feeling like they were children again, wondering how the years had zoomed ahead to the point where they were the ones *having* children.

"Evelyne has not had an easy life. I know on the surface it is all privilege, but surely you understand just how...ugly things have been for her."

"Yes." Gabriel gave Alexandre the only truth he had in him now. "I will do everything in my power to shield her from all the ugly from here on out."

Even if the ugly was him.

Evelyne was starving when she woke up. When she glanced at the clock, she couldn't be surprised Gabriel was not in bed. She'd nearly slept the morning away.

"All the books say to enjoy that now," she said, running a hand over her stomach. "That you will be keeping me up at all hours of every night soon enough. You wouldn't do that to me, my darling, would you?"

She got out of bed and moved into the closet. She frowned at her options. Since she hadn't had a chance to pack her maternity clothes, she only had items that suited a much thinner and different woman.

"What I have back in Maine will be suitable sometimes, but I will need an entirely new maternity wardrobe for royal events and the like, if your Uncle Alexandre has any plans to announce my marriage and pregnancy to the public."

She smiled at the idea of *Uncle Alex* as she found a pair of soft, stretchy pants that were a bit tight as such, but she rolled the waistband down under her stomach. What had once been a dress now fit like a somewhat odd tunic. She studied herself in the mirror, chuckled in spite of herself.

"Not very princessly, I must say."

"Who are you talking to?"

She glanced up at Gabriel. She hadn't heard him come in, and now he stood in the entrance to her closet. "The baby."

He looked dubiously at her stomach.

"You should give it a try."

He did not respond to that invitation. "Alexandre has requested our attendance at lunch since you slept through breakfast."

"Good. I'm starving."

She slipped on the sneakers she'd worn yesterday, which made her clothes look even more ridiculous. Then followed Gabriel out into the hall. She tucked her arm into his. He stiffened, though he didn't pull away.

"Are you afraid you'll lose all control and take me on the table in front of my brother and sister-in-law if we touch arms on the way?" she asked him lightly.

"You are such a comedian, Evelyne."

She laughed in spite of herself at the disgusted note to his tone, but then she was distracted by her surroundings. She came to a stop in the hall, stood there for a moment, absorbing all the details that remained the same despite her father's absence in the light of day.

"Is everything all right?"

She looked up at Gabriel. "Yes. Better than. I was just thinking how it's all the same even without Father here, and yet…it *feels* different. Lighter. Like I can breathe."

"Strange how a lack of threats of beatings might allow a person to breathe."

Before she could decide how to respond to that, she heard her name being called. She turned and saw Ines bustling toward them.

Ines smiled brightly at her and greeted her with a light

kiss on Evelyne's cheek. "It is so good to have you back. My world has been *very* masculine since you left." She held Evelyne at arm's length. "And look how pretty you are. Glowing."

"I don't know about all that. The wardrobe certainly leaves something to be desired."

"Excuse me, ladies. I have a quick call to make. I'll meet you in the dining room."

They nodded as Gabriel took his exit and the women tucked their arms into each other's as they walked down the hall to the dining room.

"I told Alexandre already, but I did want to apologize. It never occurred to me that… Well, I wasn't thinking about heirs and such. Especially all the way over in America. It was not my intention to take this from you and Alex."

"Of course not," Ines soothed.

"I'm sure Alexandre could change the law!" She grabbed on to Ines's arm, because the truth of that occurred to her. "Oh, that's it! It's so hard to believe he's king now, but since he is, he can change anything he wishes. He can certainly make your future baby the heir instead."

Ines smiled tightly and said nothing, which made Evelyne realize she was being…horribly insensitive. Alexandre and Ines had been married for nine months now, and there was no discussion of a pregnancy.

"I'm sorry. I…" She shook her head, squeezed Ines's arm. "I've read so many different women's accounts, it should have dawned on me that it might not be… That this may be a delicate subject for you. I'm so sorry, Ines. Tell me to shut up."

Ines shook her head. "You have nothing to apologize for. According to the doctors, everything is fine. No fertility issues, for either of us. It simply hasn't happened yet.

They've encouraged us to be patient. Alexandre and I have not discussed it yet, but for me, I do not care if our child… should we have one, is heir or not. I know it is why Alexandre married me. To have an heir." Ines swallowed, but though she was friendly toward her sister-in-law there was a careful wall between them. They were not real friends.

Evelyne hoped someday they could be.

"Everything will be just fine." Ines patted her arm and led her into the dining room. "Alexandre will handle it as always. You don't need to worry at all. Now, let's eat."

Alexandre was already there, and they exchanged pleasantries, sitting down. Gabriel came in as the food was being put out. The conversation was superficial, friendly and *weird*.

Evelyne kept expecting her father to come storming in. Any time the door opened—whether it be someone to bring in more food, take away dishes, or bring Alex a message— she flinched.

She hoped it wasn't noticeable, but knew it was when Gabriel put a hand on her leg. He would not offer comfort unless she was very obviously doing a bad job.

"I suppose we must have some formal ceremony for Father," Alexandre said as the meal wound down.

"Must we?" Evelyne muttered, earning a bit of a chuckle from Ines. When Alex gave them both a cool, kingly glare, they sobered.

"Why not tell the truth?" Evelyne suggested. "He was an awful man, and we do not mourn him, and they shouldn't either. They've lived under his reign. I'm not sure anyone would be surprised to find their war-mongering king a violent and vicious man everyone is glad is dead."

"What does the truth get us, Evelyne? I am afraid all it does is make us look complicit. Which isn't wrong, but I'd rather not advertise it."

"It *is* wrong. What were we supposed to do? Foment a bloody coup?"

"Instead, we did not rock the boat and people suffered. It is not so simple."

There was that word again. *Simple.* No, nothing was simple. People had suffered. *She* and Alex had suffered. Suffering seemed to be the theme.

She glanced at Ines and Alexandre. They did not look at each other, regard each other, or seem to connect in any way. Did they suffer too, in this marriage they had not wanted?

The thought depressed her.

"Perhaps we can do a three for one. Coronation-funeral-royal wedding ceremony," Evelyne said on a hefty sigh.

Alex *tried* to keep his frown in place. She *watched* his lip twitch ever so slightly though. She'd amused him in spite of himself.

And that's how she knew she was finally, really home.

CHAPTER ELEVEN

GABRIEL HAD NEVER minded a royal event before, but he'd never had to attend one as *part* of the royal family. In the past, he'd shown up as a guest, which required almost nothing from him.

Now he was involved in a flurry of events, meetings, debriefings, fittings, plans. Because he was to be an *earl*. Gabriel tried not to be bitter about such things. If he'd wanted to steer clear of royalty, perhaps he should have kept his pants on.

First, Alexandre had announced the king's passing and Evelyne's return. He let the people draw their own conclusions about that and enacted a small, private funeral that was photographed for the Alis papers. No videos were permitted. No public ceremonies were planned.

None of the former king's citizens protested, though there was some grumbling from the general and his army. Gabriel did not know what Alexandre did to handle it, but it was handled.

And then coronation arrangements went into full force. The planning was giving Gabriel a headache, and he could only take so many work calls to get himself out of fittings and meetings to go over protocol. Because it wasn't just Alexandre's coronation. The marriage and Evelyne's pregnancy would be announced and then Gabriel would also be given his title.

It was to be a day of looking forward to a positive future, so Alexandre and Evelyne said. Gabriel felt mostly dread. With his parents due to arrive tonight, the festivities beginning tomorrow, he did not know what else to feel.

This was not the life he'd planned—which only reinforced the strange notion he hadn't *really* had a plan. Work. Be successful. Skate through life without following into the depths of rage and obsession that might otherwise grip him.

Was that a life? He didn't like to think too hard on that question that lingered.

After ducking out of a protocol meeting to deal with some work, he tried to escape to Evelyne's room, hoping she would be off with her own meetings and fittings.

But when he strode in, he found she was having a fitting right here. Someone had set up mirrors and one of those awful platforms, and two women were bustling about Evelyne dressed in her royal finery. They pinned this, tutted over that, made notes on little pads of paper.

But Gabriel simply stood and watched her. She looked so regal and at ease. A princess through and through. That tight fist of need centered in his solar plexus. He didn't know how to fight it. Days and nights with her only seemed to make the band tighter and tighter.

Her gaze met his in the mirror. Her mouth curved like she could read his thoughts, and they pleased her. Did she not understand the ticking time bomb inside him?

"We'll make these last-minute adjustments, ma'am," one of the women said as the others began to tidy.

"Thank you, Joan." The other woman helped her out of the dress. It looked like it must weigh as much as armor. Gabriel frowned a bit, wondering if he should intervene. She should be off her feet more, not worried about these frilly royal events. One of the attendants helped Evelyne into a robe, and she finally stepped off the platform.

Once finished, the women gave him little bows as they left the room.

Gabriel nodded at them, but his gaze stayed on Evelyne. She belted the robe above the swell of their child.

"Are you hiding from your protocol meeting?" she asked, her smile amused rather than disapproving.

"I do not hide, Evelyne."

"Of course not," she agreed, making him want to smile.

He resisted. "Are you sure you should be putting yourself through all of this?"

"I feel fine," she returned. "I always enjoyed this part of royal life. I know it sounds silly, but when Father was alive, I liked to think of it as a symbol. If I looked royal, then behaved as kindly and charitably to everyone I met, it meant that even though *he* wasn't those things, there was some hope. For anyone who looked at me and saw those things." She sighed heavily, looking away from her reflection in the mirror. "Perhaps Alexandre was right, and we were just complicit, and I like wearing fancy dresses."

She didn't look miserable exactly, but he could see just how Alexandre's words at lunch the other day had disturbed her. Gabriel knew Alexandre carried ridiculous weights on his shoulders that weren't his, but he hadn't expected such from Evelyne.

"It's far more complicated than that, as I think you know," he told her with some force. "Complicit victims are still victims."

She looked up at him, a smile on her face. "I'm glad you think so."

When she looked at him like that, a hint of vulnerability in her happiness, he wanted to say a million things that would cause her to look at him just so. Like he was always her savior.

"I don't like to think of myself as a victim though. Look around, Gabriel. It was hardly a hardship."

"Your father beat you."

She inhaled, held it there for a moment. "Well. Yes."

"Did you think you deserved it?" he demanded, because the thought she might not know it was just wrong, simply wrong, and no amount of *amenities* made up for it, filled him with a rage he had no outlet for.

The king was already dead.

"Well, no. I mean..."

"Can you imagine laying a hand to...our child?" He tried to avoid discussing the baby too much, interacting with the idea of a child too much. Whatever securities he could implement to keep himself detached, surface level.

She met his gaze, searching for something. He turned away before she answered.

"No," she said quietly.

"Then that is all you need to know." He stared out the window, wished it was the Maine house with the terrace doors and cold whipping wind outside. He'd go stand there and watch the storm and be stilled.

He felt her come to stand next to him. He didn't dare look at her.

"I suppose your parents never..."

"No. Not once. It never occurred to me that they might. My father's disappointment held much more weight than any threat he might have given me."

She tucked her arm into his, leaned her temple against his biceps. "I am excited to meet them. I'm so happy our child might have one decent set of grandparents."

They would be that. Gabriel hadn't spoken to them much. They were overjoyed—not so much at the royal side of things, but that he'd met a nice woman and settled down— their words.

They did not know about Gia, about what was inside him. They did not know obsession could turn to violence. That every step of loving Evelyne and their child was a chance he'd become his own version of King Enzo and his parade of destruction.

So they only saw the positive. Gabriel was glad for it, but it made him dread their arrival more than look forward to it as he might have otherwise.

Gabriel left her, but his words, his assurances didn't. It was a comfort that he didn't try to undermine the abuse. Alexandre didn't do it on purpose, but sometimes she thought since he considered it *his* due, he considered it hers as well.

Which wasn't fair. Alex had protected her and spared her as much as he could. She knew one of the weights on his shoulders was that he had not done *more*, but sometimes it felt like he thought of her like...another country he had failed.

Rather than a sister he had done his level best to protect.

She sighed a little wistfully. Perhaps she could convince Gabriel to have the same talk with Alexandre that he'd just had with her. Perhaps Gabriel could get through to him and allow him to realize that no amount of abuse was their *due*.

She patted her stomach. "And that, my sweet baby, is just the kind of man your father is. For all his faults."

She should start getting ready for dinner. She was eager to meet Gabriel's parents, as he spoke so highly of them, but she was tired and achy and procrastinating.

When the room phone rang, she thought about ignoring

it, but guilt and responsibility were too much to ignore it. "Hello."

"Your Highness, Mrs. Marti has requested an audience before dinner. I have her in your sitting room, but I can tell her you are not ready for visitors if you prefer."

Evelyne sat up in her bed. Gabriel's mother wanted an audience *before* dinner. Without Gabriel? Nerves danced around her chest. But she could hardly say *no*. "I'll…be there momentarily."

She moved out of bed quickly. Luckily she'd already picked out the dress she'd wear for dinner. Since tomorrow would be full of formality, it was far simpler. And comfortable. She hurried through getting dressed and took enough time to brush out her hair and make up her face a bit.

Once ready, nerves battling around inside her, Evelyne forced herself to enter her sitting room. She was a princess. She was incredibly used to walking into meetings with people she didn't know what to expect from.

But she had never wanted to impress someone so much as she wanted to impress Gabriel's mother. She couldn't help but think that would go a long way in…something.

When she entered, Mrs. Marti stood and curtseyed prettily, making Evelyne feel a bit awkward even though she'd been curtseyed to often in her life.

"Sorry to keep you waiting," Evelyne offered, plastering a tight smile on her face and walking over to Gabriel's mother. She was a small woman, trim, her dress a beautiful plum that surely made her look younger than she was.

"A pregnant woman never need apologize for that." She crossed to Evelyne. Took her hands. Her smile was wide and welcoming, and there was an array of emotions in her expression Evelyne couldn't all parse, but she recognized them as happy ones.

"He has your eyes," Evelyne blurted out, then felt heat creep up her cheeks. What a silly thing to say.

But Mrs. Marti beamed. "Yes. My eyes and temper. Hopefully the baby will escape the temper part." Before Evelyne could think about *temper* and *Gabriel*, his mother continued. "You are looking lovely, Your Highness. You probably do not remember when we met before."

"I'm sorry. I didn't realize we had."

"It was the last time my husband and I visited Alis, before we decided to not return ever again. You were only three or four. And pretty as a picture, as you are now." Mrs. Marti squeezed her hands then began to bustle her to the couch. All the while talking.

"I didn't want our first meeting to be some formal royal affair. I know Alexandre means well, but he is just a man and cannot understand such things sometimes."

Evelyne smiled in spite of herself as she was nudged into a sitting position. "Yes, he is just a man."

Mrs. Marti laughed and sat next to Evelyne. "I wanted just a few moments to meet the man my son married without telling me."

"We are sorry."

"I understand that things with King Enzo were…complicated. I can't hold it against you, as much as I might like to." She smiled though, like she really did understand. Then she picked up a small package from the table. "I brought this for you."

"Oh…"

"For *you*. Not a baby gift, though I will shower my grandson as well when he arrives, but I always thought the woman carrying the child never got enough attention."

Evelyne felt overwhelmed with too many emotions to

name. She didn't know what else to do but open the gift when Mrs. Marti urged her to.

The box was small, the beautiful pendant inside delicate and stunning. And it reminded Evelyne of Gabriel's eyes.

"You're a princess so no doubt you have access to the most beautiful jewelry, but this is an heirloom. It has been passed down in my family for many generations."

"Mrs. Marti—"

"Bianca."

"Bianca… I couldn't possibly—"

"Gabriel is my only son. My only child. I had always planned to present this to his wife once he married—unless I hated her."

Evelyne looked up at the woman, a little desperate to have this connection but not feeling like she deserved it. "You don't know me."

"I know Alexandre. I knew your mother. And I know my son. I won't hate you, Evelyne."

Evelyne's breath caught. "You knew my mother. I suppose I knew that, but I didn't realize…"

Bianca smiled sadly. "I'm not sure I knew her *well*, but we were friends as much as anyone can be friends with a queen. Manuel brought me to Alis after we were married. The king had not fully ended Alis's relationship with Italy yet, so Manuel was still working as a diplomat. Your mother and I were pregnant at the same time, so she would invite me to teas and such."

"Alexandre always says she was…perfect."

Bianca laughed. "No one is perfect, though I'm sure she was perfect to Alex. Poor boy. She was very good. Very, very kind. Too soft for the likes of this place." Bianca's smile went sad at the edges. "She would have loved you very much."

Tears filled Evelyne's eyes. She swallowed at the lump in her throat. She didn't have the words. She didn't have… anything. *She would have loved you very much* would stick with her for all her days.

"And since she is not here, *I* will be. Manuel and I have a life in Italy, but now that King Enzo is gone, there is no reason to fear coming back to Alis whenever it is wished. We will be at your beck and call, I promise." She patted Evelyne's stomach. "And his."

"Mrs.… Bianca… I…" She flicked a tear off her cheek. "I'm overwhelmed."

"You've had so much thrust at you, and so quickly. Of course you are." Bianca scooted closer, put her arm around Evelyne and squeezed. "And growing a little one is hard work—physically *and* emotionally. It's a study in overwhelm, but you'll handle it beautifully. I have faith in the woman my boy chose."

Chose. Not really, but Evelyne could hardly lay that at Bianca's feet. So she changed the subject. She pulled the necklace out of the box, fastened it around her neck. "How does it look?"

"Beautiful." Bianca beamed, her own eyes a little wet. "You're such a beauty, it's no wonder you caught Gabriel's eye, but you have your mother's kindness. It shines through you."

Evelyne didn't know what to say to that. It put a lump in her throat she couldn't speak around. She had this angelic idea of her mother, thanks to Alexandre, and even though Bianca did not consider her *perfect*, to hear a nice account, and that Evelyne might take after the woman she'd never met… It was just too much.

"I have worried about my Gabriel, you know. He used to be so driven as a young man. He and the prince so…full of determination and plans. Something happened when Gabriel was younger, I do not know what. I have never been able to understand, but he changed. Not at his heart, thank goodness, but just in how he moved through the world. Such a…lack of direction. Oh, he was successful, that business of his. Good at it, for certain."

Evelyne wondered if whatever happened was what Gabriel had referred to Alexandre saving him from. Whatever darkness might have ended him. What might have happened to Gabriel that even his mother did not know about? That would have changed him so deeply?

Would he ever tell her? It was hard to imagine a situation where he let her in that intimately. He was always holding himself just a little bit back. Claiming obsession and acting… She didn't know.

"But he lacked an…anchor, I suppose," Bianca continued. "He does a wonderful impression of a man who knows what he's after, but I'm his mother. I can see it. All I've watched him do for over ten years is *run*." She beamed at Evelyne. "And now he has you. The both of you. Do you mind?" She held her hand over Evelyne's stomach.

Evelyne shook her head, and Bianca put a hand on the swell of baby.

"I would so like to be his anchor. I'm not sure…" Evelyne struggled against the need to lay all her fears out on this woman she barely knew. This woman who would always be just a little bit more dedicated to her actual son than to Evelyne. She forced herself to smile. "He's been very good to me. I hope I'm as good to him."

"Let me tell you, Evelyne. *That* is a good first step to a loving, successful marriage." She said it so approvingly, Evelyne felt buoyed, even knowing the marriage wasn't real and likely would never be.

Even knowing Gabriel didn't love her so there was no *loving* marriage on the horizon.

But she was beginning to realize that she didn't just like him or enjoy him. She *loved* him. The man he was, even when he was trying to hold himself apart. His strength, his desire to protect. His intelligence and irreverence when he wasn't so worried about protection. He was just…exactly what she wanted.

Oh, he would not like her being in love with him. Not at all.

But there was nothing to be done about it now. Except decide how to deal with it. But first, dinner.

Evelyne swallowed at the lump in her throat, blinked away the moisture that threatened to fall. She straightened her shoulders. "Shall we walk down to dinner together?"

"I would like that."

CHAPTER TWELVE

"I LIKE YOUR WIFE."

Gabriel tried to smile instead of tense at his father's warm approval. "She is…" He watched her move around the room, talking to people at this interminable coronation where people wanted to congratulate him on his earldom and he wanted to jump out a window.

But Evelyne positively glowed. She spoke to anyone and everyone. Despite the baby bump, she seemed to simply glide through the room. People responded to her. They lit up right back. She had a warmth about her that Alexandre and Ines could not quite pull off.

Father chuckled, reminding Gabriel he was standing there, then patted him on the back.

"Your mother was worried this was some sort of…ploy to help Alexandre out, but it's clear you quite enjoy her."

Enjoy. Obsess. Was there a difference? "She is having my child."

Father made a noncommittal kind of sound Gabriel did not know what to do with. "Well, with all these changes to Alis thanks to Alexandre's rule, and a child on the way, your mother and I are pleased we will be able to spend more time with you and your new family here."

Family. Gabriel tried not to grimace at the word. At the idea that he would never be able to create the kind of family his parents had. That nothing would ever be safe if he let himself fall too deep into it all.

Still…

"I am glad you two will be able to make the trip more often. Evelyne is quite excited by the idea of our son having such good grandparents."

"I'm not sure how you spoil a prince rotten when you aren't royalty, but we'll figure it out."

Gabriel smiled in spite of himself. Though he tried not to look forward, to imagine what it would be like to have a son, to watch his parents be grandparents, he could not deny that making his parents happy always eased something inside of him.

But more, the *easing* came from the fact that Evelyne was now making her way toward them. Dangerous, dangerous woman.

"It is a good thing, son," his father said, somewhat cryptically by Gabriel's estimation. "Not always easy. Certainly not something you can skate through, but it is good."

Gabriel looked down at his father. *Skate through* felt a bit like an accusation.

Before he could decide what to say, Evelyne approached them.

"I hope you are enjoying yourself, Mr. Marti. Pardon me, Manuel."

"It is so good to be home, Your Highness, and not worry for my or my family's safety. Your brother will be a good king and make Alis the country I remember as a boy, I have no doubts." He turned to Gabriel and grinned. "And my son shall be quite the earl."

She beamed at him. "I have the utmost faith in the both of them."

"As do I. If you'll excuse me, I must find my wife. Make

sure some young man hasn't tried to abscond with her." He gave Evelyne a little bow and then moved off.

Gabriel watched Evelyne watch his father go. She had a bright smile on her face. No signs of exhaustion when no doubt she had to be. She had been running herself hard these past few days. It was clear she was determined to take some pressure off Alexandre's shoulders.

She finally looked up at him, her smile bright and her eyes full of happiness. "I love them," she said emphatically.

Gabriel made a noncommittal noise, realized it sounded like the one his father had made. Would his son take on this tradition?

Would Gabriel know how to handle the weight of that? Ever?

Evelyne took his hand in hers and gave him a bit of a tug forward. "I am afraid you are required by princess law to dance for at least one song with me."

"Are you not tired yet?"

"Not yet. Wired. I'm sure I'll crash when it's all over, but for now I would like to dance with my husband."

Husband. It was a farce, but the more Evelyne acted like it was real, the more it *felt* real. And he had to do a better job of keeping that wall up between them. Some kind of *formality.*

But she led him to the dance floor, and he did not know how to deny her when she looked so happy. He had promised Alexandre that he would *ensure* her happiness.

And he *wanted* to. "You look beautiful. I have not been able to take my eyes off you."

"I know." She moved in easy rhythm, that content and somewhat smug smile never leaving her face as he pulled her close for the dance. "I like having your eyes on me."

That ever-present heat crackled between them. He thought

if this did not exist, perhaps it would not all feel so peril-
ous. If he simply *liked* her. But he did not know how to save
her from this combination of every feeling—like and lust
and need and frustration and this strange, bubbling light-
ness that reminded him far too much of hope. So much like
when he'd been a young man, but worse somehow. Deeper
and more complex.

What was there to hope for here? That he somehow controlled himself for the rest of his life and never did anything
violent and dangerous in an obsessive rage? Never reminded
her of her evil father?

What impossible amount of control would appear out
of nowhere considering an impossible lack of one had led
him here?

"I think I felt the baby move earlier," she said as they easily moved on the dance floor to the music. "You're going
to call me silly, but I swear I felt this flutter of him when
Alexandre announced you earl."

"Yes, I will call you silly. If you felt anything, I'm sure
it was coincidence."

"Well, I will choose to consider it a son's approval of
his father."

"Ridiculous."

She laughed and lay her head against his shoulder on a
content sigh. "I knew you would say that."

They danced for the rest of the song and into the next.
For the first time today, amid the chaos and attention and
stress, he found himself relaxing. He held her close and enjoyed the bump of their child between them.

He did not allow himself to think of the way she spoke
to the baby growing inside her, the way she thought a *fetus*
would hear the worlds *earl* and do some little internal jump
for joy. He was afraid if he thought too much about any of

it, fell beneath that surface he was trying so desperately to hold on to, all he would create was ruin.

He needed space, and with the celebration winding down, and in her condition, he knew he could find it.

"Come, let me take you to bed." He cleared his throat. "To *sleep*."

She tilted her head up to study him. Smiled. "Perhaps I should not like to sleep."

He wanted to smile back. He wanted to get lost in the gold flecks in her eyes. He wanted so many things.

But he kept that wall up, that detachment. He fought with everything he had to keep that erected.

He made their excuses, escorted her back to her rooms and right to the bed—not for anything but *rest*.

"Sit," he ordered her.

She looked up at him through her lashes. "I only follow orders if I like where they're going to lead."

"They're going to lead to rest. You've pushed yourself these past few days. Fine enough if it were just yourself, but you are carrying around an extra human being."

"Boring," she muttered, but she sat down on the bed as he'd ordered.

He knelt and enjoyed the way her breath caught in spite of himself. But he was *not* giving in to the nagging want that hounded him constantly. He was going to ensure she got some rest.

He undid the fanciful buckle of her heels and removed one shoe and set it aside.

"Gabriel?"

He glanced up at her, saw there was a seriousness in her dark gaze that had him pausing. He did not encourage her to continue, but he watched her face as wariness crept into him.

"What happened when you were younger?"

He stiffened in spite of himself. He didn't know what she was getting at, except that of course he knew. He removed the other shoe and got to his feet. "You'll have to be a bit more specific." He picked them both up and walked over to her closet.

"The thing that changed you. That Alexandre saved you from. Your mother mentioned a change. I think they're one and the same, and I think I should know what they are."

He turned to face her slowly. She sat on the bed, a beautiful, stunning delight. He wanted to touch her, glut himself in her, over and over again forever.

He could distract her with that, avoid this question, but it would not be avoided forever, he knew. She simply wouldn't let him avoid it forever, and then what?

Did he lie? Did he get angry? Or did he do the one thing he'd never really done—because Alexandre knew what had happened because he'd been there, witnessed it. Gabriel had never had to explain it.

Perhaps…he should. Perhaps this had been the answer all along. Instead of a secret to hide, a tool to keep her from falling any deeper into accepting this obsession that would only hurt them all.

She would be frightened by this story, and he did not want that. With a bone-deep reaction, he did not want her to look at him differently than she did now.

But wants were dangerous, weren't they? If she didn't hero worship him, perhaps they could solve this problem. He wouldn't run away, she was right. He would not desert her or their son, but if there could be barriers…

To keep them both safe. They could have a marriage like Alexandre and Ines. For the greater good. A workable partnership, but none of this passion, none of these time bombs ticking inside him.

He had been depending on himself and himself alone to have control, but if Evelyne knew, if she understood, perhaps their control *together* would solve this.

He held on to this hope with a surge of determination. It *had* to be the answer. So he went about telling her something he'd never truly explained to anyone.

"I met a girl during my last year at St. Olga. She was a little bit older than I was. Perhaps a little bit more…worldly to my more privileged life. But I was quite taken with her."

"What was her name?" Evelyne asked softly.

"Gia."

"I hate her." She did *not* say this softly, and there was something…amusing about the simple jealousy that shouldn't exist and certainly shouldn't be *funny*. Nothing about this was a laughing manner.

He scrubbed his hands over his face, trying to put himself back there so he could adequately convey the depths and breadth of his lack of control, lack of sanity and decision-making.

This *thing* inside him that endangered her. *And* their son.

"She was beautiful, charming, fun. She…was exciting. Everything about her. I wanted to spend…all my time with her and the worlds she opened up, but she worked at the café we studied at, so she had responsibilities of her own. So there was…pining, I suppose."

Evelyne only scowled. In any other situation, Evelyne's expression would have amused him. She looked a bit like a spoiled princess, thwarted, when she was none of those things.

"But when she did have time for me, we enjoyed each other. Early on in our relationship, she confided in me that she had a stalker. A man from her neighborhood who followed her around, harassed her, though he'd never touched her. I promised to protect her. Happy to do anything for her, feel powerful and…" A savior. Just as he'd felt with Evelyne.

There was simply no way he could fool himself into thinking he could handle all that warred inside him when he dove beneath the surface of feeling. He would hold on too tight. He would scare and hurt her.

He had perhaps saved Gia from one awful thing, but he had only introduced another. How could he expect any different when it came to Evelyne?

He would be the monster Gia had once told him he was. Because he *was* that, deep down. His need to protect or save was only a function of some dark, horrible part of his psyche.

"As much as I don't relish thinking of you protecting any woman you slept with aside from me, that's hardly something to be ashamed of. You wanted to help. You always want to help. You're a good man, Gabriel."

He shook his head. "You are very, *very* far off, Evelyne. I… There is the same violence in me that was in your father."

"Don't be ridiculous, Gabriel. My God."

"It is true. I do not revel in it the way he did. I am not *proud* of it as he was, but it is there. One day I came to pick Gia up from her shift, and he was there. Her stalker had cornered her, put his hands on her, was trying to get her into his car."

Gabriel hated to relive this, but surely she had to see what a risk she ran. If he could get it through to her that surface was all he could ever be, then both her and their child would be safe from this dangerous, destructive thing inside him.

"I do not remember everything in that moment. Just the rage. In the aftermath, I know I pulled him off her, and I…"

Gabriel swallowed. "I cannot say I fought him, because he didn't fight back. I simply beat him."

"But he was hurting her," Evelyne said softly.

Gabriel shook his head. "Yes, but there were alternatives. Beating this man did not save her. She stood there, watching. Violence on top of violence. She was screaming at me to stop by the end. Thank God for Alexandre. He waded in, pulled me off, and asked if I wished to be the same kind of man as your father. It was the only thing that saved me from killing that man."

Evelyne was quiet for a very long time. He did not dare look at her. This story would have to change things for her. It had changed things for *him*. *Everything*.

"Gia called me a monster. And I *was* a monster. Even Alex saw it. He just knew how to stop it."

Still Evelyne said nothing. Gabriel realized he was breathing heavily, winded almost. Like something was happening inside him. Some great force of change.

He shook his head, pushed the heel of his palm to his chest. There was no change. Only the truth. "It is all I have in me, Evelyne. Obsession or nothing. Drowning or skating. There is no middle ground for me. And once the switch is flipped, I cannot be trusted to make the correct decisions."

She slid off the bed, moved over to him even as he held up a hand to ward her off. She took that hand in her tiny one.

"Gabriel, how silly to think so."

He pulled away from her hand, took steps back. Regarded her with as much ice as he had left in him. "I was hoping you'd be mature enough to understand."

She regarded him with that royal superiority he found infuriating. Because it made her seem infinitely *mature*. "You were hoping I'd run away. Since, this time around, you cannot."

"You'd be surprised what I could do, Evelyne."

She shook her head. "Perhaps this feeling you have inside you is true. I cannot believe it. I cannot buy into this story you've told yourself. Or perhaps Gia and Alexandre told you. You are no monster. You are *nothing* like my father. Rushing into *save* is not wrong."

"It is if you are willing to do worse." Would he have had any remorse in killing that man? In the moment, there had been *none*. Not until Alex had told him what he was in danger of becoming.

All because he had wanted to save Gia and make her love him.

Evelyne sighed heavily. "I cannot see this the way you do, Gabriel. I have been the woman in that scenario. And while Alexandre stepped in and stopped it when he could, I would have not called you a monster if you'd done to my father what you did to that man. I would have cheered. And I cannot find a way to feel guilty about that."

He shook his head. "You don't…" Of course, he couldn't say she didn't understand. Even though she *didn't*. She could only see this from her own eyes. Not from his. Not from Gia's. Not from Alexandre's. So while she might understand what it felt like to have someone step in and save her, she did not understand it to his degree.

"Perhaps you thought this story would change my mind about you, but it doesn't. And more, it doesn't change our reality. You have a responsibility to all the people you love, and no matter how you might wish to, you cannot walk away from it."

People you love… He looked at her in horror as that clutching feeling in his chest threatened to make it fully impossible to breathe. "Do you think I love you?"

"No," she said, with a sadness that cut through him like

a knife. "But I think if you let yourself fall from the surface, you could. I have certainly fallen in love with you."

The pain of that simple, easy revelation was unbearable. She couldn't… "Evelyne, what a mistake."

She shrugged. "People make mistakes. I have seen the width and breadth of mistakes people can make. For good reasons and for bad. I cannot… I cannot feel the way you feel about this. I'm sorry. I know you want me to, but I remember what it feels like to be eighteen and wanting to exact revenge. Older, in fact. If you recall, not that long ago, I was ready for poor Jordi to suffer my father's consequences because he had refused to run away with me."

"That is not the same."

"You're right. It's worse. Jordi simply disappointed me. He didn't try to *harm* me." She lifted an eyebrow. "Do you recall what my father was capable of?"

He shook his head. Yes, the king had been dangerous, and yes, Evelyne's flippant remark about blaming Jordi for her disappearance had not been a decision made with clear-headed thinking, but she hadn't *insisted*. She hadn't actually planned or plotted or done anything about it.

"Do you think I fear you? Because when you were young you hurt someone in an effort to save a woman you loved?" Evelyne demanded. "You think I fear *you* as much or more than I feared the man who *actually* put his hands on me in violence? His own daughter? Not a stranger harming others?"

Gabriel could not look at her. He hated when she brought her abuse up as if it was such a simple fact of life. But she was changing the subject, and he could not let her. "You should fear me. That potential that marred your childhood is inside me. I saw it. I felt it. You must fear me, Evelyne. It is our only hope."

She shrugged, so nonchalant. "I will not."

"And if the monster I have learned to repress threatens our son because that chain breaks? Perhaps I would never lay a hand on you or him, but that is not the only way to traumatize someone with violence. Gia saw a monster in me. She could never look at me again. She was right."

She heaved out a sigh. Frustration dug into her expression but not what needed to—that fear, concern, worry. *Anything.*

"I lived with a monster all my life, Gabriel," she said very directly. "Monsters do not have remorse. They do not concern themselves with the feelings of others. They do not listen to friends who intervene. You can try to convince me that somehow you are a threat, but I *know* threats."

"You cannot know every threat simply because your father beat you, Evelyne."

She inhaled deeply, eventually nodded. Some agreement that allowed a ray of hope to pierce through all this worry. "You are right."

Thank *God*, he thought, sure the heavy weight on his shoulders was just relief.

"But let me ask you this, Gabriel. Do you think I would have done anything but applaud if you'd been the one to kill my father, even in front of me?"

Gabriel didn't know how to fully engage with that question. It was different. She was conflating things, but he did not know how to get that through her thick skull. Because clearly it was just stubbornness that she didn't understand.

She couldn't possibly be *right* about things he'd been living with for over ten years. She could not see more clearly. She didn't understand.

"You wanted to protect a woman you loved. I cannot fault you for that. I cannot fault you for being angry enough to do something about it."

"I would have killed—"

"You do not know what you would have done, because you did not get the chance. Alexandre may have stopped you with his words, but *you* allowed those words to matter, Gabriel."

"I allowed nothing. I still *wanted* it, Evelyne. But I knew it would be the end of my life, and I did not want to hurt my parents. Thanks to Alexandre, I finally put something else ahead of my impulses, but only because of his interference."

"I suppose it's quite *simple* then," she said, the word *simple* dripping with sarcasm. "If you are in the wrong, then so am I. Because that doesn't bother me. Do you know how many plans I had to kill my own father? How I would have done it if I'd thought I could actually accomplish it?"

He wanted to shout. She was so frustrating. And purposefully so. Her wanting to kill her abuser was not the same. Could not be the same. "You...do not understand. You are young and naïve. This is more complex."

Evelyne had the nerve to roll her eyes. "Ah, yes, back to my simplistic views on life. How's this for simple? I think *you* are naïve, Gabriel. I think you stopped maturing in that moment. All your surface, all your...keep yourself apart. All it is is a childish desire to control...how you feel. How *I* feel. Instead of deal."

He found himself speechless. She was *wrong*. He didn't have to engage with her accusation to know she was just... flat-out dead wrong. Confused. *Sheltered* for all the pain she'd dealt with.

She would not accept this. She was too stubborn. Too certain of herself. Too used to having her own opinions verified. She could not understand.

It was unfathomable.

"Good night, Evelyne. Get some sleep."

She laughed, the sound a bit caustic. Harsh enough he felt himself wince. "Good night, Gabriel."

And he could have sworn he heard her say, as he left her room, *run away again*.

But surely he was imagining things.

CHAPTER THIRTEEN

EVELYNE HAD *NOT* slept well. She had been worked up in too many different ways. First and foremost, angry at the rigid thinking that didn't allow Gabriel to *understand*. That he would find fault with *her* rather than question his own misguided feeling.

But there was a sadness, a regret, underneath all that. Because she didn't know how to get through to him. She had known his issues had kept this barrier between them, but she hadn't understood how deep and how long he'd held these issues. Nursed them.

She wanted to have hope that when their baby was born, he would see life for what it was: complicated and difficult. There was always guilt and wrong choices, but on the other hand, there was always hope and good choices too. That he was not forever cursed by something he hadn't even done.

She did not understand punishing oneself for a choice they *hadn't* made.

But now she worried even the birth of their child would not soften him if her confession of love hadn't so much as slowed him in his tracks. If he could not admit he loved her, or accept she loved him, he would always hold this wall between them. Out of fear—not for himself, of course, but for those he loved.

And he did love, whether he admitted it or not. Just as she loved.

Funnily enough, this was her concern. That the deep abiding love he felt would be their undoing. It would maintain that wall, even in the face of their child. Perhaps especially in the face of their child.

Because he thought himself a monster.

He wasn't. At *all*, but he'd made her afraid now, that if they went on as they were, their child would only get glimpses of the real Gabriel. Forever. The loving man who existed underneath his need to be distanced from such feelings would be all they ever knew.

She tried to look at it from an unbiased point of view. Maybe she was letting her feelings for Gabriel soften the blow of this admission of his. Maybe he really would have killed that man had Alexandre not intervened. Maybe he *was* a monster, and because that was what she'd grown up with, she loved a monster. Maybe these were her own traumas and issues at play.

But Evelyne just kept coming back to what she'd grown up with. Men who wielded power and force to get what they wanted. Familiar? Yes, but not what she sought out.

This was not in Gabriel's heart, no matter how much he feared it. She had been the driving force in everything between them. Not *him*. And everything he'd done for her had either been in service to Alexandre, her, or his need to keep that wall between them erected.

Even when he'd been mean to her, tried to discard her, he hadn't done it with his fists. He hadn't even really done any damage with his words.

Or does love and lust cloud your judgment?

She didn't have any answers, but the idea of clouding her judgment gave her an idea. There was someone's judgment she always trusted. She got dressed for the day, forced herself to eat despite not feeling hungry at all.

"I will take care of you no matter what," she murmured to the baby.

Then she headed for Alexandre's office. Despite his assistant's many protestations that the king had an important meeting soon that he was readying for, Evelyne walked right in, closed the door behind her before his assistant could follow and interfere.

She flipped the lock.

"Alex. I need you to tell me about what happened with this Gia woman."

Alex looked up from his computer. He blinked once or twice, no doubt to focus on her instead of the screen. "Pardon me?"

"This Gia woman Gabriel was involved with when you both were young. This man he beat so badly. I want to hear your version."

Alexandre was quiet for some time. When he finally spoke, it was with an annoying lack of emotion. "It is not my place to tell his story."

Evelyne shook her head. "*He* told me his story. And expects me to…fear him now, or something. I want your point of view. I want your side of the story as an observer. So I can understand. So I can…figure this out."

Alexandre studied her for quite some time. When he asked his question, it was completely devoid of emotion. "Do you fear Gabriel?"

She rolled her eyes. "Don't be ridiculous. He is almost as good and honest as you."

"You say that like an insult, Evelyne."

She merely raised a brow.

Alexandre sighed, pinched the bridge of his nose. Eventually he got to his feet, came around the desk and took her arm. He moved her around his desk, nudged her to take the seat he'd left.

"You've been on your feet all week. You should be taking today to rest." It wasn't just admonishment. It was meant to be a kind of distraction.

It would not work. "Alexandre, tell me what happened back then. I know he says you stopped him from murder."

Alexandre shook his head. "I do not know that it would have been murder. It's…complicated. And in the past."

"Not his past. He's so convinced he's a danger. Something that's patently ridiculous as the worst he's ever done is speak a few harsh words to me—out of this same fear that he is bad. I just don't see it. He is so good, and I *love* him, Alexandre. I truly do."

She thought of the way he'd reacted to those words. By not really reacting. By essentially despairing of her. Calling it a *mistake*. But he did not seem blindsided by the admission. He did not deny those feelings.

"I've had my reservations about the two of you, but I am glad to hear you say so. You both deserve…the warmth in each other."

For a moment, she considered asking about Ines, about *warmth*—or lack thereof, but she could only deal with one problematic relationship at a time.

"So what am I missing?" Evelyne demanded. Maybe begged. "What isn't he telling me? Why can't I understand this?"

"What was his version of events?" Alex asked, very patiently.

She went through what Gabriel had told her, hoping she didn't leave anything out. She used the same words he'd used. Described it just as Gabriel had, without any of her own commentary.

"Do you feel like you are the only thing that saved him?" she asked.

Per usual, Alexandre took his time answering, but this was how Evelyne knew he would tell her the truth, not just pat her head and tell her not to worry.

"It is impossible to say. He did harm that man, but considering the man had been dragging Gia into his *car*, I do not see what the alternative in the moment would have been. I always thought... He was much too hard on himself. In that moment, there was only reaction."

"You told him he was the same as Father."

Alexandre's eyebrows drew together. "That is *not* what I said. I told him the man was unconscious—something he didn't realize because he was trying to neutralize a threat. All I said was that continuing was something our father would do."

It was Evelyne's turn to frown. It was essentially what Gabriel had said Alex had said, but...the way Alex said it now was...softer. Not an accusation. A reminder.

"Gia called him a monster."

Alexandre's expression flattened. A hint of his rarely freed temper flickered in his eyes for a moment. "He did not tell me that."

"And that is what he has thought of himself all these years. You were there, but you do not believe him a monster, or he would not have been in our lives. You certainly wouldn't have trusted him to save me from marrying the general."

"We know what a monster looks like, Evelyne."

"That's what I told him." Feeling despair that this wasn't actually getting her anywhere, just the same conclusions, she looked up at Alex imploringly. "Why won't he listen to me?"

Alexandre moved across the room, and back, pacing with his hands clasped behind his back. As though he was going over it all in his mind. "It has been many years, Evelyne. I have not been able to get through to him. I assumed marriage meant... He had dealt with it finally."

Evelyne looked down at her baby bump in spite of herself. She could tell Alexandre the truth of how her and Gabriel had come to be married, but it seemed neither here nor there. "I suppose a child...brought those feelings back instead."

Alexandre made a noise Evelyne didn't know how to characterize, and worried if she asked, he might start poking into places she didn't want him to be. Like how exactly she had come to marry his best friend.

"Regardless, Gabriel is not a monster," Evelyne said firmly. "He was not in the wrong."

"I do not agree with his characterization of events, but there *is* violence in him, Evelyne. I have seen it. I cannot deny that."

"To protect. Not like Father. *I* would have killed Father if given the chance. What does that make me?"

"Human, Evelyne," he said very gently.

"You wouldn't have."

Alex sighed. "It was certainly a thought that occurred to me a time or two. I am not immune. But I always knew...it would create more problems than it would ever solve. And lo and behold, a blood clot did the work for me instead."

"God bless it."

Alexandre's mouth almost curved.

Evelyne pushed to her feet, grabbed her brother's hands, squeezed. "How do I get through to him, Alex?"

He met her gaze with a sadness that had her heart sinking. "If I knew, I would have done it by now."

Evelyne wouldn't allow herself to cry, but she certainly *felt* like crying. Why should this be hopeless? Why should a good man be so convinced he was not one? When she'd grown up with men convinced of their righteousness that was nothing but madness and cruelty.

The door opened and Alexandre's assistant poked his head in. His expression was pinched, his gaze accusingly on Evelyne. "Your Majesty. The diplomats are *waiting*."

"Yes, I will be right there," Alex muttered, waving him away. "I'm sorry. I do have to go. And I'm sorry I could not give you a better answer, Evelyne. Perhaps time and this child will be what he needs. I have never given up on him. I know you won't either."

Give up on him. She couldn't imagine what would have to happen for that to occur.

Alexandre leaned in, gave her a rare show of affection with a brush of lips against her hair. "You will make an excellent mother, Ev. Your care for people is truly a gift. I hope Gabriel can accept it." He pulled back. "If you'll excuse me." Alexandre strode from the room, leaving Evelyne standing there moved. Teary.

And considering.

Alexandre had never given up on Gabriel. She knew just talking to his parents that they had never done so either, even if they didn't know about what had happened. No one who really loved him had ever really given *up* on him.

So if no one had, then maybe that was the answer, the things that would change his mind. Not the answer she *wanted*. Nothing warm, kind, supportive like she wanted to be.

Maybe this time someone needed to be strong enough to choose an answer that would hurt.

"But it might be the only thing to do," she said, running her hands over her baby bump.

She was going to have to give Gabriel exactly what he wanted.

And hope he realized how wrong it was.

CHAPTER FOURTEEN

GABRIEL SPENT THE next few days sleeping in the sitting room and considering his options. He was surprised and, if he was honest with himself, a bit disappointed that Evelyne had let him be.

She did not come to him to make arguments and further propose he wasn't a monster. She did not try to entice him back into her bed.

If he saw her, it was only in glimpses. They didn't eat together, sleep together, or even attend royal meetings together.

He thought she spent most of her time with Ines, but he wasn't certain. It ate at him, but he told himself it was for the best. Perhaps he had gotten through to her.

And wouldn't that be a boon?

He told himself it was indeed, even as he looked for her around every corner, at every table, and even in the sitting room at night. Because no matter how he tried to convince himself he had *won*, everything was unsettled.

It was a bit like watching a storm approach in that house in Maine. You could see it in the distance, feel it crackle with power, long before it ever made it to shore. In the peace between now and then, you could almost convince yourself this was it. This was the new normal.

When he came back to the sitting room one evening to find her sitting on the sofa, reading a book, he knew the storm had reached shore. Because she was never here, certainly this late, when she knew he might arrive to take his proper place on the couch.

But she didn't look like a storm. She was dressed in a flowy ensemble the color of bubblegum. It somehow made everything gold in her shimmer brightly, including her hair piled atop her head in some large clip.

She held up a finger to him, continued to read her book, then once she'd finished the page, presumably, folded the edge of the page over, closed the book and set it down on her lap. She met his gaze with hands folded over the book.

She looked so regal sitting there regarding him with a cool kind of detachment. Radiant and beautiful and like she alone ran the world.

He wanted to kneel at her feet, a great howling impulse he ruthlessly fought back.

His wants would serve neither of them. *Obviously.*

She did not invite him to sit, and he felt much like he had in Alexandre's office those weeks ago, explaining himself while Alex sat behind his desk. She had certainly picked up a few tricks from her brother.

"I have given your story much thought," she said by way of greeting.

Ah, so she was here to convince him he was wrong. Satisfaction wound through him. Not because she was finally fighting it, of course, but because… Because… Well, the fact it had taken her days to come up with a suitable rebuttal just proved his point, didn't it?

He would be damn glad to be proven right, he was certain of it. And how could she argue with it? She couldn't.

"Perhaps you are right."

He opened his mouth to argue with her before he realized she'd…said he was right.

She wasn't fighting. She wasn't telling him he was good. That his violent tendencies weren't unimportant.

She was saying he was *right*.

He did not have the words to respond to *that*.

"As much as I am not convinced, how can I be more certain of your feelings, the truth of you, than you are?" she said, with the wave of a hand. "You live in your body, your mind. I do not. Perhaps there is no evidence for *me* to believe this monster exists inside of you, but if you have determined it does, I cannot argue with you." She held his gaze, still cool and direct without a hint of any other emotion. "I have to accept it."

Accept... He was having trouble keeping up with her. She spoke so...decisively, dispassionately, as though they were having a meeting about royal protocol. Not...dissolving whatever this was that existed between them.

"We cannot have the marriage annulled, not with a child on the way. Not with how it might reflect on Alexandre and our son's future reign," she said flatly. "So I'm afraid that is out of the question."

"Annulled." The word echoed through him like some sort of bullet—causing damage as it ricocheted through his insides. Who had said anything about...

"And having grown up without a mother, I do not think I want my son to grow up without a father. Though Alexandre would be a fine stand-in. I do not think you wish to banish yourself from your child's life completely."

"Stand-in." She was talking about him...not being involved in their child's life? Talking about all this ending? *Banish yourself?* No... That was not exactly what he'd meant. Exactly.

It is for the best, some vicious voice inside him whispered. But that whisper had nothing on the howl of pain that echoed through his soul. Here she was, their child tucked up inside her, talking about annulments and banishments as though they were…choices on a menu. Considered. Rejected. Of no real import.

"But we do need to come up with *something*, don't we? To handle this…problem as you see it. I think I have come up with an answer. If you watch Ines and Alexandre, everyone thinks they are married, and they are legally, but they don't…behave as a couple. They sleep in separate rooms. They busy themselves with different parts of being king and queen. They are cordial, they support one another, but there is no…love. And certainly no passion. I have decided we will follow in their example."

She had *decided*. The princess's decree. And she left no room for argument, for this crumbling inside him. She simply kept talking about *plans*.

"We will move chambers. There are adjoining rooms we will settle into. We will keep our lives separate in private and come together when needed in public. When the baby comes, he will be with us until and unless we feel the need for a nanny. You may go back to traveling, using work as an excuse. You can spend time in Italy if you see fit. You do not need to clear it with me, because we will live separately. Your responsibility will only be to your son, your friend and your title. Not me."

They already had been living separately, so this was hardly a blow, even if he could not get that message through to his body. It throbbed with a pain he could not seem to talk himself out of.

"You must be available for royal events. You must still behave as a married earl. I hope it won't be too much of a hardship for you, but it is too late to undo that which is already done. Not without hurting Alexandre or the kingdom.

At least for now. But within those constraints, you may…do whatever you need to do to keep this *monster* to yourself."

She did not say it with derision. She was being perfectly reasonable. So reasonable she didn't even seem like herself. So reasonable… She was right. This was all well and good, and the best course of action.

Still, he stood, without the words to agree, to accept, feeling a bit like a soldier stuck in no-man's-land.

"Do you have anything to say?" she asked. Dry-eyed and detached. She was not being mean or cruel or kind or anything. She was… She was treating this like a business. Which he should appreciate and do in kind, but when he spoke his voice was little more than a rasp.

"And when the baby comes?"

For the first time, she did not meet his gaze. She looked down at her belly, picked something off the fabric of her shirt. "We will have to reconvene and discuss next steps once we understand the reality of having a newborn. If you feel yourself some kind of danger to our child…"

She let that hang there, the sentence not fully spoken, but the meaning clear. Her mouth curved, but it was not a smile. Not from Evelyne. She raised her gaze back to his. "This is what you wish, is it not?"

He stared at her, those dark eyes, never looking away from him. She had taken days to think this through, and she had decided to agree with him, just as he'd hoped. Just as he'd *known* was right.

But he hadn't expected it, so he did not know how to feel. And he realized… He did not know what he wished, except to protect her. And this would accomplish that. These dangerous, uncontrollable feelings inside him could not win, could not *hurt* if they essentially lived separate lives. If *she* agreed to these separate lives.

She hadn't just agreed. She'd planned it all out. Nothing could be better. Even if his body somehow felt as though it had been cracked in half, opened in front of her, everything inside him spilling out at her feet.

But he let *nothing* out. He had to control all that whirled inside him. "Yes, this is ideal."

She gave a sharp nod. "I will always be grateful you brought me our son. The future king of Alis." She moved to get to her feet, but here she was not quite so graceful or elegant. She struggled to push herself up, and before he'd thought it through, he moved to help her.

One hand on her elbow offering leverage, one hand somehow landing on her stomach. For a moment, they both froze in the warmth of physical connection. And then something under his hand seemed to...jerk.

He pulled his hand back in reflex, then immediately pressed it back to the same spot on her stomach. "Was that..."

"He kicked." She let out a little laugh, looked up at him now with the vibrant shine of *life* in her eyes. "I have been feeling flutters but nothing so certain as that yet, though all the books say I should start. And now..."

He could not help but grin down at her. A kick. It was so...real. So bafflingly real. A reminder that in short months this life inside her would be *outside*. Real and his. He would hold his son in his arms and...

Or he would be miles away. In Italy. Living a separate life.

He watched her swallow, look away. Because it did not matter how beautiful the idea of holding their son in his arms was. Their lives would be separate. Everything would be separate.

For Evelyne and the boy's own good. And since it was, he should start now.

He took two careful steps back, clasped his hands behind him. He regarded her with the same cool detachment she had been giving him. Or tried. "I think I shall fly to Italy tonight. Handle some business."

She did not say anything at first. Just stood very still. Eventually she inclined her head though. "Of course. Have a safe journey, Gabriel." She even smiled at him.

He could not seem to manage the same. "Stay well, Your Highness."

And he left. The palace and Alis and *her*.

For her own good.

Definitely not for his.

Evelyne cried herself to sleep. That night. And the next. And the next. She tried to tell herself all would be well. She had her brother, her sister-in-law and in two months or so she would have her child. She lived in a kingdom no longer ruled by her father.

All was *well*.

She tried to plan. Decorate the nursery. Decide on a name. Focus on the positive parts of the future.

But everything felt as though Gabriel should have some say, even though he had given up his say and gone to *Italy*.

She would have spent all her time alone, wallowing, but Ines insisted on sharing meals, and since she did not often eat with Alexandre, Evelyne felt honor bound to be company for her.

But now both Ines *and* Alexandre joined her in one of the parlors in the evenings. She must not be hiding her misery very well.

"I can require him to return, you know," Alex muttered one evening as he read something on his tablet.

Evelyne looked up at Alexandre. Not only was he watching her, but so was Ines. They were both worried about her. She knew this because they were spending their evenings together. With her, to be sure, but usually they did not simply sit in the parlor like this together.

So she smiled. "I think I should only like you to require his return if it were to throw him in the dungeons."

"I'm sure that can also be arranged," Ines offered, earning her a sharp look from her husband. Which Ines ignored, going back to the blanket she was knitting for the baby.

Evelyne put her hand over her stomach. She felt some movement and tried to be comforted by his existence. Comforted by the reality of *life*.

She was used to not getting what she wanted, wasn't she? A few weeks of having what she wanted shouldn't change things.

"I do not want him forced into anything. He has made his choices. I will make mine." Even if she was struggling to make *any* choice. It didn't matter. She didn't want to think about this. She stood. "I think I shall go to bed," she announced.

And knew their gazes followed her all the way out.

Almost like they knew she was going to cry herself to sleep again.

King Alexandre Enzo Rodrigo Lidia was used to being told what to do. His father had ruled him with an iron fist, and Alexandre had learned how to develop his own sense of duty under the chains of that evil man thanks to his mother. So he liked to think he knew what to do with orders—how to determine if they were the appropriate course of action, if he should give the person doing the ordering the satisfaction of thinking they ordered a prince—now king—or if he would make it clear they had no say over him.

But he did not know what to do with his wife, standing here in this parlor, telling him what to do after Evelyne had trudged away.

"You must interfere," Ines told him, with quite a bit of fire and determination he had never *once* seen from her in these near ten months of marriage.

She never told him anything. Never insisted upon anything. She was usually exactly as he'd expected she'd be, what King Enzo had wanted the princess to be. Beige. Malleable. Deferential. She was such a tiny little thing, Alexandre hadn't given thought to the fact there might be any room for much else.

And now she stood, looking down at him in his chair. Telling him—a *king*—what to do.

He rather wanted to refuse her out of principle, but she was talking about Evelyne and... Well, it was all too clear his sister was miserable, and though he'd seen little of Gabriel, there was no doubt he was the same.

If he knew how to fix it, he supposed he would. The problem was the not knowing. He wasn't about to admit that to his wife.

"And how do you propose I do that? Evelyne has made it clear she does not wish to *make* him do anything."

Ines huffed impatiently. He'd had no idea she could *be* impatient.

"You need to convince him he is not this danger he seems to think. It's utterly ludicrous."

Alex frowned. "Evelyne told you..."

"Evelyne has told me *everything*. Because she is lonely and miserable and heartbroken. She needs a friend, and I have been that for her. And as perhaps the only impartial bystander here, I can tell you with certainty your friend is being an idiot. You must interfere, Alex. For your sister's sake."

She never called him Alex. He did not quite know what to do with this strange turn of events. And he always knew what to do, no matter the turn of events.

Ines inhaled deeply. When she spoke again, she sounded more herself. Her expression was calm, her words rational. "The truth of the matter is, we know what a loveless marriage looks like. We are quite happy to spend our time apart. Evelyne is miserable with Gabriel away. I would wager a guess Gabriel is miserable *being* away. But they cannot quite see past their own misery. *We* can. We can help them. We must."

She did not say *if we cannot be happy, at least they can be*, but he felt it all the same.

"If I require him to come back here, Evelyne does not need to know it was at my insistence. Perhaps simply spending time together will…"

Ines was shaking her head. "You need to find some way to prove to Gabriel who he really is, not who he thinks he is. He is *your* best friend. You should know how to do this."

Alexandre would not admit he didn't have a clue. And he didn't have to, because Ines whirled away, leaving him alone in the parlor. Chewing over her parting shot. And perhaps this new side of herself she'd shown him.

It wouldn't do to consider that, though. Not when they no longer needed to create an heir. Thanks to Evelyne. And Gabriel.

So he focused on them.

It took him a little bit, but when he saw he had a meeting scheduled in the morning with the general, Alexandre began to form a plan.

CHAPTER FIFTEEN

THE MISSIVE FROM Alexandre was a surprise. Gabriel looked at the email requiring his return for a few days of "royal protocol" meetings and frowned.

Gabriel did not wish to return to Alis. The longer he was away, the more he worried his return would end in…poor choices on his part.

He missed Evelyne like a limb. He wasn't sleeping. His work suffered. His personal assistant had asked—repeatedly—if he should set up a doctor appointment for Gabriel.

No doctor could cure this *sickness* inside him. Nothing could. But if he went back to the palace, what might he convince himself would?

Luckily, though it felt nothing like luck, his reaction to being away only brought home one clear and important point. This pain and suffering proved everything he'd told her. Because if he had a reasonable, rational connection to Evelyne, if love could be normal and safe for him, wouldn't he be handling a separation much better? Perhaps with *some* pain but not feeling as though his very life had ended.

But he was dangerously obsessed, and he had to accept this pain and stay away. For *her* sake.

Except Alexandre was *requiring* his presence now.

What choice did Gabriel have? A king's edict meant he had to obey, particularly now that he was an earl. If he found himself…energized by the flight to France, and perhaps *enjoying* the drive across the border…

He would handle it. By avoiding Evelyne at all costs. Yes, that's what he'd do. No anticipation at seeing her because he *would not*. Perhaps he could even convince Alexandre that whatever needed his attention could be handled in one day and he would not need to spend the night.

He pulled up to the private entrance to the castle, frowned at the three guards who stood there, hands on their weapons, like they were barring entrance.

He got out of his car, handed his keys to the waiting valet. "Is everything all right here?"

The valet looked from the keys to the guards, then bowed and got in the car. Saying nothing. He drove away, leaving Gabriel with the guards.

Concerned that something bad had happened inside the palace, something dangerous or threatening, Gabriel approached the guards quickly. "Gentlemen," he greeted. "Is there a problem?"

They did not answer, but the door behind them opening was an answer. Because out stepped General Vinyes. Dressed in his military regalia. He had been openly critical of Alexandre these past few weeks, but he had not mounted any actual attacks, nor did he defy any of the new king's orders.

The general knew a good thing when he had it, or so Gabriel thought. Gabriel could not imagine what *this* was about though. Nothing good.

"Good afternoon, General. You seem to be in my way." Gabriel smiled at him. The sharpness in the smile was not likely to be construed as friendly.

"Alas, I am afraid you will have to come with me, Mr. Marti."

"Ah, but it isn't *mister* anymore, is it? I believe you are to address me as *my lord*?" Gabriel hadn't had cause to use his new title, but if ever there was a time to flaunt it, no doubt it would be to this vicious general.

The general's expression darkened. "It has come to my attention that you were the person who kidnapped the princess."

Gabriel studied the man before him. Pompous and smarmy, those were the two main descriptors that came to mind. Him even mentioning Evelyne soured Gabriel's mood even further. "You mean my *wife*?"

"She was not your wife when you illegally absconded with a member of the royal family. We have evidence. You will be arrested."

Gabriel found it odd he wanted to laugh. Instead, he stood where he was and acted bored. Because he was. "Have you brought this evidence to the king? Have you come up with charges?"

"We shall arrest you first." The general's chin moved up. "Once we have, we will present the facts to your *friend*. Even kings have to admit when their friends are in the wrong when presented with evidence. Because if he does not use said evidence to punish you, the people will know."

Gabriel pretended to mull this over. "A word of advice, General? I would not recommend this course of action. Whatever it is you think you're going to accomplish, I can assure you, you won't." The public loved Evelyne. They did *not* love the general. While this plan might cause a bit of a headache for Alexandre, and Gabriel regretted that, he also knew Alex could hardly arrest him for what he'd done at Alex's behest.

Especially when Gabriel was currently *married* to the princess. Perhaps he *was* going to have to see her after all. It was certainly dread he felt at that realization.

Not hope.

The general leaned in, his eyes flinty and soulless. "If

the king were still alive, you'd be tried for treason. And sentenced to death."

"What a shame he's six feet under instead," Gabriel returned. He took a step to move around the guards, but their grips on the guns changed. Moved.

Aimed.

"I do not think the princess should be married to such a man. Perhaps there's even a bit of Stockholm Syndrome happening. The king will sort it out, but you must be held while we do so."

Gabriel looked from the guns, to the general.

"Have no concerns, *my lord*. I will ensure your…wife's safety in the ensuing weeks as we sort this out."

It was the most veiled of threats, but it was a threat. Gabriel looked down at the man, wondering what on earth gave him the gall to punch so completely out of his weight class.

"Mark my words, *General*, if you so much as look at my wife the wrong way, I will end you."

"Your friendship with the prince—"

"The king, General. You forget yourself. And I am an earl now, as I have reminded you." He smiled at the older man, though the expression held nothing but malice. "I believe that ranks me above you these days. Now get out of my way before this becomes an embarrassment."

"You do not give me orders." The general stood a little taller, the men held their guns a little tighter.

Gabriel surveyed the soldiers. The gleam in the general's eye. And in a flash, saw this for what it was.

Bait. A trap. If he reacted as he wanted to—that roiling physical violence inside him—he *would* be arrested, perhaps even attacked if the general's expression was anything to go by. And while Alexandre could easily absolve him of kidnapping charges, clearing him of attacking a general might require some more work.

Gabriel did not wish to require this of his friend. It would be a mess, and it would risk things for Alex that need not be risked.

No matter how Gabriel would like to plow his fist into the general's nose.

Instead, he smiled once more. He breathed. And he spoke, very carefully. "I suggest you let me go talk to our king without such theatrics." And with that, Gabriel walked past them. There was no point in giving them the satisfaction of a fight. Though his fists clenched in spite of himself.

They did not stop him, and they did not follow. Gabriel could *feel* the general's angry gaze on him, but nothing happened. It had been posturing at best, though Alexandre would need to know about it.

And nip it in the bud.

Gabriel marched his way through the palace and though he ached to see Evelyne, he would not give in to that. He was here at Alexandre's behest, and he had to warn his friend about a general with a vendetta.

He was *not* here to see his wife.

So he went straight for Alex's office, though his gaze moved toward the hallway that would take him to his—to *Evelyne's* rooms. Or maybe she'd moved by now, to their connecting rooms. For their separate private lives.

Alexandre's assistant greeted him as he approached. He gestured toward the office door. "The king will see you now."

"Thank you," Gabriel murmured, letting himself in. He shut the door behind him, lest the general decided he wanted to attend the meeting.

Alex flicked a glance up from his computer. "Thank you for coming so quickly, Gabriel," he greeted. He typed a few more words before shutting his laptop. He stood. "There are some things that needed to be done in person."

Gabriel nodded. "Very well, but first we must discuss the general."

"Vinyes? What of him?" Alex looked down at some papers on his desk, eased a hip against it.

"He claims he has evidence that I kidnapped the princess. He made some noise about *Stockholm Syndrome*, and about arresting me."

Alex glanced at him then. "Is that one of your concerns and why you stay away?"

For a moment, Gabriel was speechless. "What? No. Evelyne isn't... Her feelings are genuine. I..." Gabriel could not remember a time he'd ever floundered in such a way, but the idea Evelyne might be *swayed* from a voluntary kidnapping...

"I know you took her at my behest, but you were her only contact," Alexandre continued, like this was a normal conversation. "Perhaps that is why you do not trust yourself, because you do not trust *her* feelings?"

"Evelyne is in love with me," Gabriel said firmly, temper snapping in every word. Until he reminded himself he didn't *want* her to be. "Which...is ridiculous, but I don't doubt that... Why are we talking about... I do not care what accusations the general throws at me," Gabriel insisted, not sure why he felt the need to defend Evelyne loving him when he wished she didn't. It wasn't the *point*. "General Vinyes is a fool. I simply wanted you to be aware he's skulking around making trouble. Not just with me. He made vague threats about *watching after Evelyne*."

For a moment, Alexandre studied him. When he spoke, it was with an odd carefulness Gabriel didn't recognize in his friend.

"So, he threw accusations at you, vaguely threatened that he'd be watching Evelyne, and you handled all of this without losing your temper, and instead came to me to address the situation. Is that correct?"

Gabriel blinked. It was correct, but… "I… I could have started a fight if I'd wanted to. I considered it." Not really, but a little bit. He'd *wanted* to hurt the general, but he knew…

"But you didn't. You didn't react with violence or anything over the top. You came to warn me. How odd. I thought violence was all you had in you when it came to those you loved?"

Gabriel could only stare at his friend. Speaking as though this had all been some…ridiculous setup.

"You…" Evidence. The only one who could have had evidence was… Alex. "This was a trap?"

Alexandre shrugged. "More or less."

"And if I'd fought him? If I'd created the scene that I'm very capable of creating?" Gabriel demanded.

"I would have sided with you," Alexandre returned, as though he'd thought it all out, but had already known what the outcome would be. "It might have even given me cause to dismiss the general, which would have been welcome indeed. But mostly I trusted you to make the right decision, Gabriel. Because you learned something all those years ago, whether you can accept that or not. You're not the same man you were. Because even then you were a *boy*."

Gabriel stood there, feeling a bit like he'd been stabbed through. Not the same man. But he was. How could he have changed?

Evelyne.

He shook away that thought. Perhaps some things had felt different, but that didn't make *it* different. His reaction to the general didn't make *him* different.

"I would like to think Evelyne and I could have made that clear to you," Alexandre continued. "Neither of us are fools, and neither of us find you to be a *monster*, but it turns out Ines was right. I had to show you."

Gabriel shook his head, trying to find some anchor amid all this crumbling inside him. If he listened to the crumbling, he'd have to believe he could…be what Evelyne and their child needed.

And he wanted that far too much to trust anything. "You tricked me. It shows…nothing."

Alexandre lifted a shoulder, reminding Gabriel a little too much of Evelyne. "Doesn't it?" Alex asked casually. "You didn't know it was a trick. You reacted. Handled it. Seems to show me quite a bit, honestly."

Gabriel was utterly speechless. He didn't have an argument. As much as he might have liked a scene, he had rationalized it out. Because he did not wish to hurt or complicate life for Alexandre or Evelyne, he had…resisted those urges inside him.

As though he could. As though he would, when it mattered. He had *done* it.

"She is miserable," Alexandre said, his voice quiet and serious. "She sits in the nursery and makes no decision. She ignores the staff trying to prod her into making decisions about the baby's name so we can begin the royal decrees necessary."

Gabriel rubbed at his heart, where an ache had not left him for some time but seemed to dive deeper now.

"And you are no better," Alexandre added.

"I have been working."

"You have been *hiding*. You have been *wallowing*. Why must you both insist on your own misery? You love one another."

Gabriel did not know what to do with this *word*. Love was for people who could handle such things.

Had he handled something? Could he... He shook his head. It all felt too dangerous, too...fragile. If he gave in, he'd spend the rest of his life walking the edge of violence.

Except General Vinyes had pushed all of his buttons and Gabriel had...handled it. Could it really mean what Alexandre wanted it to mean?

Gabriel eyed his friend, trying to understand where this had come from. Trying to find some old handle on his fear. "It is not like you to interfere."

Alexandre pulled a face. "No indeed. But here I am. Take that as a sign things are dire indeed, and now it is up to *you* to fix it. You are rather good at fixing things."

He was. He *was*. He'd built a career out of fixing people's security problems for them in different ways.

But this was...

"You knew I would not make the wrong choice," Gabriel said, very carefully.

"Of course I knew, Gabriel," Alexandre said, very seriously. "I have been your friend our entire lives. I have also spent most of Evelyne's life doing what I could to protect her. I would not have allowed you anywhere near her if I thought that you also could not do the same. Just because you fell in love with her and got her pregnant under dubious circumstances doesn't mean you didn't protect her."

Gabriel sucked in a breath. There were few people he trusted as deeply as Alexandre, because Alex had always been there—and because he knew what exactly had happened with Gia. And Alex was right, there was no one he protected more fiercely than his sister.

"There are no protocol meetings to attend, are there?"

"Of course not. Go apologize to Evelyne. Make her happy. Or perhaps I will throw you in the dungeons after all...one of Evelyne's suggestions. Ines was a fan."

Gabriel chuckled in spite of himself. Yes, Evelyne would suggest that, but she wouldn't mean it. Because she loved him. She wanted him to be the man she thought he was. Not the monster he was so afraid of.

And if his best friend in the world could believe that of him, enough to set him up with the very real chance he might fight a *general*, Gabriel supposed he owed it to the both of them to decide to be the man they thought he was.

In every way possible.

"I will…see what I can do," Gabriel said a bit haltingly. He stepped forward, too many complicated emotions swamping him. "Thank you, for always being the brother I needed. Always."

Alexandre gave a sharp nod. "Likewise," he muttered, clearly uncomfortable. But meaning it.

Gabriel left the office, the anticipation he'd felt at seeing Evelyne tenfold now that he wasn't going to fight it.

Alexandre was right about Evelyne's misery. Gabriel found her in the future nursery, surrounded by wallpaper samples. Crying.

His heart cracked in two at the misery pouring out of her. Because of *him*. Because of his fears. His weaknesses.

He never wanted to watch her cry out of sorrow for him again. If there was any monster still inside him, he would remember Evelyne crying before he gave it any credence.

She looked up at him as he stepped into the room. Her expression showed no signs of surprise.

Or excitement. Or warmth. Just…resignation.

She wiped the tears away, made no move to excuse them or apologize for them. "I have been trying to decide between a zoo theme or an alphabet theme. It is quite a difficult choice."

She looked at the walls, clearly miserable. When she

should feel joy and hope and excitement. All things she'd had before he'd inserted himself into her life.

Or all things she'd had until you ran away from it.

There could be no more of this. Not if it hurt her in such a way. It was no better than being a monster.

Gabriel cleared his throat, fighting past the tightness there. "I quite liked dogs when I was a young boy."

"Dogs," she repeated. She blinked. She looked around the room as if picturing it. "I have always wanted a dog."

"I imagine we could have one now." He used the *we* on purpose. And he let himself see it. Her. A baby. Their son. A dog running around. A family that he would protect, love, cherish.

Never run away from.

For a moment, she looked like she was considering it, then she shook her head and closed her eyes, more tears landing on her cheeks. "I wish you weren't here," she said, sounding a little petulant. "Go away."

But the words hurt even if he knew why she said them. He never wanted her to wish that again. "I… I'm sorry."

"You should be. You should be sorry about everything. Every damn thing."

This was his *principessa*. No cool looks, no detachment like those weeks ago when she'd *agreed* with him. And he could see it for what it was now. Fake. Trying to get through to him, trying to get him to realize his mistake.

Instead, he'd doubled down.

But he was here now, a new truth inside him. And she was being *herself*. Emotion and truth and just…*her*.

All those aches and pains and desperate cracks inside him that he'd been so sure were his due, were *necessary* in order to know he was doing the right thing, eased.

He moved closer to her, then crouched next to her. She eyed him with a scowl.

"What if I told you I was?" he asked. "Sorry. For all of it."

She looked up at him, tears on her cheeks he could not help but wipe away.

"I would not believe you," she said, but she didn't move away from his hands on her face.

"Why not?"

"Because I'm mad at you and I want to stay that way."

"Do you?"

Her lips trembled and she shook her head. "Why are you here?" she asked, her voice trembling.

"Alex…set me up. He put me in a volatile position, and when I did not react violently and obsessively, he pointed out that perhaps… I had learned something all those years ago. That actions have consequences, and I care about the result of mine."

She lifted her chin. Sniffed. "*I* tried to set you up and you stayed away. Why should I be impressed Alexandre got through to you?"

"Because you love me."

She said nothing to that, so he knew he needed more. All.

"I knew from the moment I danced with you at your eighteenth birthday ball that you would be a trouble to me. You were so vibrant and funny—even though I knew behind the scenes you were treated deplorably. I kept you at a distance from then on because there could never be surface. I felt that, even then."

She sniffed. "Well, I thought you were pompous and too skinny."

He grinned at her in spite of himself. "No, you didn't. You had a crush on me."

Her mouth twitched a little, though she did not smile. "Perhaps I thought you handsome, in spite of the pompous and the skinny. But I didn't hold a torch."

"No, you had the impressive Jordi."

She laughed, and he felt all those last worries melt away. Yes, he would do anything to protect her, protect *this*, the family they were creating, the love that existed between them. But that did not have to mean…

He was not a young man with too many emotions and not enough sense. He had grown into his sense, his control. He had learned, in part thanks to Alexandre, and in part thanks to life.

He could trust himself. He *had* to trust himself if he was to be a father.

And a good husband to the woman he loved.

"I love you, Evelyne. And I have been afraid to feel anything so deep as love, but it is undeniable, and I… I am not a boy. Perhaps you are right that I stopped maturing in that moment, but I would argue I *did* mature and learn and grow. I was just stuck thinking too little of myself because I was so ashamed of what I was capable of."

"And now you're not?"

"I am still ashamed, but I can accept that I have grown and learned. I can accept I am not the boy I was, even if some of his impulses live inside me. More, I want to accept those things, so that I can truly be your husband, and a father to our child. A good one, like mine was. Like you've always trusted me to be."

Evelyne had not prepared for this. She had a few fantasies—mostly where he begged on his hands and knees to come back and she sent him away, crushed and crying.

Then there were the ones where he swept in and demanded to be back in her life. They fought and argued like they had in Maine and ended up in her bed like then too.

She'd gotten some mileage out of both fantasies, but this was real life. And so this was more.

This was rational and adult and real. The things he'd learned or realized. The work he was willing to put in to… make this *love* work.

Love. He'd…said he loved her. Looked her right in the eye while he did. Like he was doing now, crouched next to her sitting on the floor. It could not be a comfortable position.

"What do you want, Evelyne?" he asked. "If it is for me to go away, I'm afraid I cannot abide it. But if it is all the things you said you wanted before, then I am here and ready to work for those things. Love and a life. I will work as hard as I can to earn this love you've given me. I will dive under every surface, fight any fear. For you." He put one hand over her stomach. "For him. And whoever else may come along."

Whoever else. Whatever tears she'd managed to fight back spilled forward again at the idea of more children. A real life. A real marriage. A real *future*.

"I love you, Gabriel. All I've ever wanted was for you to see yourself as I saw you. And admit you loved me back."

"I will still worry that I will…fall back into the boy who took things too far. That this love I have for you, for our son, is too much. Too big."

"Love is never too much," she told him, trying not to tremble apart. Trying to be strong, because they both needed it. They *all* needed it. "But should it be, you could trust me to pull you back."

"I could." He framed her face in his hands, held her gaze so directly and resolutely. "I do."

She was tired of crying, but she *did* have hormones to blame on some of it. "Don't leave again," she managed to croak.

"No. No, I won't." Then he was kissing her—the tears on her cheeks, her jaw. Her mouth. "I love you, Evelyne. You are mine and I am yours. Forever."

"Forever," she agreed.

EPILOGUE

THEIR SON WAS born on a stormy night in the palace. Evelyne said it reminded her of Maine, and that she pictured that balcony looking out over the ocean when the pain was too much.

Gabriel had never felt more helpless in his life. The nurse and midwife took him to task more than once for insisting they do more for his wife, but watching Evelyne suffer was his own suffering.

Until he heard his son cry. Then everything seemed to melt away. The nurse put a wriggling, mewling creature on his wife's chest, and their gazes met over his head. For a moment of pure, unadulterated bliss.

They were parents. They had a son.

When his son was placed into his arms, clean and bundled up, he knew there would be no running away in fear. No, from here on out, there could only be love, strength, support and doing whatever was required of him to be there for his son. Fight or acquiesce, support or lean, and always love.

Hours later, cleaned up and cuddled in together on the bed, the princess and her earl invited the king and queen to meet their nephew.

Alexandre and Ines entered together, but even in his blissful state Gabriel noticed there was something…odd about them.

But they dutifully oohed and ahhed over the baby—from

opposite sides of the bed. Alexandre expressed some frustration over the fact there was still no name to go out on the royal decree, but Evelyne only told him to be patient.

When they left at the nurse's insistence that Evelyne needed her rest, it was without ever once having looked at one another.

"They're awfully icy with one another," Evelyne murmured, her head on Gabriel's shoulder, her gaze on their baby.

"I believe they had a bit of a row earlier," Gabriel murmured, stroking the babe's cheek.

"But Alexandre and Ines never fight," Evelyne said, lifting her gaze—briefly—to Gabriel. Then back to their son, like she couldn't bear to look away for more than a minute any more than Gabriel could.

"I heard shouting this morning," he told her. "And Alexandre was very distracted during our morning meeting."

"Hmm." But the troubles of Alexandre and Ines had nothing on the beautiful, sleeping boy in her arms. They both watched him in fully content silence.

"He is perfect," Evelyne said after a while.

Gabriel would have to insist she sleep soon, but he couldn't quite bring himself to take the baby away from her. Not just yet.

"He is at that. We have to name him, Evelyne. No more putting it off."

She pouted. "It's just so permanent. What if we pick the wrong name?"

"No name is wrong. Because he is perfect regardless."

"I guess this is true." She tucked the blanket under his chin, stroked a finger down his cheek. Then she looked up at Gabriel. "Do you remember back in Maine when I said I would not be naming him after you?"

"Vividly, *principessa*." He kissed her temple, and she leaned into him even more.

"Perhaps that is our answer. Let us give him the names of all the good men in our lives. Your father. Alexandre. *You*, who saved me."

While he still struggled to consider himself a *good* man, Gabriel liked the idea, because it would be a constant reminder of what he *should* be.

So their child was christened Gabriel Manuel Alexandre Marti, and both his parents knew he would someday make Alis a most wonderful king.

But more importantly, he would be a good man, surrounded by love. Always.

* * * * *

Did Secretly Pregnant Princess
*sweep you off your feet? Then you're sure to enjoy
the next installment in the Babies for Royal Brides duet,
coming soon! And why not explore these other stories
by Lorraine Hall?*

Princess Bride Swap
The Bride Wore Revenge
A Wedding Between Enemies
Pregnant, Stolen, Wed
Unwrapping His Forbidden Assistant

Available now!

MILLS & BOON ®

Coming next month

ENEMIES UNTIL AFTER HOURS
Natalie Anderson

Mia drew on a defensive smile and headed into Sante's office—leaving his door wide open behind her.

Trying to steady her heartbeat. The appalling thing was that increasingly her body responded with chaos to his proximity. It didn't seem to care that he was a heartless jerk who'd betrayed her brother, her body just wanted his near. So, she was ignoring her body. Controlling it.

'You've screwed up my scheduling.' He glared at her.

'Where?'

He jabbed a finger at the screen, and she was forced to round his desk to study it. Big mistake. There was nowhere near enough of a barrier between them and she desperately needed to calm her overexcited response.

'You've blocked out a significant portion of my day tomorrow.'

She leaned closer and he turned his head toward her, meaning his mouth was only inches from hers. It was *searingly* intimate. It would take nothing to lower hers and—

What the hell was she thinking? Why had the idea to kiss him popped into her head? She stared into his brown eyes for three seconds too long.

Continue reading

ENEMIES UNTIL AFTER HOURS
Natalie Anderson

Available next month
millsandboon.co.uk

COMING SOON!

We really hope you enjoyed reading this book.
If you're looking for more romance
be sure to head to the shops when
new books are available on

Thursday 26th February

MILLS & BOON

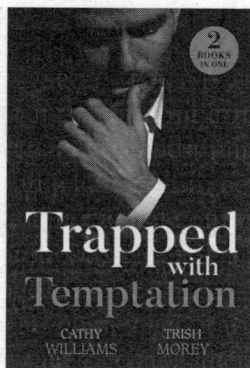

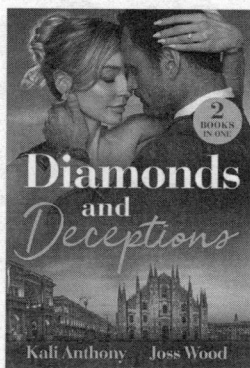

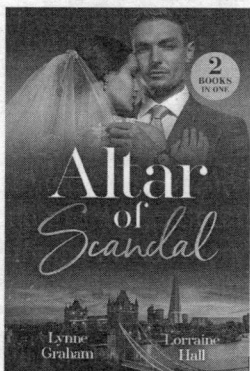

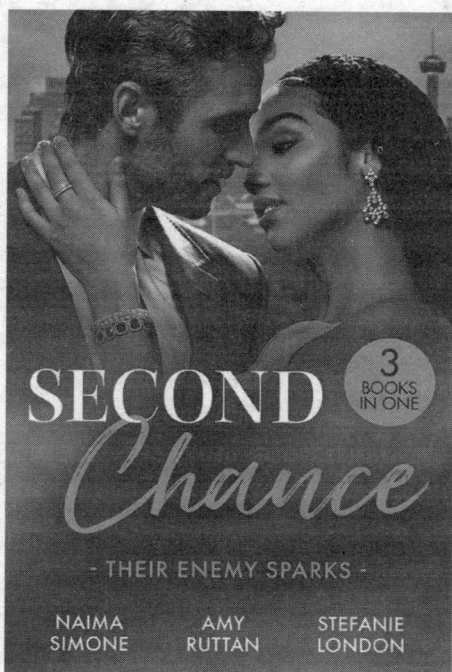

LET'S TALK

Romance

For exclusive extracts, competitions and special offers, find us online:

f MillsandBoon

X @MillsandBoon

@MillsandBoonUK

@MillsandBoonUK

Get in touch on 01413 063 232